"Eisler's new thriller is as smart, dark, and tough as his others. This one, however, is also all too real and all too close to home." —CHARLES FERGUSON, Oscar-nominated writer, director, and producer of *No End in Sight*

"A modern *Heart of Darkness,* with Special Ops veteran Ben Treven taking a rip-roaring ride through jungle shootouts and up a sinister Potomac into a world of assassination and torture, made more frightening because it's all too real." —JEFFREY KEYE, blogger on AlterNet, FireDogLake, and Invictus

"A fantastic thriller! What Le Carré and Clancy did for the Cold War, Eisler does for the shadow government of politicians, corporations, and spies that continually sacrifices America's core values in the name of national security."
—ROGER MCNAMEE,
managing director, Elevation Partners

"Extremely well researched, and what Eisler posits as fiction feels terrifyingly like fact. It's about time fiction began to reflect the reality of rendition, detention, and torture.... *Inside Out* is a gripping thriller, but it also serves an important purpose." —CLIVE STAFFORD SMITH, founder of Reprieve, author of *Eight O'Clock Ferry to the Windward Side*

"As our once trusted leaders took the nation to the 'dark side' with policies akin to those of Mafia consiglieri, Barry Eisler lights up their dungeons with blazing insights packed in his thrilling narrative."
—PHILIP ZIMBARDO, author of *The Lucifer Effect*

Fault Line

"Eisler, who has training in covert operations and is well known for his John Rain series (e.g., *Requiem for an Assassin*), presents a winning first stand-alone work."
—*Library Journal* (starred review)

"Rich characterizations and family dynamics blend seamlessly with gripping action scenes. Eisler has himself another winner." —*Booklist*

Requiem for an Assassin

"Mr. Eisler brings detailed knowledge of the covert world and his books' verisimilitude boosts their appeal. . . . Aficionados will find plenty to enjoy: the action is slick and fast, and the plot tightly choreographed." —*The Economist*

"Along with the high-tech gadgetry and low-tech blood and guts, Eisler has also let us into the head of a brilliant and extremely conflicted protagonist." —*Kirkus Reviews*

"This one is as good as its five forerunners, and here's hoping the author has a few more stories to tell." —*Booklist*

"Eisler proves himself to be as coolly efficient a writer as his protagonist is a killer." —*Entertainment Weekly*

"An exciting, fast-moving tale . . . [Eisler] writes good dialogue and action scenes and gives his characters a fair amount of depth. . . . A skillful spy novel."
—*The Washington Post*

The Last Assassin

"The depth of characterization, the seamless transitions between the different points of view, the brilliant choreography of the action, all demonstrate that Eisler is one of the most talented and literary writers in the thriller genre."
—*Chicago Sun-Times*

"A rousing success." —*Booklist*

"Wicked action sequences, smoothly delineated local color and moments of introspection capture Rain in fine, fraught form." —*Kirkus Reviews*

"It's an action thriller that will appeal even to readers who think they don't like action thrillers."
—*The Philadelphia Inquirer*

By Barry Eisler

INSIDE OUT
FAULT LINE
RAIN FALL
HARD RAIN
RAIN STORM
KILLING RAIN
THE LAST ASSASSIN
REQUIEM FOR AN ASSASSIN

INSIDE OUT

a novel

BARRY EISLER

BALLANTINE BOOKS • NEW YORK

As of press time, the URLs displayed in this book link or refer to existing websites on the Internet. Random House, Inc., is not responsible for, and should not be deemed to endorse or recommend, any website other than its own or any content available on the Internet (including without limitation at any website, blog page, or information page) that is not created by Random House. The author, similarly, cannot be responsible for third-party material.

2011 Ballantine Books Mass Market Edition

Copyright © 2010 by Barry Eisler

All rights reserved.

Published in the United States by Ballantine Books, an imprint of The Random House Publishing Group, a division of Random House, Inc., New York.

BALLANTINE and colophon are registered trademarks of Random House, Inc.

Originally published in hardcover in the United States by Ballantine Books, an imprint of The Random House Publishing Group, a division of Random House, Inc., in 2010.

ISBN 978-0-345-50511-8
eBook ISBN 978-0-345-51929-0

Cover design: Scott Biel
Cover photograph: Panoramic Images / Getty Images

Printed in the United States of America

www.ballantinebooks.com

9 8 7 6 5 4 3 2 1

Ballantine Books mass market edition: August 2011

For the bloggers.

By definition, establishments believe in propping up the existing order. Members of the ruling class have a vested interest in keeping things pretty much the way they are. Safeguarding the status quo, protecting traditional institutions, can be healthy and useful, stabilizing and reassuring.

EVAN THOMAS, NEWSWEEK

Of course, the United States is unique. And just as we have the world's most advanced economy, military, and technology, we also have its most advanced oligarchy.

SIMON JOHNSON, THE ATLANTIC

L'état, c'est moi.

LOUIS XIV

PROLOGUE

Ulrich stared at Clements, wanting to believe he'd misheard. Even in the grand panoply of CIA incompetence,
this one would be a standout.

"Let me get this straight," he said, deliberately speaking slowly and clearly so Clements and the rest of the
Langley contingent assembled before him would understand exactly what Ulrich made of their collective mental
acuity. "Ninety-two interrogation videotapes, and you're
telling me they're just . . . missing?"

Clements shifted his weight from one foot to the other,
the frozen grass crunching under his wingtips. "We think
there were ninety-two. We're still trying to get an accurate
inventory."

Ulrich looked past Clements at the precise rows of
thousands of white markers, their expanse dazzling in
the brilliant morning sun. Well, at least now he understood why Clements had wanted to meet here. No one
was going to notice, much less overhear, a small group
of men paying their respects to the honored dead of
Arlington National Cemetery. No records, no witnesses,
no proof this conversation had ever happened.

"All right," Ulrich said, running the fingers of a gloved

hand along his thick gray beard. "First thing I need to know. What's on these tapes?"

Clements glanced at the man to his left and then at the one to his right. Stephen Clements, Michael Killman, John Alkire. The deputy director of the CIA, the director of the National Clandestine Service, and the director of the Counterterrorism Center. Half the bureaucratic firepower of the entire Agency, huddling in their dark overcoats like an incipient union of funeral directors.

"Are you going to tell me? Or are we all just going to stand out here and freeze?"

Clements said nothing, and Ulrich was suddenly concerned at how meekly the man was taking his licks. Ulrich was used to being deferred to—after all, in this administration, chief of staff to the vice president was an exceptionally powerful position. On top of which, Ulrich was a big, imposing man, accustomed to intimidating bureaucratic rivals with his loud voice and blunt manner. But Clements looked beyond intimidated. He looked . . . scared. Which was itself unnerving.

Ulrich sighed. He took off his wire-framed spectacles, closed his eyes, and massaged the bridge of his nose. When he felt calmer, he slipped the glasses back on.

"Just tell me," he said, his voice a notch softer.

Clements blew out a long, frozen breath. "Waterboarding, for one thing."

Ulrich closed his eyes again. "Crap."

Waterboarding was a problem. In the public mind, it was the one enhanced interrogation technique that was most arguably torture. But even for waterboarding, the mainstream media had done a nice job of sanitizing the public's imagination of what the practice entailed, carefully describing it as "torture" only with scare quotes, or as "a practice some describe as torture." Actual footage of helpless, shackled men sobbing and begging and pissing themselves while American guards repeatedly drowned and revived them could cause a change in sentiment.

"What else?" Ulrich said.

"Walling. Stress positions. A lot of the stuff we had to stop using after Abu Ghraib."

Well, they'd survived photos of this kind of stuff coming out of AG. The public wanted to believe it had been just a few bad apples, and anytime the public wanted to believe something, the job was already ninety percent done. It could be done again here.

"What's the worst of it? The parts that'll be on the blogs."

"I don't know, we're talking about hundreds of hours of footage. It's—"

"The worst, goddamn it."

The three Langley men exchanged glances. Alkire said, "The dog stuff is pretty bad. The waterboarding is worse. There are people at Langley who couldn't even watch it on video. And the beatings—some of these guys, they had edema from being manacled to the ceiling for a week straight. You ever see someone with edema, hanging by his wrists, getting the shit beaten out of him? Half the time, their skin splits open."

Ulrich considered. He knew these three had every reason to make it sound as bad as possible. They wanted him to know that if any of this got out, the fire would be so big they'd all burn together. But even if they were exaggerating, it wouldn't be by much. He knew what was being done at the black sites. He'd long ago made his peace with it, of course, as the price that had to be paid in the shadows so the rest of America could go on enjoying the light. But asking the secret guardians of American liberty to live with the truth was one thing. Force-feeding it to the entire public was different. It wasn't the public's burden to bear.

"When did you learn the tapes were missing?" Ulrich asked.

"Just this morning," Killman said. "Another FOIA request in federal court. You're following these cases?"

Ulrich nodded. Of course he was following the cases. The ACLU had filed multiple Freedom of Information Act requests for information on treatment of terrorist detainees and then sued when the Agency refused to turn anything over. God, he hated the ACLU. If they had even half the concern for the safety of Americans that they did for the rights of terrorists . . .

"Well, recently our people monitoring the FOIA cases have been getting alarmed. We've got a detainee in court claiming his interrogations were videotaped. Now it looks like we're going to receive a court order specifically for video—and not just for Guantánamo, but covering the black sites, too. If that happens, we won't be able to dodge the order the way we have before. So we decided to do a complete inventory, assess our exposure, get ahead of the order. That's when we discovered the problem."

The problem. If nothing else, the CIA always had a flair for understatement.

Ulrich stroked his beard. He supposed it was possible one of these jokers was less stupid than he seemed, that he'd destroyed the tapes himself and was going along with this meeting just to obscure his own actions. Or that someone else, some patriot, or even just someone wise enough to have a modicum of self-preservation instinct, had done what needed to be done. After all, it wasn't as though anyone was going to take the credit for it. All that would earn him would be a silent prayer of thanks from the people whose asses he'd saved, a prayer that would last only as far as the first congressional investigation into the latest CIA cover-up, at which point his circle of silent fans would immediately point their fingers inward, ensuring their benefactor would be crucified for their collective sins.

So yeah, it was possible there was someone inside the

CIA smart enough to have demonstrated the proper initiative. That was his immediate working theory. But he had no way to prove it. And even if he did, it wouldn't solve the immediate crisis.

"There's something else," Clements said, glancing at the other Langley men.

"Is that even possible?" Ulrich asked, unable to resist.

There was a long pause. Clements said, "Some of the tapes are of the Caspers."

Ulrich could actually feel the blood drain from his face. "You . . ." But he couldn't finish the sentence. He'd only just gotten his mind around what that very morning he would have believed was impossible. Now he was dealing with the unthinkable.

We're done, he thought. *We're really done. I can't spin this one. Nobody could.*

Yes, you can. You just have to focus. The Caspers don't matter. They don't change the dynamic. They just raise the stakes. You handle it the same way regardless.

But handle it how?

They all stood silently. Ulrich's mind raced furiously, examining options, gaming out plans from multiple angles, pressure-checking vulnerabilities. He felt both terrified and weirdly exhilarated. If he could put a lid on something this big, they'd have to invent a new name for it. Damage control? Hell, he was trying to control a cataclysm.

He kept going—*yes, no, too dangerous, if, then*—conducting an orchestra of alternatives just behind his eyes. A minute went by and a narrow possibility began to emerge, a little sliver of hope. It was crazy, it was audacious, it would require luck. But it could be done. It had to be done. Because there was simply no other way.

"Here's what you're going to do," he said, looking at Clements. "You call one of your contacts in the media—"

"Ignatius?"

"No, definitely not Ignatius. At this point he might as well be an official CIA spokesperson, and everyone knows it. And not Broder or Klein, either—they're known to be too sympathetic, too. Too eager to please."

Clements frowned, obviously not getting it. "We don't want someone pliable?"

"Just listen, okay? For this, we need a news article, not an op-ed. At least to start with. From a paper that's considered liberal. So . . . make it *The New York Times*. Yeah, the *Times* is perfect, they won't even use the word 'torture' in their coverage but they're still thought of as an enemy. Call them. You're a whistle-blower. The CIA made some interrogation tapes, tapes that include footage of detainees being abused."

Clements's mouth dropped open. "What?"

"I'm not finished. You say the CIA destroyed the tapes. Clear case of obstruction of justice. You're calling because you're a patriot, this won't stand, something needs to be done."

They were all looking at him as though he'd lost his mind. Christ, they were slow. They didn't deserve to have him save their asses. Unfortunately, his ass was next in line. These morons happened to be his primary defensive wall.

"You're crazy," Clements said. "There's no way—"

"Shut up and listen if you want to survive this. The liberal media will jump all over the story. Obstruction of justice, cover-up, rogue CIA, the whole thing. There's going to be pressure. And under pressure, the CIA admits—no, no, you *confess*—yes, we destroyed the tapes. But no more than two of them for now. Two, you understand?"

Clements shook his head as though he was trying to clear it. "What . . . why two?"

"Because it's too soon to go public with ninety-two. Two is a nice, finite number, it makes it sound like you've been exceptionally careful and selective regarding who gets subjected to enhanced interrogation techniques. You can tie the number to just a couple of high-profile detainees, right? Khalid Sheikh Mohammed, Abu Zubaydah, Abd al-Rahim al-Nashiri, just the worst of the worst. Listen to those names. You think anyone outside the ACLU will complain if you've maybe been a little rough with a couple terrorists named Mohammed al-this and Khalid al-that?"

"But . . . what are we going to do later on, if the real number comes out?"

"Later on won't matter, don't you see? You'll already have established the principle that the destruction wasn't a big deal by attaching a low number to it. You can always increase the number afterward, at which point you'll just be applying the established principle to a new number. You say something like, 'Oh, did you think I said two videotapes? I meant two terrorists on one of the tapes. Sorry for the confusion.' You get it? For Christ's sake, you don't have to sign a fucking affidavit that there were only two tapes, this is just to ease the idea into the public mind. Are you telling me you don't know how to put a number in play in a way that gives you room to walk away from it later?"

No one said anything. Ulrich couldn't tell if they were getting it or if they were drifting into shock. Well, nothing to do but keep going.

"Understand? Two interrogation videos, you think. Keep it a little vague, and you can get them to report two while giving you wiggle room for later."

"Okay, fine," Killman said. "But what do we do when they start asking about waterboarding? You know they will."

"Of course they will. And when they do, you reluctantly admit it. It's already out there anyway, the vice president himself acknowledged it. This is your chance to tie the waterboarding to just a small number of detainees, your chance to minimize it. That's actually a win."

"Doesn't sound like a win," Alkire said.

Idiots. "You can't cover this up, don't you understand that? If you try, the whole thing comes out. What you can do is channel the information, shape the narrative. You need to manage this story or it'll manage you. Do it right, keep it simple, and you'll be fine."

"But it's not simple," Clements said. "It's not just videos. There are also records of what's on the videos, who had access to them—"

"Good, now you're thinking. You need to destroy all contemporaneous records describing what's on the tapes because that's the next thing the court will ask for if the tapes are unavailable. You destroy all records of who had access to the tapes, of who might have knowledge of what was on them. And you create a paper trail of the proper authorizations that predates the court order. You claim the tapes had no further intelligence value, and . . . yes, yes, you say you had to destroy them because if they ever leaked, they could compromise the identities of field agents, patriotic men and women who are risking their lives every day on the front lines of the war on terror to keep America safe. Fox, and Broder and Klein and Krauthammer and Hiatt and Ignatius and the rest, they'll pick up that angle and run interference for us, attack the patriotism of anyone who questions the decision to destroy the tapes. They'll make it a political issue, it won't be a legal one. 'Only the angry left would want to put our soldiers and spies in danger,' that kind of thing."

None of them spoke.

Come on, Ulrich thought. *Man up. We can do this.*

"Look," he said, "you're not going to be alone, okay? We'll get someone highly placed in the administration to leak the same talking points."

Clements looked doubtful. "The vice president?"

"Definitely possible. But if not him, me or someone else who can speak for him. We'll give the background not for attribution, the papers will publish it, and then the DCI, the vice president, whoever, they'll go on all the Sunday morning talk shows and cite as evidence for our positions the articles the newspapers wrote based on what we fed them."

Clements nodded, a glimmer of understanding in his eyes. "Information laundering."

"Exactly," Ulrich said, rather liking the phrase. "Just the way drug traffickers pass their money through corrupt banks to make the money usable in society, we need to pass our talking points through the mainstream media to make the talking points seem objective. You see? The mainstream media turns our talking points into news stories. They love the access we give them, it makes them feel savvy. And we love the coverage they give us in return. It's a good system and it always works. It'll work here, too."

"It's still going to be a scandal," Clements said, apparently determined not to keep up.

"Of course it's going to be a scandal," Ulrich said, disgusted that his *Hey, we're all in this together* pep talk apparently had accomplished nothing. "And you might even have to resign for it. Would you rather own up to not even knowing where the tapes are or how many there actually were or what the hell happened to them? How do you think the Fourth Circuit would respond if you said, 'Sorry, we don't know where the tapes are, we can't find them'? You think they'd actually believe you could be that inept? You and I know better, but the court? They'd think it was a cover-up because no one could be so stupid as to misplace ninety-two tapes that, if they ever see the light of day, would be the most damaging national security leak in the history of the nation. You'd have so many outside investigations up your ass you'd spend the rest of your life trying to shit them out."

Clements glared, but took the rebuke. "I still don't see what this gets us."

"Number one, it gets us time—time to conduct our own investigation, from the inside. If we do that, with a little luck we recover the tapes ourselves, do what should have been done in the first place, and the truth never gets out. The only way you're going to cover this up is by 'confessing' to a lesser crime. How can you not see that? The media will jump all over the confession because for Christ's sake, no one would confess to destroying those tapes if he hadn't actually done it. No one will suspect the confession is actually concealing something worse, and for now the revelation of a few destroyed tapes will obscure the existence of just how many tapes there really were and what actually happened to them. Think the Forest Service, starting small, controlled fires to prevent the big ones, all right? How much more do I need to spell this out for you?"

"It'll never work," Clements said. "Someone will smell political opportunity. We'll never avoid an investigation."

"No? Haven't you been briefing Congress on the program?"

"Just the gang of eight," Clements said, using shorthand for the Democratic and Republican heads of the House and Senate, and the chair and ranking minority member of the House and Senate Intelligence Committees. "But we've been deliberately fuzzy on the details."

"The details don't matter," Ulrich said. "What matters is that the briefings took place. You think the Speaker of the House wants to get into a public fight over what she was told and when she was told it? She loses that battle just by having to fight it."

Were they getting it? He still wasn't sure.

"Plus, I know how you guys work. What did Goss testify to Congress that time? 'It may be only a matter of time before al Qaeda attacks the United States,' wasn't that it? May be, but maybe it won't be? My God, how many positions can you take in the same sentence? Go back to your records, I'll bet you can find something in a briefing about videotapes and whether they should be preserved. I guarantee someone dropped some casual mention just in case there was ever a problem later. Work this right and you can use the media to implicate anyone. And the gang of eight will know it."

There was a pause while they absorbed the diagnosis. Dire, with a brutal treatment regimen, but not without hope.

"I'm not taking all the heat for this," Clements said. "I'm not going down alone."

Ulrich could almost have smiled. Clements was in. Now they were just negotiating price.

"Then find someone at CIA who will. Who's in a position to have authorized the destruction of those tapes? Get to that person. Use whatever leverage you need to. And make sure he's on board."

"There's no one else. That would be a decision for the director of the National Clandestine Service. Anything else will look like bullshit."

"Then pin it on Killman's predecessor. He's got a nice cushy job in the private sector now, right? Intelligence contractor, making four times his government salary? You can't provide him with the right incentives to play ball? You don't have any dirt on him?"

Clements smiled, the smile of someone who's been smelling blood in the water and only just realized it was coming from someone else. "I'll see what can be done."

"But remember," Ulrich said, "all this is doing is buying us time. The most important thing is that we find those tapes, or verify their destruction."

"How are we going to do that?"

Ulrich closed his eyes and suppressed the urge to

shout. If he could work with just one competent organization. Just one.

"You need to put together a team," he said. "Comprised of people with the right talents and the right incentives."

"Meaning?"

"Meaning, how many field interrogators are featured in those videos?"

Clements shrugged. "Maybe a half dozen."

"Military experience?"

"Of course. They're all Spec Ops veterans, now with Ground Branch."

"Good, then they have the talent. And they'll understand that if those videos ever get out, the least they can expect will be public ostracism. More likely, prison. That means we can trust them."

The three Agency men were nodding now. They were getting it. Slow as ever, but educable if you took the time and trouble to spell things out, if you showed them the one narrow route that offered a chance of saving them.

"Recall those men from the field. I don't care what they're working on, I don't care what their priorities are, as of this moment they have a new assignment. You run the investigation, reporting directly to me. You manage the field, I manage the political cover. There are a lot of people, people from both parties, who have a reason to want those tapes secured. If we need their cooperation, I'll make sure we have it."

Clements nodded. "How much are you going to tell the vice president?"

"Let me worry about that. For now, everything is need-to-know. And speaking of which, communication on this is face-to-face or by secure phone only. No writing, no paper trails."

Ulrich glanced down at a small sign in the pathway next to him. Through the frost obscuring the face of it he read *Silence and Respect*.

He took off a glove, reached into his coat pocket, and clicked off the Dictaphone he'd been running since this otherwise off-the-record meeting began. Then he came out with a tube of ChapStick to conceal what he'd really been up to. He rubbed the ChapStick across his lips, dropped it back into his pocket, and pulled the glove back on. It wasn't the first time he'd taped these sorts of conversations and he doubted it would be the last. He knew he would never need the recordings, but it would still feel good to have them. If his enemies ever breached all his other defenses and threatened to close in on him, he could brandish his recordings like a suicide bomb. A last-ditch threat in case the worst should ever happen. And the worst had never looked more likely than it did right now.

Still, on balance he was starting to feel a little better. He'd been rattled there for a moment, true, especially when they'd mentioned the Caspers, but that was before he'd had a chance to consider the options. Now, the more he thought about it, the more he realized he had assets he could deploy. Everybody was exposed on this, if not legally, then at least politically. The main thing was, he had a plan. And no one could work a plan the way he could.

"Remember," he said. "*The New York Times*. Two interrogation tapes, as far as you know, destroyed years ago. Now go. Get it done."

The New York Times, December 6, 2007

CIA DESTROYED TAPES OF INTERROGATIONS

WASHINGTON — The Central Intelligence Agency in 2005 destroyed at least two videotapes documenting the interrogation of two al Qaeda operatives in the agency's custody, a step it took in the midst of congressional and legal scrutiny about the CIA's secret detention program.

The videotapes showed agency operatives in 2002 subjecting terror suspects—including Abu Zubaydah, the first detainee in CIA custody—to severe interrogation techniques. They were destroyed in part because officers were concerned that tapes documenting controversial interrogation methods could expose agency officials to greater risk of legal jeopardy.

The CIA said today that the decision to destroy the tapes had been made "within the CIA itself," and they were destroyed to protect the safety of undercover officers and because they no longer had intelligence value.

PART ONE

All told, more than three thousand suspected terrorists have been arrested in many countries. And many others have met a different fate. Let's put it this way: they are no longer a problem to the United States and our friends and allies.

GEORGE W. BUSH

They literally were chaining people up for days. . . . If they ever had videos of this, it's something out of the thirteenth century.

BOB WOODWARD

So it appears we now have evidence Ghul was in a CIA prison. Where he is today is still a mystery. . . .

JUSTICE DEPARTMENT OFFICE OF LEGAL
COUNSEL MEMO

The New York Times, March 2, 2009

U.S. SAYS CIA DESTROYED 92 TAPES OF INTERROGATIONS

The government on Monday revealed for the first time the extent of the destruction of videotapes in 2005 by the Central Intelligence Agency, saying that agency officers destroyed 92 videotapes documenting the harsh interrogations of two Qaeda suspects in CIA detention including the simulated drowning technique called waterboarding.

1 ABOUT A HUNDRED PERCENT

Ben Treven could feel the Australians looking at him again, sizing him up for whether he'd make a good victim tonight. He brushed his blond hair out of his face and kept his gaze on nothing in particular, nodding his head slightly as though he was enjoying the pulsing house music. He knew the smart thing was to ignore them, but part of him couldn't help hoping they'd take their wordless interview just a little further. It had been a hell of a day and he could feel that old, crazy urge to unload on someone. If these guys wanted to give him a reason, it was up to them.

The three of them were in civilian clothes, but he'd heard the accents and seen the swagger and took them for sailors on shore leave. Manila's Burgos Street, an eternally crumbling matrix of neon and girly bars and massage parlors, had ingested them as it had ingested generations of sailors and marines and sex tourists before them. It would appropriate their money, alleviate their lust, and expel them afterward like pale effluent into the dank Manila night.

The burliest of the three missed his shot at the spotlit pool table, and as he stepped away to make room for his buddy, he squinted and waved a hand up and down in Ben's line of sight, palm forward, as though wiping a window. The gesture read, *Hello? Anybody there?*

Ben kept his expression blank. *Oh yeah, pal, somebody's here. And believe me, you don't want to meet him.*

A petite Filipina waitress in heels and a microscopic skirt sauntered over to the pool table, balancing a tray of San Miguels one-handed. Ben hadn't seen her earlier—she must have just started her shift. She took the Australians' pesos, distributed their beers, and studiously failed to respond to their leering smiles. Then she turned and headed in Ben's direction, the Australians' eyes following her ass.

"You need another drink, sweetie?" she asked Ben, smiling, her eyes dark, her teeth white against the smooth brown skin of her face.

He was standing with his back to the bar and she would have known he could have just ordered from the bartender. He didn't know whether her interest was personal or professional. He wondered whether it would irritate the Australians.

He shook his head and offered only a polite smile. "Thanks, I'm good."

She leaned a little closer. "Are your eyes . . . green?"

"That's what people tell me."

She smiled again. "It's my favorite color. If you need anything, just tell me, okay?"

"I will. Thanks."

He told himself that as long as he didn't do anything to provoke them, it wasn't his fault. But he also recognized that he was ignoring them almost ostentatiously now, that a more effective way to avoid a problem would have been to raise his Bombay Sapphire and give them a cold smile: *I'm aware of you, I'm not afraid of you, I'm being friendly so you can now look for trouble elsewhere without having to acknowledge you've backed down to the guy you were initially assessing.*

He took a swallow of the gin and set the glass down on the bar. Yeah, that would have been the better way.

But that afternoon his ex-wife had told him she never wanted to see him again, that their daughter, Ami, believed the man now raising her was her real father, that he shouldn't have tracked them down in the first place, and what could he have been thinking after they hadn't heard from him in nearly three years? She hadn't even seemed angry when he'd approached her in the rain in front of Ami's suburban Manila school, just uncomfortable, as though he was no more than an old acquaintance she would have preferred not to run into. She'd countered his protests, ignored his entreaties, and dismissed him with obvious relief. And instead of doing the minimally dignified thing and just leaving, he had lurked around the corner, getting wetter and angrier, until he heard the school bell, and then he had watched pathetically from behind a tree as his ex-wife collected their small daughter, kissing her and taking her by the hand and leading her away before Ben even had time to get a good look at her face. And now he was on his third double Bombay Sapphire, and these chumps were giving him the stink eye, and the bar was too noisy and the spotlights too glaring and Manila was too fucking polluted and humid and he was sick of it, he was sick of all of it, and someone was going to pay.

The burly Australian waved again. Ben maintained his thousand-yard stare. The Australian cocked his head and said something to his buddies; over the music and the noise of conversation at the bar, Ben couldn't hear what. The three of them started walking over. Ben noted they hadn't put down their pool cues. His heart kicked a little harder and he felt his mouth wanting to twist into a smile.

The Australians took their time, watching him, continuing to gauge him as they approached. None of the bar's patrons, generally young, mostly western, universally stupid, seemed to notice. Ben remained motionless.

The Australians weren't sure what he was, and Ben knew they would bark before they got up the courage to bite. Amateurs.

They stopped an arm's distance in front of him, three abreast, the burly one in the middle, the pool cue in his left hand, his right arm draped across his buddy's shoulder. He said, "Looking out of it there, mate. Too much to drink, eh?"

Ben kept his gaze unfocused, noting the placement of their hips and hands, smiling now as though at some private joke. The burly one was clearly the leader. Drop him suddenly and violently and the other two would be useless for anything other than hauling his carcass home. There were so many ways to do it, too, it was almost sad to have to choose. The guy's weight was on his right foot, exposing the instep to a stomp. His knees were open, too, and so were his balls. Or start with the throat, move to the head, then work your way down in whatever time you had before the guy collapsed.

The guy leaned in, his eyes trained on Ben's face. "You hear me, mate? I'm talking to you."

Still Ben didn't look at them. "I know. It's making it harder for me to ignore you."

The guy furrowed his brow. "You're trying to ignore us, is that it?"

In a different mood, Ben might have felt sorry for the guy. He might have just met the guy's eyes and let him know with a look what was a second away from happening. Then maybe give them a face-saving way out, maybe tell them he was just here to chill, sorry if he'd done anything to offend them, fair enough?

Yeah, in a different mood.

The guy glanced left and right at his buddies as though sharing his amusement, but in fact seeking reassurance. "You believe this guy?" he said. Then he turned back to Ben. "Hey. Look at me when I talk to you."

Ben felt it coming. He wasn't even trying to stop it anymore.

The guy raised his right hand and went to jab his outstretched finger into Ben's chest. "I said—"

Ben shot his left hand out and wrapped the guy's finger in his fist. He stepped in and bent the finger savagely back. There was a sound like snapping tinder. The guy shrieked and plummeted to his knees. The sounds of conversation and laughter ceased and Ben could sense people reorienting, trying to figure out what had caused that bloodcurdling sound. Ben bent what was left of the finger farther back and twisted it. The guy shrieked again, his face contorted in pain.

The guy to the left choked up on his pool cue and started to bring it around, and Ben instantly realized he'd been wrong about them turning tail. A klaxon went off in his mind and some deep-seated setting instantly ratcheted from *bar fight* to *combat*. He snatched his glass off the bar and flung gin into the guy's face. The guy recoiled and started to turn away. Ben grabbed a bar stool and swung it in a tight arc, going for center mass, getting his hips and full hundred and ninety behind it. The guy made the mistake of trying to duck, and the stool caught him in the head instead of the shoulder and blasted him sideways.

Somebody shouted. People started scrambling away. The third guy was backpedaling, his left arm out, his right hand reaching for the back of his belt, obviously going for a weapon, trying to gain an additional half second to deploy it. Ben bellowed a war cry and lunged forward, swatting away the guy's outstretched arm, grabbing and securing his right wrist, attacking his eyes with his free hand. The guy screamed and tried to shake free and something clattered to the floor. Ben shot a knee into his balls. The guy doubled over and Ben let him go. He saw the first guy was coming shakily to his feet. He stepped

in, wrapped his fingers in the first guy's hair, yanked him
forward, and clubbed him in the back of the neck. The
guy's arms spasmed and Ben felt something crack under
his fist.

He spun to face the other two. They were twisting and
groaning. The first guy was splayed on the floor, motionless.

A thought flashed through his mind, sobering in its
clarity: *did I kill him?*

He looked toward the exit. The patrons had scattered
to the periphery and the center of the bar was clear, but
ten feet away, between Ben and the door, four wiry Filipi-
nos were pointing pistols at him. Off-duty cops? Another
thought flashed through his mind:

Shit, what are the chances?

Two of them were starting to fan out to his flanks
now, the two in the center moving forward, pistols still
forward, one guy producing a pair of handcuffs from
the back of his belt.

Right now? Chances look about a hundred percent.

Even if he'd been armed, and he wasn't, dropping all
four without getting shot in return would have required a
hell of a lot of luck. He briefly considered raising his arms
to show he was no threat and just walking past them to
the exit. But their quick reaction to the disturbance, and
the tactical way they were approaching him now, told
Ben these guys were experienced, that they'd be happy to
shoot him before suffering the humiliation of letting him
just walk on by.

Ben looked around and saw people holding up cellphones. They were taking his picture. Or video.

He glanced at the Australians again. Two were still
twisting. The other was still inert. The red haze was suddenly gone and a chill rippled through him. He raised his
hands, palms forward, and thought, *Oh, shit.*

2 FALLING

Ulrich looked through the floor-to-ceiling windows and watched the K Street traffic twelve stories below, his feet perched on his mahogany desk, a wireless headset snug against his ear. "Thanks, Jim," he said. "Really appreciated your time last week. And my client is just delighted the senator understands how counterproductive any additional regulation would be on top of what the industry is already burdened with. If you have any other questions, I know it would be their pleasure to arrange another golf outing. And of course you can count on their complete support. You bet. Thanks again."

He clicked off and thought, *Done and done.* Lobbying wasn't so different from governing, really. He was making ten times his public-sector salary, which was nice, and his office furniture was a hell of a lot better than what he'd had in room 268 of the Eisenhower Executive Office Building, too, but other than that? Well, his work was no longer stamped secret, true, but nor would it have done for the public to have too close a peek at the way lobbyists made laws. The main thing was, the priorities were the same, and so were the methods. It was all about who you knew, and how you could get who you knew what they wanted.

His other phone buzzed—the secure line that went straight to his desk and not through his secretary. He put his feet down and picked up the corded handset. "Ulrich."

"It's Clements. Are you alone?"

Clements was still the number two guy at CIA, having been passed over for the number one slot by the new administration in favor of an outsider. He was a good contact—one of many Ulrich used to maintain his influence among the city's elite.

"Yeah, I'm alone. What is it?"

"We have a problem."

Ulrich's chest tightened and he immediately thought, *the tapes.*

"Go on."

"You know how in the end we all assumed the tapes had been destroyed by a patriot?"

God, he hated being right all the time. "Yes."

"The director got a call this morning telling him to go to a website. He did. The tapes are all online."

"What the—"

"Wait. They're not public. The website is encrypted. The caller wants a hundred million dollars in uncut diamonds, or he decrypts the files and uploads them to You-Tube and every media outlet in the United States and abroad."

Ulrich felt clammy sweat spring out under his arms and along his back. He was momentarily at a loss. If this had happened when he had the full authority of the vice president's office behind him, he would have instantly taken control, and taking control would have calmed him. As it was, he felt trapped, in sudden thrall to this dimwit to whom he ought to be issuing orders. He felt horribly, uncharacteristically helpless.

Which raised a question. "Why are you calling me?" he said.

There was a pause. "The director just contacted the Justice Department. They're bringing in the FBI."

"The FBI . . . no. Impossible. No one could be that stupid."

"It's not stupid. He's new. No previous connection to the Agency. He's covering his ass by following procedure."

The room was suddenly stifling and Ulrich felt like he was falling. So much time had gone by. He hadn't even thought about the tapes in . . . he couldn't remember. He really had come to believe they were gone—launch all the investigations you want, it doesn't matter because the tapes no longer exist.

He'd never been so wrong.

"You used to work with Bilton, right?" he heard Clements say. "The president's counterterrorism adviser?"

"I know him. Why?"

"Call him. He's got the ear of the national security adviser. We're going to stonewall the Bureau, and the Bureau will go to the national security adviser to mediate. When they do, we want a sympathetic ear. All we need to do is keep the Bureau on a leash for a few days while we go after whoever is behind this."

"This is what we did last time. We didn't find anything, remember?"

"That was last time. This time, something new—something major—is in play. This guy, or this organization, whoever it is, they're calling us. Creating websites. Issuing instructions. At some point, they'll have to tell us how to deliver the diamonds. All that adds up to a whole series of opportunities we didn't have before. The director's made me point man on this and I've already assembled a team—same kind of discreet team we used last time. So we can handle it quietly—but not if the Bureau gets involved and starts treating it as a criminal case."

Ulrich exhaled a deep breath. Clements was right, he had to admit. Embarrassing to have him point out something Ulrich had missed, but he was right.

"Yeah, I can get in touch with Bilton. He'll understand. What's our window?"

"The caller agreed to give us five days to put together the diamonds."

"What? You've only got five days to find this guy and air him out?"

"It's more complicated than just airing him out. He says he's got the video rigged to an electronic dead-man switch. If he fails to disarm the switch at a preset interval, the video gets uploaded."

Hot bile surged into Ulrich's throat. He pulled a bottle of Maalox Maximum Strength from a desk drawer, unscrewed the cap, and took a huge mouthful. He grimaced, his eyes watering, and swallowed.

"Anything else?" he managed to ask.

"Yeah. If this thing goes south, we'll want to have our stories straight."

"If this thing goes south," Ulrich said, his mouth pasty with the taste of the Maalox, "it won't matter what our stories are."

He realized when Clements didn't respond that he'd been hoping he would. Nothing could have confirmed Ulrich's point more emphatically than the silence on the other end of the phone.

"I'll get in touch with Bilton right away," Ulrich said. "Let's keep each other posted."

He hung up, put his glasses on the table, and sat for a moment with his face in his hands.

There was nothing he could do. The Agency was in charge, Ulrich's involvement was reduced to that of a messenger boy . . . They were done, they were all done. Ever since the tapes were first discovered missing, he'd been living on borrowed time. No, since before then, even. Since he'd first figured out what to do with the Caspers. That's what had killed him. He just hadn't realized it until now.

It wasn't fair. For so many years, he'd tried so hard to protect the nation, and he just . . . he just couldn't anymore. And without him, who would?

And then some deep part of himself cut through the thickening mists of despair. He wasn't helpless. He didn't need to defer to the idiots at the CIA who had caused this catastrophe in the first place. He didn't have the power he'd once wielded, true, but he still had the contacts. In the end, the contacts might matter more. All he had to do was use them. Use them well.

He put his glasses back on, took another swallow of Maalox, and picked up the secure phone.

3 LUNGS OF A DRAGON

On his second day in the Manila city jail, Ben was still telling himself it could have been worse. But it wasn't easy to figure out how.

Out of habit, he'd been traveling sterile. His passport, his wallet, anything that could identify him—it was all inside the safe in his room at the Manila Mandarin Oriental. Even the magnetic room key was under a loose cobblestone on Paseo de Roxas, where he'd left it when he first set out that evening. The Philippines didn't fingerprint visitors at immigration, at least not yet, so at the moment of his arrest, the only clue to his identity was the five thousand pesos and change in his jeans pocket. Which was no clue at all, thank God.

His mind had been a shambles of conflicting emotions: exultation at having fought and prevailed; worry that he'd accidentally killed someone; fury at having been so stupid and incompetent; fear about what was going to happen to him. On top of everything else, humiliation. Being arrested by the local third world gendarmerie was about the biggest embarrassment a black ops soldier could suffer. He'd laughed at stories of guys it had happened to, thought they were fuckups and incompetents. But look at him now. He was one of them.

He was determined to keep his options open, to say nothing that might unwittingly preclude subsequent possibilities. He didn't respond when the cops told him one of the men he'd fought was dead, his neck broken. Maybe they were lying, though his gut told him, sickeningly, it was true. He was silent when they pretended they were his friends, he was silent when they knocked him down and beat the shit out of him. Part of him was aware that his silence was probably making things worse. But having lost control of everything else, he found himself clinging to whatever pathetic sense of dignity and power he could derive from the simple ability to deny his interrogators his voice.

Eventually they told him they didn't care, the guy he killed wasn't Filipino and he wasn't Filipino so why were they wasting their time? They'd dumped him in the Manila city jail, which Ben quickly learned from some of its English-speaking inhabitants had been built for a thousand inmates and currently housed more than five times that number. There were people of all ages, mostly Filipino but a few foreigners, too, convicted murderers serving life sentences alongside ordinary people who couldn't afford bail and were just waiting for their day in court. It was so hot the concrete walls caused second-degree burns, so crowded the prisoners had to sleep side by side on the ground in shifts, and stank so badly from the accreted decades of concentrated piss and nonstop sweat and endemic diarrhea that you could feel the miasma on your skin like something moving and alive, something trying to worm its way into your pores so it could dissolve you from the inside out.

There was an open-air pavilion where the prisoners were served food. Twice a day, the same watery, yellowish gray porridge smelling like rotting fish. On his first morning, Ben choked it down, knowing he had to eat to stay strong, then barely made it to the corner of the pavilion before throwing it all up. A bony but tough-looking Thai guy with brown skin as drawn and dried as jerky laughed and said, "No worry! Everyone do first time, sometime second time, third time. Soon-soon, okay, yum-yum."

"Yum, huh?" Ben said, wiping his mouth with the back of his hand.

"Not yum-yum, you die," the Thai guy said. "So you make yum-yum."

No one messed with him—his size and demeanor took care of that—but so what? Dummying up, he began to realize, was just a multiplication of his initial stupidity. Had the cops even filled out any paperwork? He couldn't remember seeing any. Looking around at the shifting ranks of scrawny, gap-toothed prisoners, all of them filthy and haggard and sweating bare-chested in the heat, he could easily imagine himself being forgotten here.

On the third day, with the magnitude of his fuckup gnawing at his mind and fear settling like some dark obstruction deep in his chest, he approached the guy who looked like the head guard and asked to call the U.S. consulate. The guy didn't even look at him, he just laughed to himself and tapped his truncheon. Ben told him he was an American citizen, there'd been a mistake, he needed to talk to the consulate, okay? The guy's laugh drifted away and his gaze shifted to Ben. His eyes were flat and his fingers curled around the hilt of his truncheon. Ben felt a surge of anger and pictured himself snatching the puke's truncheon off his belt and braining him with it. But he managed to shove the anger back, knowing it was what had landed him here in the first place, knowing that as bad as things were, uncorking on a guard would make them infinitely, permanently worse.

As he lay down that night on the radiant, piss-stained concrete floor of the small cell he shared with a dozen other prisoners, he remembered a moment from his jungle training. They'd dropped him in a part of the Everglades so dense that even at noon the sun was just a dim green glow at the top of the tree canopy. He had three days to reach his objective, alone, and a day in he started wondering, if he didn't make it out, how would anyone even find him? He remembered the feeling of being lost and alone, monumentally insignificant in an indifferent, alien world. And now he was fighting that feeling again, that creeping, childlike dread at having been abandoned somewhere, orphaned, marooned.

He crossed his arms and rubbed his shoulders as though trying to prove he was even still there. Nobody knew what had happened to him. Eventually, when he didn't report in, the military would go looking, but where? He'd been inhaled like a dust mote into the lungs of a dragon. And every breath the dragon took carried him deeper into its body and farther from the light. He was in so deep already, how was he ever going to get out? In his few nightmarish days within the beast, he'd already run into guys who'd been here for years—*years*—without being sentenced, without even a hearing. He imagined that once you passed a certain point in a system like this one, the overseers wouldn't let you up for air even if by some amazing coincidence they became aware of your case. At that point, after all, your story would be an embarrassment to them. And the worse your treatment, the more sympathetic your circumstances, the more egregious the entire story, the more culpable they would all be. After a certain amount of time without a hearing, being innocent would probably be the worst thing that could happen to someone in a place like this. What were they going to do, admit that for three, five, seven years, they'd caged up a guy who—*oops*—hadn't even done anything, and never even gave him a hearing? Yeah, fat chance of that. Better to just leave you where you are. You'd been there that long already, and it wasn't like anyone was asking about you. Let sleeping dogs lie, baby. Wait long enough, and eventually they'd be sleeping for good.

The next morning, as he dozed on the concrete, he

was awakened by a hard poke in his ribs, which were still bruised from some well-placed kicks delivered by Manila's finest. He shot to his feet, his back to the wall, adrenaline rocketing through him. Three guards regarded him, their truncheons out. He looked from one to the other. Reasonably good odds, maybe, but what was he going to do—cut through these three and then levitate over the wall?

One of the guards motioned with his truncheon. Ben nodded and started walking.

They took him to a small room with faded green cinderblock walls and a single rattling fan that in its uselessness seemed only to worsen the clinging wet heat. A black man in jeans, sneakers, and a red polo shirt, obviously fit and somewhere in his fifties, was sitting at a peeling linoleum table in the center of the room, his shaved head beaded in perspiration. He shook his head in mild disapproval as Ben entered.

"Damn, son," he said in his gravelly Mississippi Delta baritone. "You look like shit warmed over."

Despite everything that had happened between them, and despite the humiliation of having his commander find him like this, Ben was so flooded with relief his legs went rubbery. He knew his situation was bad, but until this moment he hadn't realized just how near he'd been to actual despair, how convinced he was beginning to feel that no one would ever find him.

He breathed in and out a few times, pulling himself together. When he trusted himself to speak, he said, "What are you doing here, Hort?"

Hort laughed, the sound deep and not at all unfriendly. As always, Ben was struck by the man's complete ease and confidence, by his natural command presence. Colonel Scott Horton was a legend in the black ops community. He had personally designed and now commanded Ben's secret unit, the absurdly blandly named Intelligence

Support Activity, and his exploits in Nicaragua, Afghanistan, and elsewhere were such that he was held in awe not just by his men, but even by the Joint Special Operations Command brass who were his nominal superiors.

The laugh slowly died away, a paternal grin lingering in its aftermath. "When I heard they had visiting hours in hell, I just couldn't stay away."

"I don't need you to bail me out."

This was so obviously untrue Ben immediately felt like a blustering child for saying it, and expected another baritone chuckle in response.

Instead, Hort said, "It's not a question of what you need. I'm responsible for you."

Ben knew he was being stupid, but anger was the only thing keeping him together and he was afraid to let it go. "Got a funny way of showing it."

"Don't ask me to apologize for putting the mission ahead of the man, son. I already told you, it was the toughest call I've ever had to make."

Hort had been tasked with securing and erasing all knowledge of an encryption application called Obsidian. The op started with the liquidation of the inventor and the patent examiner, and would have taken out Ben's younger brother, Alex, too, who was the inventor's lawyer, along with Sarah Hosseini, an associate at Alex's Silicon Valley firm. But Alex had realized he was in over his head and had called his big brother for help. Together, they'd managed to turn things around, though not before Hort, in the service of putting the mission before the man, had tried to erase all three of them.

"Yeah, well don't ask me to apologize for not forgetting."

Hort nodded, his expression grave. "That seems fair."

Ben walked over to the chair opposite Hort, pulled it away from the table, and sat. He knew Hort would read it as a concession, but he didn't care. He'd never felt so wrung out. His ribs ached, he'd only half slept since all this shit had started, and much as he hated to admit it, he was terrified Hort would leave as suddenly as he'd materialized. It was a ridiculous fear, but he couldn't shake it no matter how much he blustered.

"How'd you find me?" he said quietly.

Hort nodded, as though expecting the question. "Pressure from the Australians. You're lucky you killed one of theirs. If it had been a local, they'd have just dumped you here and no one would ever have heard from you again."

Ben felt something sink in his chest. He realized he'd still been hoping the cops had lied to him. The hope suddenly felt stupid, and he knew he just hadn't wanted to admit it to himself, admit what he'd done.

"The guy was a sailor?" he said.

"Royal Marine, yeah."

He'd known as much already, but somehow having Hort confirm it eliminated Ben's ability to deal with the guy as an abstraction. Having this little window opened on the guy's humanity made part of Ben want to push it open further, but he knew better. Still, even the speculation was no picnic. Had he been married? He'd been pretty young, so maybe not. And Ben hadn't seen a ring, though he supposed the guy might have removed one before a night of carousing on Burgos Street. Regardless, he would have had parents. Maybe brothers or sisters. He thought of Katie, his younger sister, who'd died in a car accident as a high school junior, and what her death had done to his family. The thought that he probably had caused something similar to someone else's family because he was too sullen to just walk away from some woofing was suddenly making him feel sick. Not to mention the guy himself was never coming back, either.

"Anyway," Hort said, "the Aussies made local law enforcement go to all the hotels in Makati, asking whether there was a guest who was supposed to check out but who'd ghosted off instead. It didn't take them long to find the right hotel, the right guest, to have the room safe opened, to check the guest's passport. When they found out you were American, they contacted the U.S. embassy. When the embassy realized who you were, they contacted JSOC. And here I am."

It made sense. But it answered only how Hort had found him, not why. He knew he should ask, but he almost didn't care. He had to fight the urge to blurt out, *Please, just get me out of here . . .*

He took a breath and said, "All right, you want something from me."

Hort pulled a handkerchief out of his pocket and used it to mop the moisture off his face and scalp. "You're a little more cynical than the last time I saw you."

"I wonder why that would be."

"You want me to just leave you here? I could, you know. The Australians want to extradite you. All I have to do is step aside and let it happen."

Somehow, hearing the threat out loud eased Ben's mind a little. If Hort were really going to leave, he would've just done it. And obviously, he hadn't come all this way just to say hello.

"Maybe your brother could help you," Hort said. "Good to have a lawyer in the family when you've been charged with murder. And the girl, Sarah Hosseini. Two smart lawyers. Strange to think of them protecting you instead of you protecting them, but there you have it."

Hort had no way of knowing what had happened between Sarah and Ben—the way their distrust had alchemized to passion, maybe to even more. He was fishing on that one.

"Do they need protection?" Ben asked, his voice low, his tone casual.

There was a pause. Hort said, "No."

Ben nodded, not exactly reassured. Alex and Sarah still knew a lot about Obsidian and about the failed op to disappear it. It wasn't impossible someone on the National Security Council or wherever might get sufficiently uncomfortable about their knowledge to decide to revisit the issue. But at least Hort wasn't threatening him with it. On the other hand, he'd learned from the Obsidian op that Hort could be a master bullshitter, at least when bullshitting was required by the mission. Maybe he just knew Ben well enough to know overt threats would be counterproductive. That didn't mean the threat wasn't there. It wasn't in Hort's character or his experience to display a weapon until he was ready to use it.

"All right," Ben said. "So you've pulled all these strings, you're running interference with the Australians and who knows who else, just because you care. I'm touched, Hort. Really."

"You know you're on YouTube now, right? Camera phones in the bar."

Ben looked at him, his shame so enormous he couldn't speak.

"Relax," Hort said. "You got lucky. The spotlighting in the bar was pointed at the cameras. You can barely make out the action, let alone your face."

Ben managed to nod, the whipsaw from horror to relief intensifying how sick he felt from what he did to the Aussie marine. He concentrated on his breathing, trying to get a grip on emotions that were slipping past his control.

Hort looked at him. Other than the useless rattle of the fan stirring the leaden air, the room was silent.

"So tell me, son," he said. "What were you doing in that bar?"

Ben didn't know why, but the question made him feel suddenly wary. "What do you mean, what was I doing? I was having a drink."

"Why?"

"I had a lot to think about. Some shit has happened to me recently, you might have noticed that. I just wanted to be alone and think. You never had something like that?"

"All the time. But if you wanted to be alone so you could think, you didn't need a bar. Your hotel room would have been just fine. Or you could have taken a walk. Or gone to the library."

"They don't serve gin in the library."

"No, they don't. The gin was part of what you wanted, I can see that."

Ben was getting increasingly uncomfortable. It wasn't just what Hort was saying. It was also the quietly confident way the man was looking at him, as though he knew Ben better than Ben knew himself.

"I don't know what you're talking about."

Hort looked at him. "You know exactly what I'm talking about. But maybe you need me to spell it out for you."

Ben held Hort's gaze. But why did he feel like flinching?

"What you wanted," Hort said, "was to fuck someone up. And you couldn't do that in your room, or taking a walk, or visiting a local branch of the Manila public library system. But a bar on P. Burgos Street was pretty much tailor-made. Now, maybe you didn't mean to kill the man whose neck you crushed, maybe you just wanted to hurt him. It doesn't matter. Either way, you lost control. And an operator can never do that."

"I didn't—"

"Yes, you did. Now listen. I rocked your world recently, I get that. I wish it hadn't needed to be that way, but yeah, I turned you upside down. Your commander betrayed you, you can never trust these people again, everything you believed in is wrong. That was more or less it, right?"

Ben didn't answer. He hadn't thought of it in those terms exactly, but . . . Shit, was he really that transparent? He could feel his face burning.

"So you decided it was over with you and the unit, you were done. The problem is, you're a man with a lot of energy inside you and you needed to divert it to something else. So you flew to Manila, where your ex-wife lives with your daughter. You thought you were going to be a better person, didn't you, maybe reconcile with your ex, be a father to your little girl. Attach yourself to something new, like a man falling in love on the rebound. But it didn't go well, did it?"

Ben felt his shame coalescing into anger. "Back off, Hort."

"No, I will not back off. You went to see them, didn't you? And your woman turned you away. Or you saw her with another man. Or both, or whatever. Well, that's two rejections in a row, twice your world's been rocked. Now, some men deal with rejection and humiliation and confusion by wallowing in self-pity. Some of your more self-actualized types can let it roll off their backs. How about you? How do you deal with it?"

Ben stared at Hort, his lips thinned, his nostrils flared. It was like being stripped, being stripped and laid bare. He wanted to blast the table out from between them and slam Hort into the wall, over and over until his eyes rolled up in his head and he learned to *shut up, just shut the fuck up* . . .

"For example," Hort said, as though reading his mind, "how are you dealing with it right now?"

Ben ground his jaw shut and looked away. The breath was whistling in and out of his nostrils.

"Yeah, maybe now you're starting to see it. You've got anger inside you, son. Maybe it's all-natural, or maybe something happened along the way and made it worse. Either way, it's in your nature to seek out enemies and destroy them. It's what you do. It's what you're good at. Some people play the piano, some people race cars. You destroy enemies. And that's fine, there's nothing wrong with it. The country needs men like you and I wish we had more. But you need direction. You need that violence to be channeled. Because if somebody's not authorizing enemies on your behalf, you're going to go out and create some on your own, like an attack dog off its leash. You think what happened in Manila was a one-off? It wasn't. It was the beginning of the rest of your life."

Ben realized he was gripping the edge of the table, to steady himself or throw it aside he wasn't even sure anymore. He opened his hands and flexed his fingers and concentrated again on slowing his breathing.

He knew Hort was right. If any of it had been bullshit, he'd have laughed it off. The way it was enraging him, though . . . why would that be?

Because the truth hurts.

"No one else talks to me like that," he said after a moment. "No one."

Hort nodded. "No one else cares enough to take the chance."

"What do you want, then?"

"I want you to stop this foolishness. There's a major shit storm heading our way right now and I need your help to stop it. So I need you to stop acting out like a wounded adolescent. I need you to be more self-aware and to show more self-control. Can I count on you for that?"

Ben wiped his lips with the back of a hand. He'd already spent so much time thinking, the hell with the unit, he was out, he could never trust Hort again . . . and here was the man himself, telling him not only that he was back in if he wanted, but acting like he'd never even left. Telling him he was needed.

It was confusing as hell. But also . . .

It felt good. So good.

A rivulet of sweat ran down into his eye. He blinked. "Give me that handkerchief, will you?"

Hort handed it to him. Ben unfolded it and wiped his face.

He gave the handkerchief back to Hort. "You said something about a shit storm?"

Hort nodded and stood. "I did. But first, let's get you the hell out of here."

4 AN EXTREMELY UNPLEASANT DEATH

Larison woke before dawn in another anonymous motel, this one along I-64 just outside Richmond, Virginia. He scrubbed a hand across the dark stubble on his face and considered trying to go back to sleep. Without the pills, though, the dreams were too much to face. He realized he should have weaned himself sooner, gotten used to sleeping unassisted before starting the op. But the pills would have dulled the edge he'd need if a bunch of guys in black fatigues and face masks blew his door with a shaped charge and came swarming into the room with chloroform, flex-cuffs, and a hood. Being unprepared for that possibility would be worse than the dreams. Though perhaps not by much.

The hell with it, he was too keyed up anyway. He swung his feet to the floor, picked up the Glock 18C machine pistol from the carpet next to him, and stood. He was fully clothed, all the way down to his boots and three spare 33-round magazines of armor-piercing ammunition in the pockets of his Blackhawk integrated tourniquet pants. They weren't going to take him dazed and blinking in his skivvies the way they'd done Khalid Sheikh Mohammed. They weren't going to take him at all.

He walked through the dark to the bathroom and pissed, then came back and dragged the mattress from behind the couch and back onto the bed frame. He'd moved it to the floor the night before when he arrived. A small thing, but it could buy an extra second by creating the wrong focal point when a room was breached, and a second in a gunfight was like an hour any other time.

Truth is, it was a wonder he could sleep at all. He'd been planning this thing for years, and now it was finally happening. He'd just declared war on the U.S. government. And they were going to come at him with everything they had.

If he was lucky, the CIA would try to handle the whole thing in-house and the opposition would be limited and incompetent. More likely, given the sums involved, Christians in Action would have to bring in someone from the White House, and the White House would mobilize the NSA. The public didn't really know what the NSA was capable of—didn't *want* to know—but Larison had seen firsthand the results of operations like Pinwale, where the NSA got caught illegally reading vast quantities of American emails, along with some even more impressive ones that hadn't leaked, and the thought of the puzzle palace training all that firepower exclusively on him was both exhilarating and terrifying.

And then there was Hort. Impossible to say whether JSOC would be brought into this. But even if they were kept out, it didn't mean Hort wouldn't find his way in. Not everything Hort did had JSOC's blessing, or even its knowledge. Larison had learned that the hard way and he wouldn't forget it. Behind the avuncular exterior that was part of what made men worship him, Hort was one of the most ruthless and capable operators Larison had ever known.

He set the Glock down and started doing push-ups. He wanted to go out as little as possible, so these in-room workouts were all he could afford right now. And he needed something to burn off his anxiety.

The trick was to assume the worst and act accordingly. The NSA searched for patterns; Larison would give them none. His movements were random, he paid for everything in cash, and when he had to show ID, he could draw on a half dozen identities, all of them guaranteed sterile because he'd created them himself. It had been a long time since he'd trusted JSOC.

He finished two hundred and fifty push-ups, flipped over onto his back, and started a set of sit-ups. His breathing and heart rate were slightly elevated. He felt good. Working out always took the edge off when he was feeling paranoid.

Hort represented a different facet of the same problem. Hort would try to exploit what he knew about Larison to anticipate Larison's next move and then plan an ambush accordingly. Larison had seen Hort get inside his enemies' minds and predict what they would do next. The man knew people so well, at times he seemed almost psychic. So much so, in fact, that Larison had from time to time considered eliminating the threat Hort might now represent.

A surge of latent paranoia suddenly gripped him and he wondered if he'd made a mistake, if he should have taken out Hort after all. But Hort was no soft target, for one thing. For another, Larison wanted to avoid yet another doomed face tormenting his dreams. Not that Hort didn't deserve it. But they all deserved it. Guilty or innocent, it didn't make any difference.

He amped up the speed of his sit-ups, bludgeoning back the paranoia. He cranked out two hundred and fifty and rolled to his feet. He was still breathing through his nose. He started doing squats.

He wondered whether he should have taken a chance and staked out his ex-wife. She was still in Kissimmee, the town near Orlando where they'd lived in the years before Larison had ostensibly died—she'd grown up there and her folks were still local, and with Larison traveling so much, it had been comfortable for her, especially with the baby. For anyone who managed to connect what was going on with Larison, it would be a logical spot to begin, and Larison would have liked the opportunity to run reconnaissance to get a sense of who and what he was up against. But in the end, he'd judged the risks not worth the rewards. His primary weapons were stealth, movement, and surprise. Outnumbered as he surely was, anything that put him in contact with the enemy was an enormous risk.

Squat, stand. Squat, stand. On every other rep, he leaped into the air and landed on his toes. Sweat trickled down his sides.

Anyway, Marcy didn't know anything about him. She never had. Their whole marriage had been a pathetic farce. He couldn't even blame her for the baby. Really, he should have thanked her. It made everything he had to do afterward easier. The main thing was, operationally, she was a dead end. He was fine.

Then why was he pushing the workout so hard?

Because you're keyed up, that's all. Who wouldn't be?

He finished the squats and went straight into lunges. Two fifty, five hundred, it didn't really matter. He could go practically forever, it was just a question of time.

It was all so strange. He was officially dead, he'd been hiding for years, he'd severed all contact with anyone who'd known him as Larison. And yet it was only now that he felt everything was about to irrevocably change. He had the overwhelming sense of being perched on the edge of a dark precipice. He had no choice but to leap, not seeing what was on the other side, knowing only that it would be everything he always wanted, on the one hand.

Or an extremely unpleasant death, on the other.

He wondered for a moment whether he really had a preference. Did it matter?

He decided it didn't. After the sobbing, the begging, after the awful . . . *sound* they all made, the men he'd interrogated had all eventually reached that point of surrender, of not caring how they were released, wanting only for it to be over. It was strange that he should feel a kinship with them now.

And then he thought of Nico. If this didn't go well, Nico would never know what had happened. He'd probably assume Larison had abandoned him and gone back to his wife. The thought of Nico left that way, forever wondering, doubting, was like a vise around his heart.

No. It wouldn't end that way. He had all the cards. And he was playing them well. He'd gotten this far, hadn't he?

He wondered again whether Hort would be involved. And if so, what dumb young fool Hort would set against him. Whoever he was, Larison might have felt sorry for him. But he didn't. They'd burned the pity out of him. The only pity he had left he would save for himself.

5 SOMEONE ELSE WOULD WORRY ABOUT WHY

Less than an hour after his arrival, Hort walked Ben out of the Manila city jail. A sedan with a driver who looked like Diplomatic Security drove the two of them back to the Mandarin Oriental, where Ben showered, vacuumed down two plates of pasta and a beer, and passed out. Hort woke him at eight. The car took them to the airport, where they checked into adjacent first-class seats on a Philippine Air flight to Los Angeles. The luxury was anything but standard, and Ben took it to mean that whatever Hort wanted, it needed to be done ASAP. This would likely be Ben's last chance to sleep for a while.

The moment they were in the air, Hort took out an ordinary iPhone and selected an application that would pump out random subsonic signals to scramble any listening devices. The military called the application the Susser, meaning subsonic signals scrambler, but like so much other military hardware, such as the GBU-43/B massive ordnance air blast—more widely known as the Mother of all Bombs—this one, too, had its own nickname: the Cone of Silence. Everyone knew the national carriers allowed their nations' spy services to bug the first-class seats for industrial espionage.

Hort set the phone down on the armrest between them and put a Bluetooth earpiece next to it. "These are for you," he said. "There's more information on the phone, but we'll get to that."

"Okay."

"Two days ago, someone contacted the new director of central intelligence," Hort said, his voice so low it was almost inaudible over the background roar of the engines. "This someone has gotten hold of some extremely sensitive materials and wants to be paid for their safe return."

Ben pinched his nostrils and cleared his ears. "How sensitive are we talking about?"

"A hundred million dollars sensitive. That's what our blackmailer is asking for. Payment in uncut diamonds, none larger than three carats. Small, anonymous, easy to move."

"What do they have, photos of the president in flagrante?"

"I wish that's what this were about. No, what they have is interrogation videos."

Ben thought for a moment. "I read somewhere the CIA had destroyed a bunch of waterboarding videos. First there were just a couple, then they admitted closer to a hundred, something like that?"

Hort nodded. "That's the story they told the papers. Truth is, they never destroyed anything. The destruction story was just disinformation they put out when they discovered the tapes were missing."

"Yeah, but this story broke . . . I forget, but it's been years."

"December 2007. That's when they discovered the tapes were missing, that's when they started trying to cover it up."

"And then . . ."

"And then in March 2009, they changed the story. Ninety-two tapes, not just a few."

"Why?"

"A throw-down to the new administration. The word was, the newbies were going to investigate the tapes' destruction more seriously than the previous one was inclined to. So the message was, 'This is much worse than you think. Investigate and you'll never get anything done on the economy, or health care, or global warming, or jack shit. An investigation will go in a hundred directions you don't want. It'll eat you alive.'"

"I don't get it. In the end, what did they think was going to happen? Were they hoping the tapes really were destroyed?"

"That's exactly what they were hoping. And it wasn't a bad working theory, if you think about it. Someone should have destroyed those tapes—can you imagine what would happen if they got out?"

"Why the hell make tapes in the first place? Are they crazy over there?"

Hort shrugged. "The signal-to-noise ratio wasn't great on the information they were getting from the program. Truth is, most of the people we were picking up, we weren't even sure who they were. Informants were accusing people we'd never heard of, dirt-poor Pakistani farmers turning in some Arab just because they didn't like him or didn't want to pay him the money they owed. Settle a grudge by accusing your enemy of terrorism and collect a bounty at the same time—who could resist that? And with the methods the CIA was using, fabrication was a problem. So they tried to develop a mosaic, cross-referencing everything they extracted in the interrogations. Fabrication is random; the overlaps have more credibility, that was the theory. So every new bit of intel extracted meant they could look at previous intel in a new light. For that, they needed records, something they could go back to."

"Yeah, records. Transcripts. Not video. Not if you don't want to get crucified on CNN."

"Transcripts miss things. They needed to be able to examine the totality of circumstances: when did the subject say what he said, what was being done to him at the time, what were his facial expressions at that moment, his body language, were there other indices of fabrication? They were trying to mine every bit of value from the information they managed to extract. That was the whole point of the program. The tapes were a key part of it. And there was supposed to be an element of intimidation, too. You know, 'What are your tough-guy terrorist friends going to think when they see this video of you crying and begging like a baby?' "

Ben had heard corridor talk about the program. Most of it sounded pretty stupid to him, but that was true for a lot of Agency initiatives and it wasn't his problem. Until now, anyway.

He cleared his ears again. "These tapes . . . were there copies?"

"No. One set of originals, and that's what the blackmailer has."

"Even so, do we know that whoever took them and whoever is using them are the same? If they've been brokered, every middleman in the chain would have made copies."

"My gut tells me they haven't been passed around. First, because in all these years, no one's heard a peep about these tapes being circulated. Second, if you're smart enough to steal the tapes, you're smart enough not to broker them. The risks are similar, but the real payoff only comes when you hit up Uncle Sam. Who else is going to come up with a hundred million dollars in diamonds?"

Ben couldn't find any fault in Hort's reasoning. "All right. What do we have to go on about the blackmailer?"

"So far, nothing. Initial call placed from a cloned sat phone. Communication through an anonymous private email account established at the caller's instruction after that. We traced the points of access, of course. They're all over the eastern United States. We've tried to triangulate. No luck. No tie-in with surveillance cameras outside an Internet café, nothing like that. The people we're dealing with are good, no question."

"So working backward from the blackmail doesn't get us anything. What about from the initial theft? Assuming we're dealing with the same person or group."

Hort nodded slowly. "There, I think I might have a lead or two."

Something in Hort's tone, and in his use of "I" instead of "we," contained a world of subterranean meaning. Ben paused, knowing Hort wanted him to figure it out.

"You haven't told the CIA."

Hort looked at Ben and nodded again, obviously pleased. "Go on."

"You don't trust them?"

Hort snorted. "You could say that. Right now they're running around like a bunch of hyperactive retards. They're going to fuck this up if we let them. So we're not going to let them."

Ben thought for a moment, sensing he was missing something, not sure of what it was. "Is it just the CIA? Who else knows about this?"

Hort smiled. "The DCI contacted the Justice Department. Federal blackmail case, standard operating procedure."

"And if the FBI recovers those tapes . . ."

"Exactly. Their goal will be prosecution. They'll preserve the tapes as criminal evidence. Eventually, they'll leak. And you've got Abu Ghraib all over again, multiplied by about a thousand. You put those tapes on Al Jazeera, forget about just guaranteeing al Qaeda's monthly recruitment numbers—it'll ignite the whole Muslim world."

"Oh, man."

"So now we have three overlapping investigations. The CIA, which caused this monumental goat-fuck to start with. The Justice Department, which if they recover the tapes will, with all their good intentions and by-the-book behavior, wind up doing the same damage the black-mailer is threatening."

"And me."

"I'd call that *us*. But yes."

Ben nodded. He couldn't deny, he liked the sound of the plural better. "Us, then."

He thought for a minute. The whole thing had been so smoothly delivered. But there was something missing at the center of it. Something obvious.

"Why?" he said.

"I told you, I can't trust the others."

"No, I'm asking you why not one of the other guys in the unit. Why'd you come to me?"

"Well, for starters, I had to get you out of a hellhole in Manila."

"The real reason."

Hort sighed. "I'm dealing with manpower issues right now, that's why. Most of the ISA is tied down in Afghanistan and Iraq. Among the ones who aren't, two are recovering from injuries you inflicted when you met up with them in California. And another operator you might remember, Atrios, isn't reporting in again, ever."

Ben was glad Hort hadn't tried to bullshit him about how special he was. The truth was, there wasn't a man in the unit who wasn't in some way the best.

He thought again. There was something nagging at him . . . and then he realized.

"This whole time, we've been talking about 'the black-mailer.' Singular. You used it. And you didn't correct me when I did."

Hort smiled. "Is that right?"

"You know who it is."

Hort's smile broadened. "Just don't forget who trained you, son, all right?"

Ben felt an absurd flush of pride and tried to ignore it. "Who?"

"A good man with a lot of demons, demons that finally got the better of him. His name is Daniel Larison. You never knew him, but he was part of the unit. One of the originals, in fact. He was one of the few people who had access to the tapes."

"So why isn't everyone looking for him now?"

"Because he died in the bombing attack on Prime Minister Bhutto in Karachi on October 18, 2007."

There was a long pause. "He faked his death?"

"I believe he did. He had contacts in Pakistan's ISI and he could have had foreknowledge of the attack."

"And not warned anyone?"

"I told you, the man has demons."

"Damn. How many people died in that attack?"

"About a hundred and forty, and three times that burned and maimed. Larison was in Karachi on temporary duty. Shortly before the attack, he reported he was going to meet a contact at Bhutto's rally. But that might have been deception, and he could have left the country under a false passport after. The bomb was big enough to make it impossible to identify all the remains, one of which was assumed to be Larison's based on knowledge of his movements and on other factors. Anyway, we couldn't inquire too closely without getting into a pissing match with the ISI about placing operators unauthorized on their soil."

"Yeah, but they know we—"

"They know, and they don't want us to remove their ability to deny that they know. Anyway, if anyone could have pulled this off, it was Larison."

"What's his motive?"

"Well, there's a hundred million dollars in play. That's a lot of motive right there."

"Would you do what he's doing for a hundred million?"

"It doesn't matter what I would do. It's what Larison would do. Like I said, the man had demons. He saw some shit in the course of his work that mandated time with a shrink, but he would never see one."

Hort paused, and a ripple of sadness seemed to pass across his face.

"Yeah, he shouldered an unfair burden, and the weight was causing cracks. He was a serial steroid abuser, for one thing. He had anger management issues, for another. Too many times, he stepped over the line in the field. I won't lie to you, either—a lot of this is my responsibility. I saw the signs, I knew he'd been in the field for going on way too long. He needed a reprieve, he needed help. But with two active war theaters and shadow operations like we've never seen before, we've been stretched. Hell, we've got National Guard deployed in Iraq and Afghanistan, grunts on their fifth tour of duty, politicians asking more and more and giving us less and less to do it with. Put enough pressure on the system, you're going to start seeing cracks. Cracks in the system, cracks in the soldiers."

Interesting. Hort had read the anger in Larison as he'd read it in Ben. Well, it wasn't like the unit attracted a lot of Zen Buddhists.

"Why are you so sure it was him?"

"I'm not sure. But there's no one else that makes any sense."

"Then couldn't the other players—the Agency, the Bureau—figure out Larison, too? That he had the access, faked his death—"

"They could, but they won't. They don't know him the way I do. Larison was the best. He's what you'll be in ten years if you keep developing the way you need to. Right now, you've got the confidence and the instincts. What you need is judgment. And control."

That was a rebuke for Manila. Ben couldn't deny the justice of it.

"If it's just the Agency and the Bureau on this, how did you find out? What's your connection?"

Hort smiled as though pleased that Ben was considering all the angles, asking the right questions. But he said only, "I've been around for a while, son. I know people."

Yeah, a guy like Hort had contacts everywhere: Pentagon, State, all the spook services . . . probably even the White House. Couldn't really expect him to reveal his sources and methods.

"So, what's our time frame?"

"Five days. And he says he has an electronic dead-man trigger. Even if we find him, we can't just take him out."

"A bluff?"

Hort shook his head. "It's exactly what he would do. Or you or I would do, for that matter."

"What do I do when I find him?"

That ripple of sadness passed across Hort's face again. "You don't do anything. Your job is just to find him and fix him. Not to finish him. Not yet, anyway. For the time being, we're going to have to play this one by ear."

Ben wasn't sure what playing it by ear would be about. Up until now, "find, fix, and finish" had always constituted a half-redundant description of what Ben did, with "finish" being the real point. He wanted to ask what Hort had in mind, and why he thought they might be able to end this without ending Larison in the process. But he'd asked the important questions already, and that kind of "why" wasn't in his job description anyway. His orders were to find and fix Larison, and he would carry them out. Presumably, at that point, he'd get some new orders. In the meantime, someone else would worry about why.

6 DON'T WANT TO WIND UP LIKE HIM

The next morning, Ben was slowly circling Belthorn Drive in Kissimmee, Florida, a half-hour drive southwest of the airport in Orlando. According to Hort, this was the current residence of Larison's "widow," now going by her maiden name, Marcy Wheeler. For the moment, Wheeler was pretty much the only actionable thing they had to go on.

He drove, his head sweeping back and forth, absorbing information, looking for the detail that didn't fit: a parked car with a couple of hard-looking men inside, a van with darked-out windows, a man in shades strolling along and somehow not from the neighborhood. Nothing tickled his radar. Belthorn was a sleepy collection of modest ranch houses being inexorably replaced by more imposing McMansions. But for the heat and the occasional palm tree, it could have been a suburban street in just about any lower-middle-class American neighborhood transitioning from older families and long-standing homes to younger, more aggressive colonists, newcomers with more of a need to make a statement and more appetite for the housing debt such statements required.

Wheeler lived in one of the older, smaller homes, a one-level yellow rectangle that looked like it contained one or at most two bedrooms and that badly needed a fresh coat of paint. Ben parked at the end of the street, far enough to keep Wheeler from seeing the license plate on his rented car, near enough to watch the house. Hort had told him Wheeler had a son, and it was almost time for school.

He watched and waited, hoping he was doing the right thing. He knew he couldn't trust Hort the way he once had, not after what had happened with Alex and Sarah. But at the same time, when the op was blown, Hort had immediately stood down. He could have killed all three of them—should have, in fact, from a strictly operational perspective—but instead, he had let them walk away. Why leave all those loose ends? Ben could only surmise that it had been personal, that Hort had almost been looking for a reason to not follow his orders. But was that enough reason to trust the man now?

On the other hand, what were the alternatives? Leave the unit and join a private outfit? He could, he supposed. With the government stretched so thin, men with his credentials were making a mint as contractors. Even elite groups were having to offer retention bonuses, bonuses that more often than not didn't work.

Yeah, he should do it. Three years as a contractor in someplace like Somalia and he could practically retire.

Ah, bullshit. The truth was, he liked being in the unit. Partly it was the training. He shot with Delta, jumped with the Smokejumpers, and learned his tradecraft from grizzled CIA survivors of Denied Area operations. He enjoyed the pride, the quiet swagger that came with being ISA. There were maybe three hundred men, not just in America, but in the world, who could legitimately claim to be his peers. That was saying something.

But it was more than that. He liked being on the inside. He liked knowing the secrets, the way things really worked, the real world beneath the surface everyone else inhabited. Contractors had the salary, and maybe they still had the swagger, but they didn't have the inside position. And he didn't want to give that up.

And why should he? What else did he have? A daughter who thought he was dead, an ex-wife who wished it were so . . . crap, it hurt, but when he was alone with his thoughts like this, he had to admit his life was a mess. He was glad he and Alex had managed to mend some badly broken fences recently, that was something. But what had it really changed? They weren't attached by much more than blood before, and it wouldn't be all that different now.

And Sarah? Their chemistry was pretty unbelievable, it was true. They couldn't have been more different and at first he thought she hated him. Which maybe on some level she did, but then they'd wound up in bed anyway. He'd initially tried to pass it off as the effects of shared danger and a combat hard-on, but the truth was, it felt like more than that.

Even so, the only reason she'd let herself get close was because she didn't really understand what he did. How could she understand? They were from totally different worlds. And let's face it, she was the kind of person who was more comfortable pretending his world didn't even exist. Which was ironic, because as far as he was concerned, it was her world—a world where violence never solved anything and where no one was evil, just misunderstood, and all people were fundamentally rational and could be reasoned with—that was the illusion, the pretty veneer. He knew the truth. He knew what things looked like from the inside. And he liked the view.

He thought about how he'd handle Wheeler. He knew subtlety wasn't his forte—never had been, never would be. He was better at kicking in doors than at persuading people to open them, and this was a persuasion job, no doubt. But he'd had the elicitation training at the Farm, and over the course of various ops, he'd managed to put that training to good use. It was like Hort said, he just needed to exercise a little more control. He'd be okay.

At just past eight o'clock, Wheeler's front door opened. A small boy, eight years old if Hort's information was correct, stepped outside, Wheeler just behind him, blond hair tied back, gray shorts and a navy tank top. She helped the boy struggle into a backpack, kissed him, and waved him off, then watched while he waited at the curb with a few other kids similarly outfitted. A few minutes later, a yellow school bus pulled up. There was a hiss of hydraulic brakes, a red stop sign sprouted from its side, and then it was gone, the children along with it. Wheeler watched it go, looking somehow deflated in its wake. Ben thought of Ami in Manila, another child of a dead father.

Come on, forget it. It's better like this. Put it away.

He got out of the car and started walking toward Wheeler's house, his head sweeping left and right, keying on the hot spots. He detected no problems. He was wearing an olive poplin suit, white shirt, wine-colored tie, and black wing tips, all courtesy of a Brooks Brothers in Orlando, all practically government-issue. A standard Bureau Glock 23, spare magazines, pocket litter, and FBI ID and passport in the name of special agent Daniel Froomkin had been waiting for him in a dead drop near Orlando. Hort had explained that there actually was a Froomkin on the payroll in the J. Edgar Hoover Building in Washington, D.C., that the legend was fully backstopped. They couldn't expect Wheeler to cooperate with someone who had no colorable legal authority.

The air was humid and smelled of cut grass. A thin, Mexican-looking guy was pushing a buzzing mower across one of the lawns on the other side of the street. Ben paused and watched him for a moment. The guy's T-shirt was soaked with sweat and he was wearing earplugs against the noise. His arms were weathered and brown from too much sun. A beat-up pickup loaded with gardening equipment sat at the curb. The guy felt legit.

He headed up a short riser of cement steps, the Glock creating a reassuring weight and pressure under his left armpit, reminding himself one last time that he was Dan Froomkin, FBI, investigating a crime. Even a civilian could sometimes spot the incongruity in the vibe between an operator and an investigator. One of the things they'd taught him at the Farm was that to make a cover work, you had to submerge your true self inside it. The key was to *believe* your cover, to feel it like it was the truth.

He knocked on the door, an authoritative knock, confident, but not so loud as to be intimidating or aggressive. And he kept a respectful distance from the threshold. The trick would be to make her want to cooperate in part by making her afraid of what might happen if she didn't. But she couldn't be consciously aware of the fear. It had to be in the background, obscured by a demeanor just friendly enough to enable her to believe she was volunteering and ignore that she was being subtly coerced.

A moment later, Wheeler opened the door. Either Kissimmee enjoyed a low crime rate, or she was trusting. Or maybe her mind was still on her son.

"Can I help you?" she asked, her expression uncertain. Up close he could see she was a pretty woman, midforties, hair highlighted, teeth artificially white. The shorts and tank top revealed a toned body. Ben noted in mental shorthand that despite the modest house, despite being a single mother, she still spent on the hair, the teeth, maybe on a personal trainer or yoga or Pilates courses. Her appearance was important to her. He was aware this might be useful, but he didn't yet see how.

"Yes, ma'am," Ben said, producing the FBI ID. "I'm Dan Froomkin, special agent, Federal Bureau of Investigation.

I'd like to ask you a few questions about your late husband, Daniel Larison. It should only take a few minutes, if you don't mind."

Her pupils dilated slightly, the result, no doubt, of an adrenal surge. But she seemed more surprised than afraid. "My late husband . . . what? Why?"

"We're investigating a crime, ma'am. Your husband wasn't involved, but his behavior in the time before his death might prove helpful."

Ben waited while she absorbed that potentially ominous *we*. After a moment, she said, "All right, but I don't really think I'll be able to help, Mr. Froomkin."

Ben gave her a friendly smile, a lower-wattage version of the one that had always made it easy for him to hook up in high school and in various port cities after. "Well, it can't hurt to try and find out. And please, you can call me Dan if you like. Sometimes I hate having to be so official with people."

"All right, Dan," she said, returning the smile with a slightly nervous-looking one of her own. "Come in, I guess. Would you like a cup of coffee? I just put some on."

Ben nodded. "I'd love one. Thanks."

He followed her through a small foyer to an equally small kitchen. The furniture was sparse and eclectic and looked like it had been handed down. The way she took care of herself suggested Wheeler wasn't exceptionally frugal, so from the furnishings Ben surmised Larison hadn't carried an impressive life insurance policy and hadn't left behind much of anything else. Again, he wasn't sure what this might mean, but filed it away as something potentially useful.

The kitchen smelled like waffles or pancakes. Clearing a pair of plates and glasses from the table, she said, "Sorry about the mess. Here, have a seat."

Ben noted that she made breakfast and ate it with her son. Watched him at the bus stop until he was gone. A devoted parent. He thought of Ami again, and was irritated at himself for letting the thought intrude. Ami had nothing to do with this.

He sat and considered. She was nervous, that was clear. But who wouldn't be, when the government shows up at the door flashing ID and asking about dead relatives? The nervousness felt normal. She was wary, not scared. And regardless, she'd taken him to the kitchen. That was good. People did business in the kitchen, it was where they opened up. The living room was a façade, the place for putting people off.

She brought him coffee in a plain white mug that looked like it came from Pottery Barn or the like. "Milk? Sugar?"

"No, black is good." He took a sip. "This is great. Thanks."

She smiled again, warmed up her own cup, and sat across from him.

He took another sip of the coffee. It really was good—nothing fancy, just strong and dark, the way he liked it. "Sorry to intrude like this," he said. "Probably not your idea of an ideal morning. I'll try to make it quick."

She shook her head. "That's okay. I just don't know what I could tell you. My husband died a long time ago."

The phrase "a long time ago" intrigued him. Not a date, not a number of years . . . just something vague, a reference to the indeterminate, irrelevant past. He had the sense that she had severed her memories of Larison from her life, that she now held them at a distance. Why?

"I apologize if my presence here is stirring up any sad memories. I understand your husband died in the course of service to the nation."

She smiled a tight, uncomfortable smile. "Well, he always lived for that service. Not a huge surprise he would die for it."

Ben hadn't expected her to know anything about the

blackmail, if indeed Larison was the guy behind the blackmail. If he was even alive at all. And nothing about her demeanor suggested otherwise. Just the normal amount of discomfort.

He gave her a sad smile that wasn't exactly a forgery. Just being in this homey kitchen was like some silent condemnation of his own role as a father. "Well, I know a little about that. Hard not to let the job . . . overwhelm you."

She glanced at his left hand. "Are you married?"

He shook his head. "Divorced."

He realized this was a single mom in her mid-forties, devoted to bringing up her son. What were her dating prospects in a small Florida suburb? When was the last time she'd been with a man?

He hadn't anticipated this angle before, but sensed now it might present an opening. Maybe make her more cooperative, more talkative than would otherwise have been the case. The thought helped him push back his awareness of Ami and refocus.

"Anyway," he said, smiling and shaking his head as though the conversational detour had flustered him, which in fact it had, "there's a chance your husband was in contact with some people we need to interview. Would you happen to still have his passport? Travel receipts? Correspondence? Anything about his contacts or his movements would be helpful."

She took a sip of coffee and watched him. She seemed to be evaluating him and he couldn't tell what she might be thinking.

"No," she said, after a moment. "I'm not the sentimental type, and even if I were, I wouldn't have saved any mementos from him."

Him, this time. Before, *husband*.

He looked at her, pleased she was willing to talk, disappointed at his sense that she wasn't going to have anything useful to tell him.

"I'm sorry, would you mind if I asked why not?"

She shrugged. "We didn't have a happy marriage. Is that going to go in your report?"

He shook his head, wondering where this was coming from, and feeling a little bad, too. Part of him was aware of the strangeness of it: that maybe he was more comfortable shooting people than he was manipulating them.

"I don't see why it would need to," he said.

There was a pause. She said, "If I tell you what I know about his whereabouts before he died, will you tell me what you find out?"

Ben was taken aback. "Ma'am, this is a confidential investigation—"

"Marcy. After all, I'm calling you Dan, right?"

Ben was suddenly struggling to stay ahead of her, and wondering whether he'd been ahead to begin with.

"Yes, you're right. Marcy. If there's something I can tell you at some point, I'll tell you. But I can't promise you anything. You know that."

That sounded right. Like what a real FBI guy would say in similar circumstances.

She looked at him for a long time, that evaluating look again, and he thought he'd been a fool to believe she was being friendly because she was interested in him. She was interested in something, all right. But not in what he'd thought.

"If my husband was involved in some kind of crime, I guess you won't be able to tell me. But I don't care about that anyway. It's his . . . personal life that still bothers me. It shouldn't—he's been dead a long time and mostly I've moved on. But it would help me to know. Closure and all that."

"I . . . understand," Ben said, as noncommittally as he could.

She smiled at him, an odd smile Ben judged as about equal parts sympathy and condescension, and again he was struck by how badly he'd misjudged her intelligence.

"Do you?" she asked.

He set his coffee mug on the table. "Why don't you tell me and we'll see."

There was a long pause. She said, "My husband would go away for weeks, sometimes months at a time, and wouldn't tell me where or why. What was I supposed to think?"

"Well, you know his assignments were secret—"

"Please. Other than the honeymoon and a short time after, we were barely having sex. Even when he would come back from one of these long 'assignments,' he wasn't interested. When we did it at all, it felt perfunctory. Like maybe he was thinking of someone else. What would you have made of that?"

"I suppose under the circumstances I'd suspect my husband was having an affair."

"Of course that's what you would suspect. So I hired a private investigator and had him followed."

Ben stared at her for a moment while he tried to digest that. "You . . . had your husband followed?"

She frowned slightly, and Ben realized she had misunderstood the reason for his surprise. "I mean," he said, "from what I've heard about your husband, hiring a PI to follow him would be like sending a twelve-year-old to beat up Mike Tyson."

The frown eased and she chuckled. "Yes, the investigator told me he was 'surveillance conscious,' I think that's the phrase he used. At first, the best he could do was learn that my husband had flown to Miami. Twice. But the next time, when I told him my husband was about to travel again, the investigator waited at the airport in Miami. This time, he saw he was flying to Costa Rica."

Holy shit, Ben thought. *This could be something.* "Costa Rica."

"Yes."

"And then?"

"The investigator hired someone local, in San Jose. Next time my husband went to Costa Rica, the local guy was supposed to follow him. Instead, he disappeared."

"Your husband disappeared?"

She shook her head. "Not my husband. The local guy. My investigator got scared, told me he didn't want to work on the case anymore, and gave me back my money. And my husband died after that, before I could hire someone else."

"What do you think happened?"

"I don't know. I don't want to know. My husband could be a scary man."

"Scary how?"

There was a long pause. Then she said, "He had rage inside him. I don't know what about. Maybe it was work, things he saw or things he had to do."

"He had a temper?"

"No. He never lost his temper. At least not with me. With me he was mostly just cold."

"Then—"

"I can't explain it to you. You wouldn't understand, you didn't live with him. There was something inside him he was struggling to keep from exploding. Maybe it finally did. I don't know. I look back now, and I realize . . . he was very controlled. He only let people see what he wanted them to see. Even his wife. So I don't have anything else I can tell you."

They were quiet for a moment. Ben said, "Do you still have the contact information for the local investigator?"

"Sure. Harry McGlade. He operates out of Orlando.

Or at least he did—we haven't been in touch since he dropped the case."

Ben couldn't rule out the possibility that she was in some kind of collusion with Larison. But if so, they'd have to be in collusion with the PI, too, or at least they would have had to manipulate the hell out of him years in advance. All of which he judged highly unlikely. His gut told him she was telling the truth.

"What else?" he asked, reminding himself to use the kind of open-ended questions they'd taught him at the Farm were best for general elicitation.

She laughed. "What else were you expecting? That's got to be more than you were hoping for right there."

He was half impressed, half irritated by her spunk. He wondered what she'd been like as Larison's wife. A handful, that much was clear.

He looked at her. "If you think of anything else, will you call me?"

She smiled, a faint, sad movement at the corners of her mouth. "If you learn anything else, will you do the same?"

Why not, he thought. *She's still in pain over this. You can call her, tell her anything you want, and make her feel better.*

"If I learn something that would be personally helpful to you," he said, "then yes, I'll try to find a way to let you know. Off the record." It felt good to say it. It wasn't even a lie exactly.

"I just want to know about Costa Rica. You understand?"

He nodded. "Yeah."

"Was he seeing someone there."

"Got it."

She closed her eyes and shook her head. "I doubt it. That's a very hard thing not to know about the man you were married to. If you're decent, you won't even put what you find in your report."

"I don't . . . I'll try not to."

She looked at him and nodded gravely, as though grateful for his gesture and doubtful of its worth. "Well, if you happen to come back here and want to fill me in in person, that would be fine."

He nodded, wondering whether he'd been wrong after all about her initial interest. "I can't promise anything," he said. "But . . . I think that would be nice." Again, he wasn't exactly lying.

She walked him to the door. He opened it and took a quick glance through the crack—first right, then sweeping left as he opened it wider. Everything looked all right. The gardener and his truck were gone. Other than that, nothing had changed since he'd arrived.

"My husband used to do that," she said from behind him, her voice cold.

He stepped out onto the stoop and glanced back at her. "Well, I don't want to wind up like him."

Even before the words were out, he realized it sounded harsher than he'd intended. As he tried to think of a way to soften it, she said, "Don't, then," and closed the door between them.

7 THE EASY WAY

Ben walked down the steps, scanning the street. The information about Costa Rica sounded promising. He would check with Hort on ops in South America, and if they could eliminate business, he would assume Larison had been traveling for personal reasons instead. A lover? The wife certainly seemed to think so.

And he'd follow up with McGlade, the investigator. Guy had to have been mildly brain damaged to try to tail someone like Larison, but he'd at least had the sense to figure out at some point the job wasn't worth the per diem.

Marcy. He had to admit, even beyond operational necessity, he was intrigued. She was a strange combination of savvy and honesty, openness and mystery. He wanted to do right by her, if he could. Not because he was interested in her. Or at least, not only because of that. It was something about the way she'd watched her son. That . . . sadness he'd seen in her face when the bus had pulled away. Initially it had made him think uncomfortably about Ami, but now it was summoning images of his own childhood, the breakfasts his mother would serve her three kids and her slightly absentminded engineer husband. Happy breakfasts, mostly, even though Ben had little patience for little brother Alex. Or at least they'd been happy until Katie's accident. Happiness had fled the Treven household after that, with Ben close on its heels.

Forty yards from his car, he noticed another one parked behind it, a brown Taurus that hadn't been there before. His heart rate kicked up a notch and his alertness level moved from orange into red. He slowed, watching the car, aware of the weight of the Glock.

Thirty yards out, the passenger-side door opened. A big white guy with close-cropped hair in a suit a lot like his started to get out. The driver-side door opened, too, and a black guy emerged, as big as his partner and also in a dark, forgettable suit. Ben slowed more, his readiness now completely at condition red, his heart pounding, his limbs suddenly suffused with adrenaline. They started walking toward him, their hands empty. He sensed, without having to consciously articulate it, that this wasn't a hit. If it had been, they wouldn't have moved on him while he was this far away.

Ben's head tracked left to right and he scanned his flanks to confirm the primary threat wasn't just a setup— a trained response burned by combat into reflex. A petite young black woman with a short afro, shapely and well-dressed in navy slacks and a matching sleeveless blouse, was walking along the sidewalk toward them. Her vibe was civilian and he sensed no connection to the two men. He judged her not part of the threat.

Ten yards. Ben watched their hands and shoulders, not their eyes. If anyone's arm even twitched, he would have the Glock out and they'd have to skip the pleasantries.

Five yards. "Excuse me, sir," the black guy said. "We need to ask you a few questions."

Ben checked his flanks again. The black woman was watching them, but with no more than normal curiosity. When she saw Ben looking, she glanced away, just another civilian recognizing possible trouble and not wanting it to recognize her back.

Three yards. "Who's 'we'?" Ben asked.

"FBI," the white guy said. "You need to come with us."

They stopped, close enough to try to grab him now, if they were that stupid.

"Nah, I don't feel like going anywhere right now," Ben said. "Better just ask me here."

"Look," the black guy said, his hand easing his jacket back, thumb first. "We can do this the easy way—"

Ben didn't give him a chance to finish the move, or even the sentence. He shot an open-hand jab into the guy's throat, catching his trachea in the web between his thumb and forefinger, feeling the cartilage shift unnaturally behind the blow. The guy's teeth slammed shut and his head snapped forward.

The other guy started to shuffle back to create distance, his hand going for something under his jacket. But he was on the wrong end of the action-reaction equation. Ben caught him by the lapels and smashed his forehead into his face. He felt the guy's nose break. He took a half step back and shot a knee into the guy's balls.

He turned back to the black guy, who was clutching his throat with his left hand and groping under his jacket with his right, his eyes bulging. Ben closed the distance, caught the guy's right sleeve, and yanked him past in the kind of arm drag he'd once favored as a high school wrestler. He hoisted him from behind, rotated him over an upraised knee, and slammed him facedown into the sidewalk.

The white guy was on his knees, his face a bloody mask. He snaked a jerky arm inside his jacket. Ben took a long step over and kicked him in the face. The force of the kick lifted the guy's supporting arm clean off the sidewalk and he dropped the gun he'd been fumbling for. Ben swept it up—a Glock 23, just like his. He checked the load. Good to go.

He tracked back to the black guy, aiming the Glock with a two-handed grip. No movement. Track back to the white guy. Same.

He stepped over to the black guy and bent to take his gun and check for ID.

A voice came from behind him, feminine, sweetly southern-accented but with steel underneath. "Put the weapon down, sir. Now. Or you're dead right there."

He looked up. Son of a bitch, the black woman. She'd taken cover behind a parked car and was pointing a pistol at his face.

"I'll be damned," he said, slowly lowering the Glock. "You're with these guys. I didn't spot that."

"Drop. The weapon. Now."

Ben didn't know who they were. They felt like law enforcement. From the way they were armed and what the black guy had said, they could have been FBI. And Hort had said the Bureau was investigating.

But he'd be damned if anyone was going to take him into custody again. Not today. Not ever.

He eased the Glock into his waistband. "Yeah, I heard you the first time."

"Sir, I will shoot you."

He looked at her. "Then shoot me."

The black guy groaned and started to get up. Ben kicked him in the face and he went down again.

"Stop that!" the woman yelled.

"You want to ask me your questions, ask," Ben said. "Otherwise, I've got places to go."

There was a long pause. The woman continued to watch him through her gun sights and for a tense moment Ben wondered whether he'd miscalculated, whether she might actually shoot him.

She watched him for a moment longer, and he could see the tension in her face. Incongruously, he found himself noticing her skin. Smooth, light brown, with a sprinkling of freckles across her nose and cheeks. There was a hint of Asian in the shape of her eyes.

She lowered the pistol and muttered, "Goddamn it."

She came out from behind the car and approached him, the gun in a two-handed grip but pointed at the ground. Ben noted that she was watching his torso, not his face. She was well-trained.

She walked over to the fallen white guy and knelt next to him. "Bob," she said, "are you okay? Bob."

Bob groaned. He got a hand on the street and started pushing himself up. The woman helped him. While she did, Ben reached inside the black guy's jacket.

"Hey!" the woman called.

Ben extracted a Glock from a shoulder holster. "Too late," he said. "Doesn't look like you're going to shoot me, but I don't know about this guy."

The woman walked over. "Drew," she said. "Goddamn it, Drew, talk to me." She looked at Ben. "If you killed him, I swear to God you're going down."

Drew wheezed, then broke into a coughing fit. He rolled to his side, his hands on his throat.

"Well, he's breathing," Ben said. "What were you saying there, chief? Something about, what, doing this the easy way? Well, you were right, it was easy."

"Shut up," the woman said. "Drew. Look at me. Can you drive?"

Drew sat up and massaged his throat. Ben didn't think the guy looked good to drive. He looked good to puke.

But Drew managed a nod.

"Then go."

Drew wheezed. "That's not—"

"Just go. I'll interview this guy and fill you in later."

She stood up and holstered her gun. "All right," she said. "Let's go."

"Go? Where are we going?"

"Wherever you like. A coffee shop. A park. Somewhere we can talk."

"I don't think—"

"Just shut up and drive your car, okay? Before I get sorry I didn't shoot you."

8 NO ONE EVER SEES ME COMING

They found a Starbucks in the direction of Orlando. At the counter, Ben told the girl at the register, "Just a black coffee. Tall." Then he walked off and found a table that put his back to the wall.

A minute later the black woman set a couple of coffees on the table and joined him. She looked miffed, whether at having to buy and bring him his coffee or being stuck with her back to the door or both, he didn't know. It was satisfying either way.

"Who are you?" the woman said.

He picked up the coffee and took a sip. "It's not going to work that way."

"What way is that?"

"The way where you ask the questions."

"Look, if I wanted to—"

"But you don't want to. Otherwise you would have already."

She drummed her fingers along the table. He couldn't help noticing how attractive she was. That great skin; close-cropped, natural black hair; full lips; perfect teeth. Maybe that's why he'd instantly written her off as a potential threat when he'd first spotted her. Stupid.

She opened her purse and took out an ID. The ID read, *Special Agent Paula Lanier, Federal Bureau of Investigation,* along with a photo.

Ben looked up from the ID. "Well, Paula, it's good to meet you."

"Sorry I can't say the same. And now it's your turn."

Ben didn't want to get into specifics. The Froomkin identity was backstopped, but someone within the FBI itself could debunk it easily enough.

"Why don't you just call me Ben," he said.

"All right, Ben, who are you with?"

"With?"

"Stop messing around with me, okay? I want to know who you are and what you were doing at Marcy Wheeler's house. And I want to know whatever she told you."

He took another sip of coffee. "That's a lot to ask, on short acquaintance."

"It's not, really. Not when you consider that you can tell me here, or I can arrest you right now and we can conduct the interview at the Orlando field office instead."

"Is this the hard way or the easy way again? It didn't work out well for Bob and Drew back there. You sure you want to go down that road, too?"

"I'm the one who had the drop on you, remember?"

"Then why haven't you just arrested me?"

"Because I'd rather do this off the record for now."

"Why?"

"Look, I know who you are. Or what, anyway. You've got spook written all over you."

Ben couldn't help smiling. "I could say the same about you, you know."

She cocked an eyebrow. "Funny. I know you're CIA. Could have been DIA, maybe, but I know they're not involved in this thing."

Interesting that she would assume that. Well, Hort told him the CIA would be conducting its own off-the-books investigation, trying to beat the FBI to the tapes. Looked like the Bureau was aware of the problem, too.

He felt a momentary unease. These missing tapes were

big. Maybe the biggest thing he'd ever worked on. A lot of players were after them, maybe for a lot of different reasons. A part of him wondered why all these agencies were circling one another the way they were, and the thought was as unfamiliar as it was uncomfortable. He was accustomed to thinking in terms of who. And when. And where. And how. But *why*? For the second time in as many days, he reminded himself that why was someone else's problem.

"What are you, Ground Branch?" she said. "You're former military. I can tell by the way you move."

"Yeah? Well, I took a look at you and couldn't tell anything. Until you were pointing a gun at me."

She smiled. "That's right. No one ever sees me coming."

An unprofessional double entendre popped into Ben's mind and some vestigial sense of judgment saved him from giving it voice.

"I'll bet they don't," he said, keeping it neutral.

"So don't blame yourself too much."

"I'll get over it."

They sat in silence for a moment, watching each other, and Ben knew she was evaluating him the way he was her.

"All right," he said, "so why off the record?"

She smiled just the tiniest bit, and he realized she'd been using the silence to draw him out. Damn, he had to stop underestimating women.

"Because I've never seen interagency cooperation worse than what we have on this case. Not even compared to what I've heard it was like before 9/11. And look what all that distrust and rivalry caused back then. When we don't work together, Americans die. It's that simple, but you people never seem to wake up to it."

"'You people'? What about your side?" Weird to suddenly find himself pretending to be an FBI guy pretending to be a CIA guy, but he went with it.

"Oh, there's plenty of blame to go around, I'm sure. But we're getting next to zero from the Agency on this one. We had to threaten a subpoena just to get a few records. And your presence at Wheeler's house confirms you've been holding back. If you know something about her, if she's relevant, why haven't you told us?"

"Well, it's not like you told us, either."

"The only reason my team was staking out Wheeler's house in the first place is because the Bureau thinks she's a dead end. If they thought she was important, someone else would have been assigned."

"You mean you, Bob, and Drew aren't the A-team?"

She cocked an eyebrow again. "You keep up the sarcasm," she said, her voice sweet, "you might get smacked."

"I don't know. That might be nice."

She went to take a sip of coffee. Halfway to her mouth, she snapped the cup toward him. Hot coffee hit him in the face. He shot to his feet, spluttering and wiping his eyes.

"What the fuck?" he said.

He looked around. A few patrons were staring, but quickly glanced away.

"Oh, what, did I not smack you the way you were hoping?" she said.

He wiped his face and flung coffee droplets from his palms. "You've got nerve, sweetie, I'll give you that."

"Sit your ass down and recover your pride. Unless you want me to school you again."

He sat down, his ego smarting much worse than his face. "I like when you get all ghetto-talk on me. Really, it's sexy."

"Oh, a little racist patter to go with the sexist. You trying to bore me to death now? You think I haven't heard it all before, mostly from people a lot more clever than you?"

Goddamn it, she was right. She'd won the round. Now he was just being an asshole.

"Well," he said, "you were right. That's twice I didn't see you coming."

She smiled, and despite her evident amusement there was something gentle and even forgiving in her eyes. "I told you. Now listen. I like your dimples but I don't have time to flirt with you. I'm not here to play games."

"Yeah? What do you have in mind instead?"

"A little word association exercise to start with, to establish our bona fides. You ready?"

"Sure," he said, not knowing where she was going.

"Detainees."

Ah. Now he understood.

"Interrogations," he said.

She nodded. "Now we're making progress. Video-tapes."

"Missing."

"Diamonds."

"A hundred million U.S."

"Bingo."

They were quiet for a moment. "All right," he said. "We're both looking for the same thing."

"Exactly. And the brick wall your people are throwing up is going to make it impossible for either side to find it."

"Then tell me what you need," Ben said, hoping to learn more from the questions than he was willing to provide with answers.

"I need Larison."

"Larison's dead."

"He's supposed to be dead, yes."

"What makes you think he's not?"

"Look, the only thing we could get from CIA were some records, probably incomplete, on who had access to what we're looking for. I was up for two nights straight cross-referencing the data. A black ops guy named Larison, deceased, had the access. I asked the Agency and they stonewalled me. That told me I was on to something. I told my superiors we needed to look into it. How sure are we this guy is dead? And even if he is, maybe he had an accomplice who got the tapes before Larison died. They all blew me off. They're all looking for an analyst, trying to adapt their serial killer profiling tools to predict the kind of personality that would do something like this. And let me tell you, once an orthodoxy takes hold at the Bureau? It's like religion, nothing's going to shake it. So they told me fine, you want to stake out a dead guy's widow's house? Go right ahead. They gave me Bob and Drew, who you might have noticed aren't the sharpest tools in the shed, and shooed me away. They were just glad to get me out of their hair."

Well, Hort had been wrong about another agency not getting curious about Larison. He'd read the Bureau right, it seemed, he just hadn't known about this tenacious woman.

"Why didn't you interview her yourself, then?" he said.

"I was going to. But first I wanted to watch her. See if someone like you happened to show up."

"Might have cost you time. Pretty big gamble."

"Not so big, really. Because here you are. So what did she tell you?"

"Not much."

"You're lying."

Well, it felt like he was lying, but technically he was afraid he might be telling the truth. "She might have told me one thing that was useful. I'm going to check it out now. Leave me alone for a while and I'll let you know what I turn up."

"That's your idea of interagency cooperation? I knew you were CIA."

"Look, I'm under a lot of pressure. It's the best I can do right now."

"Fine. You can explain while I'm booking you in the Orlando field office."

"You want to know something, Paula? I like you. You're smart and you've got balls. But if you make a move to arrest me, you're going to wind up like your buddies Bob and Drew. The only difference might be that with you, I could feel bad about it after."

She watched him for a moment, amused or seething he couldn't tell.

"You're right," she said, with that sweet, soothing tone that to him was beginning to sound like a rattlesnake's tail. "You're a hard man. Even if I arrested you, I bet I couldn't get you to cooperate. Guess I'll just have to interview Wheeler myself. When she mentions someone has already been to see her, I'll say, 'Really? That's awful. Who was he? Did he tell you he was FBI?' 'Cause I know you didn't just waltz into her house and tell her you were CIA. 'He did? No, ma'am, he wasn't FBI. I don't know who he was, we've never heard of him. But impersonating an FBI agent is a crime punishable by no less than ten years in a federal penitentiary. I'd like to assist you in registering a complaint with the Bureau so we can conduct a formal investigation into who this man could be. We'll need to release a description to the media, too.' That kind of thing."

"You're bluffing."

"Then call."

He watched her. She didn't blink.

He asked himself why she wouldn't do it. And couldn't think of a single good reason.

"All right," he said, "we need to visit a private investigator in Orlando. But your pals Bob and Drew stay behind, got that? They need medical attention, for one thing. For another, I don't want to have to worry about one of them stewing over what happened, and doing something stupid to get his mojo back. They don't strike me as the bygones-be-bygones type."

"No, they're not. So, yes, we'll make it just the two of us. But give me their guns first."

Ben looked around. "Hand me your purse."

She did. He held it under the table and slipped Drew's and Bob's weapons inside it, then put it on the table. She went to take it back, but he didn't let it go.

"I'm still armed, Paula," he said, looking into her eyes. "And I'd hate to have to shoot you just as we're getting to know each other. I really would feel bad about it."

She smiled and patted his hand. "I'll bet you would, sugar. I'll bet you would."

9 SOME KIND OF MILITARY SPOOK

Harry McGlade's office was located in Orlando's Parramore district, home of the Amway Arena, a U.S. federal courthouse, police headquarters, and a number of other state buildings. The area was awake and bustling when Ben and Paula arrived. At nightfall, Ben knew, the daytime population would roll away like drops of mercury, revealing a sad substratum of winos, whores, and madmen beneath.

Paula had called McGlade from the road and told him she had a case, that he was highly recommended though she couldn't say by whom, that she needed to see him right away. McGlade was amenable.

The building was a ramshackle second-floor walk-up with a stairway that smelled like someone had been using it for a toilet. Paula went in first. McGlade was just beginning to stand from behind an enormous metal desk when Ben followed her in. Crestfallen would be too strong a word for the look on his face, Ben thought, but not by much. His age was hard to guess—ballpark, sixty—and he was overweight in a way that looked more liquid than fat, with Gollum-pale skin that suggested this squalid room was as much a cave to him as it was an office.

"Didn't realize there were two of you," he said, in a nasal voice.

"I'm sorry," Paula said. "I didn't want to say too much over the phone."

Ben looked around. The place was like an experiment in entropy. Papers so scattered that but for the settled-in stink of sweat and tobacco you'd think a wind had blown through. Two overflowing ashtrays. An algae-covered aquarium with no fish that Ben could see. It was hot, too, and Ben realized the guy must be too cheap or too destitute to use the air conditioner.

There was a pair of metal folding chairs in front of the desk. McGlade came around, swept up the piles of paper on each, and made a show of stacking them neatly on the floor. "Here," he said. "Have a seat. Coffee?"

Ben and Paula both said, "No," simultaneously and equally emphatically.

McGlade circled back to an incongruously fancy leather office chair Ben suspected he'd stolen. "All right," he said, "what can I do for you?"

"It's not what you can do for me," Paula said, reaching into her purse and taking out her credentials. "It's what you can do for the FBI."

McGlade examined her ID, his expression suddenly sewn up tight. "All right. What can I do for the FBI?"

"You can tell us about a case you were working on a little over three years ago," Ben said. "Guy named Daniel Larison. His wife thought he was having an affair."

McGlade's face lost a drop of color. "I'm sorry, but all my client matters are entirely confidential."

Paula smiled at him. "Mr. McGlade," she said, her tone exceptionally sweet, "we're very busy, so I'll get straight to the point. Tell us something useful, and you'll have a contact and friend inside the Bureau for life. Fuck with me, and I'll crawl up your ass and chew my way out."

Ben thought, *What?* He had to clamp his jaw shut to keep from laughing. At the same time, he was beginning to realize McGlade would have to be a fool to think she was bullshitting him.

There was a long silence while McGlade assessed the probabilities. Then he said, "All right. Three years ago, a woman in Kissimmee contacted me, told me she thought her husband was having an affair."

"Marcy Wheeler?" Paula asked.

"Yeah. Wheeler. Happens all the time. Usually it's a wife who calls me, but sometimes a husband. Ninety percent of what I do is domestic. Anyway, I get what I need from her—photograph of the husband, car registration, that kind of thing—and I go to tail the guy, see where he's going. SOP. Except, it turns out the guy is almost impossible to tail."

"Watching his back?" Ben said.

"You could say that. Now I see a little of this kind of thing all the time. People who are up to no good can be jumpy, sometimes they pay more attention than your average honest citizen. I'm used to it and it's not a problem for me. This guy was way beyond that. His wife told me he was some kind of military spook, but when I saw how surveillance conscious he was, I knew he was something really special. Counterterrorism, Delta, something like that. I told Wheeler this one could take a while, he was too watchful and I couldn't get close. I quoted her a long-term rate and she was okay with it."

"A little annuity for you, huh?" Ben said, and he realized he felt weirdly protective of Marcy. "She the first client you fed that story to?"

"As a matter of fact, smart guy, she was. I don't charge by the hour. My business is about results."

"Okay," Paula said. "So you backed off. But you stayed on him."

"That's right. His wife would tell me when he was traveling. Now here's the interesting thing. Most times, even though I couldn't stay on him long, I could confirm he was going to Patrick Air Force Base. Figured from there, he was getting a military flight to wherever he was going. But other times, I confirmed he was going to Orlando International. When I'd get the word from the wife, I'd set up at the airport in Orlando, wait for him there. Didn't matter that he was watching his back if I could get set up in front of him, right?"

Ben popped a knuckle. "You figured the civilian flights were the illicit ones."

"Exactly. So twice in Orlando, I watched him board a flight to Miami. Next time the wife told me he was traveling, I went to Miami, started staking out the arrivals gates for flights from Orlando."

Paula leaned forward in her chair. "And?"

"And twice I saw him boarding a flight to Costa Rica. San Jose, the capital. I told Wheeler it looked like he was up to something in Costa Rica. As it happens, I have a contact there, someone who could pick Larison up when he arrived. She said do it. So I did."

Paula said, "Who?"

"Guy who goes by the name Taibbi. I know him from the service. He's a surfer, or was when I knew him, anyway. Now he owns a bar in Jacó, near Playa Hermosa, a big surfing beach. Freelances in this and that, if you know what I mean."

"No," Ben said. "I don't know what you mean."

"Look, Jacó's got three draws: surfing, drugs, and whores. You get it now? I asked Taibbi if he wanted to be my local liaison on this case. Follow a guy, confirm whether he's got a mistress, I get a finder's fee, he gets the balance. I warned him the guy was military, surveillance conscious. Taibbi says don't worry, I've got a crew."

Paula glanced at Ben, then back to McGlade. "What happened?"

"I don't know, exactly. All Taibbi told me was that Larison did one of his crew. Cut his throat."

"My God," Paula said.

"Yeah. Whatever happened, it spooked Taibbi bad, and Taibbi, let me tell you, has seen his share of shit."

"That's not what Wheeler told us," Ben said. "She said your guy in Costa Rica disappeared."

"Yeah, that's what I told her. I just wanted to keep it vague, you know? The fewer questions the better. Anyway, Taibbi told me he was done, called me a few choice words for not adequately warning him of what Larison was all about—like I knew, for fuck's sake—and told me he was out. I started thinking about what I'd gotten myself into, what it would be like if Larison ever learned some PI had been following him. Well, the hell with that. So yeah, I told Wheeler my Costa Rica guy had disappeared and I gave her back her money. And that's the last I heard of any of this, until now."

Paula said, "And Taibbi didn't go to the police?"

"Taibbi lives the kind of life that doesn't mix well with law enforcement. And if your next question is why I didn't go to the cops either, what was I supposed to do? Tell the Costa Rican police I heard there was a murder that the guy who might have seen it will never testify about? Please."

"So you saw Larison traveling from Miami to Costa Rica," Ben said. "What were the dates?"

"Are you shitting me? It was three years ago."

"You don't have records?"

"Oh, yeah, I have records," McGlade said, looking around the office. "I'm sure they're here somewhere. I'll just get some excavation equipment and we'll turn them up in no time."

Ben tried not to let his impatience show. "What was the season?"

"First time was . . . shit, I can't remember. But wait. Second time . . . I remember the Magic had just made the play-offs. It was a big deal, their first time since 2003. So that would have been . . . April. Yeah, April 2007. Yeah, they beat the Celtics the night before, I remember that. So . . . hold on."

McGlade leaned forward and worked his computer for a moment. "April 16, 2007. That was the day Larison flew from Miami to San Jose the second time. So the first time would have been . . . maybe three months before that. Four at the most."

"Remember the airline?" Ben said.

"Lacsa. Costa Rican carrier, United affiliate, I think."

Ben nodded. It wasn't perfect, but it was a pretty good start. Hort could check the passenger manifest on the day Larison traveled. Ben doubted the man would have been traveling under his own name, but now they had a good shot at uncovering an alias. Or one of them, anyway.

McGlade said, "All right? That's everything I know. You don't have to crawl up my ass now. Unless you're into that kind of thing."

"One more question," Paula said, smiling. "The name of your friend's bar."

10 SOMEONE ELSE'S DREAMS

Larison stepped off the bus at the Greyhound station in Harrisburg, Pennsylvania. The ticket he'd bought was for Scranton. One was as good as the other, he just didn't like going where the ticket said he would. He knew no one was watching—paying cash and moving by bus was the most secure and anonymous means of travel left in America—but there was no downside to layering in another level of security, either.

He slung his bag over his shoulder and started walking, his boots crunching quietly on the cement sidewalk. The sun was setting behind the tired-looking buildings to his right, but the air was still suffused with a stagnant heat. He didn't care. A little sweat, a little body odor would make it less likely that anyone would take an interest in him or recall his passage after he was gone.

He headed south along Market Street, knowing he'd find a hotel soon enough. In his worn jeans and faded flannel shirt, his unshaven face obscured by a Cat Diesel hat, he knew he looked like a tradesman of some sort who'd lost his job in the hollowed-out economy and was looking to find another. Nobody important, but not a criminal, either, just a down-on-his-luck guy moving away from something sad and toward something maybe a little better, interesting to nobody, not even to himself.

More than anything, he wished he could have spent

these days with Nico in San Jose. Or better yet, on the beach in Manuel Antonio, where they'd first met. Costa Rica had become a kind of symbol in his mind, a shorthand for forgetting everything about his past and living the way he wanted to, with the person he wanted to. But he couldn't afford to go there now. He was too tense, for one thing. Nico, who could read his moods like no one who'd ever known him before, would intuit something was wrong. Also, for now, Larison preferred not to cross international borders. He wanted his remaining few contacts with the government to come from a variety of entirely random eastern seaboard locations, including the last contact, when he would instruct them on how to deliver the diamonds. After that, he would vanish like smoke.

For a moment, the thought of vanishing made him feel almost giddy. Because it would seem like vanishing only from his enemies' perspective. From his own standpoint, it would be more like . . . more like being reborn, like his real self finally stirring to wakefulness. And once that part of him, the real him, the self he'd denied and obscured and hidden for so long, was awake, the dreams would stop, wouldn't they? Yes, that would be one of the best parts about waking up, that the dreams would finally end. They'd belong to someone else then. They couldn't touch him in Costa Rica.

He'd gone there for the first time five years earlier, while on temporary duty training the Honduran government's praetorian guard in intelligence gathering and interrogation. He'd heard of Manuel Antonio, supposedly a gay paradise on Costa Rica's Pacific coast. It was a short flight to San Jose, and from there, a short drive to Manuel Antonio. Of course he hadn't told anyone where he was going, he was just taking a few days to himself. He was married, and people naturally assumed he was being tight-lipped because he was chasing whores and wanted to be discreet. No one cared about that sort of thing. Getting a little strange tail was considered one of the perks of temporary duty and was ironically protected by its own informal "Don't ask, don't tell" policy. He was happy to have people think it of him. It wasn't so terribly far from the truth and was therefore perfect cover.

Manuel Antonio lived up to its billing: white sand beaches framed by swaying palm trees to one side and blue surf to the other; dozens of lively bars and clubs and restaurants; nothing but young, toned men, all relaxed, fearless, looking to hook up. He remembered thinking the moment he arrived he would have to find a way to get back, it was that good.

He'd met Nico on Playita, one of the surfing beaches. Nico was riding a board in and then paddling it back out, sometimes with some other surfers, other times alone, and Larison was watching from the sand, admiring the way Nico got the most out of his waves, enjoying the occasional flash of brilliant teeth against smooth, cappuccino-colored skin, the lean muscles that stood out whenever he cut back against a wave or moved his arms to recover his balance. A few times, as he got close to the beach, Nico caught his eye and smiled. Larison smiled back, wondering. He guessed Nico was at least ten years younger. Some guys liked hooking up with someone older, more experienced. Some didn't. He knew which he hoped the gorgeous creature on the surfboard would be.

After about a half hour, Larison had walked down the hot sand and stood with his feet in the cool, clear water. He watched Nico surfing in, glad to see he was heading right in his direction.

Nico rode in about twenty feet from the beach, then slowly sank into the water as the wave's force depleted. He picked up his board and waded over to Larison, smiling, rivulets of water running down his skin, his chest and shoulders broken out in gooseflesh.

"You like to surf?" he asked in Spanish-accented English.

Larison was surprised. When he didn't want to be spotted as an American, he was adept at projecting something else, and thought he had been. "How do you know I speak English?" he asked.

The smile broadened. "You seem so happy. I think maybe you've never been here before."

Larison should have been irritated or on guard that this guy had made him. But he wasn't. In fact, for reasons that just then he didn't really understand, he felt secretly glad.

"Well, you're right about that," he said.

"So? You like to surf?"

Larison smiled. "I like surfers."

A blush appeared behind Nico's tan cheeks, a blush Larison found surprisingly disarming, even endearing.

They had dinner that night, then made love in Larison's hotel room. Larison was ordinarily aggressive in bed, and usually attracted men who sensed the conflicted rage in him and wanted to be on the receiving end of it. But Nico brought out something different in him, something much more gentle, even tender. They'd spent the next two days and nights together, and Larison had concocted an excuse to delay his return to Honduras for two days more. He would have tried to stay even longer, but Nico had to return to San Jose, where he had a small architectural practice. They drove back to the capital city together in Nico's old Jetta. As they sat in the idling car at the curb of the airport passenger drop-off, there were a dozen things Larison wanted to say, none of which he could find the courage to articulate.

"Do you want to see me again?" Nico asked, as Larison hesitated, his hand on the door handle.

"Yes," Larison said, meeting his eyes and then looking

away, both hopeful and terribly afraid of what might be said next.

"I want to see you, too."

Larison looked at him again, hoping Nico would see how much his words meant, and understand why Larison couldn't answer.

"You're married, aren't you?" Nico said.

Larison looked away, ashamed but also strangely grateful for Nico's ability to read him, to understand what other people could never see.

He wanted to lie. Instead he found himself nodding, unable to meet Nico's eyes.

"It's okay," he heard Nico say. "I thought so. I'm glad you told me."

"It's . . . complicated."

"Of course it is," Nico said, without a trace of sarcasm or condescension.

"Can we . . . let's just see what happens. I want to see you again. This feels different." He couldn't believe what he was saying. He swallowed. "Special."

"I'm out, you know. Everyone knows I'm gay—my family, my firm. I don't really want to go back to halfway in the closet, you know?"

Larison nodded, his mind a roiling mass of emotions. He'd never had this kind of conversation before, with anyone. He'd never even imagined having it. He never would have dared.

"But I would do that," Nico said. "For you."

Larison looked at him. He couldn't speak. He felt an excitement that was becoming indistinguishable from panic.

And just then, in that mad moment, gripped by impossible hope, Larison felt something bloom in his mind. An idea—no, not even an idea, just a possibility, a possibility he'd never considered before but whose contours he was immediately able to recognize.

"Give me some time," he heard himself saying. "There are some things I can do . . . to find a way out of what I'm in. Can you do that? Can you be patient?"

Nico smiled shyly and said, "For you, Dan," and Larison was immediately glad he'd told Nico his real first name. Ordinarily he wouldn't do that, but from the first instant there had been something about Nico that had made Larison want to be honest with him. About the things he could be, anyway.

He took Nico's card but didn't embrace him. He knew Nico wanted him to, but also knew Nico sensed that he was already melting back into his public self and that any contact in that guise would be unacceptable.

After that, he was able to find a way to visit Costa Rica at least twice a year, sometimes as many as four. He traveled only under legends he himself had developed. He was extremely paranoid about communication, creating an encrypted email account for each of them under false identities and instructing Nico how to use it without establishing any possible connection to either of them. The security procedures were unfamiliar to Nico, but he understood Larison's fanaticism to be an outgrowth of his fear of being outed, and was always exceptionally careful as a result. In fact, Nico displayed an aptitude and even eagerness for some of the security tools of the trade, which gratified Larison not only for the obvious substantive reasons, but also because he knew it was a sign of Nico's devotion and desire to please him, as well.

Of course, meeting repeatedly in Costa Rica and staying in Nico's apartment was suboptimal from a security standpoint, but Larison didn't have the money to fly both of them to neutral locations or to pay for hotels. It was all he could do to conceal from Marcy the money he was diverting from his military salary for coach travel to Costa Rica. More than that would have risked causing suspicions.

But now they would be able to travel anywhere, live anywhere. He'd come to love Costa Rica and what it represented, but he thought it would be wise to move on, at least for a while, when this thing was done. He'd asked Nico before about someplace new—Barcelona, maybe, or Buenos Aires. Nico had been reluctant because his practice was based in San Jose. So Larison had told him he was working on something big, a sale of his company that would set them both up for life. Larison would finally leave his wife, buy them land somewhere, and Nico could design the house while he worked on establishing a new practice. How did that sound? Nico said it sounded wonderful, though Larison sensed he didn't really believe it could be true. Well, he'd see soon enough.

The sun was now completely blotted out by looming office buildings and darkness was seeping into the sky. He came to a Hilton hotel and decided it would do as well as any other. He walked in, hoping he'd be able to sleep a little better this time than last.

PART TWO

The people in government who made mistakes or who acted in ways that seemed reasonable at the time but now seem inappropriate have been held publicly accountable by severe criticism, suffering enormous reputational and, in some instances, financial losses. Little will be achieved by further retribution.

JACK GOLDSMITH, FORMER ASSISTANT ATTORNEY
GENERAL IN THE JUSTICE DEPARTMENT'S
OFFICE OF LEGAL COUNSEL

That is not to say presidents and vice presidents are always above the law; there could be instances in which such a prosecution is appropriate, but based on what we know, this is not such a case.

JON MEACHAM, NEWSWEEK

If you're going to punish people for condoning torture, you'd better include the American citizenry itself.

MICHAEL KINSLEY, THE WASHINGTON POST

11 ROUGH MEN

Three hours after leaving McGlade, Ben and Paula were on a flight to Costa Rica. Hort had arranged for a small jet to take them from Orlando International. Ben didn't ask and Hort wouldn't have told him, but Ben suspected the jet was part of the Jeppesen/Boeing–supported civilian fleet used to render and transport war-on-terror detainees through a series of black site prisons.

Ben had never been to Costa Rica and hated the idea of a hot landing in a place he didn't know and didn't have time to reconnoiter. Ordinarily, he would arrive in a place several weeks before the actual action to thoroughly familiarize himself with the terrain. No chance for that this time around, but he'd bought a guidebook in Orlando and was perusing it on the plane. Far from ideal, but it was a start. And he'd picked up some sneakers and a Tommy Bahama short-sleeved button-down shirt and cargo shorts that he figured would blend better than the faux-FBI outfit he'd worn to visit Marcy Wheeler. Paula was still in her navy pantsuit, and he figured she was most comfortable looking professional and governmental. Fine for her, but he generally liked to look like whatever would be least noticed in the environment at hand.

He'd called Hort after leaving McGlade's office. Lanier's credentials checked out: FBI special agent, joined the Bureau out of SMU right after 9/11, currently working out of the J. Edgar Hoover Building in Washington, D.C.—same as one Dan Froomkin. Known for being a maverick and a pain in the ass, but also for getting results. Hort agreed with Ben's assessment that her threat to kick up a public fuss about Ben's visit to Larison's wife wasn't a bluff. Meaning for the time being, it was best to keep her close.

"Now, listen," Hort had told him. "Maybe Costa Rica will turn out to be a dead end. But if it's something, if Larison has someone he cares about there, if part of his plan is to disappear with her afterward to a private island or who knows what, and he figures out you're keying on that someone, he'll feel cornered. You'd be threatening his op, his girlfriend, everything. This is personal to him. So you watch yourself, son. I told you, you're good, but you're not in his league. Not yet."

The "not yet" removed the sting. "I'll be careful."

"Good. And hang on for a minute . . . okay, while we've been talking, I got a printout of Larison's travel records from the ICE database. Looks like he did travel to Costa Rica, spring of 2005. Flight from Tegucigalpa, where he was TDY at the time. But nothing in April 2007."

"He traveled that first time under his own name?"

"Yes, and it fits. Say something happened while he was there that first time, he met someone. After that, he wouldn't want to keep going back under his own name. With one data point, there's no pattern, nothing for anyone to look for. He had no way of knowing he'd get placed in Costa Rica through something else. Now, you say this McGlade claims Larison killed someone on one of these trips?"

"That's what he told us, yeah. The one where Larison traveled from Miami on April 17."

"Okay, that would be an Airbus A320, hundred and fifty seats. Figure two-thirds full, half the passengers women . . . my guess is, we'll have to sift through something like forty or fifty names before we spot the one that isn't like the others. Once we know what legend he was traveling under that day, we can cross-reference, see if he's been using it for something else. This is promising. Good work, son."

Ben was annoyed at himself for needing the man's approval. He wondered if Larison had been this way, or if that was something an operator grew out of. Maybe that's what Hort meant about him becoming like Larison, if he kept developing this way. He wondered.

Hort had also checked up on Taibbi. Vietnam combat veteran, three tours with the 82nd Airborne, and an LRRP—long-range reconnaissance patrol. Meaning he was self-reliant, understood stealth, and would be handy with a variety of close-range weapons. A conviction in 1982 on arms-trafficking charges. Pleaded guilty, served three years, moved to Costa Rica in 1987, and hadn't had a problem with the law since then. According to his current passport and cellphone records, he was presently in Jacó, and Ben could reasonably expect to find him at his bar.

He looked at Paula. She was asleep in the seat facing his, her head dipped forward. The cabin was aglow with the sun setting ahead of them and her face was obscured by shadow.

He watched her, enjoying the opportunity to do so unobserved. He liked her hair, liked that she kept it short and natural. Though with her face, he supposed she could do pretty much anything she wanted with her hair and things would be just fine.

He wondered what it must be like for her at the Bureau, a black woman, clearly smarter and more capable than most of the people she had to answer to. Did she have to work twice as hard as her peers? Did she use her sex appeal, or did she try to suppress it? She didn't wear a ring. Was she single? Did she date? Were guys intimidated about going out with a government agent? Did she ever have a thing for someone at work, and have to fight to try to hide it?

He rotated his neck, cracking the joints, still watching her. What would she be like in bed? Would the professional façade be so important she couldn't ever let it go? Or could she allow someone to see her naked, not just literally, but figuratively, too?

She said no one ever saw her coming. If it was true, he decided, it was also a shame. He decided Paula coming would be a very fine thing to see.

And then he thought of Sarah and was immediately ashamed of himself. But what could he really share with her? He never felt so alive as he did when he was hunting. Not a politically correct thing to admit, probably, and Sarah would have found it repellant, but wasn't it true for everyone? That everyone loved to do the things they were good at? Yeah, he wasn't the smoothest guy in the world, and sure, he had some development ahead of him, but Hort was right, there was nothing he was suited for like ops. He'd survived shit that would have killed most men, most good men, even, and he'd survived it because he was better. How could he not enjoy—how could he not exult in—what he did, what he was? And who was Sarah, or anyone else, to judge him for that?

What was that saying? *People sleep soundly in their beds at night only because rough men stand ready to visit violence on those who would harm them.* Something like that, anyway.

Well, he was one of those rough men. And he wasn't going to change that, not for Sarah, not for anyone. And fuck anyone who had a problem with it.

12 A MASSIVE DEDUCTIBLE

Ulrich could no longer see the K Street traffic below him. It was dark outside, and his windows were now effectively mirrors. It was too late to make any more phone calls, and he was too agitated to get any work done anyway, but still he lingered. His two sons were in college and his home life had long since settled into a sexless kiss hello, followed by a perfunctory recitation of the minutiae of the day, followed by the sounds of the television in the next room, followed by sleep. He and his wife had become strangers, bound mostly by past and progeny, acquaintances who continued to share the same space merely out of habit, the result of some long-ago momentum that itself was slowly dying, as, he supposed, were they.

Not that it had been so terribly different even before the boys had left for school. He was the vice president's special assistant back when the vice president had been the secretary of defense, and after that he'd served as the Defense Department's general counsel. Cynthia had put her foot down about the hours after Timmy, their second, had been born, and Ulrich had joined a law firm to placate her. The money was better but the work was boring, and he'd missed being on the inside. So returning as the new vice president's chief of staff when his old boss was tapped as the president's understudy was impossible to resist. Cynthia had put up a few pro forma arguments, but she knew not to fight the battle she couldn't win.

So for eight years he'd arrived at his sons' basketball games only in the last quarter, if at all, and the family had maintained the fiction that dad was mostly home for dinner by moving the meal hour to eight, then to nine . . . and even then, more often than not, he'd had to call with an apology and another useless promise that everyone knew he'd break next time, too. Mostly by the time he'd get home in the evening the boys had been asleep, and often he was gone again the next morning by the time they woke. Weekends he tried to be around. But with two active war theaters and so many initiatives to keep the country safe . . . it was just all-consuming. How would he have explained it to his family if there had been another attack on his watch? They told him they understood and he hoped it was true. And Cynthia, whatever resentments she might once have harbored over his absences, seemed to have long since let them go. He was grateful to her for that. But none of it changed the fact that his children had grown up and left the house, and he'd barely been around to see any of it. And nothing would ever bring that time back for him, or give him a chance to relive what he'd missed. Nothing.

He tried to let it go. Ruminating about the past, happily or otherwise, wasn't a luxury he could afford just now. It was the future he needed to worry about. He tried running worst-case scenarios in his mind. Ordinarily, this kind of exercise would calm him. This time, though, the scenarios were exceptionally horrific. If Clements screwed the pooch on the tapes, and if Ulrich's backup failed, too, he was going to be left with not much more than the gobbledygook Condi Rice had been caught stammering in response to those little Stanford shits. What was it again? *The president instructed us that nothing we would do would be outside of our obliga-*

tions, *legal obligations, under the Convention Against Torture . . . and by the way, I didn't authorize anything. I conveyed the authorization of the administration to the agency. That they had policy authorization subject to the Justice Department's clearance . . . so, by definition, if it was authorized by the president, it did not violate our obligations under the Convention Against Torture.* People laughed at her at the time. But what else could she say? She had to say something.

Yeah, it was feeble enough when Rice said it. In Ulrich's case, it wouldn't work at all. Because his name—his *signature,* for God's sake—was all over the authorizations.

He heard the chime of incoming email and checked the message. Damn, this was good. Daniel Larison, former JSOC operator. The name sounded familiar . . . one of the people they'd suspected when the tapes first went missing? But hadn't that guy been dead? He'd look into it, figure out the discrepancy. He tried not to hope, but maybe, just maybe they actually had a shot at getting this genie back in the bottle.

At the bottom of the message, he noticed an attachment. It was a photo of a blond guy, mid- or early thirties. The guy's eyes were closed, but even so, somehow there was a hard look about him. Ulrich thought for a moment, then moved the photo into a new email—*Who is this? One of yours?*—and forwarded it to Clements. He'd send the rest of the information after he heard back. These days he trusted the CIA less than ever.

He blew out a long breath. It was going to be a long five days. Well, with a little luck, or a lot of luck, more likely, maybe this could be resolved more quickly.

He opened his office safe, removed an encrypted thumb drive, and popped it into his computer. He was like a home owner with a raging fire bearing down on his house. It made sense to take a fresh look at his insurance policy.

On the thumb drive were unredacted copies of the Office of Legal Counsel memos, the secret opinions the administration had made the Justice Department draw up to legalize enhanced interrogation techniques. Everyone involved understood that worst case, no matter what else happened, the memos would give them legal cover: *Senator, we were just doing what the Justice Department told us was legal.* The CIA certainly understood the game. They'd had it played on them not long before: *Senator, we were just following the CIA's intelligence about weapons of mass destruction in Iraq.* Hell, if you were in Washington and didn't know this was the way the game was played, it meant it was being played on you.

But Ulrich understood the memos would serve an additional purpose, one most people didn't recognize. Ulrich was familiar with the concept of "force drift," which was basically the notion that when you set a fifty-five-mile-per-hour speed limit, you did so knowing that in fact people would drive at seventy, instead. So when he had instructed the Justice Department to create the memos, he knew two things. First, that no matter what the memos authorized, looked at properly, the authorizations could be construed as limitations. Second, that no matter what the limitations were, men in the field would exceed them. And when they did, and should those excesses come to light, Ulrich could shape the narrative away from *The administration authorized torture,* toward *Field personnel exceeded the administration's clear legal limits.*

The plan had worked nicely to contain the damage from the Abu Ghraib photos. The question was, would it also work now, if the interrogation videos came to light?

He considered. There was an unwritten rule of American politics: the sacrifice had to be commensurate with the scandal. For Abu Ghraib, it had been enough to sacrifice a few enlisted personnel. Watergate, on the other hand, had required the resignation of a president. And the rule had an important corollary: the more the politician could invoke national security as a justification, the more the impact of the scandal could be blunted. That's why Clinton's blow job almost killed him, while war crimes accusations were so easy to deflect.

The question was, where along that continuum would the tapes land him? He could play the national security card, certainly. It wasn't as though he had much else. But the Caspers . . . it was hard to see how even national security was going to get him around that. Yeah, the tapes alone would be a God-almighty fire, but the Caspers . . . the Caspers would dump gasoline onto the blaze. Against a conflagration like that, a few enlisted personnel or some field agents would be a pretty puny firebreak. Something bigger would be required. And why not him? After all, his name would be at the center of the interrogation program. He would be a big enough sacrifice to sate the public, but not too big to cause undue discomfort. Certainly the public would prefer the sacrifice of a high-level facilitator to, say, the trial of a former president and vice president, and because they would prefer it, it would be easy for everyone who might otherwise be vulnerable to make it so.

Yeah, they would come after him. And he'd make an appealing villain, too, like Jack Abramoff in his black fedora. He could imagine the descriptions already, how he'd "traded on his government service" to become a "lobbyist fat cat" . . . and the way his enemies would ply the media with not-for-attribution tales about his periodic outbursts at idiots, his judgment . . . Yeah, he knew the way it would be played. He'd played it that way dozens of times himself. Of course, knowing how the game was played and being able to defend yourself when you had become the game's object were two different things.

He pulled the thumb drive and put it back in his safe. Well, he'd checked his insurance policy, only to discover a massive deductible. Only to realize he *was* the deductible.

But that was okay. He had the one other policy, the ultimate policy. The audiotapes that thank God he'd had the sense to make that morning at Arlington National—and other times, too.

But he'd play that card only if he had to. Only if he'd run out of every other option.

His secure line buzzed and he snatched up the phone. "Ulrich."

"Okay to talk?" It was Clements.

"Go."

"The photo you sent. His name is Ben Treven. He's an army guy."

"So not one of yours?"

"Definitely not."

Ulrich should have known the guy wasn't Agency. If he'd been Agency, he would have been bringing up the rear, not closing in on the target.

He stared at the photo on his screen. "You think he's one of Horton's?"

"Hard to say. His MOS is classified. Even just the photo took some doing to match. I could try to find out, but asking would reveal that we know."

"Well, it really doesn't matter what he is. He wasn't part of the original program, he's answering to I don't know whom, and it looks like he's already five steps ahead of you in finding whoever is trying to leverage those tapes. Now, listen. I've got other information to forward you. How fast can you get your Ground Branch team to San Jose, Costa Rica?"

There was a slight pause. "Four hours, if that. Where are you getting this information?"

"Don't worry about that—the information is solid, that's all you need to know."

"No, that's not—"

"I don't know what name Treven is traveling under, but now that you know what he's looking for, you should be able to anticipate him. Find out what he knows and who he's working for, get him out of the way, and find those fucking tapes."

There was another pause. Clements said, "Let me clarify something for you, Ulrich. You don't give me orders anymore. You're just a lobbyist now. The only reason I'm even talking to you is out of courtesy."

"Yeah?" Ulrich said, his voice rising, some dark part of his mind suddenly joyous at the prospect of having someone to bully, to dominate. "Well, let me clarify something for you. You're talking to me because you need me to run political interference for you, which I have. And because without the information I just gave you, you couldn't find your own ass with both hands and a flashlight. And because if someone smarter than you doesn't tell you what you need to do, you're going to be in newspaper headlines in less than five days and in a prison cell not long after that. You got it? Are we clarified now?"

Silence on the other end of the line. Ulrich slammed down the receiver, stood, and paced back and forth for a minute, concentrating on his breathing, trying to calm himself. He knew he shouldn't have snapped at Clements: it would chafe worse now than in the days when one of his tirades had been backed by the power of the Office of the Vice President, and so was apt to be counterproductive. But damn, it had felt good to be in charge again, giving orders and not suffering idiots, if only for a moment.

He went back to his desk and forwarded Clements the information he would need. He hoped he was making the right call. Treven was obviously cleverer than the CIA, and so logically stood a better chance of recovering the tapes. The question was, what would he do with them if he did? Ulrich decided he couldn't take that chance. He didn't trust the CIA, but at least he understood their motives.

JSOC just felt like a wild card. He'd deal with them accordingly.

13 THE SOUND WAS ALWAYS THE SAME

Larison shot bolt upright on the mattress, his body slicked with sweat, the awful screams still ringing in his ears. His heart was pounding combat hard and he was practically hyperventilating.

A dream. Calm down, it was just one of the dreams.

He grimaced. God, if he could only take a pill. Anything to dull the sound of those screams, to obscure the terrorized faces behind them.

He realized he was gripping the Glock. Must have snatched it up without realizing as he woke. A protective reflex, useless now. Against the dreams, the gun wasn't even a talisman.

He could still hear it. A naked man, strapped to a table, eyes bulging in panic, past words, past screaming, just making . . . that sound. He was awake now, but he knew it would be hours before the echoes would fade from his brain.

He got up, turned on a light, and started pacing. He kept the Glock in one hand and compulsively touched surfaces with the other—dresser, walls, a lamp shade—pressing, patting, poking, anything to remind himself he was awake, he wasn't in the dream anymore.

People didn't know. They didn't know that sound, the sound a man made when you took him past the point he could endure. Every man made the sound, and it was always the same. It started with bluster. Then there would be begging. Then bawling and babbling. Child-like sobbing, shrieks for mercy. And finally, when everything had been tried, every remaining human effort and desperate stratagem and fervent hope, and all of it had failed, there would be nothing but that sound, that wordless, keening wail, the melody of a soul being snuffed, a psyche cracking open, the birth cries of an animal devolving from a man. And no matter how many times you heard it, it never pierced you less. The hair on the back of your neck would stand up no less, your scrotum would retract no less, your nausea afterward would subside no sooner. Once you heard the sound, you could live to a hundred and you would never, ever get it out of your ears.

And God help you if you were the one who did what produced it.

And all that bullshit about how it was for a good reason. As though a reason would have made any difference, as though a reason could do anything to make you forget even one single moment of it. It was worse than the stink of blood and the slime of viscera. You could acclimate to killing. Torture was different.

He slowed his pacing, breathing deliberately, in and out, through his nose. He could feel his heart rate beginning to slow. Okay. Okay. He was okay.

If he could only sleep.

He remembered one guy, one of the Caspers, they called him Bugs, for Bugs Bunny, because he had these big, protruding ears. They'd run a routine on Bugs: sleep deprivation, hypothermia, stress positions, beatings. They buried him alive in a box. The box is what broke him. Afterward, just seeing his captors approaching his cage, he would scuttle into a corner and fetal up and start making the sound. It was some Pavlovian thing. No one thought he was acting. No actor could make that sound.

And the Pavlovian thing worked in reverse, too. Just seeing Bugs scuttle off and hear him start making the sound . . . it was like someone pressing the nausea button in Larison's brain. He'd come to hate Bugs for the way he felt about himself. As though Larison's own agony had been Bugs's fault. And Jesus, what he'd done to the guy as a result. Jesus.

He'd tried to rationalize it all by telling himself it was to save lives, prevent attacks. But they never got anything useful. And so much of what they were being tasked with wasn't even about attacks. It was about whether there'd been a link between Saddam Hussein and al Qaeda. He remembered the first time they'd issued him a list of Saddam-AQ questions. He'd done it. It wasn't as though he'd been in the habit of thinking much then, it was easier to just do what he was told. But afterward he wondered what the hell he'd just done. He'd just endured the sound again, and for what . . . to provide someone political cover? That was his job now? That's what he was being used for?

And if they would use him for that, what else would they use him for? And what would they do when they were done using him?

Despite his fearful secret, somehow he'd always believed the military would do right by him. He'd given the army everything, endured horrible things, the kind of things you could never utter, not even to other men who had done them, too. Things that made him wonder whether there was a God, that made him fear some inevitable reckoning he sensed but couldn't name. He needed to believe the military would reciprocate, that in return for his sacrifice they would support and protect him.

Then Abu Ghraib happened. He saw the way the brass

and the politicians closed ranks to blame the enlisted personnel. He remembered reading an article by a guy named Jonathan Turley, about how the rank and file always got scapegoated, about the abdication of command responsibility. He started to think about what he was doing, and about what the politicians would do if it leaked. Graner, England . . . how was he any different? He'd be the perfect fall guy, especially for the Caspers.

He didn't want to accept it. He wanted to believe what he was doing was different, that *he* was different, and that anyway it would never leak, it was too closely held. But he knew that was all bullshit. Nothing was more important in combat than avoiding denial and engaging reality, and the habit of combat helped open his eyes to political reality, too. Eventually it would all come out. They'd need a fall guy then. The fall guy would be him.

Once he realized it, he could see it clearly. They'd talk about his temper, which ironically was why they'd had him working the Caspers in the first place. They'd call him a steroid freak. They'd dig for other dirt. If they discovered his secret, they'd crucify him with it. Rogue. Sadist. Nutcase. Homo. They'd say he volunteered for this detail so he could be alone with detainees, so he could work out his twisted fantasies on naked, helpless men. And then, to prevent him from talking, to prevent him from revealing what he knew about the Caspers and taking everyone else down with him, one morning he'd be found hanging in his cell.

Yeah, that's the way it would happen. If he let them.

So he found a way to not let them. A way to protect himself, bring down the hypocrites who were going to set him up, and create a new life for himself—and for Nico—all at the same time.

His heart rate had returned to normal. He turned off

the light and lay back down on the mattress. He kept the Glock in his hand.

All he had to do now was stick to the plan. After that, Costa Rica. Costa Rica was where the dreams would stop.

He just had to get there.

14 PROJECTION

At some point during the flight, Ben nodded off. He was still recovering from three near-sleepless nights in the Manila city jail and a lot of time zone shifts after, and he was glad for the chance to get a little shut-eye.

When he woke, Paula was looking at him the way he'd been at her earlier. "What?" he said, scrunching up his face and blinking. "Was I drooling?"

She cocked an eyebrow and gave him a bored look. "Not that I noticed."

He saw she was holding an iPhone, like his. "You like it?" he asked, gesturing with his head.

"Love it. Does just about everything but shoot bullets."

He laughed. "iBullets. Maybe one day."

He looked out the window. The sun was low in the sky. He checked his watch. Damn, he'd been asleep for almost an hour. They didn't have far to go.

"So how'd you get into this line of work?" he asked, sitting up and cracking his neck.

"What, you mean a nice girl like me?"

"I don't think you're nice."

"Oh, but I am."

"All right, a nice girl like you, then."

She looked at him for a long moment. He couldn't tell what she was thinking, and he thought maybe she wasn't going to answer. But then she said, "Nine-eleven happened during my senior year of college. I was planning to go to grad school for an M.A. in psychology—psychology was my undergraduate major—but I decided to do something to make a difference, instead."

"How's that working out for you?"

"Making a difference?"

"Yeah."

"It's hard, sometimes. Getting anything done in this bureaucracy is like trying to swim in molasses. But I've found ways."

"You work in the D.C. headquarters building?"

"I do. Do you know it?"

"Visited on a school field trip when I was a kid."

"You grew up in the area?"

"For a while. Among other places."

"But you know Washington."

He remembered a family excursion to the city when Alex had still been in a stroller. The five of them had stayed in a single room in a cheap hotel off Dupont Circle. Alex wanted to start at the zoo. Katie wanted the ballet. Ben wanted the war memorials. Their dad wanted the Smithsonian. Their mom had tried to negotiate the resulting hairball. It had rained the entire weekend and even Katie couldn't stop the fights. Ben had been back maybe a half dozen times since then, never staying for longer than he had to.

"I know it well enough to know I'd rather be somewhere else," he said.

"And where is that?"

"Why, you thinking about visiting me?"

"Just making conversation."

Her questions were innocuous enough, but they were making him uncomfortable. He didn't want to tell her too much. Harmless details could sometimes be assembled into a meaningful mosaic.

"How about you?" he said. "Why the FBI? Why not CIA, or the military?"

"Because I believe in law and order. Plus I don't like violence. Law enforcement's about breaking the cycle of violence."

He briefly wished someone had told that to the Manila cops who'd exhausted themselves beating the crap out of him. With every passing hour, the memory of those four days felt increasingly bizarre and improbable. But still, every time he thought of it, the cops cuffing him and later whaling on him, the heat and stink of the prison, the feeling of being swallowed up by some huge, insentient beast, cut off from anyone who knew him, anyone who cared—

"And you?" she said.

"What about me?"

"Why the military?"

"Military? I don't know anything about the military."

"My ass, you don't," she said, shaking her head.

He liked the thought of her ass, which he'd had a few opportunities to appreciate during their unlikely time together. He smiled to let her know.

She cocked an eyebrow and gave him the bored look again. "My God, you're really just fourteen years old, aren't you?"

"It feels like sixteen, actually, but I could be off by a little."

"Actually, I think fourteen is generous."

He smiled. "I thought you said before you didn't have time to flirt with me."

She snorted. "What makes you think I'm flirting with you?"

"Aren't you?"

"I certainly am not."

"Yeah, you are. Otherwise you wouldn't have denied it so fast."

"Oh, dear. Romeo here can't go wrong. When a woman says she's interested, she's interested. When she says she's not interested, she's still interested. Did you know that grandiosity and megalomania are primary characteristics of narcissistic personality disorder?"

"Don't get me wrong. I don't mind."

"Well, I'm glad you're enjoying yourself."

"So, are you married?"

She squinted at him. "Are you for real?"

"You don't have to answer if you don't want to."

"Oh, thank goodness. For a moment there, I thought you had subpoena power or something."

"Well?"

"Let's just keep this professional, all right? I don't think we need to start getting to know each other's personal lives and all that."

"Suit yourself. You're the one who was flirting."

"Please."

"So you're not married."

"No, I'm not married."

"Why not?"

"What are you, my grandmother?"

"Does she ask you that?"

"All the time. But she has an excuse. She's senile."

"Do you date?"

She laughed. "What is this, twenty questions? Why are you asking me this bullshit? Seriously."

"I'm interested in you."

"You're not interested in anyone but yourself. You've got that written all over you."

She seemed to mean it, and because it wasn't the first time he'd heard such a thing, the comment bothered him enough to make him want to ask what she meant. But he knew if he did, he'd lose the initiative. Initiative toward what, he wasn't really sure.

"I'm just wondering what it's like to be a young,

attractive, female FBI agent who's smarter and got more moxie than most of the men around her."

"Oh, is that me? Smarter and with more moxie?"

"Don't forget the attractive part."

"Yes, I heard that, too."

"So, are they intimidated by you? Do they hit on you?"

"You know what you're doing right now?"

"What?"

"It's called projection. Do you know what that is?"

"I think I've heard of it."

"You've heard of it, but you don't recognize it. It's when you attribute to others a behavior you sense but can't face in yourself."

"Is that what I'm doing?"

"Of course it is. You're intimidated by me and it's making you uncomfortable. You deal with the discomfort by being sexually passive-aggressive with me. Hitting on me, that is, which makes you feel dominant. But rather than recognize any of that and deal with it like an adult, you suggest that it's other people who must do what you yourself are doing right this very minute."

Ben puffed up his cheeks and blew out a breath. "That's a pretty sophisticated analysis."

She looked at him, and once again he was struck by an incongruous gentleness in her eyes. "It's actually pretty simple," she said. "You're hurting inside, Ben or whatever your name really is. That's where all the adolescent bluster comes from. You don't want anyone to see what's really going on in there, so you act like a jerk to push them away. I expect it works really well for you, too."

After everything that had happened with Alex, that one stung. He thought of Hort, stripping him bare with his commentary in that filthy prison. A few rejoinders came to mind, but because he sensed that maybe she was right, they all made him feel pathetic.

"I guess it does," he said.

But she didn't catch that he wasn't sparring anymore. "Now listen," she said, "we're busy now, we have a job to do. But you know what? When this is over?"

He raised his eyebrows.

"When this is over, I want you to make a little time for yourself and look up some of the disorders we've been talking about. Projection, for example. Maybe you can get some insight."

He didn't answer. He'd had about as much insight as he could handle.

15 BREAKING THE CYCLE OF VIOLENCE

Ben and Paula landed at Quepos, a small airport on the Pacific coast with an open-air pavilion handling both departures and arrivals. Hort had taken care of customs, and they hadn't needed to transit through San Jose.

At the curb, a young, fit-looking brown-skinned guy in shorts, a polo shirt, and shades was leaning against a dark green van. Ben and Paula walked over.

"Where are you heading?" the guy asked.

"Up the coast," Ben responded, using the bona fides Hort had provided. "Hoping to see some crocodiles."

The guy nodded, handed Ben a set of keys, and walked off without another word. Paula watched him go. "We don't have to sign for anything?"

"I guess not."

"If I didn't already know you're a spook, that's pretty much the proof. If you were FBI, we'd be waiting in a rent-a-car line now."

Ben smiled and opened the driver-side door. Paula rolled her eyes and moved around to the passenger side. "I know, I know, the man's got to drive," she said. "What does this thing do, shoot Hellfire missiles? Turn into a boat?"

"No, but if it's what I'm expecting, in back it's got one-way glass on the windows, a couple of comfortable swivel seats, and even a portable toilet. Perfect for all your mobile surveillance needs."

Paula entered the coordinates for Taibbi's bar in Jacó on her iPhone. As soon as they were clear of the airport, Ben reached under his seat and pulled out the Glock 23 that was waiting for him there. Better this way than taking a chance on trying to bring one directly, in case Hort hadn't managed to handle customs.

"Well, that's handy," Paula said. "I don't suppose you'd like to share."

"Check under your seat."

Paula did. There was a Glock waiting for her, too.

"Now that's the kind of interagency cooperation I'm talking about," she said, smiling and checking the load.

"I don't want you walking around unarmed. But don't point it at me, okay? Once was enough."

"Well, that would be ungrateful of me, wouldn't it?" she said, and Ben noted that she hadn't actually agreed. Not that it would have mattered anyway. They weren't exactly on their way to a lifelong friendship, but he was pretty sure they were past the point where they'd be throwing down on each other.

They headed north up the coast, the sun setting to their left, the road shifting from one lane to two and then back again as it twisted past jungle and plantation and rickety roadside towns. Occasionally they would crest a hill and catch a glimpse of the ocean, its surface scored with gold and pink as the sun slipped away beyond it, but mostly the route felt more tunnel than road, a passage sealed off in all directions but forward and back by the indifferent, impenetrable green of the rain forest all around.

When they passed a sign telling them they were ten kilometers from Jacó, Paula said, "Now listen. I know you like to be the driver, I know you like to be in charge. But let's not go into Taibbi's place bristling with attitude, okay? If we have to ratchet things up, we'll ratchet things up. But let's start sweet. Which means I'll do the talking, okay?"

Ben chuckled. "Was that sweet when you told McGlade you were going to climb up his ass and chew your way out?"

"It's what was called for at the moment. But I started nicely and evaluated him first."

"Don't get me wrong, it's a great line. I'm going to use it myself first chance I get."

"Do we understand each other? You're too much of a hard-ass all the time, and I don't want you getting in people's faces and antagonizing them unnecessarily. We won't get any cooperation that way. You have to know when to use sugar and when to use spice. You're all spice."

"All right, whatever. If you want to take the lead, it's fine with me. All I care about is the results."

"I don't think that's true, but okay."

"What do you mean, it's not true?"

"I mean, when someone uses a hammer for every job he's presented with, he's not just trying to do the job."

He glanced over. "What's he doing, then?"

She looked at him. "He's enjoying the hammer."

Ben didn't answer. Like a few of her earlier observations, like what Hort had told him in the Manila city jail, the latest comment chafed, and he knew that must mean there was something to it. But not something he was inclined to consider at the moment.

By the time they pulled into Jacó, the last light had leached from the sky. They rolled along the main drag, two potholed lanes hemmed in on either side by low-slung buildings, some new, others ramshackle. There were open-air restaurants and dim nightclubs, souvenir shops and cheap hotels, construction sites and vacant lots and everywhere palm trees, swaying as though to silent music in the murky dark.

"There it is," Paula said, pointing to an enormous illuminated sign for Bottle Bar, the name they'd gotten from McGlade.

"I know," Ben said, watching three curvaceous Latina prostitutes going inside. "Just want to get a feel for the street before we go in."

He continued down the strip. Small knots of tourists, some Tico, others foreign, wandered the sidewalks and zigzagged back and forth across the street, not aimlessly, exactly, but more with the air of people who would know what they were looking for only when they found it. The contours of the town changed somewhat as they drove, but overall, Jacó was a fractal, each part possessing and revealing the character of the whole. Which was, obviously, the bartering of pleasure—surf and sun by day, booze and sex at night. Burgos Street in Manila, Pattaya in Thailand, Orchard Tower in Singapore . . . they all looked different, and they all felt depressingly the same.

They drove back toward Bottle Bar and parked a little way down the street. Paula started to get out. "Wait," Ben said. "Let's just watch for a minute."

"Why?"

"Because you never know what you might learn."

A group of five pudgy white guys approached the entrance. A security guy in a black Bottle Bar T-shirt stood up and waved a wand over them, but perfunctorily, just their waists and shoulders. The guy reached out and patted a pocket here and there after wanding it, probably to confirm that what had set off the detector was just a cellphone.

"See that?" Ben said. "We can't just go in there with shoulder-holstered Glocks."

"All right, fine, we'll leave the guns in the van."

Ben shook his head. Even on his own time, he didn't like to go unarmed. When he was operational, there was just no way. "Not yet," he said. "Let's just keep watching for a minute."

They did. "Look," he said. "They're not wanding the girls."

It was true. Another collection of prostitutes, black, Latina, and mulatto, went right past the security guy, who nodded and didn't even stand up.

"He probably knows those girls," Paula said. "They're probably there every night."

"Maybe." He looked at her.

She frowned. "What?"

"We need to get you a costume change."

She looked at him, not understanding. Then her eyes narrowed as his meaning became clear. "No. No, that's ridiculous."

"It makes perfect sense. Have you seen even one non-professional woman go in there in the last ten minutes? Civilian women don't go to places like Bottle Bar—it's not that kind of joint. The system is, the hookers get in free and the bar charges the men a cover for the privilege of paying for overpriced beer while they take their time deciding which girl they want to take home that night."

"I see you know a lot about places like this."

"I know enough to tell you you can't just march in there in your FBI pantsuit. You look all wrong. You'll draw attention and at a minimum they'll wand you. It won't work."

"So you want me to dress up like a sex worker, is that it?"

"Well, you've got the body for it, from what I can tell."

She looked at him. "You're repulsive."

He sighed, realizing something. "You've never worked undercover before, have you?"

"What's that supposed to mean?"

"It means you're used to people taking you seriously because you're the FBI. You're used to relying on the badge to get what you want. But you're not in Kansas anymore, Dorothy. You don't have automatic authority out here. You need to learn to blend, to use stealth."

"Stealth? All I've seen you use since the moment I met you is force."

"The point is, if your sweet-talk routine falls flat, and if no one here gives a shit that you're with the big bad Bureau, force might be all we have to fall back on. We're going to be on unfamiliar ground, with a guy who I gather from McGlade and otherwise is no cupcake, in a place that deals with enough troublemakers to justify a metal detector at the door and probably more security inside. I don't want to go into an environment like that without a gun if I don't have to, and if all we have to do to slip one inside is dress you like a streetwalker, it seems like a pretty small price to me."

She glared at him for a long moment, then said, "Fine."

They got out and walked to an open-air souvenir shop down the street. Along the way they were approached twice by scrawny locals offering weed and Ecstasy. Each time Ben shook his head and the dealers peeled off.

In the shop, amid ¡Pura Vida! T-shirts and Imperial Beer baseball caps and postcards of beach sunsets and surfers carving waves, they selected a black sarong and a red halter top. Ben looked at the halter Paula was holding, checked the sizes, and grabbed another one, one size down. He held it out. Paula looked at him as though he was offering her a turd.

"I won't even be able to breathe," she said.

"And no bra."

"Are you trying to be funny?"

He wasn't. Maybe, on another occasion, he would have been enjoying the whole thing, but he wasn't in that mode now. He didn't know what was inside that bar and whatever it was, he wanted to be carrying when he found it.

"I'm being one hundred percent professional when I tell you there's going to be a direct correlation between the doorman's eagerness to examine you with his eyes and his failure to examine you with the metal detector."

She looked at him for a long moment, as though trying to detect some glint of humor or mockery in his eyes. When she saw none, she said, "All right, then," and took the smaller halter into the changing room.

A few minutes later, she emerged, and despite himself, Ben's mouth dropped open a little. He could tell before that she had a good body, but . . . damn.

"How's this working for you?" she asked, smiling and stepping unusually close.

"It's . . . you look good. For the role, I mean."

She stepped closer. "You sure there's nothing else I need to do, just to make sure I'm properly in character?"

He hadn't noticed earlier that she'd been wearing perfume, but he could smell it now, and as much as the revealing clothes, maybe even more, it stirred his awareness of her as female. He'd contemplated her sexually from the moment they'd driven off from Kissimmee together, of course—she was an attractive woman, and some level of sexual contemplation of attractive women was a reflex for him. But it had been more of an intellectual thing initially, driven partly by curiosity, partly by antagonism. Seeing so much of her actual skin, her body revealed in the ridiculously tight halter and clinging sarong, smelling her perfume from how close she was standing . . . there was nothing intellectual about it.

She stepped so close he was sure he could feel the heat from her body. She put a palm on his chest, and he was acutely aware of its warmth and slight pressure. "What, nothing to say? That's not like you."

"What do you want me to say?" he said, horrified to feel himself getting hard and searching for some way to regain control.

She looked into his eyes. "Anything you like," she whispered. "Whatever it is you want."

He swallowed. "Come on, knock it off. We've got something to do."

He took hold of her hand. She allowed him to remove it from his chest, but as soon as he'd done so, she replaced it, this time on his hip. Tilting her head back so that she was still looking into his eyes, she stepped all the way in and pressed her breasts and pelvis against him. His lungs wanted to suck in a breath and he barely managed to refuse them.

She shifted slightly, and the feeling of her breasts moving against him, separated only by a pair of inconsequential pieces of fabric, the friction of her crotch against his hard-on . . .

"Oooh," she cooed. "Feels like you have something nice down there."

Within the severely curtailed drop-down menu of his mind, he recognized a possible option. Call and raise. See how far she would go with this before she blinked.

And was suddenly certain she wouldn't blink. Not for anything.

She wet her lips with her tongue and moved her hand around to his ass. He grabbed her wrist and stepped away. "Okay, enough," he said. "You've made your point."

"My point? What's my point?"

He blew out a long breath. "I don't even know, but I'm sure you've made it."

And suddenly the coquette was gone, vanished, and he was looking at Paula again. "The point," she said, "is don't assume I can't work a cover."

She was right. Just because she didn't know the details of playing a role didn't mean she didn't have an instinct for it. She'd fooled him outside Marcy Wheeler's house, and again now.

And damn, he was blushing, he could feel it. "Big mistake," he said. "Clearly."

"Now let's go talk to Taibbi."

They found a shadowy place under a palm in an empty lot. Paula put her gun in her purse and slung it over her shoulder so the bag rested against her ass and the strap pressed diagonally across her cleavage. The look concealed the bag and its unusual weight, and also further accentuated her breasts, something a moment earlier Ben would have sworn impossible. They waited until they saw another group of prostitutes approaching from down the sidewalk. Paula fell in behind them as they passed and joined them at the entrance. The security guy waved them through with professional indifference, though he did take a long moment to look Paula up and down in a way that had nothing to do with his job description. All right, good to go.

Ben concealed his own Glock in the grass at the base of the palm. He judged the risk of someone breaking into the van greater than that of someone stumbling across the gun here, and besides, if things went hairy inside and one of them made it out, the quicker the access, the better. He also left behind the SureFire LX2 LumaMax flashlight he carried. It was a little longer than the width of a man's hand and as thick as a thumb, with a length of duct tape wrapped around its middle to make it easier to hold in the teeth. Useful for a variety of tasks, not all of them involving illumination, and a little too recognizable as special ops everyday carry by anyone with an eye for such things. He took the souvenir shop bag they'd put her jacket and pants in and moved off.

He imagined himself as just another horndog tourist, liberated from the strictures of work and church and family and on the cusp of a night of memorable Jacó debauchery. With the scent of Paula's perfume lingering in his nostrils and the feel of her breasts still vaguely electric against his torso, getting the vibe right wasn't too much of a stretch.

The doorman wanded his waist, shoulders, and the

souvenir shop bag he was carrying, patted the cellphone in his back pocket, and waved him in. Ben pushed open the door and a pretty woman pointed to a sign in English and Spanish—cover charge for men two thousand colones, or four dollars U.S. Ben gave her the money in colones and she taped a fluorescent paper bracelet to his wrist, a pass to show he'd paid if he came back later and wanted to pick another girl.

The place was a long rectangle, with an island bar up front and a second bar against the left side farther back. The lighting was low—just a collection of small blue and red bulbs dangling from a black ceiling, plus the glow of a half dozen wall-mounted flat-screen monitors all displaying the same soccer game, all inaudible over the thumping house music. Ben estimated the crowd at about thirty, but the place looked like it could accommodate ten times that, assuming local fire codes were interpreted with the appropriate leeway. Well, it was early still, and places like Bottle Bar didn't really get going until a bit later in the evening. He noted an alarmed emergency exit on the right, and had a feeling there would be another in back.

He moved inside, keeping the island bar to his left, avoiding the bold eyes of the hookers. He spotted Paula at the end of the bar and walked over.

"You come here often?" he asked, raising his voice over the music, his eyes sweeping the area behind her.

"Yes, it's my favorite place. Give me my clothes now, okay? I think we're more likely to get some cooperation from Taibbi if I look like the Bureau than if I look like a Jacó streetwalker."

"No problem. Just step in close first and slide the barrel of the Glock into the back of my pants, okay?"

"I'll hang on to the gun, thanks."

"I don't want to argue about this," he said, suppressing a little surge of irritation. "I'm sure you're a good shot, but you probably expend as much ammunition in a year on the range as I do on an average day. And I won't even ask how many gunfights you've been in. You're trained for law enforcement, Paula, not combat shooting. So do me a favor. For both our sakes. Give me the gun. And I'll give you your clothes."

She glared at him, and he was suddenly unsure whether having her stick a gun in his pants was such a hot idea. But then she was stepping in close, standing on her toes, her breath warm against his ear, one hand under his shirt on his abdomen, the cold gun metal on the skin of his back, and she slid her front hand around and eased his pants back and he felt the barrel of the gun slide into his waistband.

"You're lucky I don't shoot your ass off," she said. She took the bag with her clothes and moved off to find the bathroom.

Ben watched her go. He adjusted the Glock, then did another circuit of the bar. He counted a total of six security guys, including the one with the portable metal detector out front, all in Bottle Bar T-shirts. Three of them were behind the island bar, working alongside an equal number of petite Ticas, and didn't look like much, though probably they could be mobilized if there were a problem that required a show of force. And probably the number of security personnel, like the number of bartenders, would increase as the hour grew later and the bar more raucous.

He walked. Rear emergency exit—check. Next to it, a black curtain with a sign next to it that said *Privado*. Presumably Taibbi's office. And if there had been any doubt, the muscleman in dreadlocks and the black Bottle Bar T-shirt sitting on a stool next to the curtain would be an important clue. Okay. He stood a little ways off and watched the scene in the bar and waited. He thought of the last bar he'd been in, the one in Manila. But it was different now. He was operational. If violence was called for, he'd use it purposefully.

Or at least for the right purpose.

After a few minutes, Paula appeared. She was back in her regular clothes.

"I think I'm going to miss that outfit," Ben said.

"I'm sure you will."

"I should have taken a picture."

"Yeah, you should have. Because that's the last you'll be seeing of it."

"You ready?"

"Let's go."

They strolled over to Dreadlocks. The guy watched their approach and didn't get up. Ben wasn't impressed. If he'd been Dreadlocks and seen himself walking over, he'd damn sure be on his feet before the threat had closed the distance.

Paula said, "Hello there. Do you speak English? *¿Habla mejor Español?*"

Dreadlocks looked at her and said in American-accented English, "What do you want?"

"Oh, thank you. My Spanish is so rusty. We're here to see Mr. Taibbi."

"Is he expecting you?"

"I don't believe so, no. But I'm sure he'll want to talk to us anyway. We have some information about Harry McGlade."

Dreadlocks looked at her for a moment longer, shifted his eyes to Ben, then shrugged. He got up, parted the curtain, and disappeared behind it. Ben heard a door open and close.

A minute later, Dreadlocks appeared from behind the curtain. He stood closer to Ben and Paula than he needed to, crossed his massive arms across his chest, and said, "He's not here."

Ben looked at him. "You had to go back there to figure that out?"

"Guess I did."

"When's he coming back?"

"Don't know. Maybe never. Main thing is, he's not here. Now you need to not be here, too. You understand?"

"Of course we do," Paula started to say. "It's just—"

Ben cut her off. "Actually, I don't. I can be a little slow about that kind of thing. Maybe you can explain it to me."

Ben could tell by a dozen tiny signals the guy wasn't a fighter, just someone who'd gotten used to intimidating people with his size and demeanor. Some guys like that, when they realized they'd treed a bad one, would find a lame way to back off and save face. But Ben didn't see any of that kind of recognition in Dreadlocks's eyes. Well, every would-be hard-ass fucks with the wrong guy eventually. Looked like Ben was going to be this one's first.

Dreadlocks looked at Ben and frowned. Ben thought of something one of his instructors had once taught him, something he'd already known from innumerable street fights as a kid. But he liked his instructor's formulation anyway:

When faced with violence, make sure you hit first, soon, early, and often.

Didn't look like Dreadlocks had received that particular memo. Well, it was never too late to learn.

Dreadlocks uncrossed his arms and stepped in closer. Ben knew the stance was supposed to look confident, and he supposed it did. But it was also extremely stupid. It left the guy's whole body open to attack.

"I'm gonna ask you—"

Ben didn't wait for the rest of the question. He threw a hand forward like a guy pitching a softball. There was a nice, satisfying impact as his palm connected with Dreadlocks's package. Dreadlocks made an *oomph* sound and doubled forward, his eyes bulging. Ben spread his fingers, raked in everything in the neighborhood, and squeezed extremely hard. The sound Dreadlocks was making changed to *huuunnnhh,* and his face turned as scarlet and stricken as that of a man having a coronary. He wrapped his hands around Ben's wrist but Ben didn't let up for a second.

Ben looked around to make sure Dreadlocks didn't have plainclothes backup and that they hadn't drawn the attention of any of the uniformed security up front. He didn't see anyone. They were lucky the bar was relatively quiet at this hour, the security posture accordingly relaxed.

"I'm sorry, what did you want to ask me?"

"*Hnnnnuuuunnnnnhhhhh,*" Dreadlocks said, grimacing.

"I'm sorry, I don't speak *hnuh.* But let me ask you something. Answer in English, okay? Is Taibbi here?"

"He's . . . here . . . ," Dreadlocks said, sounding like a human steam kettle.

"Good, I thought so. Now, in a second, I'm going to let you go. You try asking me any more questions after that, I'm not going to be so easy on you. Okay?"

"Okay," Dreadlocks wheezed.

Ben let go and Dreadlocks dropped to his knees, clutching himself and making retching noises. Ben stepped past him through the curtain. Paula caught up and said, "What the hell was that?"

Ben glanced at her. "Just trying to break the cycle of violence."

"You call that breaking the cycle of violence?"

"Well, there's no more violence, is there?"

"How are we going to get any cooperation after that?"

"I don't know. I don't usually think that far ahead."

Ben swung open the door and stepped into a small, rectangular room, only slightly better lit than the bar outside, Paula just behind him. A man was sitting in an enormous leather chair facing the door, leaning back, his legs up on a wooden desk, tooled-up cowboy boots crossed at the ankles. He had a head of shaggy gray hair and small, strikingly blue eyes set back deeply under a craggy, protruding brow. He didn't flinch when Ben and Paula walked in. Instead, he pulled a few leaves off a plug of chewing tobacco in a pouch and casually eased them up between his gums and cheek. He closed the pouch and tossed it onto the desk. Then he slowly worked the wad into place with his tongue, watching them silently.

Taibbi, Ben thought. In his experience, any man who could be as relaxed as this one when two strangers barged into his office had a weapon within arm's reach. If the guy's hands went under the desk or into a drawer or anywhere else, Ben was ready to upend the desk and dump it on him.

"Who are you?" Taibbi said after a moment, in a deep Texas drawl.

Ben looked at him. "Friends of Harry McGlade."

"Harry McGlade doesn't have friends."

Ben realized that was probably true. "Acquaintances might be a better word."

Taibbi squinted. "All right, Harry McGlade's acquaintances. What the fuck do you want?"

Ben said, "Information."

Taibbi cocked his head and regarded them for a long moment, as though trying to figure out how two people this stupid could also draw breath. "Well, sure, absolutely, just ask whatever you want, I'll tell you everything I know."

Paula said, "We were hoping if we ask nicely, Mr. Taibbi."

Taibbi spit a wad of tobacco juice into a cup. "The way you asked my bouncer?"

Either Taibbi was just coming to the logical conclusion,

or he'd overheard the confrontation. Either way, it didn't matter. Ben said, "He started it."

Paula looked at him disgustedly, like he was the world's biggest child. Ben looked back and shrugged.

Taibbi said, "He's supposed to start it. He's the bouncer."

Paula was still looking at him, and Ben could almost see fumes coming out of her ears. He thought, *all right, all right.*

He glanced at Taibbi. "Well . . . I regret the misunderstanding."

Taibbi smiled. "No, you don't regret it. But you will."

Ben was about to kick the desk over and straighten the clown out, but Paula said, "We really do apologize for what happened. My name is Special Agent Paula Lanier, FBI. We're investigating a homicide, and have reason to believe you may be a material witness."

Ben saw Taibbi's pupils dilate from a little adrenaline dump. Either the guy had reason to be generally antsy about the FBI, or he was specifically nervous about what Paula had asked him. Or both.

Taibbi looked at Paula, then Ben, then back. He squirted tobacco juice into his cup. "Show me your credentials."

Paula reached into her purse, pulled out her ID, and put it on Taibbi's desk. He put his feet down, picked it up, squinted at it wordlessly, then handed it back. He looked at Ben. "And you?" he said.

Ben would have preferred to refuse, but he could tell from Taibbi's demeanor that if the guy got the idea he was faced with other than legitimate law enforcement, he wasn't going to tell them shit. He hadn't said anything when examining Paula's ID. It was a good bet that he'd read and return Ben's silently, as well.

Ben handed him the Dan Froomkin ID. Paula glanced at it as it changed hands. Whatever she saw, she said nothing. The main thing now was that Taibbi feel a little cooperation would be in his interest.

The bet paid off. Taibbi looked, squinted, and handed it back. Ben slipped the ID into his pocket and said, "Now, what were you saying, about how we might regret something?"

There were footsteps behind them. Ben spun, ready to draw down. It was Dreadlocks, still somewhat hunched over, and two other guys in black T-shirts.

"It's fine, Bobby," Taibbi said. "We're fine. All of you, go on back out to the bar."

Dreadlocks Bobby gave Ben what he must have thought was a menacing look and turned to go.

Ben said, *"Hnnnnunnnh."*

Dreadlocks's face reddened. "Motherfucker," he growled.

"Thanks, Bobby," Taibbi said. "We'll talk later."

Dreadlocks limped out, the other two security guys just behind him. Taibbi said, "Okay, apology accepted. Now, what's this about a murder?"

Ben was about to respond, but Paula beat him to it. "Our acquaintance, Mr. McGlade, explained to us how he retained you to follow the subject of an investigation of his, one Daniel Larison, whom Mr. McGlade had traced to San Jose. Mr. McGlade informs us that Mr. Larison murdered an associate of yours. We'd like to learn more about that."

Taibbi was silent for a long moment. He drummed his fingers along the desk. Ben watched his hands.

He looked at Ben, then back to Paula. "Mr. McGlade told you that, did he?"

Paula nodded. "Yes, he did."

Taibbi squirted a brown stream into his cup. "Well, McGlade is a grade-A scumbag. If I had time, I'd get on a plane, fly out to Orlando, and personally put a boot straight up his ass."

"I can't say we found his company particularly pleasant, either," Paula said. "Now, I'd be very grateful for anything you could tell us about Larison. Our investigation doesn't otherwise concern you, your bar, or any of your affairs. Even if we were to see something untoward here, narcotics, for example, or any other illicit thing, we'd be too focused on the information you give us to care, or even to remember."

Taibbi leaned back in his chair and crossed his ankles on the desk again. "Like you guys have any jurisdiction here in Jacó anyway. Please."

Paula smiled, and Ben wondered if Taibbi, who seemed to have good instincts, would recognize just how dangerous her smile could be. "Oh, Mr. Taibbi," she said, in her most honeyed voice, "I hope a smart man like you would know better than that. There's jurisdiction, and then there's jurisdiction. It's the second kind that can really bite you on the ass. Especially if you give someone a reason."

Taibbi looked at her for a long moment. Ben could tell the man was tough. But he could also tell he was smart. He knew what Taibbi would do.

"Well," Taibbi said, with a grudging smile, "I don't see any reason we can't have a conversation. Just about some hypotheticals. Nothing that really happened. And off the record, of course."

Paula returned his smile. "That's all we're asking."

Taibbi scrunched up his face, worked his chew around from inside his cheek, and spat it into his cup. He got up and sauntered over to a bureau. "What's your poison?"

Ben thought it extremely unlikely the man would try to drop two FBI agents in his own bar. Still, he watched him closely, ready to draw and use the desk for cover if Taibbi did anything the least bit froggy.

"We're on duty," Paula said. "But thank you."

"Suit yourself," Taibbi said. He pulled the stopper out

of a decanter and poured a large measure of what looked like whiskey into a glass. "How about you, tough guy?" he said, looking over his shoulder. "You look like a whiskey guy to me."

"Nah, milk's more my speed."

Taibbi chuckled. He picked up his glass, took a swallow, and let out a long breath. He turned his back to the bureau and leaned against it, looking Ben up and down. "The FBI must have been short on decent wiseasses when they hired you."

"Yes, sir," Paula said, shooting eye daggers at Ben. "That's about right. Now, those hypotheticals you were going to tell us about?"

Taibbi took another swallow. "What's the worst thing that happens if you get made on surveillance?"

Ben looked at him. "Depends on the target."

Taibbi's eyes narrowed. "'Target,' huh? Not 'subject'?"

Ben thought, *shit*. Paula said, "My associate here did some other things before joining the Bureau. You might have noticed that."

My associate, Ben thought. She didn't know what name Taibbi had seen on the ID, so she didn't use one. She was good. At the moment, he had to admit, better than he was.

"Did he now?" Taibbi said.

"Well?" Ben said. "What's the worst thing?"

Taibbi rolled the glass between his palms. "In my experience? You're embarrassed. Maybe you blow the case."

Ben waited.

"So you understand, that's all we were expecting. That was the limit of our downside. McGlade told us this guy was surveillance conscious, sure, but that's like saying someone with the fucking Ebola virus is feeling a little under the weather. It doesn't exactly prepare you for what you're about to face."

He took another swallow of whiskey, and Ben was fascinated to see the way real tension was creeping into his expression and posture. The man didn't like what he was remembering.

"We followed Larison from the airport. He took the bus and we used a four-person tag team. All we needed to do was track him to his mistress's place, if there was a mistress, get a photo, email it to McGlade, back at the bar by midnight. Easy money for an evening's work. Well, let me tell you about our easy money. We'd been rotating the point to keep Larison from getting a fix on anyone. My guy Carlos went first, and rotated out when Larison changed buses in San Jose. By the time we'd tracked Larison to Barrio Dent, a suburb on the east side of downtown, Carlos was on point for the third time. We'd been careful as hell, but Larison must have made Carlos anyway. I had visual contact with Carlos, he had the eye on Larison. All of a sudden, Carlos stops under a streetlight, looks confused. Looks left, looks right. I'm thinking, fuck, Larison slipped him. We blew it."

He took a swallow of whiskey and let out a long breath.

"And just as I'm thinking that, Larison appears out of the dark like a fucking apparition. I know how that sounds, and I don't care. I'm telling you, the man was gone, and then he was there. He did something, it looked like, just touched Carlos lightly from behind, and then he was gone again, like fucking vapor. Carlos starts staggering around, clutching his neck, there was this slurping sound. I ran over. Fucking blood like I've never seen—and I promise you, I've seen blood—blood is geysering out of Carlos's neck, just shooting out all around his hands and between his fingers. Larison must have used a punch knife or something, you got that? Something sharp as a razor. Opened Carlos up like a fucking beer can, he knew exactly where to put the cut. Jesus,

I'm telling you, I never saw anything like it. Carlos went down and bled out in ten seconds. I had blood inside my shoes, my socks were soaked from standing in it."

He took another swallow of whiskey and shuddered. "Hypothetically, that is."

Ben had no doubt Taibbi was telling the truth. First, because unless he had natural Oscar potential as an actor, he couldn't have feigned what Ben had just seen. Second, because Ben understood Larison. He knew the training. The reflexes. The mind-set.

Ben said, "Why didn't you go after him?"

"What, that night? I told you, we might as well have been chasing the humidity under that streetlight."

"No, another time. You'd traced him to Barrio Dent. And you're local. You could have found him."

Taibbi's expression was grim. "Maybe one of us did."

Ben and Paula said nothing. Taibbi finished what was in his glass and refilled it.

"Yeah, Carlos had a brother, they were both part of my crew. The brother's name was Juan. Juan was a tough little bastard, and he worshipped his big brother. He was out of his mind from what Larison did. It was all, 'Let's get that motherfucker' this, and 'Let's get him' that. I told him we needed to keep cool heads and cut our losses. That this guy was out of our league and we'd gotten off lightly, see? I've been around long enough I can make that kind of call. But Juan was young and stupid."

"And it was his brother," Ben said, thinking of Alex.

"Yeah, it was his brother. Hard to let that go. Well, he stormed off, telling us how we were pussies and cowards and could all go to hell. Which I'm sure we all will, eventually, it's just Juan found a way to get himself there first."

"What happened?" Ben asked.

"Don't know what happened. My guess is, Juan went back to Barrio Dent looking for Larison. Somehow, he found him. Maybe he got lucky, if you can call it that.

They found his body in a sewer in Los Yoses, another little suburb adjacent to Barrio Dent. Skull crushed from behind. Larison must have come up behind him, just like he did Carlos. Only difference was, Juan's wallet was missing, so the police wrote it off as a robbery. Juan wasn't exactly an honest citizen, by the way, so it's not like the police knocked themselves out trying to figure out what happened to him."

"His wallet was gone?" Ben said, imagining Larison.

"Yeah. I figured it was Larison's way of making it look like a robbery instead of an execution. Less interesting that way to the gendarmerie."

"You say the brothers were named Carlos and Juan?" Paula said.

"That's right. Carlos and Juan Cole."

"The deaths occurred in Barrio Dent and Los Yoses?"

"Yeah, like I said."

"Close to each other?"

"Maybe two kilometers apart."

"Can you tell us where precisely?"

"He did Carlos across the street from a restaurant called La Trattoria in Barrio Dent. Just north of the Citibank on the central avenue leading from San Jose to the suburbs. You can't miss it, there's only a single streetlight, the rest of the street is dark. That's why Larison chose it."

Ben knew that's why Larison chose it. He'd spotted the tail and then led them into an ambush.

"And Juan?" Paula said.

"Around the corner from a restaurant called Spoon in Los Yoses. One block southeast from the restaurant. The corner with the sewer."

"Any other contact with Larison after that?" she asked.

"Are you kidding me? Let me tell you something. I think you can surmise that I don't have a whole lot of rules in my life. But I've got one: you don't fuck with the angel of death."

"Angel of death?" Ben said.

Taibbi looked at him, squinting slightly as though try-ing to decide something. "Don't pretend like you don't know what I'm talking about, amigo. I can tell you do."

He took a swallow of whiskey, then looked into the glass. "I served in Vietnam, and I've known some pretty tough customers along the way. But I've known only three men who I'd call death personified. One was a guy named Jake, and he's long dead. Another, went by the name of Jasper, is supposed to be in business for himself now, and believe me, you don't want to be the subject of that business. The last was a part-Japanese guy named Rain, and no one knows what happened to him. Larison is in that league. He killed Carlos about as casually as I spit tobacco. And Juan, too. Snuffed them out and then evaporated like some evil fucking mist. Like I told Juan before he went and threw his life away, we were lucky. With a guy like Larison, it could have been worse."

Paula said, "So you never saw him again."

"No. And I sure as hell haven't been looking."

She said, "You don't know what he was doing here?"

"I don't know if he was on holiday, or he had a mis-tress, or if he wanted to go hiking in the fucking rain for-est. I don't know how long he was here or whether he's ever been back. I don't know anything more than what I just told you. And I don't really want to, either."

They were all quiet for a moment. Ben said, "I want to know something."

"What?"

"Why'd you tell us all this?"

Taibbi glanced at Paula. "Because your partner asked so nicely, remember?"

Ben shook his head. "I don't think so."

Taibbi took a swallow of whiskey. "I told you, I don't want to cross paths with Larison again. But that doesn't mean I want him to live happily ever after, either. So whatever you're planning to do with him, I figure now it's your risk, and maybe my reward. That's a division of labor I can live with."

Paula frowned. "What do you mean, 'whatever we're planning to do with him'?"

Taibbi laughed. "What I mean is, if you're FBI, I'm Doris Day." He nodded at Paula. "You, maybe." Then he looked at Ben. "But you? No way."

"Yeah?" Ben said. "What am I?"

"I don't know, exactly. But I'll tell you what you look like. You look like him."

16 NOT A COMFORTING THOUGHT

In the van on the way to San Jose, Paula was fuming in the passenger seat. "I told you I was going to take the lead. Why can't you listen?"

"We got what we wanted, didn't we?"

"Despite you, not because. Every time you open your damned mouth, you antagonize people."

"Yeah, and then you got to do your sweet southern girl routine. Isn't that what you guys call 'good cop, bad cop'?"

"That's right, 'you guys.' That was an FBI ID you showed Taibbi, wasn't it?"

"What difference does it make?"

"I want to know who the hell you're with."

"That doesn't make any difference, either."

"Then why won't you tell me?"

"Because it doesn't make any difference."

"It's all personal for you, isn't it?"

"What are you talking about?"

"You say it's the job, but it's not. You'd already gotten past that bouncer, but no, you had to make fun of him afterward, also. And Drew—you'd already disarmed and disabled him, why'd you have to sass him, too? Does the sass help you get the job done?"

He frowned. It was like Hort again, asking him why he went to that Burgos bar.

"Look, a Zen monk can't do what I do, okay? Not that you would know."

"Oh, those are the only two possibilities? Zen monk, and you?"

He didn't answer. He'd never longed to be working alone as much as he did right then.

They drove for a while in silence. Ben said, "Did you catch what Taibbi said about the wallet?"

"Of course I caught it."

"I mean, what did you make of it?"

"Just what Taibbi said. Larison was trying to make the second killing look like a robbery."

"Wrong. Larison didn't give a shit what the second killing looked like. He'd already vanished like a ghost and no one was going to connect him to the body whether the guy died of blunt trauma or a heart attack or was abducted by aliens."

"Why, then?"

"Because once is happenstance, twice is coincidence, three times is enemy action."

"Will you please stop talking in riddles?"

"Put yourself in Larison's shoes. You arrive at the airport. You're good—you're the best, in fact—so you remember faces, especially ones that belong to anyone who puts out any kind of operational vibe, no matter how slight. At the airport, you log dozens of faces, knowing most of them, probably all, will turn out to be false positives. The ones you see now are happenstance. Then, a half hour, a bus change, and five miles later, one of those faces pops up again behind you. The guy definitely has the vibe. Okay, that's twice—coincidence, maybe. Now you get to Barrio Dent—long way from the airport, small part of the city—and you see the guy *again*. That's enemy action."

"Tell me again how you've never been in the military."

"So now Larison knows for sure he's been followed.

But he's got no reason to think there's any way he could have been followed from the States. In other words, he's not being followed because he's Larison. He's being followed because he's something generic."

"You mean, like a tourist."

"Exactly. He figures that he drew the attention of a gang whose MO is to follow a tourist from the airport, hit him over the head when he's alone or somewhere dark, and make off with his bag, his wallet, his passport, his watch. It happens. And the pattern fits what Larison realizes is in his wake. So he decides to disrupt the pattern."

"All right, that's Carlos. Then what?"

"Then what, I think, could be our break."

"How?"

"Larison was in town for a few days, maybe longer. Say he was shacking up with his mistress. They're going out a lot, enjoying the local nightlife, the restaurants and bars. Carlos's brother Juan knows Larison had business in Barrio Dent or nearby because that's where they tracked him to. He knows it's a long shot, but he's obsessed and he's got nothing else to go on anyway. So one night, he cases every watering hole in Barrio Dent, Los Yoses, and San Pedro. They're all right next to each other and none is particularly big. I read it in the guidebook. Systematically, one by one, starting in Barrio Dent, go back to the beginning, repeat. If he doesn't get bingo the first night, he does it again the next."

"Okay, one night, like Taibbi said, he gets lucky."

"Yeah, although again, lucky might not be quite the right word. He spots Larison and his lady, say, having dinner. Now, he thinks he's being a cool customer and that no way Larison's going to make him. Even after what happened to his brother, he doesn't get what he's up against. Like Taibbi said, he's young and hotheaded."

"And Larison made him."

"Right. And I'll give you good odds, too, that Juan was liquored up when he found Larison the second time, so he'd be sloppy and radiating all his inner badassedness. So Larison spots the problem and says to his girlfriend, excuse me, I need to step outside—a smoke, a little air, whatever. Wait here, babe, I'll be right back. He walks outside, and dumb young Juan follows him. Larison leads him along a little, then doubles back on him, just like he did to Carlos. He doesn't have time or the opportunity to interrogate him, but he wants to know who are these guys who've been following him. So he does him, takes his wallet, puts him in the nearest sewer so he won't be found until later, and is back inside without even breaking a sweat."

"Taibbi said Juan's skull was caved in. How did Larison do that? With some table linen he borrowed from the restaurant?"

Ben reached into his pocket and pulled out the Sure-Fire flashlight. He handed it to Paula. "Feel the bezel, around the glass. That's Mil-Spec hard-anodized aluminum. Now hold it in your hand like a hammer, with the bezel protruding at the bottom of your fist. Now imagine smashing it into the back of someone's head with an overhand blow. What do you weigh, a hundred twenty, a hundred twenty-five pounds? You could put a hole in someone's skull that way. A guy like Larison could do an entire lobotomy."

She handed the SureFire back to him. "Larison would carry something like this?"

"Like this, or an ASP tactical baton. Or he picked up a rock. It doesn't matter."

"How would you know what a guy like Larison carries?"

Ben ignored the probe. "The point is, he does it, takes the wallet, and sees the guy he just killed is named Juan Cole. He would have checked the papers after he did

Carlos, so now he knows he's dealing with brothers. Taibbi suggested these guys were petty criminals, they probably have records, and the papers would have said as much. So Larison's working hypothesis becomes, two brothers, or maybe a gang of which two brothers were a part, followed him from the airport hoping to mug him. He killed one brother, the other decided he wanted revenge, Larison killed him, too."

"Damn."

"Yeah, Taibbi was smart to steer clear—guy's a survivor type, you can tell. Anyway, after he did Juan, Larison would watch his back even more carefully than usual just to make sure the rest of the gang, if there was a rest of the gang, wasn't on his ass. Nothing happens, though, and anyway he's only in San Jose sporadically. And all this was three years ago. So at some point, he figures these were the only two guys he had to worry about. And he doesn't have to worry about them anymore."

"What did Taibbi mean when he said 'whatever you're planning to do' with Larison?"

Ben glanced at her, then back to the road. "He meant, what do you think happens to someone who tries to read the angel of death his rights?"

"What are you going to do if we find him, then?"

"I'm not going to wind up like Carlos and Juan, I'll tell you that."

"What are you supposed to do?"

"All I'm supposed to do is find Larison. So if we tree him, I hope you're not going to try to arrest him, okay? You bring that mind-set to the job, you'll be at a lethal disadvantage. And I don't want to fill out the paperwork."

"I'm touched that you care, really."

They drove in silence for a few minutes.

Paula said, "Where'd you get that ID?"

Ben glanced at her, then back to the road. "You knew

there were other alphabet soup agencies involved in this. You said so yourself."

"I want to know which one you're with."

"I told you, forget about it."

"You're some kind of assassin, aren't you?"

"I'm just here to find Larison," he said again. The weird thing was, it was the truth. So why did it feel like a lie?

"Taibbi said you looked like Larison. What did he mean by that?"

Ben looked at his watch. "Why don't you tell me what our next move is. You know, don't you?"

"Are you talking down to me?"

"Not that I was aware of. But I can if you'd like."

"Our next move is, we canvass restaurants and bars around the sewer where Juan's body was found. Larison couldn't have moved him far—the body would be heavy, for one thing. He wouldn't have time, or concealment, for another. So wherever Juan was found, Larison was nearby that night. If we show his picture in a few places, and if Larison's been back or if he was a regular, we might just catch a break."

Ben nodded. "How's your Spanish?"

"I can get by. You?"

Ben's Farsi was fluent, his Arabic decent, and his Spanish high school rusty. "I think we'll need to rely on you in that department," he said. "And by the way, it's not just that Larison must have been close by to where he did Juan. It's also that, when he killed Carlos, it wasn't in a place that mattered to him."

"What do you mean?"

"He'd already spotted the surveillance. He wasn't going to lead them all the way to his correct address. He'd either get off the bus early, or ride it well past his actual destination. Barrio Dent comes up before Los Yoses on the way from the airport. My guess is, Larison's real destination that night was Los Yoses, or maybe the next stop, San Pedro, or maybe somewhere farther east. He got off in Barrio Dent to make sure the killing wouldn't be too close to a place he was connected with. The second time, he wouldn't have that luxury. He wasn't being followed, he'd been discovered. It's a whole different dynamic."

"So you think the fact that both killings happened near a restaurant is a coincidence."

"I think the first one was a coincidence. The second one, maybe not. Anyway, most of the streets in San Jose don't have names. People use restaurants and other landmarks to describe locations. That's all Taibbi was doing."

"How do you know that?"

"Read it in a guidebook on the plane."

"Well, that was a good idea."

Ben nodded. He didn't mention that reading extensively about a place before going operational was ordinarily only the beginning of area familiarization, and that not having had time to do more than read this time made him feel like he was groping and stumbling in the dark.

"So you think his girlfriend lives in Los Yoses?" Paula said.

"Or farther east. But not Barrio Dent. Otherwise he wouldn't have gotten off the bus there. Now, tell me this. You think he'd still be dining out a hundred yards away from where he put Juan in a sewer?"

"From what Taibbi told us, I don't think we're dealing with someone who gets indigestion from murder."

"What about tactically? He'd practically be returning to the scene of the crime."

"Yes, but like you said, he's only in San Jose sporadically. A month, or six months after the murder, he knows the case is closed. Juan was some sort of street criminal. I can pretty much guarantee that if they didn't have a suspect within seventy-two hours of the crime, they dropped the file into a cold cases basement drawer. Which would be like dropping it into the Bermuda Triangle. And Larison would know that."

Ben nodded, glad she wasn't asking any more assassin questions.

He ran it all through his mind again, and felt pretty sure they were looking at it the right way. And although canvassing restaurants was going to be a long shot, it wouldn't be any longer than what Juan Cole was up against when he'd gone looking for Larison.

Which was not a comforting thought at all.

17 HIS FRIEND NICO

The drive from Jacó took three hours. The road zigzagged up through the jungle and then down again, the diffused glow of the moon behind the clouds from time to time silhouetting mountains in the distance. Here and there they passed the odd roadside *soda* selling tacos or a bodega advertising fresh mangoes and avocados, and the light from these tiny and invariably empty establishments would shine in the distance like a promise of permanence and then fade away behind them, leaving nothing but the headlights pushing feebly against the dark again, the jungle close on either side, the van feeling small, enclosed, improbable, a bathysphere exploring an accidental canal along some ocean's lightless floor.

They passed the time talking about pistols, loads, and their favored carries. For someone who took a dim view of violence, Ben had to admit, Paula knew her hardware. Paula used the iPhone to find a hotel in San Jose—the InterContinental, in Escazú—and to confirm there were vacancies. Ben told her not to make a reservation. The hotel wasn't going to sell out its remaining rooms this late, and he saw no advantage to possibly alerting someone to where he would be spending the night. Not that anyone was looking, but . . . he just had this weird feeling, like there were forces moving around and beneath him, forces he could sense but not understand, and the feeling was keeping his usual low-grade combat paranoia at a healthy simmer.

They arrived in Barrio Dent at close to eleven. The iPhone's GPS function took them straight to La Trattoria, where Taibbi said Carlos had been killed.

Ben parked the van and they stepped out into the sultry night air. There was an audible whoosh of traffic from the central avenue a block away, but other than that the neighborhood was quiet, its colonial houses decaying in stoic dignity beneath the swaying palm trees.

A streetlight across from the restaurant cast a sickly yellow cone of light on the crumbling sidewalk beneath it. Outside the illuminated pall, the street was cloaked in shadow. Ben stood at the edge of the light and glanced around.

"Yeah," he said, nodding. "He got off the bus on the central avenue, took a couple turns, walked past this light . . . yeah, he could have come at Carlos from anywhere in the dark, and disappeared as easily. Okay."

They walked back to the van. "What does that tell us?" Paula said.

"Maybe not much. I just need to get in his head."

"Is it working?"

Ben nodded, imagining what Carlos would have looked like spotlighted under that streetlight. "Plug in the coordinates for that restaurant Spoon, will you? Let's see if we can figure out what happened there."

Paula did. It wasn't much more than a kilometer. They drove the short distance, parked just down the street from the restaurant, and walked over. Spoon was on the corner of two reasonably busy streets, cars parked on both sides, an auto body repair place across from it, the neighborhood a weird mixture of small restaurants and light industry, overgrown lots behind rusting chain-link fences, high-tension wires clinging to low buildings, plaster façades giving over to creeping mold feasting nonstop in the incessant tropical moisture.

Ben looked inside the restaurant. A neighborhood joint, brightly lit, cacti in the windows, plastic chairs and vinyl booths, locals talking and laughing over what looked like desserts and coffee. He could hear eighties American pop playing incongruously from inside. Windows ran the length of the place on both streets it was facing, and Ben was on the verge of deciding this wasn't where Juan Cole had seen Larison—he wouldn't have needed to go inside—when he saw there was a back room that wasn't visible from the windows. So he would have gone inside to check. Okay, Spoon was a possible.

He turned and watched the street for a moment, imagining Larison inside with his girlfriend. Juan Cole pops his head in, you spot him, but he doesn't spot you spotting him. What do you do? You make the decision. You come up with an excuse and get up. You go outside, and . . .

He looked around. Not the street facing the entrance. Too busy. You'd make a right, instead, toward what looked like a more residential part of the neighborhood. Yeah, that felt right. And according to Taibbi, it was where they'd found Juan Cole.

He walked down the cracked sidewalk, Paula just behind him. As soon as he was beyond the light cast through the restaurant window, he was enveloped in darkness. It felt right. So right he was nearly convinced this was exactly how it had gone down.

The block was short. He passed a rust-colored, two-story apartment building on the right, its windows, like all the others he'd seen in San Jose, barred. Then a windowless wall. The sidewalk curved right onto the cross street, and on instinct, Ben followed it rather than crossing the street, and bam, there it was, he saw exactly what Larison had done. There was a staircase and an entranceway immediately to his right. Larison had ducked into it the second he'd turned the corner. If he had any street sense at all, Juan Cole would have realized what had happened just an instant after turning the corner and seeing that Larison was gone, but in that instant Larison had already stepped out from the shadows and broken open the back of Cole's head. An instant could be a hell of a long time against a guy like Larison.

He looked around. Taibbi had said southeast corner, right? That meant across the street. Ben waited for a car to pass, its headlights momentarily cutting through the darkness, then crossed over.

Yeah, there it was. A corner sewer, the cement lip eaten away by time and humidity and lack of repair. It would have taken Larison all of five seconds to drag Cole across the street and shove him inside. If Cole hadn't been a big man, he would have fit easily enough. If he had been big . . . Ben knelt, took hold of the metal grate, and lifted it. It came free easily.

Yeah, brain him, take his wallet, wait for any cars to pass, drag him, dump him . . . he wouldn't have been gone longer than three minutes. People left for longer than that when they got up to take a leak.

"I think it was in Spoon," Ben said, standing up.

"Where Cole saw Larison?"

"Yeah."

"How do you know?"

Ben shook his head. "Just a feeling. Let's go see if anyone in that restaurant recognizes Larison."

They walked back to Spoon and went inside. It was lively with laughter and conversation and the sounds of Billy Idol playing through speakers in the ceiling. Yeah, a neighborhood place. The crowd—about twenty men and women, ages ranging from mid-twenties up to maybe fifty—felt like they belonged there, like they were regulars. Just a neighborhood dessert place, good when you're tired after a night out, but not quite ready for the night to be over.

The host, a smiling man with a belly and a handlebar mustache, walked over with a couple of menus.

"*¿Cuantas personas?*" he asked. How many?

Paula smiled and responded in Spanish while she showed her credentials. Ben was able to make out most of it: We're looking for a regular customer of yours, we'd be grateful if you could help us find him. He's not in trouble, we just need to ask him a few questions.

"Your Spanish is very good," the host said in English, returning her smile and wiping his hands on his apron. "But if you like, maybe English is better?"

Paula laughed. "Oh, my goodness, thank you for saving me from embarrassing myself. Yes, please, English, if that's okay."

The host's smile broadened. "All right. How can I help?"

Ben had to admit this was the right time for Paula to take the lead. When she wasn't busting balls, there was something so . . . soft about her. It was disarming. Maybe that's what she'd meant about people not seeing her coming.

Paula took out her phone and showed the host a photo of Larison.

"Sure, I know him," the man said.

Ben's heart kicked up a notch. He wanted to jump in, but reminded himself that Paula was doing fine, better than fine. He kept his mouth shut.

"You know him how, sir?"

"He's a regular. Well, not a regular, exactly. He comes in a few times a week, or two weeks, and then he's gone for a while. But he always comes back. He's a good customer."

"When was the last time you saw him?"

"I'm not sure. Maybe . . . a month ago? Two months?"

Ben felt a little clench in his stomach, that twist of

combat excitement. That was it. The first solid evidence they had that Larison was alive. And if he was alive, he had to be the one behind this thing.

"Is he . . . alone, when he comes here?" Paula asked.

"No, he comes with his . . . friend. Nico."

From the slight delay between the "his" and the "friend," and slight stress on the latter word, Ben realized instantly. He thought, *Holy shit*. He thought of Larison's wife, Marcy. No wonder she couldn't let Larison's Costa Rica excursions go. Did she know? Did she suspect?

And was Larison the father of their son? And if not, did he—

"This Nico," Paula said, "do you have any way you could put us in touch with him?"

"No, not really. He comes in a few times a month."

"Do you know his last name, sir?"

"I . . . no, I don't."

Ben sensed the questions were now making the man nervous, and that his memory would start to deteriorate as a result.

"When was the last time Nico dined here?" Paula asked.

"Maybe . . . sometime in the last month? We have a lot of customers."

"I'm sure you do, sir. Does he pay with a credit card?"

"I think so, yes. Sometimes."

Bingo. Unless the guy was mistaken and Nico paid only with cash, Ben was sure he now had enough for Hort to take to the NSA, whose supercomputers would triangulate on the name Nico and regular appearances at Spoon in Los Yoses. Ben doubted they'd get even one false positive.

And whatever Larison's relationship with this guy, it was long-standing, and ongoing. If Nico didn't lead them to Larison, it was hard to imagine what would.

18 JUMPY'S NOT MY STYLE

Back in the van, on the way to the InterContinental, Paula said, "It's him. He's not dead."

Ben nodded. "Sure looks that way."

"What's our next step?"

Ben almost pointed out that after tonight, "our" was likely not going to be applicable. Instead, he said, "We report in and try to get some sleep. And we're going to be staying in the same room, okay?"

"Say what?"

"Look, why would a man and woman with next to no luggage be checking into a hotel together without a reservation at near midnight? A spontaneous business convention? You want to appear to be what people expect you are, that's how you avoid getting noticed. So I want you to get back in that sarong and halter. Put your jacket over it. It'll look like you're a prostitute I met at a bar who's wearing a cover-up to be presentable in the lobby of a nice hotel."

She cocked an eyebrow. "And just how far do you expect we'll have to go in performing our roles?"

"Don't get your hopes up. This is just for public consumption."

"My hopes. You really are something. Anyway, why don't we just check in separately and solve the problem that way?"

"Because I don't trust you. I don't want you off in your own room, talking to I don't know who and doing I don't know what."

"You don't trust me. My God, you have nerve."

"Also, it would be natural for a married man arriving at a hotel with a prostitute to wear a baseball cap with the visor pulled low to obscure his features. Never know when you might run into a business acquaintance coming out of the bar. And to keep his head down a bit so his face doesn't get picked up by security cameras. To be reticent about meeting the eyes of any staff he encountered. And you should do the same. Keep the jacket open, show some cleavage. No one's going to look at your face."

"Why are we worried about all this?"

"It's just better not to be remembered or recorded now. You never know what's going to happen later."

Escazú was on the west side of the city. They drove through San Jose's crumbling but vital center, and after a few minutes found themselves passing every conceivable western chain restaurant and retailer. Escazú was obviously an upscale enclave of Americana, right down to the ritzy-looking shopping center across the street from the hotel.

They parked in the lot rather than taking advantage of the valet. Anyone who noticed them walking in without bags would assume they were already checked in. If they thought otherwise . . . well, a man and a woman shacking up for the night away from their spouses could be expected to be discreet. Along with the baseball cap and averted eyes, the parking lot rather than the valet fit the pattern, which was what Ben wanted.

They walked into a bright, air-conditioned lobby—stone floors, a ceiling open all the way to the fifth floor, piano music playing from hidden speakers. The bar was off to the left, and it sounded lively. On the right, three receptionists stood behind a dark wood-and-marble counter.

They strolled over to the nearest of the three, a young Tico in a navy suit. "We need a room for the night," Ben said, his voice quiet, slightly conspiratorial.

"Certainly," the man said. "We have king-bedded rooms, twin-bedded rooms . . ."

"Twin beds would be fine," Paula said.

Ben's face betrayed nothing. But inside, he wanted to smack her for being so stupid.

The receptionist worked the keyboard. "I'm sorry, the only rooms we have available now feature a single king-sized bed."

"A king-sized bed would be fine," Ben said calmly. If Paula uttered one single word of protest, he was going to find something and gag her with it.

"Very good, sir," the receptionist said. "And how many keys will you require?"

Simultaneously, Ben said, "One," and Paula said, "Two."

Ben stared at Paula and said, "One," the single syllable sounding like a growl.

Paula stared back but didn't respond.

"And what credit card will you be using?"

"I'll just use cash."

"All right. And we'll require some form of ID. A passport, or . . ."

Ben pulled out his wallet and put three hundred U.S. on the counter.

"I'd just be more comfortable if there were no record of the transaction," he said. "And please, keep the change."

The receptionist looked down at the money for a moment. He produced a magnetic key in a paper sleeve and handed it to Ben with a gracious smile.

"Your room number is here," he said, gesturing to the sleeve. "The elevator is just past the bar. Enjoy your stay."

"Thank you," Ben said, glancing at the card. Room 535. "I'm sure we will."

They walked over to the elevator. As soon as the doors had closed and Ben had inserted the room card and pressed the button for five, he said, "What were you thinking?"

She looked at him. "What's your problem this time?"

"My problem is, what do you think we look like? We're supposed to be a horny couple shacking up here to have sex. And you're asking for a room with separate beds. You can have the goddamned bed, I'm happy to sleep on the floor."

"I don't see that my request was incommensurate with—"

"With two people who came here to fuck?"

"Maybe you snore. Maybe you thrash in your sleep. There are a lot of reasons two people might want to sleep in separate beds after they make love."

"Yeah? Not in my experience."

"Well, if you can find girlfriends so patient they can tolerate your personality generally, I expect they might be able to tolerate you in other ways, too."

"Yeah, well likewise, I can think of all kinds of reasons a guy might want to get up and go home after he was done fucking you. But that's not the point. The point is, most people who come to a hotel to have sex prefer to do it in the same bed. What you did was a mistake. Mistakes like that get you noticed. Getting noticed gets you killed."

Paula took a deep breath as though to answer, but stopped when the doors opened. There was no way anyone could have anticipated them here, but out of habit, Ben swept the area with his eyes before moving out of the elevator. They walked down the corridor and Ben let them into the room.

As soon as he had double-locked the door, Paula said, "And you're lecturing me about getting noticed? The first thing you did in Taibbi's bar was practically castrate his bouncer. And then every chance you got to get in Taibbi's face, too, you did. Yeah, that's you, Mr. Invisible."

Ben walked past her into the room. Marble bathroom on the right. King bed in the room past it; dresser, flat-screen television, desk on the left. He glanced out the window at two massive, kidney-shaped pools in the courtyard below, then pulled shut the curtains and turned to her. "We've been over this already. When I need to be direct, I'm direct. When I need to be invisible, I'm invisible. If you don't know the difference, you're a goddamned amateur."

Her lips were pressed tightly together and she was breathing so hard her nostrils were flaring. Ben realized he needed to back off. Not that what he was saying wasn't true, but true didn't mean it was helpful.

"Look, you're smart in a lot of ways, I can see that. And you've got good instincts, you know how to play a role. But you need to use your head, too. Why can't you be smart enough to see this isn't your ordinary investigation? That right now you're operating outside the world you're accustomed to? Did you not hear Taibbi when he was talking about what happened to his men? When was the last time you were investigating someone who could ghost up behind you, sever your carotid, and walk away from the arterial spray before your body even hits the floor? I'll tell you when the last time was. Never. Otherwise you'd be dead. And Larison is only half of it. We don't even know who else is after him, or whether they might take an interest in us, too. Do you get it? You're smart and you're good at what you do, but right now you are out of your league and if you want to stay alive, you need to listen to me when I talk to you."

"You are so condescending, it makes me want to wipe the smugness right off your face."

"Is that how you break the cycle of violence?"

She closed her eyes and let out a long breath. "I

hate that I've let you make me this angry. You're not worth it."

He knew he shouldn't respond, but he couldn't help it. "If I'm not worth it, why are you angry?"

She opened her eyes. "Exactly. I'm going to take a bath. Do you need the bathroom first?"

"Yeah, actually, I do."

"Fine. And when you're out? I do expect you to sleep on the floor."

"With pleasure," he said, walking past her.

He closed the door, took a leak, and furiously brushed his teeth with the toothbrush and toothpaste the hotel had provided. If she had a problem using the same toothbrush, she could just go without, he didn't give a shit.

She'd been stupid in the lobby. But . . .

What was the point of unloading on her like that? He could have just pointed out her error. She wasn't thick, she would have gotten it.

Was he trying to get back at her for some of the things she'd said in the van on the way from Jacó? That crap about how he took things personally, that the job alone couldn't justify the way he piled on . . . it had stung. Which, of course, meant there was probably something to it.

And wasn't the thing she'd criticized him for exactly what he'd just done to her? If his goal was to explain operational behavior, he could have just explained it. What did insulting her have to do with that?

And if explaining hadn't been the point, what was?

You wanted to hurt her. Because she hurt you. She challenged you, so you had to put her in her place.

Was that really it? Because, when he put it like that, it sounded so pathetic.

He spat and rinsed his mouth, then looked at himself in the mirror. He wondered if anyone ever looked in the mirror and saw an angry, thin-skinned, petty reflection staring back.

Probably not.

Well, maybe this was part of what Hort had been telling him about. Getting greater self-control. Because how could you have greater self-control if you didn't have greater self-awareness?

All right, fine. But what if you wound up not liking the self you were becoming aware of?

He didn't want to think about that.

He washed his hands, soaked a washcloth, and wiped his face and eyes. That sense of unseen forces, and now all this thinking about his own behavior and what might lie behind it . . . he didn't like it. He thought maybe it was better before, when he just did what he was told and acted the way he wanted and fuck anyone who had a problem with it. It had all been working out pretty well, hadn't it?

Sure. And your daughter thinks you're dead.

"Come on," he said, out loud. "It was supposed to be a rhetorical question."

He chuckled, but without much mirth. Now he was talking to himself. He'd think a question, and a voice in his head was actually answering. And then he'd responded to the voice. What was he going to do, start having conversations with himself?

He needed a vacation. He needed something. That shit with Obsidian, and then the Manila city jail . . . he was just stressed out, that was all. Who wouldn't be?

You wouldn't be. Not before.

"Will you knock that shit off?" he said, out loud again.

He opened the door and walked wordlessly past Paula. "Everything all right in there?" she said.

"Yeah, what do you mean?"

"Sounded like you were talking to someone."

"I don't . . ." He shook his head and laughed. "I was being an asshole a few minutes ago. I'm sorry."

She looked at him, and he had no idea what she was

thinking. After a moment, she said, "Forget about it," and then went into the bathroom.

When he heard the bath water running, he called Hort and briefed him on everything that had happened. He assumed she was doing something similar on her end, but there wasn't much he could do about it.

"Nico, huh?" Hort said.

"Yeah, Nico. What do you think that's all about?"

Hort laughed. "You mean could a hard-ass operator like Larison also be a swish?"

Ben felt a little embarrassed. "Well . . . yeah."

Hort laughed again. "Of course he could. And he wouldn't be the only one, either."

"You're shitting me. There are gays in the unit?"

"Of course there are. And personally, I don't care. All I give a damn about for any soldier is soldiering. Who a man wants to sleep with couldn't matter less to me."

Ben thought for a moment. He supposed what Hort was saying was true. He'd just never considered it before. It was hard to imagine any of the men he worked with could be gay, let alone an operator like Larison.

"It fits, though," Hort said.

"What does?"

"Larison living a secret life. You asked about his motives, remember?"

"Being gay is a motive?"

"Not being gay as such. But having to live in the closet? Knowing you'll face a discharge if anyone finds out, despite all your heroism in the field, despite the personal costs of what you've endured, despite how many American lives you've repeatedly saved? Look at what happened to Dan Choi, for God's sake. The man was an Arab linguist, too. You know how badly we need those? I'll tell you, we can make a terrorist talk, but we can't get him to talk in English. And the army got rid of Choi anyway, just for being gay, a good man who wanted to serve his nation. It would take a better man than I am not to develop a grudge about that. And keeping that kind of secret, living a double life, especially with the kinds of pressures men like us already have to bear up under . . . I told you, I saw the signs. I guess I just didn't know how bad it was."

"Well, what do we do about this guy Nico? He's our connection."

"I need to get his coordinates to the NSA. We've got enough now to figure out who he is, where he lives and works, all his particulars. If we're really lucky, we'll uncover something linked directly to Larison. Even if not, it sounds like this guy could be our big break. Good work, son."

Ben felt that embarrassing flush of pride he always got when Hort praised his performance. He said, "Assume we get Nico's particulars. What do we do then? Snatch him, exchange him for the tapes?"

There was a pause. "I don't know yet. That decision is likely to be made above our pay grade."

Ben was intrigued, both by the pause and by the reference to "our" pay grade, as though the two of them were not just on the same team on this, but also somehow equal.

"Okay," Ben said.

"You should know," Hort said. "There's also been some discussion about his wife and son."

"You mean a snatch?"

"That's what I mean."

It wasn't his place to say, and he almost didn't. But the thought of taking a kid, and the wife, too, Marcy . . . it just made him queasy. It wouldn't be right.

"I don't know, Hort. Snatching a kid? I mean, come on."

"I agree. And I've made the argument that it would be worse than immoral—it would be tactically stupid. From everything you've learned, I think we can assume the wife and son wouldn't even be a pressure point. Larison didn't provide for them, the woman said it wasn't a happy marriage—"

"Marcy. Her name is Marcy Wheeler."

"I know. And after what you've learned about Larison, I'm wondering whether the boy is even his. Anyway, the bottom line is, Larison cared about them so much he faked his death and disappeared. I doubt he'd lose a whole lot of sleep if someone were threatening them now."

Okay, that was good. Didn't sound like anyone was particularly inclined to go after Larison's family. Probably just the kind of pseudo tough-guy talk he imagined suits liked to pleasure themselves with. And Hort certainly wasn't for it.

"What do you want me to do in the meantime?" Ben said.

"There's nothing you really can do, except sit tight. How's that FBI agent, Lanier? She giving you any trouble?"

"All kinds of trouble. But nothing I can't handle."

"Well, let's see what we learn about this guy Nico and what the powers that be want to do after that. After tonight, it might make sense to shake her loose."

"Roger that."

There was another pause. Ben said, "Is everything . . . are we getting some kind of interference on this?"

Hort said, "Why do you ask?" and oddly, Ben imagined him smiling.

"I don't know. Just . . . I was thinking about what's on those tapes. A lot of people must be sweating."

"They are. And I'll tell you about people who are sweating. The sweat gets in their eyes, makes it hard for them to see clearly."

"Anything I need to worry about?"

"Worrying is my job. Your job is to get some sleep

now. I might be calling you in just a few hours with an update."

"Okay."

"Again, good work, son. What you've done might have cracked this thing wide open. I'm proud to say I work with you."

Coming from Hort, this was extreme praise. Ben was simultaneously touched that he would say it, and also concerned about what was going on in the background that could be making him feel, what? Sentimental? Or like he needed an ally?

"Well," Ben said, thinking of Obsidian, "there are still a few things you and I need to work on. But . . . thank you."

"Just get some sleep now. We don't know what's going to happen tomorrow."

Hort clicked off. His parting words were of course a simple statement of fact, but they were also somehow ominous.

Ben thought about just getting in bed and telling Paula they could either share or she could sleep on the damn floor. But that feeling of unseen forces was still torquing up his paranoia. The hell with it. He grabbed an extra blanket from the closet, folded it into a sleeping pallet, and placed it along the wall on the hinged side of the door. He grabbed a pillow from the bed and tossed it onto the pallet. Yeah, he'd sleep better this way. Because if anyone breached the room, the bed would be the initial focus. It would be interesting to see Paula sweet-talk her way out of that particular cycle of violence.

And then he felt bad. Yeah, she was driving him crazy. But he didn't want anything to happen to her, either. If the room were breached, that bed would be the initial big red X. She thought no one ever saw her coming? She didn't know some of the guys he worked with. In night vision goggles, she'd show up just fine.

Paula emerged from the bathroom wearing a hotel robe, beads of water clinging to her face and neck. She looked good.

Ben sighed. "I know I'm wasting my breath, but it probably wouldn't be the worst idea to drag the mattress on the floor and put it up against the door. A bed is just too easy to key on when you breach a room."

"Are you expecting company tonight?"

"If I were expecting it, I wouldn't be here. It's just some extra insurance, that's all. This thing is big. And a little weird, somehow. Can't you feel that?"

"Well, it's definitely a little weird. My team is being treated in an Orlando hospital for injuries inflicted by the man with whom I'm spending the night in a San Jose hotel. Whose identity, I might add, remains a mystery. So yes, you could say it's out of the ordinary."

"If you want to move the mattress, I'll help you."

"It's fine where it is. But thank you."

Ben nodded and looked away. He was surprised at how much he wished he could get through to her. But he didn't see how. "Well, if you're done with the bathroom," he said, "I'm going to take a shower."

"Feel free."

He walked to the bathroom and paused at the door. "I'm going to leave it open, okay?"

"What?"

"I'm sorry, with the water running, I won't be able to hear what's going on outside the door. I can deal with not seeing or not hearing, but not both. So no peeking. Unless you want to."

She looked at him for a long moment. "Either you are a certified paranoid, or an incorrigible exhibitionist."

"Well, I'm not an exhibitionist, as far as I know."

He paused, trying to find the right words. "I know you think I'm a prick, and you're probably right. But I can tell you this: my radar's pretty good. It's saved my ass more times than I can count, and right now, it's telling me that something is . . . going on with these tapes that we can't see. It's making me jumpy. And if you were smart, you'd be jumpy, too."

"Jumpy's not my style."

He nodded, and for a moment felt unaccountably sad. "Yeah? Well, it probably wasn't Carlos or Juan Cole's, either."

19 I WILL BURN YOU

Ulrich paced in his office, tugging on his beard, continually fighting the urge to pick up the secure line and call Clements one more time. He'd heard from his contact and there was a lot of news, but he couldn't make full sense of it without Clements's input. He'd sent two emails and left three messages and the son of a bitch still hadn't gotten back to him. It was maddening. Back in the day Ulrich could have had an admin raise Clements on the phone inside a minute anytime, day or night, and Ulrich wouldn't even bother picking up the phone until he'd been told Clements was already on the line, waiting for him.

He didn't like it, and the disrespect, the not-so-subtle suggestion that somewhere along the line, someone had cut Ulrich's balls off, was the least of it. They weren't isolating him for payback, and they weren't doing it for sport. They were doing it for a reason. And he was beginning to sense what the reason was.

He considered the facts. First, that muckraker Seymour Hersh had reported about an assassination ring operating out of the Office of the Vice President. Hersh claimed the program had been run through JSOC, which meant the leak had come from one of the other participants—CIA or NSA. And then there were the leaks about the illegal surveillance program, all pointing again to the OVP. And then the leaks about the OVP's plan to override the

Fourth Amendment and use active-duty military to arrest U.S. citizens on American soil.

Then, on top of all this, the new DCI suddenly decides to brief Congress on a CIA assassination program that he claimed never went operational anyway, telling them, in effect, that there was an assassination ring, but it was someone else's. That last stunt suggested to Ulrich the other leaks were coming from the Agency, too. It all felt coordinated to him. The question was, coordinated to what end?

God, he could actually feel their machinations, could practically see them scuttling into crevices like cockroaches from a light. They were creating a framework for something, he could tell that much, and the Office of the Vice President was at the center of it. Who was the head of the illegal surveillance program? The OVP. Who was in charge of assassinations? The OVP. Who wanted to send the military into American suburbs? The OVP. Associate the OVP with enough scary things, and when the next scary thing was revealed, it would only be natural for everyone to assume, to want to believe, that it was all the OVP's doing, too. At this point, the new revelation could be anything: child molestation, malnourishment in Africa, global fucking warming . . . it wouldn't matter because the people had been primed to believe the bad stuff always came from the OVP.

Yeah, the hard part was creating the receptivity, getting the public to *want* to believe something without them actually realizing they wanted to believe it. After that, it was easy to just realize it for them.

So he recognized the setup—recognized it because he'd created ones like it himself so many times before. The question was, what was the punch line? And was the joke going to be on him?

It had to be the tapes. But how?

He continued his pacing. For any kind of executive

action, the public understood the beast had both a head and a tail—that there was management, but also labor. So what the Agency was saying, the narrative they were creating, was . . . management was the Office of the Vice President; and whoever the labor was, it wasn't us, it was someone else.

The tapes, the tapes . . . if the tapes got out, the news would be all Caspers, all the time. At which point, someone would feed the media a big, juicy chunk to connect the Caspers to the OVP. That was it, the Caspers would be the punch line, and the OVP, which was responsible for everything else, must have been responsible for the Caspers, too. But what was the evidence, the dot that would connect the other dots, the information they would slot into the expectations they'd already created? What did they have on him that wouldn't also lead back to them? There must have been something with his return address on it. What would it—

He stopped, the blood suddenly draining from his face, his chest constricting. The return address. *Jesus Christ, no.*

His hands were shaking and it took him three tries to open his wall safe. He took out the encrypted thumb drive and fired it up on his computer.

They'd told him they needed to set something up to take care of the Caspers. At the time, he thought it was brilliant, he'd never heard of anything like it. It sounded so good, in fact, that he'd actually conceived of it as a kind of pilot program. If it worked with the Caspers, there was no reason not to expand it to resolve other difficult situations, as well. So he'd signed off on the creation of a dummy corporation . . . Jesus, what had he been thinking? At the time, it hadn't even occurred to him. The corporate fronts were routine for a dozen different purposes—safe houses, air transport of rendered detainees . . . Hell, half the program was conducted through corporate false fronts. He was signing off on them every day—but now, now . . .

What was the name of the company? Eco, Ecology, something like that? He scrolled through memos and correspondence and findings . . . and there it was. Ecologia. A European company that had pioneered the concept of "ecological burials." And Ulrich had signed off on the creation of the dummy corporation that had purchased two of their units. Christ, he might as well have just filled out the purchase orders himself.

He leaned back in his chair and closed his eyes. He could see it clearly now, not just what they were doing, but the way it would all play out. They'd fingered him. They'd created the narrative, exposing one by one all the different elements of the program, each time demonstrating how that element emanated from the OVP. He knew from experience that once a narrative had achieved this much momentum, this much weight in the mainstream media and the mind of the public, it was impossible to squelch it. From here, it was only going to get worse. The other players would recognize Ulrich was vulnerable, that he'd been positioned to serve as the personification of the entire thing, the poster child for the program, and they'd realize then that it was in their interest to pile on. There would be more finger-pointing, more anonymous leaks. It would be a perfect storm: the public wanting a villain; the mainstream media wanting a fall guy to protect the powerful; the potentially culpable firmament doing everything in its collective power to deliver the villain the public was clamoring for. It would be a kind of mass cleansing, cathartic for everyone involved, a ritual stoning of a symbolic individual to bury the broader sin.

And what could he argue in response? That he was only following orders? Laughable in its own right, and worse considering how motivated people would be to not hear it. Everyone but the lunatic left understood that presidents and vice presidents, sitting or former, were above the law, that the notion of trying them was simply absurd. Lieutenants, though, aides-de-camp, were a more vulnerable class. Sure, he'd have some colorable legal arguments, but those would be useless in a trial by media. He hated to admit it, but he'd really underestimated the spooks. In the end, they'd outmaneuvered him.

Or maybe not. He still had one thing that could turn this around. His final insurance policy. His suicide bomb. All he had to do was—

The secure line buzzed. He snatched up the receiver. "Ulrich."

"Clements. Okay to talk?"

"Where the hell have you been?"

"There's a lot going on. Okay to talk?"

"Yes, for Christ's sake, go."

"We know who the blackmailer is. A former JSOC ISA operator, Daniel Larison."

Ulrich had gotten that much from his contact an hour earlier. But he didn't see any advantage in acknowledging that to this self-important moron who wouldn't even return his calls.

"JSOC?" he said, pretending he was grappling with new information on the fly. "Horton must have known. That's how he got ahead of us. But wait a minute. Larison? Wasn't he one of the people who had access, but we ruled him out because—"

"Because we thought he died in Pakistan. That's what he wanted us to think, to divert our attention elsewhere while the trail to him went cold."

"He's alive?"

"Very much so. Also very gay, and with a civilian lover in San Jose, Costa Rica."

"A lover . . . this must be why that guy Treven was on his way to San Jose."

"He's the one who developed the intel."

The pretense part was done. Now he had real questions to ask. "How the hell did JSOC get involved in this? Horton sent Treven? How did he explain his man's presence to the national security adviser?"

Clements sighed. "He was filing UNODIR reports along the way. The national security adviser never even saw them, just like Horton knew he wouldn't. They were complete CYA. And what's he going to do now, reprimand Horton after the results this guy Treven got?"

UNODIR meant "unless otherwise directed." You filed a report at the last possible minute, knowing that, by the time it was seen, whatever you were up to would be a fait accompli. Essentially, a ballsy way for gaining retroactive permission. Or, if whatever you were up to failed, for getting court-martialed. Horton had played it well.

"I told you," Ulrich said, "we don't want JSOC getting those tapes."

"Understood."

"Well, what's the plan?"

"Don't know yet. We've got an interagency meeting in three hours. I'm going to recommend we threaten the lover's family, use them as leverage. With luck, that'll bring Larison out in the open."

Leverage. Yeah, that made sense. Sometimes it was all people understood.

"You there?" Clements said.

"Yeah, I'm here. Now listen. I know what you're up to."

"What are you talking about?"

"You think I'm your Plan B, I'm going to be your fall guy if something goes wrong, if those tapes get out. And you've been taking steps to make it happen. But there's something I want you to hear. Listen carefully."

He clicked the play button on his recorder and gave Clements a few key moments from that long-ago Arlington National Cemetery meeting. When he felt Clements had heard enough, he hit stop.

"Now you understand," he said, his voice supremely calm. "If the tapes come out, we all go down. Not just me. All of us."

There was a long pause. Clements said, "You're crazy."

"And that's only one of many. So back off."

"Back off . . . I don't even know what you're talking about. Listen to yourself. Look at what you're doing. You've created . . . tapes about the tapes? This problem wasn't convoluted enough?"

"Another thing. There are copies. If something happens to me, someone I trust has instructions to release those copies."

"Someone . . . someone else knows about all this? You've lost your mind."

"Don't push me, Clements. I will burn you. I will fucking burn you."

Silence on the line. It felt good. It felt . . . subservient.

"So just do your job and recover those tapes. And you better keep me in the loop while you're at it."

He clicked off, feeling good, feeling in control again. Leverage. In the end, it was all you really needed. That, and the balls to put it to use.

20 AN INTERESTING DAY IN SAN JOSE

Ben was only half asleep when he heard his phone buzz. He picked it up in the dark by feel and saw that it was Hort. "Yeah," he said, keeping his voice low to avoid disturbing Paula. Though he was pretty sure she'd be awake and listening regardless.

"Sorry to interrupt your beauty sleep," Hort said.

Ben glanced at the screen. It was just past six in the morning local time. "That's okay. It wasn't that beautiful."

"Well, we've got an interesting situation here."

"Interesting good, or interesting bad?"

"Bad. I'm being overruled by a bunch of goddamn amoebas."

It was unusual in the extreme for Hort to comment on how decisions were made or how he received his orders. All of that had always been a black box to Ben, and now Hort was opening it, at least a crack, and letting him see inside it. It was both enticing and discomfiting.

And then he thought of Marcy and her son, and felt suddenly sick.

"What does that mean?"

"It means, first, we got everything on this Nico you uncovered. Nico Velez. He's an architect. Lives, works, and was born in San Jose. His parents still live in the city, and so do his two sisters and his three nieces and nephews. He's openly gay and he's a complete civilian."

Paula's phone buzzed. She picked up instantly, confirming for Ben that she had indeed been awake and listening. "Lanier," she said, simultaneously swinging her legs off the bed and heading toward the bathroom. In the semidarkness, Ben caught a glimpse of white panties and a matching camisole. She clicked on the bathroom light and closed the door behind her.

"Hey, the FBI woman just got a call, too," Ben said. "Are they in on this now?"

"A lot of different players have been offering their input, yeah. Makes sense she'd be getting a call about now."

"Anyway, so we know who Nico is."

"That's right. And it gets better. We isolated the alias Larison traveled under when he flew to San Jose on April 17, 2007. He's used it six times since then. So we can put him in San Jose at least eight times."

"But probably more than that, because he'd be traveling under other aliases, too."

"Exactly. So whatever's going on between Larison and Nico, it's long-term, and it's serious. This is not some casual hookup we're talking about."

"Does this mean no one's talking about Marcy Wheeler and her son anymore?"

"It means that, yeah."

Well, that was good. "So what's the problem?"

"The same problem it always is, again and again and again. Stupidity and arrogance."

"I'm not following you."

Hort sighed. "I know. I'm not making myself clear. It's been a long, frustrating night."

"You've been up all night?"

"Yeah, arguing with the Neanderthals."

Again, Ben was intrigued by Hort's openness. He didn't even know who the Neanderthals were. JSOC? NSC? Justice?

"Well, what's the plan?"

There was a pause. "The plan is for you to stand down."

"Stand down? But we're so close."

"You know it and I know it. But the powers that be think they know better."

"What are they going to do?"

"They're flying in a Ground Branch team right now."

"Ground Branch? Why?"

"They want Larison to think they're going to snatch Nico."

"To bring Larison into the open?"

"That's the idea. Snatch Larison, get him to spill his guts, recover the tapes, and call it a day."

"That's not going to work."

"That's right it's not going to work. You tell me why."

Ben thought for a moment, imagining Larison, putting himself in the man's position, assessing the same threats, gaming out the same countermeasures. "Because . . . Larison would have planned for this. He said he's got the tapes on some kind of electronic dead-man trigger. He's not going to give that up, even under duress, because he knows that wouldn't stop the duress."

"I agree. They're going to torture him to prove a negative—that there are no more copies of the tapes. No matter what he gives up, they can't know he's given up everything, so they get their doctors to keep him alive, and the torture never ends, ever. Larison knows what he's in for if he's caught. So what does he do?"

"He sets the dead man to a short fuse."

"That's right. He knows the only thing that could deliver him from his agony is having the tapes published. So by snatching him—"

"They might as well just publish the tapes themselves."

"Good. Now, tell me this. How would you handle the situation if you were in charge?"

Ben had worked with Hort long enough to know when Hort was grooming him for some new skill set. But this was different. These were management-style questions, not tactical. Again, he was both confused and intrigued.

"I'd . . . leave Nico and his family alone. And when Larison called in, I'd tell him everything we'd found out. I'd tell him the bad news is, we know who he is, we know about Nico, we know everything. And if those tapes ever get released, we take it out on Nico and his family."

"Good again. And what would be the good news?"

Ben thought. "I'd give him a bonus, I guess. Not a hundred million, that's crazy, and maybe Larison would try to use it to resettle the family and eliminate our leverage. But something. A million, five million, something to show goodwill and no hard feelings. You know, enjoy the money, enjoy your life and your good health, and as long as those tapes never get revealed, it's all live and let live. It's not foolproof, but I think it's the best we could do under the circumstances."

There was a pause. Hort said, "Remember how I told you in, say, ten years, you could be as good as Larison?"

"Yeah."

"I was wrong. I think you're going to be better, and it's not going to take that long. You're already smarter, more in control of yourself, than the people who are jerking our chains."

Ben was as intrigued by the reference to "our" chains as he was by Hort's hints regarding the people who were jerking them. And as much as he wanted to believe Hort's praise was deserved, he wondered whether there was something behind it, something he couldn't yet see.

"I told them," Hort said. "I told them we could not control this thing one hundred percent. That we need to work the odds. As long as there's even a five percent chance the tapes could be released, we can't move against Larison. And as long as there's even a five percent chance of retribution against Nico and his family, Larison can't release the tapes. Both sides indulge in a little strategic ambiguity while in fact standing down. That's the best way for us to get what we say we really want, which is for those tapes not to be released."

"What do you mean, 'what we say we really want'?"

"Look, if they really just wanted the tapes, I already told them their best course of action. The problem is, they don't just want the tapes. They also want Larison. They're scared and they're angry, and even though they don't know it and won't admit it, part of what's driving them is the urge to subdue the author of their pain and strap him to a table and exercise dominion over his body, mind, and soul. They need to feel like they're in control again, and just having the tapes out there with the lowest probability of release isn't going to help with that."

"But torturing Larison will."

Hort sighed. "I want you to remember something, son. Remember it and never forget."

"Okay."

"There are going to be times when you will be tempted to use what *The New York Times* in their chickenshit way calls 'harsh interrogation techniques.' You can call it whatever you want, you and I know what it means, and so does everybody else."

"Okay."

"A good ops man understands his real objectives, knows the right objectives, and chooses his means accordingly. So when you feel that temptation, you never forget that when you resort to those tactics, your motives are at least as much about the means as they are about the ends."

"I don't follow."

"People always say they're torturing to get the information. But there are a lot of ways better than torture to get information. So you don't torture just because you want the information. You torture because you want to torture. I didn't know this when I was your age. I know better now, and I don't want you to make the mistakes I've made. Not just for tactical reasons, either. I don't want your soul to have to bear it. I've seen what that does to a man. And I don't want you to make the same mistakes these assholes keep making, again and again and again, and never learning from them. So promise me."

Damn, he'd never heard Hort so agitated. He felt like he was starting to get a better sense of those unseen forces at work, that Hort was opening a window and letting him see inside. "I promise," he said.

"Good. Now, Larison's supposed to call in to the DCI thirty minutes from now. He's expecting to get a status update about the diamonds. Instead, someone is going to tell him the diamonds aren't coming and that if he doesn't immediately hand over the tapes, Nico's family is going to start getting smaller."

"What good would it do if he turned something over anyway? He could have made a hundred copies."

"That's not the point. They're just trying to bait him into going to San Jose."

"You think it'll work?"

There was a pause. "I think he'll come. But if he does, he'll be ready. And these Ground Branch guys, going up against a cornered, desperate man like Larison . . . they're not going to get him. They're going to get killed."

"What do you want me to do?"

"I want you to observe. Whatever happens, it's going to be hairy. Maybe you'll be able to see something or learn something that'll keep us in the game after this play is over. But you need to stay to the sidelines. These guys don't know you, and they could be trigger-happy."

"What about Lanier?"

"Your FBI friend?"

"I wouldn't call her my friend."

"Can you lose her?"

"I don't know. She's pretty tenacious."

"Well, you'll have to lose her or manage her, one or the other. You don't want her in your way."

Ben wasn't sure which would be easier. "Okay," he said.

"Larison should be calling in shortly. I'll let you know how it goes. If this plan of theirs works out, I'd say you can expect him to arrive in Costa Rica in anywhere from the next six to twenty-four hours. It's going to be an interesting day in San Jose."

21 CAUGHT IN THE CROSSFIRE

Ulrich was just heading into Trinity Methodist with his wife when he saw Clements standing by the entrance. Christ, were they watching him now? And was this their way of letting him know they were watching?

No, he was probably just being paranoid. And even if they were watching, so what? Did they really think they could intimidate him? He had the recordings, and God help them if they pushed him.

"You go ahead," he said to his wife. "I just need to make a quick call."

She smiled understandingly and went inside. She knew he viewed church attendance mostly as a matter of keeping up appearances, both in the community and, just in case, with the Almighty. More often than not, the pre-church calls he made lasted longer than just a minute.

He raised his mobile to his ear and walked back out to the sidewalk, nodding at a few incoming parishioners along the way. By the time he reached the parking lot, he heard Clements just behind him. He dropped the mobile back into his pocket.

Clements fell in alongside him. "I tried you at the office, but—"

"What, are you watching me now?"

"Please. It's pretty easy to know where someone goes to church."

Clements's denial did nothing to ease his suspicions. But it didn't matter. The audiotapes were all the protection he needed. "What is it?"

Clements glanced down at Ulrich's hands. "You taping this conversation?"

"I've got more than enough already. We're already at mutual assured destruction, Clements. I don't need more warheads."

Ulrich waited, giving Clements time to absorb the truth of Ulrich's words. After a moment, Clements said in a low voice, "The national security adviser just ordered JSOC to stand down. Larison called in this morning, we told him we know who he is, we know everything, that if he doesn't cough up the tapes, his lover and his lover's family are fucked, one at a time. We think he's on his way to Costa Rica right now."

Ulrich looked at him. "Your guys are there?"

"On their way. The national security adviser made clear this is CIA's op. Horton didn't like it, but he doesn't have the resources right now anyway."

"And you do? For a snatch?"

There was a pause. "Yes and no. No, Ground Branch doesn't have a snatch team in theater. But we were able to scramble a private team. Blackwater."

"Blackwater? We don't want contractors getting hold of those tapes. Are you crazy?"

"What were our alternatives? You want JSOC running the op?"

Shit. Clements had a point. "You trust those guys?"

"More than I trust Horton."

Another good point. "What about Horton's guy? The one in the photo. Treven."

"Like I said, he's been ordered to stand down."

"You really think Horton is just going to tell his man to walk away?"

Clements stroked his chin. "I see what you're saying.

Well, I have two Ground Branch guys there now per what we discussed previously. They're not equipped for a snatch, and two is too few anyway, but you're right, it wouldn't hurt to have them keep looking for Treven."

"Good. And even more important, make sure the contractors have the photo. If Treven shows up at the snatch point, they should assume he's there to interfere. And you know, it's not like they'd be expecting him, so it would be understandable if he accidentally got caught in the crossfire."

"You're right. I'll make sure the Blackwater operators know who to look for."

"And the Ground Branch guys. And what to do if they see him."

Clements nodded and turned to walk away. "They'll know."

22 BIG AND BAD

Paula came out of the bathroom, obviously done with her call. Ben said, "How's the Bureau today?"

She looked at him. "They say my role here is done."

"What does that mean?"

"It means I'm supposed to return to Washington."

"Is that a bad thing?"

"You know it's a bad thing. It means that's it for the law. The assassins are going to take over now."

Ben sighed. She was so earnest with the law-and-order shit.

"Look," he said, "for what it's worth, I've been ordered to stand down, too."

"You have not."

"Yeah, I have."

"What about Larison?"

"He's someone else's problem now."

"You can just care, and then not care, like flipping a light switch?"

"You're assuming I cared to begin with."

"You know, I'll bet a lot of people believe you when you tell them something like that. I'll bet there are times when you even believe yourself."

"Look, it's too early in the morning for you to psychoanalyze me, okay? Why don't you just fly back to Washington, and next time I'm in town, we can have a drink."

"I don't think so."

"You don't drink?"

"I don't think I'm just flying back to Washington with my wings clipped. And I don't think you are, either."

Ben didn't answer. It felt like it was her move.

"You're not, are you?"

He sighed. "I'm supposed to observe."

"You're not a very good liar."

"Actually, I'm an accomplished liar. It just that this time, I'm not lying."

"Tell me what's going on."

"I don't know, exactly. All I know is my team is out, and some other team has been brought in. My coach doesn't think the new team understands the game and is going to lose. Badly. He wants me to be on hand."

"In case they need a pinch hitter?"

"Just to observe."

"Well, that sounds good to me."

"Look—"

"Don't even start. I'm not going to just walk away. So we can do this separately and trip each other up, or we can keep coordinating."

"I don't know that our coordination has been all that coordinated."

"We've gotten this far."

Ben knew he could lose her easily enough. But he didn't know what her people knew. If they'd briefed her on Nico's particulars, losing her wouldn't help. She'd just be waiting wherever he arrived.

"Let's get some breakfast," he said. "I don't know when we'll get another chance. It feels like something big and bad is on the way, and I want to be in position when it arrives."

23 ONE WAY OR THE OTHER

Larison waited in front of the gate at JFK for his flight to San Salvador, his eyes moving from the announcements board to the faces of the people swirling through the area and then back again. He wanted desperately to fly directly to San Jose International, but if they had the resources to watch airports, that would be the one they'd key on. From San Salvador he could catch a nonstop to one of the smaller towns—Limón or Tamarindo or Quepos—and then finish the journey by train or bus. Or better yet, by motorcycle.

He was still shaky. He'd called from a Jersey City motel room, expecting the conversation to be brief and one-sided, expecting them to be meek, even if it was just playacting while they tried to buy themselves time. He was going to be in complete control. So he'd never really recovered from the first words they said to him:

Hello, Daniel Larison.

He'd made it through the call. He listened wordlessly as they explained how they would send contractors to rape Nico's nieces and nephews and mutilate his parents and sisters and brothers-in-law; and then, when the happiness, the coherence, the sanity of Nico's family had been torn and broken and shattered, they would explain to Nico why it had all happened. Because of the man Nico was seeing, who wasn't who he said he was. Who did a stupid thing to antagonize powerful people, who kept on doing it even after he'd been warned of the consequences to Nico and his family.

When they stopped talking, Larison had paused for a moment to demonstrate his composure. When he spoke, his voice was calm, emotionless, the same voice he would have used had he not heard a single word they'd just uttered. He said, *I'll call again on Friday with instructions on how to deliver the diamonds. If you don't deliver, I will release the tapes. And anything that happens to Nico or his family will seem mild after what I will do to you and yours.*

Then he had hung up. For a long moment he stood still, his eyes unfocused, his heart hammering. Then his legs buckled and he collapsed and curled up on the floor on his side and sobbed uncontrollably for almost ten minutes. He knew he had to move—triangulating on a cloned satellite call was almost impossible, but it was almost impossible that they'd identified him so quickly, too. But he couldn't move. Shame and horror and self-pity and fear and grief had simply overwhelmed him.

Finally, it subsided. He picked himself up, staggered to the sink, and splashed cold water on his face. He looked at his reflection in the mirror, his eyes red, his cheeks dripping and unshaven, his teeth bared, his nostrils flaring with his agitated breathing. He looked like a nightmare.

Then be a nightmare.

Yes, that was it. Make them pay. Make them pay for everything.

But first, he had to move. That lesson had been drilled into him from the start: No matter what you were hit with, no matter the pain or shock or confusion, never stop moving. Never give them a stationary target.

A corollary lesson was that when you're ambushed, your best chance of prevailing almost always involved a simple strategy:

Attack back.

They'd be expecting that, of course. In fact, as the shock of the call wore off, to be replaced by a seething determination, he began to understand they were baiting him, hoping he would be provoked.

What he would do, therefore, wouldn't be a surprise. How he would do it would be everything.

He checked his watch. He tried not to imagine what it would be like to be impossibly rich. He could have chartered a jet, he could have been on the ground in San Jose in three hours. Instead, he was glued to this seat in an airport, waiting for the interminable minutes to pass.

The worst part was that he couldn't figure out what the vulnerability had been. It was distracting him, his mind wouldn't let it go, he kept going over every aspect of his preparations and his movements and he couldn't identify a single thing he'd done wrong. The only thing he could remotely come up with was those two brothers, the ones who'd been tailing him and who he'd assumed had just been petty criminals. Maybe they'd been more than that . . . but even if so, who were they, and how had they been tailing him in the first place? He'd been so careful not to create patterns, but somewhere, he must have done something, he just couldn't understand what. Maybe the NSA had capabilities beyond even what he'd known of? Maybe he'd made some small mistake, and their supercomputers had unraveled everything from that?

He checked his watch again. He'd always prided himself on the supernatural calm he could summon before combat, but it wasn't working for him now. He'd imagined a dozen ways this might have ended badly. All of them were unpleasant, but he'd been prepared, he could have faced it. What he'd never imagined was that they'd get to him through Nico.

He scrubbed a hand across his face. He was so exhausted. The announcements and the beeping from the goddamned golf carts . . . it was all so loud and cacophonous, his head was beginning to pound from it. The dreams were killing him, too; he'd had no idea how bad it was going to be without the pills. It wasn't getting better, either—in fact, every night was worse than the one before. What had he been thinking, what monumental hubris had caused him to believe he could take on the entire fucking government and walk away from it clean? It was never going to work, he could see that now. Was it some kind of dramatic stand he was taking, Ahab slashing at the back of the whale even as it carried him down to drown in the dark and the deep? What the hell had he been trying to do?

If he was going to die anyway, he should release the tapes right now. All he had to do was log on to one of the sites he'd created, enter a password and then a command, and it would be done. Or fail to log in for a preset interval, that would do it, too. Would they really hurt Nico after that?

He decided they might. He couldn't take that chance. And besides, maybe, maybe, maybe he could turn this around. Regain the momentum. Show them who they were fucking with.

The main thing was that the tapes would be released, one way or the other. He focused on that, thinking, *one way or the other, one way or the other,* until he started to feel a little calmer. One way or the other. That was pretty much the only thing still keeping him going in the face of the suffocating knowledge that he'd screwed up and probably doomed Nico and rendered all his own most ardent hopes into pathetic, childish fantasies. Knowing that the tapes would get out, one way or the other.

That, and imagining what he was going to do to the people who would be waiting for him in San Jose.

24 HE'LL COME FROM HERE

Ben and Paula fueled up with an enormous buffet breakfast in the InterContinental's restaurant—omelettes, exotic fruits, and several cups of Costa Rica's justifiably famous coffee. Ben had a feeling the rest of the day would be nothing but granola bars, and wanted to make sure they had plenty to run on, through the night if necessary.

When they were done, they headed over to Nico's residence. Ben had briefed Paula on their cover for action—the story they would tell if anyone questioned their presence. They were Americans thinking about becoming part of the large Costa Rican expat community and were examining possible neighborhoods. They'd only break out the FBI credentials if it became necessary. Better to try something less remarkable first.

Both the residence and office were in Los Yoses, about a kilometer from Spoon, each within walking distance of the other. It all fit: the regular appearances at Spoon, and Juan Cole's "luck" in finding Larison there; Larison getting off the bus early in Barrio Dent to draw his pursuers away from the real locus of his interest in San José.

They started with a drive-by of the residence, a condominium on a narrow two-lane street just south of the main thoroughfare. The condo, gated, fronted with palm trees, and obviously deluxe, was eight stories tall and looked new. Everything else on the street was low-slung and slightly ramshackle. Directly across the street from the condo was an enormous construction site—from the size of it, the future home of another fancy collection of condos.

The street was on a short block open at both ends and with no turnoffs in the middle—the horizontal bar in an *H*. Ideally, that meant two sentries at each of the two possible access points—each end of the horizontal. The sentries' job would be to warn the primary snatch team of the target's approach. The reason for two was security in case of opposition. One sentry you could do. Finishing off two before either got a warning off was far more difficult, so the preference was always to use two on whatever point of access the target might use. The primary team would have line of sight to the building entrance or other X where they intended to actually do the snatch. If the snatch was clean, the sentries would move out fore and aft as the primary team left the scene with the target secured. If the primary team encountered opposition, the sentries could close with flanking fire.

Larison would know all this, just as Ben did. So the question was, what would I do if I were him? And the best way to answer that, Ben knew, was to look at the street as Larison knew it—as someone who had repeatedly walked it.

They parked on the main thoroughfare about a kilometer away and got out, baseball caps pulled low over sunglasses against the inevitable security camera tapes police would be examining if there were violence in the area. The sky was uniformly gray, the air heavy with humidity and the weight of impending rain. Despite Los Yoses's urban density, they were surrounded by the cries of birds and the buzz of tropical insects. By the time they reached the condo, they were both sweating.

Ben looked up and down the street. You wouldn't want to approach from either end. You might be able to drop both sentries, but probably not before they got off a warning to their counterparts opposite and to the primary team. No, the way to achieve maximum surprise here was to initially bypass the sentries. Start from the inside and work your way out.

He crossed to the opposite side of the street and stood in front of the construction site, his back to the front of Nico's building. Paula came up alongside him.

"What do you think?" she said.

He looked around the site. It sloped steeply from where they stood all the way down to the opposite block. So far, the only completed work was a foundation and a couple of skeletal concrete floors. But that, along with the foliage around it, would provide a lot of concealment. The downside was the uphill approach, the possibility of being pinned down from above by anyone who spotted you. But in Ben's mind, the concealment was the key. That, and the lack of any better alternatives.

"I think he'll come from here," Ben said. "That's what I'd do."

"So where do we wait?"

"I want to see the office before I decide that. But if we set up here, I'm thinking we'll park on Nico's street. Not at the end, where Larison would be looking for sentries; not in front of the building, where he'd be looking for the primary team. In between, in an operational dead zone, with line of sight to where the primary team would set up and maybe to the sentries, too. And to where we expect Larison to emerge."

They walked over to the office. It was a small gray building on a cul-de-sac, a sign in gold lettering on the front advertising *Gomez and Golindo, Architects*. Apparently Nico Velez wasn't a name partner. That they used English rather than Spanish on the shingle suggested a foreign clientele—or perhaps that English had some cachet in Costa Rican architectural circles. Neither of these details was likely to be operationally useful, but Ben logged them regardless, just in case.

The one-way street simplified things somewhat for a snatch team, requiring only two sentries instead of four. But still . . .

They walked to the end of the cul-de-sac. Amid the collection of modest apartments and single-family houses, some converted to professional use, there was a patch of thick grass and trees that led to a highway access ramp. Would Larison approach from there? It was either that or the street. Like everything else Ben had seen in San Jose, the buildings were all mini-fortresses, the windows and driveways gated and barred against crime, razor wire strung along potential access points. And many of the properties had yapping dogs patrolling within. No, Larison's only two realistic options here were stealth through the trees or an open approach from the street.

"I think he's going to start with the condo," Ben said.

"Why?"

"He wouldn't like the alternatives here. They're more obvious, and there are fewer of them. Plus he'd know the terrain better around the condo. Presumably that's where he stays when he's visiting Nico. Maybe he's seen the office, but I doubt he's spent much time here."

"Makes sense."

Ben looked at his watch. It was past noon. Unlikely Larison could make it here so soon after this morning's call—unless he were here already, which Ben seriously doubted. Running an op from the city of his secret lover would offer nothing but downside. Besides, Hort had said the emails and sat calls were coming from North America. No, Larison wasn't here. But he could be arriving soon. And likewise the snatch teams.

"Time to get in position," he said. "We might have a long wait."

25 COME OUT, COME OUT, WHEREVER YOU ARE

Larison flew into Limón airport, on the Caribbean coast, and at a shop nearby rented a motorcycle—a Kawasaki KX250F dirt bike. A little smaller than he would have liked for the drive to Los Yoses, but perfect for dodging traffic and jumping curbs and avoiding potholes once he was inside the city. It was an older version of the same bike Nico kept at his condo, which Larison used to get around the city while he was in town and Nico was at work. Obviously, he couldn't access Nico's bike now, but this one would more than do. Especially with the flip-up helmet, which nicely concealed his face.

The ride in took less than three hours. In a park at San Pedro, just east of Los Yoses, he stopped, his shirt soaked with sweat, his skin covered with a fine coating of road grit. He removed his helmet and wiped his face with a sleeve. It was getting near dusk and he had to hurry now. He knew the terrain but the opposition would have better tools, including night vision gear, and he didn't want to cede a single unnecessary advantage.

There was an outhouse in the park that was serviced less frequently than good hygiene might be thought to require. So it was very unlikely anyone would have been inclined to squeeze underneath the structure, the back of which was raised on wooden stilts about a foot off the dirt, and grope in the dark miasma along the beams supporting the floor. As Larison did now. It took him only a moment to retrieve his stash and squirm back out— a moment short enough, in fact, to enable him to hold his breath during the entire excursion, which was the best way to get in and out of the passage in question without vomiting en route. In Larison's experience, a good hide always provided disincentives for casual exploration, outhouses therefore often providing prime possibilities.

Outside, he looked around to confirm he was unobserved, then unwrapped the package he had retrieved. Inside was an HK USP Compact Tactical, known in the community as the CT, for counterterrorism, plus spare magazines and VBR-B .45 armor-piercing ammunition. The gun was small, powerful, accurate, and durable as hell. Perfect for storing under outhouses like this one and of course in backup locations, as well, and perfect, too, for causing extreme mayhem after retrieving it.

He loaded up three magazines from the package, popped one into the gun, racked the slide, and placed everything into the fanny pack he was wearing under his shirt, the contents riding just below his belly. He left the top open. He took the other items from the package— currency, false identification, an Emerson Super Commander folding knife—and pocketed all of it. Good to go. Just one more thing.

There was a variety of synthetic opioids used for snatches. The most popular was called sufentanil, and it was about ten times more potent than its analogue, fentanyl, which the Russians had aerosolized and used in the 2002 Moscow theater hostage crisis. Typically, the drug would be delivered via an air-rifle-fired dart, with a medical team standing by to immediately administer first aid, including breathing assistance and opioid antagonists, as soon as the target dropped. Teams tended to err on the side of too large a dose for fast action, which meant swift application of the antidote was critical.

But the medics wouldn't have to worry about Larison. Since he'd set this thing in motion, he'd been orally self-administering naltrexone, another opioid antagonist, used for detoxifying heroin addicts. The only side effect was anxiety and some enhanced receptivity to pain, because opioid antagonists blocked the action of endorphins, the brain's natural opiates. A small price to pay, under the circumstances.

The naltrexone would probably have been sufficient, but if they hit him with a big enough dose of tranquilizer, maybe not. Better not to take a chance. He opened his backpack, unwrapped a syringe from the medical kit inside it, measured off a dose of naloxone—a related antagonist, used for heroin overdoses and, not coincidentally, post-tranquilizer snatch-victim revivals—and injected it intramuscularly into his thigh, grimacing from the naltrexone-enhanced pain. He tossed away the syringe, blew out a long breath, and pulled his helmet back onto his sweat-slicked head.

He'd already gamed the whole thing out, but he went through the plan again one more time anyway. If they had the manpower, they'd cover both Nico's condominium and his office. The condo was on a residential through street. Lots of parking on both sides of the street, plenty of places to set up. But they wouldn't know which direction Larison would be moving in from, so they'd need a spotter at each end of the street or, ideally, two spotters on each end to reduce the chances of a sentry getting taken out and exposing the primary team to a surprise attack. The primary team would be three men: one with flex-cuffs, one with a hood, one with a gun. So that was seven possibles at the condo.

The office was on a cul-de-sac, so they'd only have to cover one end of the street. That meant a probable maximum of five men.

If they had the manpower, they'd field full teams at both locations. If they could only cover one . . . it was impossible to know for sure, but he guessed the condo. They'd see the construction site on the lot across the street and figure he would use it for an unexpected approach. And in fact, he was tempted to do so. He was reasonably confident that with his superior skills, and knowing the terrain as he did, he would spot the opposition before it spotted him. But he had a better idea. Something a little less predictable, and therefore substantially more lethal.

He was mildly concerned that in the midst of the coming mayhem he could actually run into Nico. But he recognized this was mostly just superstition. He'd have his helmet on for most of the op. The chances of Nico being right there on the street for any of it were slim.

He rode the Kawasaki over to Nico's street, the late afternoon air blowing inside his shirt and cooling his wet skin, the buzz of the bike's engine loud in his ears. His heart was beating hard, but his mind was calm, clear, and purposeful. It was the way he always felt in the instant before an op went critical, like a well-oiled killing machine inside had taken the wheel and he was just along for the ride.

He turned onto the street and immediately spotted a white van at the entrance—the sentries. His heart kicked harder. They were here. It was on.

He rode up the street, the 250 cc engine buzzing, knowing the sentries would have already alerted the primary team. They couldn't have recognized him through the helmet, but a heads-up would be SOP. The primary team would move in for a closer look. Larison would give them one.

He parked the bike between two cars and killed the engine. He swung his leg over the side and engaged the kickstand. He took a deep breath and slowly let it out. Then he removed the helmet, set it on the seat, and started walking toward the entrance of the condo. His face twisted into a smile and he thought, *Come out, come out, wherever you are, motherfuckers.*

26 THE ELEMENT OF SURPRISE

Ben and Paula watched the motorcyclist pull up and park not ten yards from the entrance to Nico's condominium. They were in the van on the other side of the street, about twenty-five yards away, on the crest of a slight slope in the street. Any farther and they would have lost line of sight to the entrance.

"That's him," Ben said, watching the guy kill the engine.

"You're sure?" Paula said.

Ben nodded. He couldn't have explained how he knew, but he knew. Larison had decided not to come up through the construction site. Smart. He must have realized the route would be too foreseeable, and Ben mentally kicked himself for earlier assuming Larison would do the predictable unpredictable thing. But others, it seemed, had made the same mistake Ben made, and were now committed to it. Three hours earlier, Ben and Paula had watched through the one-way glass at the back of the van as various hard-looking foreigners cased the street by ones and twos. None of them had set up in front of the condo entrance, which suggested to Ben they'd decided Larison was going to approach through the construction site and were waiting for him there. Larison, it seemed, was one step ahead of them.

But why the street? The sentries would have made him instantly, and even if they weren't sure it was Larison they were seeing through the visor of the helmet, they would have alerted the primary team to be safe. Larison had lost the element of surprise.

So what surprise was he planning?

The motorcyclist got off the bike and removed the helmet as though he had all the time in the world. He set it down on the bike's seat, ran his fingers through his wet hair, and dried his hands on his jeans.

"Oh, my God," Paula said. "You were right."

Ben moved from one side of the van to the other, looking through the one-way glass. He didn't see anyone approaching yet, but they would be. Any second.

"What the hell's he doing?" he said.

27 HEAD SHOTS

Larison stood a few yards down from the entrance to Nico's condo, facing the building. His eyes were open but he wasn't focusing on their input. All his concentration was focused through his ears. He tuned out the birds and the insects, the sounds of distant traffic. It was stealth he was listening for. And he would hear it soon enough.

He turned and walked slowly toward the entrance. He knew he wouldn't reach it.

He didn't. He heard the soft pop of a CO_2 cartridge from somewhere behind him. At the same instant there was a slap/sting sensation on the right side of his neck. His hand flew to the spot, found the dart, and ripped it away despite the barbed tip. It was already too late, of course; the dart had a small explosive charge that had instantly pumped the tranquilizer into him upon impact. Ripping it out was useless. But it's what Larison had seen countless rendition targets do before, and it was important that he mimic them precisely now.

He wobbled, then dropped to one knee, leaning forward, the way tranquilized targets always did, his right hand already inside the fanny pack. He closed his eyes and *listened*.

Three sets of footsteps, approaching fast: two from the flanks, one directly behind. The ones to the flanks would have flex-cuffs and a hood. The one in the middle would have a gun out to provide cover.

The sounds of the footsteps changed as they went from gravel to sidewalk, then to the street. Twenty-five feet. Twenty. Fifteen.

In a single motion, he stood, spun, and brought up the HK in a two-handed grip. The guy in the middle had just enough time to widen his eyes before Larison blew the top of his head off. He tracked left—*bam*! Tracked right—*bam*! Three down, all head shots.

He heard a car coming fast from his right. He moved between two parked cars and confirmed it was the white van he'd seen parked at the end of the street when he came in. He waited until it was forty feet away, then stepped out into the road, brought up the HK, and put a round through the windshield into the driver's face. The van swerved wildly and slammed into a parked car ten feet from Larison's position on the other side of the street. Larison crossed over, moved past the van, and approached it from behind on the passenger side, the HK up at chin level. A dazed-looking operator covered in his partner's blood and brain matter was struggling with the door, which must have been jammed. He saw Larison and tried to bring up a gun, but the angle was all wrong and the timing useless. Larison shot him in the head.

He walked quickly across the street, mounted the Kawasaki, fired it up, pulled on the helmet, and raced down the street toward where he knew the other sentries would be. Even if the first set hadn't contacted them already, they would have heard the gunshots, would have known something had gone badly wrong. They'd be trying to raise their comrades on cellphones right now. He noted another van, a green one, on his right as he rode, but it was in the wrong position to have been of any use operationally and he judged it just a civilian coincidence.

There it was, at the end of the street, another white van, parked on the right, facing away from him. He scanned the other parked cars and potential hot spots to ensure he wasn't missing anything. He wasn't. The van was the target.

He gunned the engine so they would hear him coming, then swerved between two parked cars, jumped the curb, and raced up the sidewalk to the passenger side of the van. He saw the passenger's reflection in the sideview. The man had heard the whine of the Kawasaki's engine and naturally assumed Larison was coming up the street, not the sidewalk. So, sadly for him, he was now facing the wrong way.

Larison pulled up to the window. The guy's ears must have had just enough time to send an urgent corrective message to his brain—*threat on right, not on left*—because his head started to turn in the instant before Larison put an armor-piercing round into the back of it.

The driver was amazingly quick. In the moment during which Larison was focused on his partner, he managed to open the door and jump out onto the street. Larison stepped back, judged the angle, and fired twice through the van. He heard a cry from the other side and circled carefully around the front. The guy was splayed out on his back in a growing pool of blood, a gun on the ground beside him, his legs kicking feebly as though to propel him from the scene of his own destruction. Larison checked his flanks—*clear*—stepped out from behind the cover of the van's engine block, and approached him, the HK up.

"Please," the guy whispered. "Please."

Larison smiled and shot him in the face.

He went back to the bike, reloaded, and roared off.

Seven down, he thought. *Five to go.*

He wished there were more.

28 SHAKEN UP

The whole thing happened so fast that Ben didn't have time to figure out what to do. In the space of a half minute, he watched Larison appear, drop five men, and disappear again. Ben could have gotten out of the van after the first three and engaged Larison from behind, but his orders were strictly to observe, and besides, the point, if anything, was to snatch Larison, not to kill him. Still, it was appalling to have to be a spectator to so much killing, to be helpless to do anything about it.

Paula was stunned by the mayhem. She watched it all with one hand over her mouth, the other around the butt of the Glock in her lap, muttering, "Oh, my God. Oh, my God."

When Larison mounted up and roared off toward the other end of the street, Ben knew the two men waiting there were already dead. A moment later, the same .45 caliber gunshots he'd already heard confirmed it.

Ben started to pull out his phone to call Hort. And then he realized.

Larison wasn't done. He was heading toward Nico's office. Hoping to find more prey.

Someone had to warn those guys. He could call Hort—

Who would have to call the national security adviser, who would have to call the CIA, who would have to call the field director, who would have to call the snatch team in front of Nico's office, whose bodies, by then, would already be cooling.

Fuck it.

He opened the back door. "Drive to Nico's office," he said. "Right now. I'll get there faster on foot."

"What the hell—"

"He's going to take out the second team. I've got to warn them."

He sprinted down the street, the Glock out, his eyes scanning the hot spots. He passed another van, a bloody body splayed out in the street beside it. People were looking out windows and coming to doorsteps. He pulled the baseball cap lower and ran.

He cut across corners and between parked cars and it took him less than two minutes to cover the distance to Nico's office cul-de-sac. Fifty yards out, he heard two more .45 caliber shots.

He burst onto the street just in time to see Larison pumping another white van full of bullets. Larison was standing on the passenger side, just behind the door, the angle obviously calculated to make shooting maximally difficult for the people inside. Two shots, a third. Then he calmly walked to the back of the van and emptied a half dozen more rounds into it in a pattern that no one hiding inside could have avoided.

Ben sprinted down behind a parked car. He hoped it would provide cover. He had a feeling Larison was using AP rounds.

Larison looked left and right. He took a fresh magazine from a fanny pack or belly band and swapped it into his gun. Ben had the shot. All his instincts, all his experience, told him to take it.

He ground his teeth together and fought warring impulses. He could end this thing right now. Right here. But wouldn't that mean the tapes, set to a dead-man trigger, would be released? Wasn't that exactly what he was supposed to prevent?

Larison picked up his bike and mounted it. He rode past Ben. And looked directly at him.

Somehow, even through the visor obscuring Larison's face, Ben thought he felt a kind of . . . recognition pass between them. He still had the shot. Larison must have known it. But he didn't react. He just looked at Ben, and then rode away.

A second later, Paula came barreling down the street, going right past Larison. She must have missed Ben crouching between the cars because she went by him. *Shit.* He ran out after her.

She turned around in the cul-de-sac. Her window was down. "Here," Ben called. She nodded and stopped. Ben went around the back of the van and saw her pushing the passenger door open as he came up the side. He would have preferred to drive, but if they encountered opposition, for the moment it would be better for Paula to drive and for Ben to shoot.

There was a squeal of tires from the opening of the street. Ben gripped the side of the door and watched a brown sedan rapidly approaching. *Cops?* he thought. It would have been a pretty fast arrival. And that kind of bad luck twice in a row, first Manila, now here . . . he didn't believe it.

"Keep your head down," he said. He could see a passenger and a driver, both Caucasian, both wearing shades. No one in back.

The car stopped ten feet in front of them. The driver and passenger, both in poplin suits, stepped out. Their hands were empty. Ben scanned the area. He saw faces in gated windows and people coming to their doors. But no other immediate threats.

"Paula Lanier?" the passenger asked, moving toward the driver side of the van.

Paula looked at him. "Who are you?"

Ben didn't like the whole thing from the beginning, and he was liking it less by the second. The way the car was blocking them. The fact that whoever these guys were, they wanted to have a conversation of some sort at the scene of a recent multiple homicide. The way the passenger had called out Paula's name, which felt like an attempt to lull her by establishing false familiarity. And now they were engaging in a flanking maneuver. Five more feet, and the passenger would disappear from Ben's view. Meanwhile, the driver was continuing to advance on Ben.

He didn't think these things consciously, but rather realized them in a kind of instanteous mental shorthand. Nor did he consciously weigh a decision. Rather, he simply understood what needed to be done. And did it.

He moved up from the side of the van, tacking right so he could keep the driver and passenger in a single line of vision. "Stop moving," he called out, loudly and in a flat tone that would have made an attack dog pause. He put the Glock's sights on the driver's face. "Now."

But the passenger didn't stop. And the driver said, "Relax, fella, we're here to help. Diplomatic Security. Here, let me show you ID."

The guy started to reach inside his jacket. Under more relaxed circumstances, Ben might have asked, *What part of "stop moving" don't you understand?* As it was, he shot the guy instead. A neat hole magically appeared in the guy's forehead. His body twitched once and slid to the ground.

The other guy lurched toward the driver side of the van. Ben sprinted forward to prevent him from getting to cover, the Glock at chin level in a two-handed grip. As he angled around the front of the van, he saw the guy had gotten his gun out. Too late. Ben nailed him with another head shot. Blood and brain matter sprayed the side of the van and the guy tipped over to the ground.

Ben ran up to the door and yanked it open. Paula's mouth was hanging open in shock. Her face was flecked with red and gray. He knew she wasn't going to be able to drive. Not now.

"Move," Ben said. "Passenger seat. Go."

She complied. He stepped over the dead guy, jumped into the seat, engaged the transmission, and swerved around the sedan. The sedan's front bumper clipped the open door and slammed it shut as they squealed around it.

"What . . . what the fuck . . . ," Paula spluttered.

Ben drove. They could figure out what the fuck later.

"What did you just do? They said . . . they said they were—"

"What they said was bullshit."

"How can you be so sure? You *killed* them."

"You're goddamned right I killed them. You think Diplomatic Security doesn't know enough to stop moving when a guy pointing a gun point-blank at their faces tells them to? You think DS is so inept that not only don't they stop, they reach for something unseen? There's not a cop or a DS in the world that stupid."

"That's it? You decided to kill them . . . based on that?"

Ben shot onto the highway and headed west. He slowed his speed to normal.

"Actually, no, there were a dozen things. The way they stopped. The way they approached. The way they used your name. And why wouldn't anyone have had the sense to tell us they were coming? You don't send in a B-team like that without a heads-up to the A. It's guaranteed to cause friendly fire."

"They knew me!"

He glanced at her. "Did you know them?"

She shook her head. "No."

"Then they didn't know you. They knew your name.

I'm sure they had a photograph. The rest was artifice to help them get close."

"But how could you really *know*—"

"Look, I don't tell you how to dust for fingerprints, okay? So don't tell me how a couple operators get close to their targets before drilling them with head shots. If you'd waited a second longer for the proof you want, you'd be dead now."

"Then who were they?"

Ben shook his head. "I don't know. I'm starting to think they could be anyone. That's the problem with those damned tapes."

He thought. Could Hort have set him up? He still didn't trust him, not after Obsidian. But why would he? Hort was getting overruled back in Washington, and Ben was his only set of eyes and ears on the ground. What possible gain would there be for Hort?

Besides, if it had been Hort, why would that guy have used Paula's name and not Ben's? It was Ben they needed to lull more than Paula. He was the greater tactical threat. If Hort had sent them, he would have told them as much.

And it was more than that. So soon after the emotional whipsaw of Obsidian and Manila, Ben didn't *want* to believe it could have been Hort. Some things, he decided, just had to be determined by your gut. And his gut told him it wasn't Hort.

Which didn't answer the question of who it *had* been. Backup for the snatch teams? What would have been the point? And why would they have asked for Paula? CIA? FBI? He just didn't know.

About the only thing going well for them at the moment—beyond the welcome fact that they were still alive—was that it was getting dark and starting to rain. The cars on the highway were becoming indistinct, their headlights on, their wipers pumping. Still, a van was far from impossible to spot. Fourteen people shot to death in a quiet San Jose suburb, probably a dozen witnesses describing the vehicle leaving the scene, possibly noting that a white man and black woman had been inside it. An unusual combination, one the staff at the InterContinental might remember, even if they couldn't describe the faces of the man or woman in question. He knew he'd been careful about keeping his head down in the lobby and elevator of the hotel, where the cameras were. He hoped Paula had been, too.

He pulled off the highway into a strip mall full of cantinas and bodegas. "Where are we going?" Paula said.

"We need a vehicle change. Police will be looking for this van. I don't want to be driving it when they find it."

"I *am* the police," Paula said, shaking her head as though in disbelief.

"Not here, you're not. Not now."

He drove down the parking lot until he saw what he was looking for—an early nineties Ford Taurus. He pulled up next to it and stopped.

"Take the wheel," he said. "I'm going to hot-wire that Taurus, and you need to follow me when I've got it going. We don't want to leave the van right here for the police to find when they get a stolen-vehicle report. We'll leave it a couple miles away and then drive the Taurus."

Paula nodded meekly, and he wondered whether she was going into shock.

"You okay?"

She nodded again.

"You going to be sick? That's normal. It's okay."

She shook her head. "I'm okay. I'm just . . . I've just never . . ."

"I know. We're going to get you someplace quiet. You can clean up. And we'll talk. Okay?"

She nodded again.

"Just follow me now. It won't be long."

He got out and was happy to find the car unlocked.

Not exactly a model chop shops were salivating over. He could have broken a window easily enough, but someone driving with a window down in the rain is sufficiently abnormal to draw law enforcement attention. Unbroken was better.

He got in the car, closed the door behind him, slid the seat back as far as it went, and took out his tools: the SureFire mini-light; a key ring from which a number of handy items dangled, including two screwdriver bits, flat point and Phillips head; a Benchmade 9051SBK folding knife; a short strip of duct tape from around the mini-light. An old drill sergeant had once told him a soldier with thousand-mile-an-hour tape and a few other small items was a wonder to behold, and Ben had since found it to be true.

He got down under the steering wheel, holding the duct-tape-wrapped SureFire between his teeth, and used the Phillips head screwdriver to remove the steering wheel access cover. He found the primary power supply wire and the electrical circuit wire, used the Benchmade to strip about an inch of insulation off each, and twisted them together. He stripped a half inch of insulation off the ignition wire and touched it to the wires he'd connected a moment before. The engine kicked over. He pumped the gas pedal with his hand and the engine caught. He wrapped the duct tape around the connected primary power and electrical circuit wires, put his tools back in his pockets, sat up, and nodded to Paula. He turned on the headlights and pulled out, watching Paula follow in the rearview mirror.

This time he drove southeast, in case anyone had reported a green van fleeing west on the highway from the crime scene. Ten minutes later, he spotted another shopping mall from the road and pulled off the highway. Paula pulled in next to him. He left the engine running, got out, and opened the driver side of the van.

"We need to wipe it down," he said. "We might not get everything, but it's better than nothing."

There was a canister of bleach wipes in back intended for this very purpose. They spent a few minutes going over everything they'd touched. When they were done, they got out. They left everything unlocked, the driver-side door open, and the keys in the ignition. With luck, someone would steal it, contaminate it, and drive it far away.

"It's okay," Paula said, walking around to the driver side of the Taurus. "I can drive."

"I know you can. But you wouldn't be human if you weren't shaken up by what just happened, okay? And it's also human not to realize it until later."

"You're not shaken up?"

"I've seen this kind of thing before. You haven't. Come on, I'm not trying to give you a hard time. You can drive tomorrow if you want. Let me take over for now."

She looked at him as though trying to gauge his intent, then nodded and went around to the other side. They pulled away and Ben took out his phone.

Hort picked up on the first ring. "What happened?"

"Larison killed them. Showed up on a motorcycle and dropped all seven in front of the condo. They put a tranquilizer round in his neck, it didn't do shit. What is the guy, a vampire?"

"A tranquilizer . . . goddamn, he must have dosed himself with an antagonist. Damn."

"Plus five more in front of the office."

"I told them. I told them."

Ben heard only anger in Hort's voice. Nothing that indicated he'd known about the two guys in the brown sedan.

"I had the shot," Ben said. "I could have taken him out. Not in time to save anyone, but still."

"Your orders were only to observe. Technically, you weren't even supposed to be there."

"I did. I'm just . . . saying."

"I understand how you feel. But if you'd dropped him, the dead-man trigger would probably have published the tapes already. You did the right thing."

"I tried to get to the second team. I couldn't reach them in time."

"I'm sorry, son."

"There's something else. As we were pulling away from the office, a car pulled up. Brown sedan, I didn't get the make, not that it would matter. Two guys got out. Caucasian. American, from the accents. They knew Lanier's name. It was a hit."

There was a pause. "A hit? You sure they weren't Ground Branch, part of the snatch team?"

"I'm sure."

"You're okay?"

"I'm fine. They're not. I didn't have time to check for ID, and I doubt they would have been carrying any. But you need to find out who those guys were and who's coming after Paula and me."

"Roger that. How's Lanier?"

Ben glanced over. "She's okay."

"Do you need anything?"

"No, we're good. Unloaded the van, we're going to find somewhere to bunk down for the night."

"Good. Get some rest. Stay safe. I'm going to find out what I can and get back to you."

"What's our next move? Larison's still out there."

"I know. And maybe now, these idiots will listen to me when I tell them how this needs to be handled. Before we lose any more people."

29 DOUBT

Larison rode hard to the southeast, rain splattering against his visor and soaking his shirt. He'd dosed himself with Benzedrine to counter the post-combat parasympathetic backlash and felt like he could ride forever. With light evening traffic and breaks at a minimum, he would reach the Panamanian border in about five hours. The weather was slowing him down for the moment, but the wind was blowing north and he could see breaks in the clouds ahead of him. With luck, he'd be riding out of it soon.

He wasn't worried about CIA opposition—he knew they'd thrown everything they had at him in Los Yoses and all of it was gone now. It would take them time to regroup. But the carnage in the capital was outlandish enough to possibly lead to a heavier than usual police presence at airports. Safer, for now, to leave the country by land. He'd stop late tonight, find a place to stay, shower, shave, buy some fresh clothes in the morning, and cross the border looking presentable instead of like the half-mad, juiced-up death machine he felt like now.

His working theory was that the two teams were CIA Ground Branch. He hadn't recognized any of them from ISA selection, and he'd been around long enough to have known at least a few faces if ISA had indeed been part of the op. Or maybe they were contractors. It didn't matter. If they were CIA, the opposition was now thinned by an even dozen. If they were contractors, it meant the CIA was hurting for operators in the first place and had to reach out to the private sector. Either way, he'd bought a little time.

The one thing he wasn't sure of was the guy he'd seen outside Nico's office, crouched between two parked cars, a pistol steadied against the hood of one of them. He'd looked vaguely familiar, but he was wearing a baseball cap and shades and Larison couldn't be sure. Someone he'd reviewed during selection? Maybe. But if the guy was ISA, why hadn't he taken the shot? Larison had been wide open, and the guy had just watched him go by. Was he afraid of the dead-man trigger on the tapes? He ought to have been. But who was he, and what was he doing there?

An hour outside San Jose, he stopped at a gas station and refilled the bike. And then, shivering under a dripping corrugated awning, his wet skin broken out in gooseflesh, he called Nico at the condo. The phone rang twice, then Nico picked up.

"Aló?"

Larison spoke in English. "Nicky, it's me, Daniel."

"Daniel? What . . . why are you calling?"

Larison almost never called him on the phone. Everything was by an anonymous email account, which Larison accessed only from random places. And never any proper names or identifying details.

"I . . . heard something on the news. A big shooting in San Jose." He felt a little catch in his throat and paused. "I was worried about you."

"Yeah, there were these crazy shootings right outside my condo and my office! I was in the office, we thought it was firecrackers at first. But when we looked outside, there were these people shooting at each other. But I'm fine. The police think it was drug traffickers. Crazy, huh?"

Larison swallowed and closed his eyes. God, he wished

he could just be there right now. The door locked . . . the jazz Nico liked playing softly . . . the smell of the apartment that was coffee and the old couch and Nico himself . . . the living room lit only by the light of Nico's desk lamp. Larison liked to watch him while he worked. He liked the purposefulness of it, and the innocence of the task. Sometimes Nico would look up and catch Larison watching, and his face would open up in that beautiful, boyish smile.

"Daniel?"

"I'm here."

"When can you come to see me?"

A tear slipped down Larison's face. "Soon."

"How soon?"

"I'm . . . working on something big right now. The thing I told you about before, it's almost done now. When it's over, I'll come to you."

"But you sound sad."

"I just have a lot going on. I'll explain more soon."

"Okay."

"Nicky?"

"Yes?"

"If this thing I'm working on doesn't go well, you might . . . hear some bad things about me."

There was a pause. "I don't understand."

"I can't explain now. But no matter what you hear, I don't want you ever to doubt, it scares me that you would doubt . . ."

"Daniel, what is it?"

Larison blinked hard to clear his eyes. "I love you. Promise me you won't doubt that."

"I never would. I love you, too."

Larison blew out a long breath. "Thank you."

"I wish you would say it more often."

"I know. I'm going to. I will."

"But what—"

"I have to go. I'll call soon, okay?"

"I miss you."

"I miss you, too. Bye."

He clicked off, turned off the sat phone, and zipped it up in the backpack. Then he dropped to a squat, put his face in his hands, and let himself cry hard for a minute. When it was out, when he felt purged, he got on the bike and rode back into the rain.

30 BAD IDEA

Ben and Paula stopped at a place called Villas Rio Mar in Dominical, on the central Pacific coast. Paula had found it on the iPhone. The place had separate bungalows, which would enable one of them to check in and the other to slip inside unnoticed afterward. Probably this far from San Jose it didn't matter, but Ben didn't want the staff to see a white man and a black woman checking into a hotel together. Just in case anyone had reported their general description after the shootings in Los Yoses. And besides that, though they'd done what they could to clean the gore off Paula's face and hair, she still looked like hell.

Ben checked in while Paula waited in the car. He explained to the nice woman at the counter that his bags were in the trunk, that he'd get them later because of the rain. Yes, it was a late reservation—turned out the place where he'd been planning to stay was sold out. So glad they had a room at this hour. And did they take cash? Wonderful. He paid in advance for three nights. It wasn't the kind of place anyone stayed at just overnight, and he didn't want to do anything more unusual than he already had. He'd come up with another story tomorrow, when he checked out.

He walked across the grounds to the room just to make sure there was no one around and that he could slip Paula inside unnoticed. It was all clear. Either they didn't have many guests that night or the rain was keeping people inside, or both. There wasn't a lot of illumination, either—mostly just footlights along the paths connecting the thatch-roofed bungalows, all of it surrounded by impressively dense rain forest.

The room was clean and bright, with absurdly cheerful bedspreads depicting blue night skies and yellow moons and stars. He'd gotten a double this time, and was glad he wouldn't have to sleep on the floor. Two beds, a small desk, and a chair. More than enough. He found a side path that bypassed reception, propped open the gate, and went back out to the car.

"We're good," he said. "Follow me."

He took her inside and locked the door behind them. Under the bright lights of the room, she looked at herself in the mirror. She still had flecks of brain in her hair. She closed her eyes and grimaced.

"I'm going to take a shower," she said.

"Good idea."

She pinched two spots on her shirt, pulled it away from her body, and looked at the stains. "And can you . . . is there a gift shop, or something? Can you get me something to wear?"

"No problem."

She gave him a faint smile. "Not another halter, okay?"

He returned the smile and nodded. "I'm going to grab something to eat, too. Do you . . ."

"No. I don't want to eat."

"No problem. I'll bring something anyway, okay? You might change your mind later."

She looked down at herself. "That's hard to imagine."

"I know. But just in case."

The restaurant was closed, but the bar was open, and the bartender told him they could put together a plate of this and that. *"Dos,"* Ben said. *"Estoy muerto de hambre."* Make it two. I'm starving.

While the bar put together the food, he went to the gift shop next to reception. They didn't have much in the way of clothes—mostly bathing suits and surfing regalia—but he found a blue sundress he thought would do the trick. They could worry about getting her something else tomorrow. He bought the dress, along with a short-sleeved button-down shirt for himself.

He picked up the food from the bar along with two bottles of Imperial beer and went back to the room. From the sound of it, Paula was still in the shower. He sat on the floor with his back against the bed and wolfed down an enormous plate of chicken, rice, and beans, all covered with a tangy sauce he'd never tasted before, and polished it off with a beer. It was delicious.

When he finished, she was still in the shower. He knocked on the door and said, "Paula? You all right?"

"I'm fine," she said. "I'm . . . I'll be out in a minute."

"I got you something to wear."

"Just leave it out there. There's a hotel robe."

"Okay."

A few minutes later, she came out in a white terry cloth robe. Her hair was wet and her face looked raw. Ben understood instantly. She'd been in there scrubbing under the hottest water she could stand.

"You all right?" he asked again.

She shook her head. "I'm never going to get that smell off me. Blood, and . . . it was brain, wasn't it?"

"It's just in your head now. It's not on you anymore. And it'll fade, I promise."

She nodded and stood there uncertainly. "Come on, sit down," he said. "See if you can eat something. It'll make you feel better."

She sat next to him, holding the bathrobe close as she did, and he pulled the plastic wrap off the remaining plate of food. She took a hesitant bite, then another. "Damn," she said. "That's pretty good."

She started digging in and he popped the cap off the other Imperial. He was glad she was eating. They hadn't had anything in over fourteen hours, and he knew from experience that no matter what was going on in your mind, you had to tend to your body.

"Okay if I put your contaminated clothes in a laundry bag?" he said. "We're going to need to get rid of them."

"Please. I don't want to look at them again. I'd burn them if I could."

He found a plastic laundry bag in a drawer and went into the bathroom. Her clothes were in a pile on the floor. He picked them up and dropped them in the bag. Nothing had come off on the floor. The blood was dry. He dropped the bag in front of the room door so they couldn't forget it when they left and sat down next to her again. She'd eaten about half the food and finished the beer.

"I can't eat any more," she said. "Thank you. That was good."

"No problem."

"Why are you being so nice to me now?"

"Am I?"

"Yeah. Usually you're an asshole."

"That's just a cover. Underneath, I'm really a very caring person."

She laughed. "Seriously."

He shook his head. "That's a hard thing, what happened to you today."

"But you're used to it."

He shrugged. "Yes. But that doesn't mean you are. Or that you should be."

"So you're going to stop being nice tomorrow?"

"You won't be over it tomorrow."

"When will I?"

"I don't know. It's different for different people."

"How was it for you?"

He paused, remembering. "At the time?"

"Yes."

"It was so chaotic, I didn't even have time to think. But . . . exhilarating."

"Will you tell me about it?"

"No."

"Why not?"

"It's a long story."

"I don't think I'm going to fall asleep anytime soon."

"It was Somalia. The battle of Mogadishu. Did you see the movie *Black Hawk Down*? Or read Mark Bowden's book?"

"I saw the movie."

"Well, that's what it was. Bowden did a good job. So did Ridley Scott. No one had time to think. It was just a nonstop firefight."

"But afterward."

"Like I said, exhilarated. And devastated, because I lost friends."

"I'm sorry."

"Comes with the territory."

"Stop being such a hard case."

"I'm not. It was a long time ago. I don't like thinking about it. Anyway, it was different for me."

"How?"

"I was trained. I was prepared. You haven't had any of that. You've never seen anyone die before, have you?"

"My mother."

"I mean killed."

"No."

"Well, seeing a dozen or so people shot to death in front of your eyes is shocking even if you've been prepared for it."

She nodded and didn't answer.

He got up and squeezed her shoulder gently. "Going to take a shower. Be back in a few."

He brushed his teeth, then took a scalding shower,

soaping up and scrubbing off the day's sweat and grime, the hot water loosening up his muscles and accessing the fatigue underneath. Post-combat parasympathetic back-lash was a bitch, and he was coming down from an entire day fueled by adrenaline. His mind was still on fire from all that had happened, but his body was starting to get the upper hand.

He pulled on a hotel robe when he was done, turned off the light, and went back out into the bedroom. Paula had turned off all the lights but the little one on the desk. She was lying on her side on one of the beds and Ben thought she must have fallen asleep.

He walked around to the side of the bed to see if her eyes were closed and was surprised to find her awake, her face streaked with tears that shone amid the shadows.

"Hey," he said. "You okay?"

She didn't answer.

He squatted down next to the bed and put his hand on her arm. "What is it?"

She shook her head. "I just don't know what the hell I'm doing."

He didn't know what to say. He tried, "You're doing fine."

"I mean, I'm a law enforcement officer. Fourteen people were killed today. I saw you kill two of them. And I'm not doing anything about it."

"There's nothing to be done."

"I don't know what my role is anymore."

"You're doing a good job. I didn't mean it cruelly before when I said you're out of your element. You're law enforcement, and you just got dropped into a combat zone. You're trying to learn your way."

She nodded and a fresh flow of tears ran silently down her face.

He squeezed her arm. "Paula."

She didn't answer.

He got up and walked around to the other side of the bed, then lay down next to her. He stroked her arm.

"I can't stop thinking about it," she said. "I can't get it out of my head."

"I know."

"His . . . his brains . . ."

Her voice rose on the last word and then choked off. She curled up and shook with silent tears.

"Shh," he whispered. "I know. I know."

A sob caught in her throat and she cried harder.

"That's it," he said. "Let it out. Let it out. That's what I do, when I can't take it anymore."

She coughed out a laugh through her tears. "You do not."

"Of course I do. All soldiers are crybabies, because we deal with so much shit. We just don't tell anyone. It's bad for our image."

He realized he'd acknowledged he was a soldier, but decided it didn't matter.

She laughed again, then cried harder. He put his arm around her, took her hand, and pulled her close. "Shh," he said again. "It's okay."

She gripped his hand and pressed back into him. He was suddenly acutely aware of the feel of her ass through the material of the robe.

Oh, fuck, this wasn't good. He didn't want to let her go—it would have been awkward, and anyway he seemed to be making her feel better, but . . .

She shifted slightly, and the feel of her body moving against him was like a current of electricity against his skin.

Post-combat hard-on, he thought. *That's all it is. Should have seen that coming. Don't be stupid now.*

She shifted her hand to the back of his and pulled him closer, pressing his forearm across her breasts. A shock wave of lust coursed through him.

Don't be stupid, don't be stupid . . .

She moved his hand lower. "Please," she whispered.

"Paula . . . ," he said, his mouth close to her ear.

"I just . . . I need to feel something. Please."

Somehow his hand had slipped under her robe. She pressed it tightly against her breasts. Her skin was warm and smooth. He could feel her heart pounding.

"You're upset," he said, his voice low, his throat thick. "I don't know if . . . I don't think we should . . ."

He stopped, not sure what he was saying, feeling like he was babbling. His hand moved. He felt a hard nipple against his palm. He wanted her so much it made him groan.

"No," he said, panting. "No, no, this is a bad idea. A bad idea." Somehow he pried his hands off her and sat up. "Paula, no."

She sat up and turned to him. The robe had opened partly, and in his peripheral vision he could see the muscles of her neck, her breasts contoured in shadow, the skin smooth and dark against the white terry cloth. He was massively hard and knew he'd never done anything as difficult as not reaching out and tearing the robe off her and throwing her back on the bed and—

"Fuck you, then," she said.

He shook his head, not comprehending. "What?"

She slapped him. Hard. His head rocked back and he saw a white flash behind his eyes. He was so stunned by it that she managed to slap him again before he could do anything to stop her, another powerful, stinging shot from the opposite side. A red haze misted his vision and he felt his scalp tighten with anger. She drew back her arm again, her hand balled into a fist this time, and as the punch came forward, he snaked an arm inside and deflected it. He pushed her onto her back and straddled her. She twisted an arm free and punched him in the mouth. She couldn't get any leverage behind the blow but it smashed his lips into his teeth and hurt like hell.

"Bitch," he said, turning his head and spitting blood. She tried to hit him again and he caught her wrists and pinned them to the bed next to her head.

She struggled and kicked. He slid down onto her thighs to control her legs and looked down at her breasts. He couldn't think anymore. He lowered his head and took a nipple into his mouth. She sucked in a breath and her pelvis arched and he almost let her go but then thought no way, he wasn't going to let her hit him again.

"Fuck you," she said again. "Fuck you."

He moved his head to her other breast and she moaned, and the sound of her own pleasure seemed to incite her.

"You want this, don't you?" he said, past caring about the consequences. "All right. You win."

He let go of her wrists and she hit him in the mouth again. There was a shock of pain and his head rocked back. He grabbed her wrists again and pressed his body down onto hers.

"You want to play?" he said. "Fine. Fine with me."

He slid his right hand under her waist and fed her right wrist into it. She struggled and tried to bite his ear, missing it and scoring her teeth against his scalp instead. He sat up and jerked her arm around, turning her over onto her stomach.

He sat on her thighs and with one hand pinned her arms behind her back. She kicked and struggled underneath him. He pulled the belt off his robe, slipped it under her top wrist, pulled it around, and yanked it tight with his teeth and free hand. He tied it off in a square knot, then wrapped it around her other wrist and repeated the operation so that her bound wrists were side by side.

He slid lower over her legs and tore her robe out of the way. She grunted and tried to twist loose.

He lay down on top of her and pushed his knees between hers. Then he sat up and spread her legs with his own. Her ass was a ripe, dark peach, the shadow between her legs maddening, beckoning. She turned her head and looked back at him and again said, "Fuck you."

He didn't answer. He put his weight on her bound wrists with one hand and with the other began to touch her. She was completely wet. He eased a finger inside her and she groaned.

His heart was slamming away in his chest like a battering ram. Panting, feeling like he'd lost his mind, he flipped her over onto her back. He got his knees between hers again and spread her legs. He bent to kiss her. She jerked her head to the side and again said, "Fuck you."

"Yeah," he said. "Yeah, that's right."

He moved lower and took a nipple into his mouth again and touched her with his fingers and the sound of her moaning made him insane.

He slid lower. He got an arm under one of her thighs and forced her legs farther apart. Then he put his mouth against her belly and bit her, the way she'd tried to bite him. She cried out, and before the cry was done he'd slipped his other arm under her so that her thighs rested on his shoulders, and he pushed his mouth against her so she could feel his lips and his teeth and his breath, and he slipped his tongue inside her. She gasped and the sound of it made him dizzy, the sound and her taste and how hot and wet she was against his mouth and face. He moved one hand up and rolled a thumb around her nipple. With the other, he started touching her with his fingers in time with his tongue.

She groaned. His lips hurt and his heart was pounding and he was so hard it ached.

He glanced up at her. She was watching him, panting, her head off the pillow, the muscles of her neck straining. Her body was slick with sweat.

He paused and put his fourth finger in his mouth,

coating it with his spit and her juices. He lowered his head and started up again. He kept his eyes on hers. He slid his slicked finger slowly into her ass.

Her eyes widened and she sucked in a breath. He felt her muscles clench. He worked her with his mouth and fingers. He didn't take his eyes off her.

Her panting grew faster, deeper. A low sound came from her throat. He kept going, out of his mind with the need to fuck her.

The sound deepened and rose and changed into a drawn-out cry. She squeezed his head with her thighs and pushed her pelvis into his face and shuddered and arched and cried out. Her back arched farther, and farther still, and then suddenly all the tension in her was gone and she collapsed back to the bed. There was no sound but her breathing.

He brought his arms around and moved up between her legs.

"Kiss me."

She didn't answer. He took her face roughly in his hands and looked in her eyes and pressed himself against her. She struggled but there was nothing she could do, she was too wet and too tied up and he was holding her too tightly. He pushed forward and moved a little inside her and somehow made himself stop. She grimaced and pushed back against him and he slid in a little farther. He watched her, their faces an inch apart.

She groaned again, her mouth open, her head tilted back. He eased away, then clenched his stomach and ass and drove his hips forward and buried himself inside her. She cried out and he pressed his swollen lips down on hers. She groaned into his mouth and he held her face in his hands and spread her legs wider with his thighs and he fucked her, long and deep and desperately hard, and he forgot where they were and why they were here and what had happened that day and he fucked her, and when she started kissing him hungrily and hard and fucking him back it was too much, he couldn't stop, and there was nothing else in the world but her face in his hands and her body pinned beneath him and he gripped her harder and cried out into her mouth and he came, he came and she sucked on his tongue and it went on and on until he had spent himself inside her.

When it was over, his exhaustion was so sudden and complete that he felt momentarily unsteady. He pushed himself away from her slightly, his breathing ragged, and looked into her eyes.

"Damn," he managed to say.

Her breathing was as rough as his. She said, "Untie me."

He touched a hand to his swollen lips. "Not if you're going to hit me again."

"I think I'm done with that."

"What the hell got into you?"

"I don't know."

He turned her on her side and untied her wrists, then lay down facing her. "Were you trying to provoke me?"

"I'm not sure."

"Don't get me wrong. I liked it."

"Yeah, I could tell that."

"Why, though?"

"I was just . . . mad. You were being so nice, it made me lower my guard. And I could tell you wanted to, and I told you I needed you to, and then suddenly you got all high-minded on me . . . it just really made me angry."

"I didn't mean it like that. You know I wanted to. I just thought it was a bad idea."

"Well, you changed your mind pretty fast."

"Maybe it was all that talk earlier about interagency cooperation."

She laughed. "Yeah, we're a model for the way Uncle Sam should function. 'Make love, not war.'"

He ran his hand gently along her face and the side of her head. "I like your hair. The way it feels."

"You've never been with a black woman before, have you?"

"What do you mean?"

"You're not supposed to touch a black woman's hair."

He thought for a moment. "Now that you mention it . . . I did get that vibe a few times here and there."

"They were straightened, right?"

"Yeah. You know, not like yours."

"You can touch it if it's natural. It's the straightened and hair extensions and wigs that can get you in trouble."

He eased his hand around to the back of her head. "I like yours better."

"You wouldn't believe what it takes to make black hair straight. I don't have time for it. Besides, I'd rather just be myself."

They were quiet for a moment. He said, "So . . . I guess we can sleep in the same bed tonight?"

She laughed again. "I guess so."

"Good. Because I'm so tired, I'm going to pass out."

"That sounds good."

"Tell me something first."

"What?"

"Why wouldn't you kiss me?"

There was a pause. She said, "It was too intimate. I wanted you to fuck me, not make love to me."

He'd never thought of it that way. "Does that mean you won't kiss me now?"

"It's a bad idea."

"You've got some pretty finely parsed notions about what separates a good idea from a bad one."

There was another pause. She touched his cheek with

a hand and kissed him, long and tenderly. His lips hurt but it was delicious anyway.

She broke the kiss and looked at him. He said, "Was that so bad?"

She shook her head. "It was okay. But it was the first part I really wanted."

31 SQUEAKY CLEAN

Ulrich checked his watch for probably the tenth time in an hour. Almost ten o'clock. He needed to go home and get some sleep. But he'd become so afraid of being away from the secure phone that he was hurrying back to his desk even from bathroom breaks. Anyway, it wasn't like he was going to sleep even if he left. All he could do these days was toss and turn until the sun rose and he could get up and come into the office without it being so early he would seem deranged or obsessed.

The secure line buzzed. He jumped and then snatched up the receiver.

"Ulrich."

"Clements. Okay to talk?"

"I'll tell you if it isn't, okay? What is it?"

"We have a problem."

Ulrich flinched. If Clements had been a doctor, "problem" would doubtless be his favorite way of informing patients they had inoperable brain cancer.

He closed his eyes. "Tell me."

"We lost everybody. Twelve Blackwater contractors, two Ground Branch operators. They're all dead."

Ulrich shook his head. It was unbelievable. This was just . . . this couldn't be happening to him.

"What about Larison?"

"We're pretty sure he's not among the dead."

"Why just 'pretty sure'?"

"Because there are no survivors. There's no one to report in. So all I can tell you right now is the math. We sent twelve contractors and two operators. Costa Rican media is reporting fourteen dead. Yeah, it's possible one of the dead is Larison or one of them is Treven, but if that were the case, it would mean at least one of our guys was still alive. And if one of our guys were alive, he would have reported in by now. So I think it's a pretty safe assumption that Larison killed all of them, or that he killed the Blackwater snatch teams and Treven killed the two Ground Branch."

Ulrich dropped his glasses on the desk and scrubbed a hand across his face. "What about the tapes?"

"No sign of release. Yet."

"What's our next move?"

"We don't have one. The op has been turned over to JSOC."

Ulrich didn't respond. It was really almost funny. How just when you thought things couldn't possibly get worse, they always found a way.

"You there?" Clements said.

"How did this happen?"

"The national security adviser was furious when I told him the snatch teams were Blackwater. 'You deceived me, you told me they were Ground Branch, blah, blah, blah.' I told him it didn't matter, that the Blackwater guys were all former government, anyway. I mean, he was only pissed because the op failed. If it had worked, he wouldn't have cared if we'd hired goddamn al Qaeda to do it. And I told him so."

It was actually amusing, imagining Clements growing some balls that way. "Very diplomatic of you."

"It didn't matter what I said. His mind was already made up. At which point, Horton made his move. And now he's the national security adviser's best friend."

"For all we know, Horton's people took out the snatch teams. So Horton could go back to the national security adviser, say I told you so, and take over the op."

"It doesn't matter. It's done."

"Fine. What does he propose?"

"That we give Larison the diamonds."

Ulrich laughed. "That's his plan? That's what he proposed? That we just capitulate to this psycho's demands and call it a day? That's ingenious. I can't believe no one else thought of it."

"Yeah, well, the national security adviser seems to like it. We've got an interagency meeting in his office first thing to thrash out the details."

Ulrich tried to think of anything he'd seen that had spiraled this far out of control and still been righted in the end. Nothing came to mind.

"Well," he said, "I guess we just have to hope that Horton knows what the hell he's doing. And maybe he does. It's not like he's squeaky clean on all this. After all, he's the one who took care of the Caspers."

PART THREE

There are different kinds of truths for different kinds of people. There are truths appropriate for children; truths that are appropriate for students; truths that are appropriate for educated adults; and truths that are appropriate for highly educated adults, and the notion that there should be one set of truths available to everyone is a modern democratic fallacy. It doesn't work.

IRVING KRISTOL

No, there will be no review. The President has determined that they are all enemy combatants. We are not going to revisit it.

DAVID ADDINGTON, CHIEF OF STAFF TO
VICE PRESIDENT CHENEY

Sometimes in life you want to just keep walking. . . . Don't always be issuing papers and reports. Some of life has to be mysterious.

PEGGY NOONAN, ABC NEWS

32 MANEUVERING

Ben's phone buzzed. He opened his eyes and saw faint light coming through the window. He picked up. "Yeah."

"You get any sleep?" Hort said.

Ben looked at the clock readout. Shit, he'd been unconscious for over six hours. He'd needed it. "Yeah, believe it or not." Paula opened her eyes and Ben raised a finger to his lips.

"Good. We have a task group meeting with the national security adviser in thirty minutes. We just got an email from Larison, and he says he'll be calling. I want you to listen in."

"Listen in? How am I going to do that?"

"I'm going to leave my mobile phone on. Set to speakerphone. A little oversight on my part."

"You can do something like that in the White House?"

"The meeting's not in the White House. The national security adviser wants to keep this thing as far from the president as he can. The meeting is at his house in Potomac."

Once again, Ben was intrigued that Hort was including him in management stuff, if only on a listen-and-learn basis. "Okay . . . ," he said.

"It's just him, me, and the deputy director of central intelligence, Stephen Clements. Clements is the genius who convinced the national security adviser that it made sense to try to snatch Larison. And by the way, the snatch teams weren't Ground Branch. They were Blackwater."

"Are you kidding? The Agency contracted out *this* snatch?"

"They did. The good news is, the national security adviser is very unhappy about it. With a little luck, that means he'll listen to reason."

"You mean listen to you."

"Son, believe me, on this one there's no difference."

"So those two guys who tried to drop Paula and me . . . they were Blackwater?"

"That's a little unclear right now. Clements says they were Ground Branch, there to supervise. He thinks Larison killed them along with the snatch teams. Or he's pretending to think that."

"What do you think?"

There was a pause. "I don't know what to think. There's always a lot of maneuvering between the various agencies. I'd hate to think it's gotten to the point where we're trying to bump off each other's players."

"I told you, it was supposed to be a hit."

"I don't doubt you. Believe me, there's more behind-the-scenes bullshit on this op than I've ever seen."

"Yeah, I've been getting that feeling."

"Well, for that reason as much as any other, I want you to be able to see how decisions are getting made here."

So that's why Hort wanted him to listen in—to prove that he had nothing to do with the two guys outside Nico's office. To show that, even after Obsidian, Ben could trust him. Or maybe this was more management grooming. Or both.

"Okay," he said again.

"I'll call in a half hour. Keep your phone on mute. And I'll call again after, when it's done and we can talk securely."

"Roger that."

"How's your FBI friend?"

It was the second time Hort had referred to her as his "friend." He wondered whether Hort suspected something was up. He would have seen her photo from her Bureau file.

"She's okay. A little shaken up by what happened yesterday, but okay." He looked at Paula's face, but couldn't learn anything from her expression.

"All right, good. Be ready in thirty minutes." He clicked off.

Ben put the phone down. Paula said, "What was that?"

Ben wasn't sure how to answer. He couldn't really get rid of Paula before the next call. And the thought of needing to do so, when they were lying next to each other naked, was exceptionally strange.

"It was my boss. He says Larison is supposed to call in again in thirty minutes. He wants me to listen in."

"Why?"

"So I'll know what's going on."

"Which is . . . ?"

"I don't know, exactly. But it seems like the snatch teams were Blackwater, and the two guys who showed up after were CIA Ground Branch."

She frowned. "Are you sure?"

"No, I'm not sure, but my boss's information is usually pretty good. Looks like the CIA doesn't want you to recover those tapes. And doesn't want anyone else to, either."

She didn't say anything. He thought she looked a little ill.

"I know," he said. "It's a dark day for interagency cooperation. Outside of you and me, I mean."

He thought the crack would get her to smile, but she didn't. Which was really too bad, because, after all, they had a half hour to kill.

"You okay?"

She shook her head. "I just . . . I just don't know what the hell's going on."

"Yeah, I've seen some crazy shit, but this one is up there, no doubt."

"Then why are you so cheerful?"

He shrugged. "I got laid last night. That always puts me in a good mood."

That made her smile. "Yeah? Was she good?"

He felt his lips. They were swollen and tender. "Well, she's got a good straight right, I can tell you that."

She raised an eyebrow. "Really? Is that all?"

He smiled. "No, there's more. And if she joins me in the shower, I'll tell her all about it."

33 NOT A PLACE YOU WANT TO BE

Thirty minutes in the shower wasn't quite what Ben would have allotted if it had been up to him, but they managed to use the time well. Afterward, Paula got into the sundress and Ben pulled on the shirt he'd bought. He put the one he'd been wearing the day before in the laundry bag with Paula's clothes. They'd dump it somewhere far from the hotel.

"Just gotta listen in on this call," he said. "And then we'll go."

"Put it on speakerphone."

Shit, he should have seen that coming. "I don't think—"

"Don't tell me you're keeping secrets from me. Not after what happened yesterday. Not after what's happened since then."

He briefly considered telling her that was all separate, that shared danger, even a shared pillow, didn't mean he could share operational details, too. And decided that, if he did, she was going to start punching him again. And besides, it wasn't really a question of operational details. It was just a bunch of managers arguing about what to do. And hell, she knew a lot already.

He nodded. "All right. Speakerphone."

She smiled. "Now, this is Larison? Calling whom?"

"As far as I know, just my boss, the national security adviser, and a guy from the CIA."

"Who's your boss?"

Shit. Another one he should have seen coming. He was tired. Or he was distracted by what had happened with her. Either way, things were getting past him.

"Let's just listen in, okay?" he said.

"There's nobody from Justice on this call?"

"I guess not."

"Gives a whole new meaning to the phrase 'Justice is blind,' doesn't it?"

Ben shrugged. "I think these guys are more concerned about the national security implications of the situation than they are about the justice ones."

They sat on the unused bed and waited. The phone buzzed just a minute later. Ben raised a finger to his lips, answered the call, and immediately pressed the mute button.

"I'm going to explain the deal to you," said a low and raspy voice, the tone calm and confident. Given the current circumstances, Ben figured it was Larison, about to issue instructions.

"We're listening." Ben didn't recognize this one, either, but assumed it was the national security adviser, running the meeting.

"It's actually very simple," Larison said. "Nothing's changed. If the diamonds haven't been delivered to me in twenty-four hours in accordance with my instructions, the tapes will be released."

"I understand," the national security adviser said. "I'm going to turn this meeting over now to our new point man on the operation. I think you know him. Colonel?"

"How are you doing, son?" Hort said. Paula mouthed, *Your boss?* And Ben, feeling he had no choice, figuring she pretty much knew who he was at this point anyway, nodded.

There was a pause. Larison said, "Hort?"

"It's me."

"I had a feeling they'd bring you in."

"Well, I wish they'd brought me in earlier. This thing would have been handled better."

"All I want to hear is that you have the diamonds. If you do, we'll keep talking. If you don't, you're wasting my time."

"We have them."

"Where are they?"

"What do you mean?"

"Where are you holding them? What city?"

"They're here in Washington."

"Good. I'll call again in twenty-four hours and tell you how you'll deliver them. You'll use a single courier. I think you understand what will happen if you deviate from my instructions."

"You made your point in Costa Rica, son. Loud and clear."

"Twenty-four hours. You'll want to have a jet ready."

There was a click, then a dial tone, then silence.

The national security adviser said, "What do you think?"

"I think this is another opportunity," a third voice said. "We can pick him up at the point of exchange." It must have been Clements.

"I'm sorry," Hort said, "can you tell me how that's different from your previous plan? The one that cost fourteen lives and put Larison on a hair trigger. Literally, most likely, if we're talking about his dead-man switch."

"He got lucky."

"*You* got lucky. Lucky he didn't just uncork and release those tapes. In case you haven't noticed, the man is not exactly stable."

"We don't even know if there is a dead-man switch. He could be bluffing."

"He's not bluffing. I know him. And right now, I guarantee you he's got the switch set to dangerously short intervals. When he picks up the diamonds, he'll probably have it down to about fifteen minutes. Your plan is to take him, secure him, revive him, elicit accurate intel, and disarm the switch in under fifteen minutes?"

"Better that way than just handing over the diamonds and hoping for the best."

" 'That way' is a fantasy, and the only thing a fantasy is good for is jerking off."

Paula covered her mouth to suppress a giggle and Ben gave her a *yeah, that's my boss* shrug. It was weird, and a little intoxicating, to be listening in on such a high-level conversation. And to have made Paula party to it.

"Where are you going to get the men, anyway?" Hort said. "You going to go back to Blackwater? And what are you going to do if the information Larison gives you doesn't disarm the trigger, but instead sets it off? How are you going to know, until you see the footage from those tapes on the Al Jazeera nightly news and every American network?"

There was silence for a moment. Clements said, "What you're proposing means we'll have those tapes hanging over the head of the U.S. government forever. And eventually, they're going to come out."

"Maybe. But everything you've tried is guaranteed to *make* them come out. Besides, Larison is going to have something hanging over his head, too. Nico. And his family. Like I said before, we have nuclear parity now. Mutual assured destruction. Which wasn't pleasant for anyone back in the day, true, but it managed to keep the peace."

The national security adviser said, "I have to say, I don't like the idea of his getting away clean."

"Sir," Hort said, "you can always pick him up later if

that's what you choose to do. I'd advise against it even later for the same reasons I'm advising against it now, but you could if you wanted to. What you can't do is try to pick him up now, with that dead-man switch set to the kind of interval I know he's programmed it for. Give him the diamonds, let him walk away and calm down. Eventually, having to worry about resetting that trigger every hour is going to get to be too much of a risk and too much of a pain in the ass. He'll adjust it to every twenty-four hours, or every forty-eight. If you pick him up then, there's a chance. Right now, there just isn't."

There was a long silence. The national security adviser said, "Have a jet ready tomorrow. With the diamonds."

Hort said, "Yes, sir." Ben heard the sounds of papers being shuffled, people getting up, and then the line went dead. He hit the end call button.

"I can't believe they're just going to give him the diamonds," Paula said. "Blackmail, murder . . . they're just going to pretend none of this ever even happened?"

Ben shrugged. "Come on, let's go."

"Where are we going?"

"I don't know about you, but I'd like to get the hell out of Costa Rica. Just in case local law enforcement is looking for me in connection with what happened in Los Yoses yesterday."

"But Larison—"

"Larison's gone already. Probably crossed the border somewhere while we slept. I know this is hard for you to accept, Paula, but this isn't a criminal investigation. It never was. My best guess? Even in the Bureau, there are people who recognize it's not a criminal investigation, and they're leaking to people in the CIA, people who are very committed to stopping a criminal investigation. And to stopping you, if you insist on trying to conduct one. That's not a place you want to be."

"This really just . . . sucks."

"On the one hand. On the other hand, no one's talking assassinations anymore, right? The powers that be have decided to resort to diplomacy."

She shook her head and grimaced. "I don't know what the hell the powers that be are doing. I really don't."

34 COURIER

They drove north on the coastal road toward the airport in Quepos. Fifteen minutes into the drive, Ben's phone buzzed.

"All right," Hort said. "You heard."

"Yeah."

"So you know, somebody's going to need to hand over those diamonds tomorrow. I want it to be you."

Ben was surprised. "Me?"

"You know anyone better?"

"No, I'm game. I just . . . you know, it's not what I usually do."

"Well, none of this is usual. I need you to get to Washington ASAP. We don't know what Larison is planning for tomorrow. We'll have a jet ready, but beyond that, all we can really expect is that he'll be issuing instructions step-by-step to keep us scrambling."

"In case anyone tries to grab him again."

"Exactly. Although his primary defense against a snatch is still his dead-man setup. Where are you now?"

"About an hour from Quepos."

"The jet will be waiting for you there. It'll take you to Washington National. Give the FBI agent a lift if she wants it, but get clear of her after that. Stay in the area tonight, and be ready to roll by 0700 tomorrow."

"Roger that."

He clicked off. Paula said, "So you're going to be the courier."

Ben glanced over. He hadn't said that much on the call, but it had been enough. "Looks like it."

"You okay with that?"

He shrugged. "Is there a reason not to be?"

"Well, some people might consider Larison to be a pretty dangerous character, for one."

Of all the reasons Ben might have been concerned, danger just wasn't one of them. He thought about saying something about how danger was part of the business, but decided it would sound cheesy. Or that she would just accuse him of being a hard-ass again.

"I'll be careful," he said.

"I could go with you."

"Actually, you can't. Larison said it has to be a single courier."

"Did he really say that?"

"He did."

"Well, damn."

"Look, it's all over now but the logistics. Somebody's got to give him the diamonds. It could be anyone. It just happens to be me. By tomorrow evening, or the next day at the latest, this thing will be done. After that, the tapes will be released or they won't be released, but that particular problem is above our pay grade."

She didn't answer.

"Okay? Paula, this isn't up to me."

Still no response.

"Look, if anything changes, I'll let you know."

"How?"

"Well, you live in D.C., right?"

"Fairfax. Why?"

"It's just, I don't have a place to stay tonight—"

She laughed.

"—and I'm always looking for ways to improve those interagency relations."

"Yes, you've been diligent about that."

"I try."

"You know, last night was nice—"

"This morning, too."

"And this morning, too. But having you stay at my apartment . . . right now, that's too much for me."

"More of the 'you wanted to be fucked, not made love to' thing."

"Something like that."

"Well, I could just fuck you, then. I'm pretty flexible that way."

She laughed again.

"Seriously," he said. "Was this just a one-off? Because, when you weren't trying to punch me in the face and bite my ear off, I thought it was pretty good."

She nodded. "It was good. A little . . . crazy. But good."

"So?"

"So I think I need a little time to digest everything that just happened, okay? Not just with you. With everything."

They barely spoke on the flight back. Paula's eyes were closed for hours but Ben sensed she wasn't sleeping—that she was instead simply withdrawing into herself. Withdrawing from him. He watched her and noticed for the first time how long her lashes were. He noticed not for the first time how good she looked in the sundress. But neither of these observations felt relevant. It was as though she'd pulled down a steel curtain between them. She seemed as distant and unreachable as though the night before hadn't ever happened.

They went through customs and then through the terminal. Standing outside arrivals, diesel buses and honking taxis lurching past, the midday Washington sun superheating the humidity around them, Ben tried to think of the right thing to say. And couldn't.

"Are you . . . sorry?" he asked.

"Not exactly."

He chuckled. "Well, that's a ringing endorsement if ever I heard one."

She shook her head. "I'm just . . . confused."

"I tried to tell you it was a bad idea."

"I don't remember you trying all that hard."

"Believe me, I did."

"Well, maybe I should have listened."

"Yeah, maybe you should have." It came out harsher than he'd intended, but still.

She nodded slowly, then said, "I need to go." She turned and started to move away.

"Paula."

She turned back to him.

"I know you need to write some kind of report. You should . . . be careful what you put in it."

She took a step closer. "Are you threatening me?"

He felt irritation rising and pushed it away. "First of all, I don't threaten. And second, no, all I'm doing is giving you some well-intentioned advice. As a friend. Those Ground Branch guys in Los Yoses knew your name. There's still a lot we don't know about this whole thing, and what we don't know is making certain people extremely twitchy."

She didn't answer.

"But hey, write whatever the hell you want." He turned to go.

"Ben. Wait."

He turned. For a moment, she looked like she was genuinely struggling with something. Her mouth opened, then closed. She pursed her lips, and it was as though her expression were somehow . . . dissolving. For a second, he thought she might cry.

"What?" he said.

Then her face solidified again and she shook her head. "Nothing," she said, and walked away.

He watched her heading toward the Metro. He was having trouble believing she could just walk away to write a report while he delivered the diamonds to Larison. Well, she didn't have much choice. Still, if the shoe had been on the other foot, he would have been humiliated, furious. Maybe that's what was bugging her.

His phone buzzed. Hort.

"Yeah."

"Are you still at National?"

"Yeah, we just landed."

"Lanier?"

He watched. "She's gone."

"Good. Larison just called in. He's moved up the delivery. Told us to have a jet ready to leave from National at 1800."

"Where did the call come from?"

"We can't pinpoint these satellite phone calls because from geosynchronous orbit, the footprint is too big. It could have come from Costa Rica. Or the southeastern United States. Or anywhere in between."

"You think he'd have the diamonds delivered in Costa Rica?"

"I don't know. Before, I would have said not a chance, but now that Nico's known, maybe he thinks it doesn't make a difference."

"So what's the plan?"

"Larison has the number of the phone I gave you. He's going to call you at 1800 with instructions on where you'll be flying. We're refueling and servicing the jet you just came in on and it'll be ready."

"What does he know about me?"

"Not a single thing outside you're a guy delivering a

package. From his standpoint, you might as well be a pizza delivery man."

"Hell of a pizza."

"Yeah. I'll meet you on the Crystal City Metro platform in one hour with the diamonds. Yellow Line, in the direction of Huntington."

Ben wondered if Hort was choosing such a public location to reassure him again. It wasn't really necessary. If Hort had wanted to set him up, there had been plenty of opportunities already. Or he could have just left him in the Manila city jail.

"I'll be there," Ben said.

An hour later, on the Crystal City platform, amid bored, oblivious commuters walking and waiting beneath the science fiction hush of the vaulted cement ceilings, Ben spotted Hort coming toward him in civilian clothes, a backpack over his shoulders. He saw Ben and walked over.

They shook hands. Ben eyed the backpack. "Is there really a hundred million dollars in there?" he said.

"There is. Twenty-three pounds, in case you're curious. Don't lose it." He slipped the pack off and handed it to Ben.

"Don't I have to sign for this?"

"Are you kidding? We give out bricks of hundred-dollar bills in Iraq and Afghanistan like we're handing out lollipops and solicit work through no-bid contracts and there's that three-trillion-dollar stimulus . . . at this point, a hundred million in the black ops budget is nothing but a damn rounding error. The only thing unusual is that we're using diamonds instead of cash."

A train pulled in with a hiss of pneumatic brakes and a recorded announcement of its arrival at the station. Ben watched commuters flowing on and off like zombies in a horror movie.

"The Fed had a hundred million worth of diamonds just lying around?"

"No, what you have in that bag is another triumph of government–private sector cooperation. Someone at the CIA had the admittedly excellent idea of engaging Ronald Winston."

"Winston?"

"Son of the late Harry Winston. World's premier diamond expert. We needed someone with deep contacts in the markets in Africa, Amsterdam, Tel Aviv, New York, someone who could cajole a few Saudi princes. And also someone monumentally discreet. Apparently there's only one man who fit the bill, and that's Winston. He personally certified every stone in this bag and I took possession directly from him."

"What was Winston's cut?"

"I'm sure he was well compensated. Being indispensable, and discreet on top of it, puts a man in a position to charge a premium."

"I guess that's true."

"Now, listen. It's just you on this. There's no one else. So if anyone tries to interfere with you, you stop him. Any way you have to. Remember, you're carrying a hundred million in there in untraceable, easily convertible stones. Plenty of people would like to get their hands on that, never mind the tapes."

"Roger that."

"You're armed?"

Ben nodded. "Same Glock you set me up with when I was Dan Froomkin, FBI. It was on the jet where I left it."

"Good. We can't have Larison thinking we're fucking with him again. The connection you uncovered in Costa Rica gives us a lot of leverage, and that's important, that's our insurance that if we let him walk away happy, he won't release the tapes. But no sense antagonizing him, either. If another team from Blackwater shows up and tries to take him again, he might just decide the hell with it, we're never going to give him what he wants, he might as well just release the tapes and the hell with the rest. We don't want him in that frame of mind."

His phone buzzed. He glanced down, saw the caller's number was blocked. He looked at Hort.

Hort said, "Anyone else have this number?"

"No. Just you, as far as I know."

"It's him, then. Calling early again to keep us jumping. Go ahead."

Ben accepted the call. "Hello."

"Is this the courier?"

The same low, raspy voice Ben had heard on the conference call. The same confident tone. It was him. Larison.

Ben looked at Hort and nodded. "Yes." After all the circling around, the listening in on other people's calls, it was strangely satisfying to be engaging Larison directly.

"You're going to start off by driving."

"I thought I was flying somewhere."

"Maybe you are. But first, you're going to drive. Do you have a navigation system?"

"On my phone."

"Good. Head west on Interstate 66. I'll call you again in a little while and tell you what to do next. Now, listen. I'm going to be watching you. I might be tailing you, I might be having you drive past static checkpoints. I might have video installed on the route to monitor you that way. If you're being followed, if you're not alone, I'll put a bullet in your brain and pick up the diamonds that way. Understood?"

The threat made Ben want to answer in kind, but he caught the reaction and suppressed it. "Understood."

The line went dead. Ben repeated the conversation for Hort.

"Shit," Hort said. "Should have seen that coming. We don't have a car ready. All right, take mine. The driver's outside."

They left the station and walked over to a dark gray

Crown Victoria parked at the curb. Hort told the driver, a crew-cut Asian too young to be part of the unit, that they'd be taking the Metro. The guy got out and Ben got in. He put the backpack on the floor of the passenger side and made sure the door was locked.

Hort held open the driver-side door and leaned in. "Remember," he said. "It's just you. And be damned careful with Larison. He killed twelve operators in Costa Rica. One more isn't going to make a difference to him."

35 MIRROR

Ben slipped in the Bluetooth earpiece, opened the iPhone navigation function, and followed Route 1 north to I-66. He checked his mirrors, but in the late afternoon rush hour traffic, there was no way to spot surveillance. It was entirely possible Larison could have ghosted up behind or alongside him and snuck a peek in the car. But Ben had a feeling he hadn't. No, if Ben had been Larison, he'd have planned a route involving increasingly quiet streets and residential neighborhoods with multiple points of ingress and egress—the kind of route that reveals a tail by winnowing him out of traffic and forcing him to stay close—and set up there. A standard surveillance detection route, in fact, the only difference being that this time, the person trying to spot the tail would be not the driver, but someone running countersurveillance from a static location.

On the other hand, he'd thought he knew what Larison would do in Los Yoses. And hadn't even been close.

The iPhone buzzed. Ben accepted the call through the earpiece. "Yeah."

"Go north on Glebe Road. Then west on Sixteenth Street North, past the hospital. Then right on George Mason."

Ben input George Mason into the phone. A map came up. It was what he expected: the street cut through a residential area and offered multiple outlets leading to a half dozen major arteries. If someone were following him, they'd have to reveal themselves there. Probably Larison was set up nearby, watching.

"I'm turning onto Glebe now."

"Just keep going."

Several cars took the exit behind him. He marked the makes and colors as he drove past several blocks of brick and stone houses and well-kept lawns. The hospital came up on his right, multiple buildings along an entire block, surrounded by parking lots. He made a right on George Mason and continued past the west side of the hospital. Two of the cars that had followed him off the highway turned with him—a black Cadillac and a blue Toyota behind it. Nothing definitive—Glebe and George Mason were both busy streets, and it would have been surprising if no one else had turned off onto them from 66. As for Larison, he could have been watching from anywhere inside. Or from one of the cars parked along the street. Or from behind a tree. There was no way to know.

"Okay, I'm on George Mason now."

"Make a left on Twentieth Street. Then zigzag over to Nineteenth. Left, right, left, right."

"Doing it now."

The Cadillac continued straight on George Mason. The Toyota made a left behind Ben. Still nothing definitive—the western sun was reflecting off the Toyota's window and Ben couldn't see inside, but someone who lived in this neighborhood might have followed the same route. Still, suspicious enough to warrant some simple countermeasures.

"Got a possible problem here," Ben said. "I'm alone, per your instructions. But if that's not you in the blue Toyota, I think someone's following me."

"It's not me."

"Okay, I'll go around the block and see what he does."

Ben made a right on Greenbrier, then a right on Patrick Henry. The Toyota stayed with him. He could make out a driver and a passenger, both in shades. He made a right again, back onto George Mason. The Toyota stayed with him.

"Okay, it's official," he said. "The blue Toyota is a tail. Looks like two men in the car. I'm telling you so you'll know I didn't put them there. Also, from the route I just drove, they know I'm aware of them now."

"How did they follow you?"

Ben wished he knew. He thought of Hort again, but it just didn't make sense. A tracking device in the car, then? Satellites? And who were the guys behind him, anyway? Blackwater? Ground Branch?

"I have no idea," he said. "I'm just the courier. I was told to follow your instructions and that's what I'm doing."

There was a pause. Larison said, "Is your navigation system up?"

"Yes."

"Head west again. You see the high school at Washington Boulevard and McKinley?"

Ben dragged the phone's touch screen to the right. "I see it."

"The parking lot behind it?"

"Yes."

"Turn into the parking lot from Madison and circle around it."

"All right."

Ben drove and the Toyota stayed with him. Even if he'd known who was behind him, and he didn't, he wouldn't have liked the idea of the parking lot. There was no way to know where Larison might be waiting inside or along the way, and the man seemed to have a penchant for high-caliber, armor-piercing ammunition. Overall, though, Ben judged it unlikely that Larison would try to greet him with a bullet. He'd want to first confirm that the courier actually had the diamonds. It was post-confirmation when things were maximally likely to become unpleasant.

As for the occupants of the Toyota, of course, that was a little harder to say. He patted the Glock in the shoulder holster and drove.

He headed south on Madison and turned into the parking lot per Larison's instructions. The lot was a rectangle, bordered by a chain-link fence, with the entrance and exit on one of the short sides. It had four rows—two along each of the long sides and two up the middle—and might have held fifty cars full, though there were only a half dozen at the moment. Ben drove along, the Glock in his hand now, his head swiveling, scanning for Larison. The Toyota pulled in behind him.

He passed a white pickup parked to his right. No occupants. He checked left. Right. Forward. Nothing. He checked the rearview—

Larison, in jeans and a windbreaker and a baseball cap, popping up from the bed of the pickup like a deadly jack-in-the-box—

Shit, shit, shit—

Pointing a pistol at the Toyota, two-handed grip—

Ben's head snapped left, snapped right, looking for a way to turn, trying to determine whether, how to engage—

Bam! Bam!

He checked the rearview. Damn it, whatever he was going to do, he was already too late. Larison had put two rounds through the windshield. The Toyota veered to the right and crashed through the chain-link fence into a tree. Larison dashed up behind it, the gun up at chin level. A shot came from inside the car, blowing out the driver-side window. But the guy must have been aiming over his shoulder and the shot went wild. Larison fired again, came closer, and fired twice more.

It was like Costa Rica again. Every reflex, every self-preservation instinct Ben had was screaming, *Get out of the car, engage.* But he couldn't. Larison's dead-man trigger was protecting him like a bulletproof vest.

Ben peeled around the far end of the lot, his tires screeching, and got the car pointed north, toward Larison, keeping one of the parked cars between them. He reached across and opened the passenger-side door. If Larison tried to circle behind him the way Ben had seen him do to so many deceased-immediately-thereafter people already, Ben would be out the passenger side and laying down fire in a heartbeat.

But Larison didn't try to maneuver. Keeping his gun on Ben, he walked calmly over and went around the front of the car. Ben tracked him with the Glock, his finger firm against the trigger, but didn't fire.

Larison leaned over and looked into the open passenger-side door. He was carrying an HK, Ben noted. The Mark 23. Forty-five caliber, maybe the same he'd used in Costa Rica. Up close, Ben could see dark circles under his eyes.

"Hand over the gun," Larison said, pointing the HK at Ben.

Ben had known men in his professional life who naturally radiated quiet danger. It was nothing they said, and nothing they did, at least not overtly. You could just feel it about them, that they were capable, competent killers. It's what Taibbi had been talking about, with those soldiers he'd mentioned. Ben had thought the guy was being melodramatic when he called Larison the angel of death. But he got it now. The man just exuded lethality, a kind of uncomplicated readiness to kill. Combined with everything Hort had told him and everything he'd seen, it was intimidating. So it took a certain level of discipline and determination for him to respond as he did.

"Sorry, that's not going to happen."

Larison didn't respond. He just looked at Ben, his eyes

as flat and emotionless as mirrored sunglasses. Ben had never been faced with this much immediate danger while simultaneously being prohibited from engaging it. All his instincts were screaming, *Shoot! Shoot!* He gritted his teeth and his hand shook.

Larison squinted slightly. "You were the one in Los Yoses, weren't you?"

Ben nodded.

"Why didn't you take the shot?"

"Same reason I'm not taking it now. The diamonds are in that backpack. Just take it and go."

Larison looked down at the bag. Then he got in the car and pulled the door shut. "Drive."

Ben thought, *What the hell?*

They sat there, mirror images, each pointing a pistol at the other.

Another few seconds, and Ben would either have to shoot the guy or leap out of the car and bolt for cover. What he couldn't do was endure the tension of neither.

"You want me to drive?" he said. "Holster that fucking HK and wedge your hands palms down under your thighs. Deep under."

"You're not paying proper attention."

"No, *you're* not paying proper attention," Ben said, struggling to ignore the *Shoot! Shoot!* alarms screaming in his mind. "You know I'm not going to kill you. If I'd wanted to, I could have in Los Yoses. Or again just now. But there's nothing preventing you from trying to kill me. Except this gun. Which is why I'll be holding on to it and you'll be putting yours away. Otherwise, we can just sit here until the police show up to investigate reports of gunshots. Or you can take the diamonds and go. It's your call."

There was a long, tense pause. Larison swiveled and looked through the rear window. He did the same to his right. Then he slid the HK inside his windbreaker. He looked at Ben, and Ben could swear the man was sup- pressing a smile.

"Drive," he said.

Larison hadn't sat on his hands, but Ben hadn't really been expecting that much and decided he could live without it. The truth was, he wasn't much more eager to be sitting there when the police showed up than he imagined Larison would be. He switched the Glock to his left hand and hit the gas. If Larison lunged at him, he could grapple with his right and shoot with his left.

"Where are we going?" Ben said.

"Get on Lee Highway. Head west."

That made sense. Not a neighborhood street where they would stand out; not an Interstate where suspects in a shooting might expect to be fleeing. Just enough traffic for them to blend while they drifted in the direction of the Beltway, and from there, to anywhere.

"You can have the car if you want," Ben said, check- ing the rearview, making sure no one was behind them. "You really need me driving you?"

"I need you to confirm you have what you're sup- posed to have."

"The diamonds are in that backpack, right at your feet. You can see for yourself."

"I'll let you take care of that."

Ben got it. Larison was afraid of a nerve spray or a dye pack. He didn't want to open the backpack himself. Smart. He looked at his phone and saw it had no signal. Larison must have been carrying a jammer, something that would take out the phone, GPS, and anything else anyone might have used to track the car. Again, smart.

They got on Lee Highway and headed west. Ben was paying the bare minimum of attention to driving. Most of his concentration was on Larison, whose hands had been resting on his knees since Ben had driven off. He knew what Ben would make of it if his hands went anywhere else, or if Larison made any sudden movement at all, for that matter. The good news was, that meant if he *did* move, Ben wouldn't have to waste any time trying to interpret his intentions. The bad news was, Ben had seen how fast the man was. And if he made a move, Ben would have the action/reaction disadvantage. And Ben would be shooting left-handed.

One piece of good news, three bad. It would have been a lot easier to just shoot the guy and be done with it. Orders were a bitch.

Larison said, "How long have you been in?"

Ben glanced at him, trying to judge whether it was just a distraction. He decided the hell with it. If he didn't talk to the guy, he was going to shoot him. He had to do something, or the tension was going to make him explode.

"The unit?"

"Yeah."

"Six years."

"You like it?"

"Yeah, I like it."

"Why?"

Ben shrugged. "I'm good at it."

"I can see that. You think that's enough?"

"It has been so far."

"Yeah, it was good enough so far for me, too."

"What happened, then? Hort said you were the best."

Larison smiled slightly. "Did he?"

It was amazing. Even over Larison, even after everything that had happened, Hort just had that power. "Yeah. It's part of what made him suspect you. He said no one else could have pulled this off—taking the tapes, faking your death, all of it."

Larison's smile faded. For a moment, he looked almost wistful. "I don't know about the best. But I was up there."

"Still are, from what I can see."

"Thanks."

"Not sure it's a compliment, given what I've seen you do with it."

"You talking about Los Yoses?"

"Yeah."

"What do you think they were going to do to me?"

"Well, it's not like you've given people a lot of choices."

Larison glanced left, then right, then behind. "People always have choices. They say they don't to enable themselves to do what they wanted to do anyway."

"You sound like Hort."

"Hort said that?"

"Something like that."

"Well, maybe he's learning from his mistakes, too."

"What do you mean?"

"Nothing."

"How'd you do it, anyway? I saw them hit you with the tranq."

"Opioid antagonist."

"Nicely done." He couldn't deny it.

Larison nodded. "You know who they were?"

"Blackwater, supposedly."

"Contractors? For me? Who sent them?"

"The Agency, from what I hear."

"Shit, I thought they'd at least care enough to send the best."

Ben laughed, and Larison joined him. It was bizarre, but there they were, driving along, possibly on the brink of gunplay, cracking up.

"There were two more," Ben said, when the laughter had faded. "After you left."

"Who?"

"Ground Branch, supposedly. But I don't think they were there for you. They were setting up for a hit—on an FBI agent who's been investigating this thing, or on me, or on both of us. I didn't have time to clarify all the details."

"Yeah, the Agency wouldn't want anyone else to get the tapes. You dropped them?"

"Yeah."

"Good for you."

They drove in silence for a minute. Ben said, "You miss it?"

"The unit?"

"Yeah."

"Why would I miss being lied to and used and manipulated? And set up and discarded, when they were through with me?"

"So you miss it."

They both laughed again.

Ben said, "Why'd you do it?"

"Take the tapes?"

"And everything else."

"Long story."

"Well, we're just driving along. Shooting the shit."

Larison chuckled. "I saw what they were going to do to me. I did it to them first."

"Sound tactics."

"I wish there'd been another way. But they didn't give me a choice."

"You said people always have choices."

Larison checked the surroundings again. Ben had been doing the same. Normal traffic, no apparent tails.

"I guess I did. All right, maybe it was my fault. Maybe I was the one who foreclosed all the choices. Maybe I was stupid along the way to get in that position, to get in so deep I couldn't find my way back, only out."

Ben wanted to ask more, but Larison seemed to be getting agitated, and generally speaking, Ben preferred not to agitate proven deadly people carrying HKs in the passenger seat next to him.

"You want to know something?" Larison said. "I like you. You remind me of me. When I was young and stupid."

"I don't know, man. You're the one who's got the whole U.S. government for an enemy now. How smart is that?"

"You think Uncle Sam's your friend, is that it? You think your loyalty is a two-way street?"

Ben thought about Obsidian, about what Hort had done. "Not exactly, but—"

"You don't even know what this is about, do you?"

"What, the tapes?"

"It's what's on the tapes."

"You mean the interrogations. Torture."

Larison shook his head. "Hort hasn't told you, then. No, of course he hasn't. Likes to keep people in the dark. 'Need to know' and all that."

"Hasn't told me what?"

"You really want to know?"

"I don't even know what you're talking about."

"Because only a few people in the world know. And you've seen what they're willing to do to prevent anyone else from finding out. You really want that knowledge? You really want people suspecting you have it?"

It was weird. Not so long ago, he honestly wouldn't have cared. He might even have thought Larison was trying to distract him with irrelevancies.

But now . . . he did want to know. He wanted to know what all these people had died for.

"Tell me," he said.

"All right. But tell me something first."

"If I can."

"How'd you track me to Costa Rica?"

Ben hesitated. And decided he couldn't imagine Larison retaliating against Marcy, or doing anything else that would hurt his own son.

"Your wife. Or ex-wife. She suspected you were having an affair. Hired a private investigator."

Larison was silent for a long moment. Then he said, "I'll be damned. Marcy . . . I never saw that coming.

You know, you look everywhere for the possible threat, and you miss the one right under your nose. Damn. So that's it. Those two guys in San Jose—"

"Working for the PI."

"I checked them out after the fact. They had records. So I figured it was just random street crime."

Ben nodded. "It made sense. You had no way of knowing."

"Well, you figured it out. What, did you interview Marcy?"

"I did."

"And she put you in touch with the PI . . ."

"Right."

They were quiet for a moment, and Ben knew Larison was reviewing everything, analyzing events through clarified hindsight, piecing it all together, understanding step-by-step how Ben had gotten to him.

"Marcy," he said, shaking his head. "Should've seen that coming."

Ben didn't like the direction that comment might lead in. "If you think about it, it actually worked out pretty well."

"How?"

"If the government didn't have something on you, they wouldn't have trusted you with the money. They would have just kept coming at you until they got you or killed you or the tapes were released. But the way it is, now that they know about your . . . connection in Costa Rica, Hort was able to persuade them. He called it mutual assured destruction."

There was a pause. Larison said, "Hort has a point. As usual."

"Don't you even want to know how your wife is? And your son?"

"He's not my son."

"So then . . . so your wife . . ."

"You mean, did she know about me?"

"Yeah."

"I don't know. I would have said no. But I also would have said no if you'd asked if she might have hired a PI to follow me."

"I'm sorry, man."

"Don't be. I can't blame Marcy. I was living a lie, and she was bearing the brunt of it. In the end, we're all only human."

Ben nodded, reassessing what he thought he'd known, wondering about Marcy.

"All right, I told you. Now you tell me. What's this all about?"

There was a long pause. Larison said, "The Caspers."

"Caspers?"

"Ask Hort. Ask him about Ecologia."

"What does—"

"And if Hort won't tell you, ask David Ulrich."

"Who?"

"The former vice president's chief of staff. According to *U.S. News & World Report*, 'The Most Powerful Man You've Never Heard Of.' Or 'The Hidden Power,' is how the *New Yorker* put it. Currently a K Street lobbyist, naturally. He knows even more than Hort. He knows everything. And hasn't suffered from any of it. I was going to make him suffer. But now my hands are tied."

"The Caspers. Ecologia."

"Yes. That's what's really going on here. That's what's really got everybody's panties in a wad."

"I don't know what those things are. You're not telling me anything."

"I'm giving you the tools to find out. Who do you think you're really working for? King and country, or just the king?"

"What does—"

"You have to be careful now. What do you think will

happen after you've done what they asked of you, and they decide you're some kind of threat?"

"I'm not a threat."

"Maybe not before, but you are now. Because of what I told you. Just wanting information makes you a threat. You want to know how they'll hang you out to dry before they hang you literally? I've seen it done. I don't even know you, and I can tell you how they'll set you up before they knock you down."

Ben wanted to believe Larison was just bullshitting him, but somehow . . . it didn't feel like bullshit.

"Here," Larison said, "I'll tell you first what Hort told you about me. I'm a psycho case, right? Anger management. Combat stress. Steroid abuse. Did he tell you I'm gay?"

"He didn't."

"Then he was hoping you'd find out for yourself. Conclusions you come to yourself are more persuasive. Didn't they teach you that at the Farm?"

"I don't think he knew."

"He knew. If he didn't tell you, it's only because he knew you'd find out some other way."

"I don't see what that even has to do with it."

"No? You're going to honestly tell me it doesn't make me suspect? Alien? A freak? You need all that, if you're going to hunt someone. Hort was just providing it. Probably doesn't even think of it as deception, or even as manipulation. He's just giving you the tools you need to carry out a job. You think anyone we ever tortured and killed in the big, bad war on terror was white and Christian? It doesn't work that way. You can't do that shit to your own kind. They have to be turned into the Other first. Dehumanized. You and I . . . we're like prisoners being set against each other by the guards. If you can't see that, you're nothing but a tool."

A month earlier, Ben would have laughed at something like that, thought it was demented. But now . . .

"You said you'd tell me how they'd set me up."

"Easy. You got in a lot of fights growing up, didn't you?"

The truth is, the description was an understatement. "Maybe. What about it?"

"On the one hand, nothing. Everyone in the unit got in fights as a kid. There's a correlation between childhood fights and subsequent combat capability, that's all. But to the public? It becomes 'history of disciplinary problems and violence.'"

"I cheated on tests, too. Hopefully they won't nail me with that."

"You been in any fights lately? Bar brawls, anything like that?"

Ben didn't answer. But with Manila so fresh in his mind, he knew his silence was answer enough.

"Yeah, I thought so. Now you have 'anger management issues.' 'Inability to control violent temper.' I'm guessing you're divorced, am I right?"

Again, Ben didn't answer.

"That would be 'inability to form lasting social bonds.' Likewise if you're at all estranged from any kids you have. And if you ever really uncorked and got in trouble with local law enforcement, they'll use that to crucify you. They love to mention when someone's been arrested. Who needs a conviction? An arrest is just as good."

Ben tried telling himself it was like a fortune-teller's trick, that these things applied to everyone, that Larison could have done the same with anybody. But he didn't believe it. He thought of Manila . . . of Ami, of the jail. He'd never imagined how those things could be woven into a narrative by someone else. And was the narrative even untrue?

"Ever downloaded porn? 'Deviant.' Any solitary hobbies? 'Loner.' Talked to an army shrink? 'Psychiatric patient.' Look what the brass did to Graner and the rest after Abu Ghraib. Look at what the Bureau did to that guy Steven Hatfill, or to Bruce Ivins, when they needed to convince the public they'd found the anthrax villain. You think any of those people thought they were vulnerable? You need to wake up, my friend. You need to understand the way the system works."

"You make it sound like there's some kind of conspiracy."

Larison laughed. "Conspiracy? How can there be a conspiracy when everyone is complicit?"

Ben wanted to dismiss what Larison had told him as nothing but a paranoid rant. But he couldn't. At least not until he'd learned about the Caspers. And Ecologia.

"All right," Larison said. "We're going to split up now. Find a place to pull over."

Leaving it up to Ben was smart. Larison had chosen the general direction, so he knew Ben wasn't driving him into a setup. He'd know that if he were to choose a specific spot to stop on top of it, it would make Ben twitchy.

Ben drove for a few minutes more, then saw a sign announcing National Memorial Park Cemetery. He pulled off onto an access road and went through a gated opening in a brick wall. Inside was an expanse of trees and rolling lawns that but for scores of scattered headstones could have stood in for an ordinary public park. He followed a looping drive and pulled over. They sat in the long shadows of some nearby trees, watching each other.

"Time for us to get out of the car," Larison said. "How do you want to do it?"

This was more deference than Ben had been expecting. "Why are you asking me?"

"You're not going to kill me."

"I already told you that."

"It doesn't matter what you told me. Now I know."

"How?"

"I just do. How do you want to do this?"

"I'll go first."

"Fine."

Ben eased his little finger off the barrel of the Glock and used it to open the door. He got out, stood, and transferred the gun to his right hand. He kept it trained on Larison. Other than the sound of passing cars on the nearby highway, the cemetery was silent.

Larison opened the passenger-side door and stepped out, taking the backpack with him. He tossed it onto the driver's side of the hood. It landed with a dull *thunk*. They stood there, watching each other.

Larison nodded toward the bag. "Open it."

Ben unzipped the bag. He couldn't resist a peek. Just a bunch of whitish, yellowish stones, really. Hard to believe it was worth a hundred million. And everything else it had cost.

He turned the bag toward Larison and held it open. "Okay?"

Larison nodded. "Zip it up again."

Ben did. He slid it across the hood. Larison picked it up and put it on the passenger seat.

"We're done?" Ben said.

Larison closed the door. "Unless you want me to drop you off somewhere."

"No offense, but I think I'd rather walk."

Larison laughed. "No offense taken."

Larison walked around the front of the car. Ben took a step back. He didn't think Larison had any intention of trying to disarm him, but why take a chance.

Larison stood by the open driver side. He held the door, and for a second, he seemed unsteady.

"You all right?" Ben said. "You look . . . tired."

Larison blinked. "I don't sleep well."

They were silent for a moment. Larison looked back

at the road they'd come in on. "You don't have to worry about them suborning you," he said. "They get you to suborn yourself."

"I'm not following you."

Larison held out his hand. "Let's hope you don't."

Ben hesitated, then transferred the Glock to his left. They shook.

Larison got in the car. He looked off into the distance at something Ben couldn't see.

"That sound," he said, shaking his head. "You can't imagine. Don't let them do that to you."

He squeezed the bridge of his nose and sighed. "God, I wish I could sleep."

He blew out a long breath, put the car in gear, and drove off.

Ben stood in the shadows of the swaying trees after Larison was gone. He thought, *Caspers.* Then, *Ecologia.*

He clicked on the phone and saw he had reception again. No doubt, Larison had been carrying a jammer. He brought up a map and found a Metro station—West Falls Church—less than a two-mile walk from where he stood.

He thought, *Ulrich.*

It was still early. And K Street wasn't far.

36 THINK IT OVER

Larison drove east into Arlington, where he parked the car in a strip mall and transferred the diamonds into a nylon bag. There was an envelope inside. He hadn't noticed it at the cemetery. He held it up to the dome light, saw nothing untoward, and opened it. It was from Hort. A phone number. And a message telling him to call. There was something he needed to know.

He frowned at the note for a long moment, then pocketed it. He waved a portable metal detector over the diamonds and got no reading. Okay, no tracking device in a fake stone. In a few days, maybe a week, he'd visit a jewelry store with some samples and confirm that he'd received what he'd bargained for. And God help them if he hadn't.

He hooked up the jammer to an external battery and left it in the car's glove compartment. If the car had a transmitter, it would be out of commission for at least another six hours. By then, Larison would be long gone.

He bought a backpack in a sporting goods store and put the nylon bag of diamonds inside it. He used the satellite phone to reset the dead-man trigger on the tapes. Then he found a bus stop and waited, his head down, his baseball cap pulled low.

He supposed he should have felt happy, or at least relieved. But he didn't. He'd always intended to release the tapes after he'd received the diamonds. And now he couldn't. He'd been exposed, and Nico was at risk. Yes, as long as the tapes were out there, Nico would be safe. And he'd gotten the money. But he'd also been neutralized. There wouldn't be any justice. And more than anything else, he'd wanted this thing to end with justice.

He tried to focus on what was in the backpack. At least there was that.

He took out the letter from Hort and looked at it again. He didn't need to call. What could Hort tell him, anyway?

But what the hell, there wasn't any downside. They couldn't trace the sat call. And maybe he would learn something useful, not from anything Hort intentionally told him, of course, but by reading between the lines.

He keyed in the number. Hort picked up immediately. "Horton."

Larison waited a moment. It was strange to be talking to him again, just the two of them, the way it had been so many times in the past. It felt like an impossibly long time ago.

"Why'd you want me to call you?"

There was a pause. Hort said, "I was expecting to hear from the courier first."

"The courier is fine. He's good. I hope you'll treat him better than you treated me."

There was another pause. Hort said, "You're not going to like what I'm about to tell you. But bear with me. It gets better as it goes along."

Larison felt his scalp prickle. He said nothing.

"I figured your next stop would be a jewelry store somewhere. I wanted to let you know before you got there that the 'diamonds' you're carrying are fake. They're plastic. Hold a hot flame, like a butane torch, to any of them. Or hit one hard with a hammer. You'll see."

Larison felt an icy rage begin to spread out from his

chest. It crept down his stomach and up his neck. A red haze misted his vision.

"You just made the biggest fucking mistake of your life," he said, his voice near a whisper.

"Hear me out now. There's good news, too."

"Yeah, the good news is, I'm going to listen to you scream before I let you die."

But he hadn't hung up, and he knew how Hort would read that. Well, let him. It wouldn't change the way this thing was going to end.

"Instead of the diamonds, I'm offering you a million dollars—diamonds, currency, gold, whatever you want."

"Forget it."

"On top of which, my protection and another million a year if you come back to work with me."

A bus pulled up. Two people got off. The doors closed and it pulled away.

"What are you talking about?"

"Think about it. You could never have spent that money anyway. Most of what you were going to spend would have been for security. If you're working with me, you won't need that, you'll already have it."

"In exchange for what, exactly?"

"Peace of mind, ultimately."

Larison laughed harshly. "You're offering me peace of mind. That's funny."

"I know what you planned to do with those tapes after you got the diamonds. Well, you can't now that Nico's exposed. But it was the wrong way to go about it anyway."

"What do you mean?"

"You want people to pay for what happened to you? We'll make them pay."

"I want you to pay!"

"I already have, son. I have the same nightmares you do."

"You weren't there. You didn't do it. You don't live with that fucking sound in your ears."

"I live with all kinds of things. It's the others that don't. Well, I want them to pay, too. And there's something more."

"What?"

"You need to be on the inside, son. You can't cut loose, not after the things you've done. You've tried nihilism. And it's been caustic to your soul, I know."

Larison squeezed his eyes shut. He felt like his head was being crushed in a vise. "I can't. I can't take this anymore."

"We'll get you help. The best help there is. Between the money and what's on those tapes, we can change some things that should have been changed a long time ago."

Larison opened his eyes and breathed through his mouth. He felt sick. He'd been such an idiot, thinking he could get free. An idiot.

"The million is yours no matter what. You earned it. You paid for it. Tell me how to get it to you and it's done. If you want the rest—the million a year, the protection, the power to set some wrong things right—we need to talk more."

Idiot. Fucking idiot. You could have killed him. You could have—

"Think it over. Take your time."

—killed him, you—

His stomach clenched. He clicked off the phone, leaned over, and convulsively threw up onto the curb. He gasped, his back heaving, then gagged and threw up again.

You could have killed him.

He stood there for a moment sucking wind, his hands on his knees, his eyes and nose streaming.

And not just Hort. He could have killed Marcy, too. Why hadn't he? What stupid, pathetic sentiment had permitted him to be so fatally, disgustingly stupid? He told himself he would never make a mistake like that again, and even as he thought it he knew how meaningless the vow was now, how hollow.

When he felt a little steadier, he looked around. There was a gas station across the street. He walked over and found a guy in blue coveralls in the garage.

"I need to borrow a hammer," Larison said, his voice ragged.

He could tell the guy wanted to refuse, and was almost glad for it. He looked at the guy, struggling to control his rage, wanting someone to vent it on. The guy figured out refusing would be a bad idea. He leaned over and pulled a large orange dead blow hammer off the floor. He handed it to Larison. "This is all I've got," he said.

Larison hefted it. It weighed about four pounds. He imagined the damage it would do to a man's skull. He said, "I'll be right back."

He walked around to the side of the building, took a diamond out of the bag, and set it on the concrete sidewalk. He put the bag down, lowered his stance, and gripped the hammer. He looked at the diamond for a moment. It was meaningless, inert.

He raised the hammer over his head and smashed it down. The diamond—the plastic—exploded beneath it. Shards flew in a thousand different directions.

He pulled another from the pack and smashed it with the hammer. It exploded exactly like the first. He did it again. And again. He attacked the bag with the hammer, blasting it, savaging it, beating it the way he wanted to beat Hort's brains.

He realized he was screaming. He stopped and looked up. The gas station guy was looking at him from around the corner, appalled and afraid and frozen to the spot.

Grimacing, his breath snorting through his nose, Larison stalked over to him, the hammer dangling from his hand like a war club. The guy's eyes widened and his face went pale.

Larison stopped an arm's length from the guy. He looked at him for a long moment, grinning with hate. He held out the hammer. "Thanks," he said.

The guy took it without a word or even a nod. Larison went back to the bus stop. He left the bag where he'd dropped it.

Another bus pulled up. The doors opened with a pneumatic hiss. He got on. He didn't even know where it was going.

It didn't matter. What mattered was that even through his rage and his nausea, his horror at how close he'd been and at how badly he'd blown it, he understood what he was going to do.

Accept Hort's offer.

Take the money.

And when he was ready, when he had regrouped and resettled and refocused, get to Hort. He thought the courier, the blond guy from the unit, might be the right place to start. He was good, Larison could see that much. But he saw something else, too: The guy wasn't happy. He knew he was being manipulated, and was looking for a way out. Maybe Larison could give him one.

He smiled grimly. Because when he found Hort, he would do things to him, do everything to him, until he made the sound Larison could never get out of his ears.

This time, it would be like music.

37 A DRINK

Ulrich's secure line buzzed. He looked at the phone, wondering if it would be better to just not answer. It was never good news. Never.

Still.

"Ulrich."

"Clements. Okay to talk?"

"Why do you always ask me that? Yes, it's okay. It's always okay. This is a fucking secure line, do you not know that?"

There was a pause. "Are you watching CNN?"

"No."

"There was a shooting in Arlington. Two dead."

Ulrich clenched his jaw. "Theirs or ours?"

"Ours."

Ulrich didn't say anything. He felt numb. The numbness wasn't unpleasant. At the moment, he much preferred it to whatever sensation it must have been blocking.

"We can still turn this around," Clements said.

Ulrich laughed. It started slowly and built to a cackle. He thought of these idiots, blundering about, thinking they had a clue, relentlessly ruining his life. It wouldn't last, he knew, but for now, he relished the humor element in the whole thing.

"You want to know how you can tell when a war is lost?" he said, wiping his eyes. "When people describe it as 'still winnable.' Well, that's what I've been doing with myself all along on this. I keep telling myself it's still winnable. But it's not. It's just not. There are too many idiots. I can't keep fighting them. I can't keep fighting you."

He set the phone back in the cradle and put his face in his hands. He laughed again. And then he was crying.

People wouldn't understand. He'd worked so hard to keep the country safe. Yes, he'd authorized some difficult things, some questionable things. But what looked questionable now didn't look at all that way after 9/11. Back then, no one was questioning anything. They all just wanted to be safe, never mind how. So what, he was going to be hanged now for refusing to let a bunch of rules and procedures and bureaucracy prevent him from keeping people safe? What was the alternative? Dot his *I*'s and dash his *T*'s and just let the next attack happen? That would have been the real crime.

He blew out a long breath. It didn't matter. He'd known the risks, hadn't he? He'd never been in the military, but he'd performed his own kind of service. Soldiers risked life and limb defending America. He'd risked his job, his reputation, his own freedom in the same cause. How many people could make that claim? No matter what happened, he had every reason to be proud of what he'd done. And his family did, too. Even if no one else could understand, they would.

He thought about getting a drink. It was a simple thing, really, a man stopping by a bar on the way home from work. He wished he'd done it more often.

He really ought to do it now. It might be a nice memory later.

38 PROPERTY OF THE U.S. GOVERNMENT

On the platform at the West Falls Church Metro station, Ben used the iPhone to find Ulrich's particulars. The former vice presidential chief of staff was now a "special policy adviser" for a lobbying outfit called Daschle, Davis, Baishun, one of the K Street giants, just as Larison had said. An Orange Line train would take him to Farragut West Station, a few blocks from Daschle, Davis's headquarters.

On the ride in, Ben considered a number of stratagems for getting into Ulrich's office. A back entrance, the roof, an elevator shaft, a maintenance stairwell. Or, having seen Ulrich's picture on his firm's website, just set up and wait for him in the parking garage under the building. Or outside the front door, if he used the Metro. But any of those would require reconnaissance, and reconnaissance required time. He didn't want to wait. He wanted knowledge. And he wanted it tonight.

Besides, he thought he had a better way.

When he emerged aboveground from Farragut West Station, it was dark. Commuters flowed past him down the station escalators, car headlights illuminated the street. The air was warm and soggy and smelled like Washington, a city built on a swamp. He walked a block north to K Street and found the Daschle, Davis building, an expensive-looking glass-and-chrome square dominating the entire block.

He went through the revolving doors, and instantly the sounds of outside traffic were erased, replaced by a quiet hush and cool, dry air. The expansive lobby mirrored the exterior—glass, chrome, a polished granite floor. A rent-a-security-guard, a black guy in a blue uniform, sat behind a station in front of the elevators. Ben walked over, his footfalls echoing in the cavernous silence.

"I'm here to see David Ulrich."

"Do you have an appointment?"

"I don't."

"Who should I tell him is here?"

Ben could almost have smiled. He took out his credentials and set them in front of the guard. "Dan Froomkin. FBI."

The guard picked up a phone. Explained who was here. Paused. Said, *Yes, sir. Yes, sir, I have.* Hung up the phone. Gestured to a sign-in sheet on the stand in front of him.

"Just need you to sign in, Mr. Froomkin."

This time, Ben did smile. "Happy to," he said.

He rode the elevator to the fourth floor and took the stairs from there. He didn't consider Ulrich a threat, but using the unexpected route was a habit that had always served him well before. He mentally patted himself on the back for thinking to arrive as Froomkin. He might have dropped Hort's name, or mentioned JSOC, but he expected that if Ulrich met him under a pretext like that, he would have come down to the lobby and kept Ben away from his inner sanctum. A possible interview by the FBI, though, was something you'd want conducted in private. And privacy was a funny thing. The same kind of space that could make a person feel confident could also make him feel exposed and vulnerable. Another kernel of wisdom from the Farm.

A smiling, pantsuited receptionist led him down a hushed, thickly carpeted hallway past a series of closed mahogany doors. Discretion, the place seemed to say. Quiet influence. Compartmentalization.

At the end of the hallway was a single open door. The receptionist gestured to it and went back the way they'd come. Ben went inside and closed the door behind him.

Ulrich was sitting behind a dark, massive desk. All these guys, compensating with their furniture. To the side was an ego wall covered by photos of Ulrich with the former vice president and various other political luminaries and insiders.

Ulrich set down a pen and stood, a big man, maybe a former linebacker now going to seed. "Agent Froomkin," he said, looking up, "what can I—"

He saw Ben's face and his mouth dropped open. Ben thought, *You know me. Son of a bitch.*

Ben understood Ulrich's move an instant before Ulrich did, and shot forward just as Ulrich lunged for the phone. Ben leaped onto the massive desk and kicked him in the face. Ulrich went flying backward. The phone clattered to the desk. Ulrich bounced off the wall behind him, blood flowing from his nose, and somehow managed to snatch the handset off the desk. He raised it to his ear and Ben stomped the receiver. Shards of plastic exploded under his heel. Ulrich looked at the receiver as though in disbelief that it had just been rendered useless, then drew his arm back to throw it at Ben. Ben eliminated that possibility by jumping down from the desk directly in front of him. Ulrich dropped the receiver and turned to run the other way. Ben grabbed him by a wrist and the back of his neck and slammed his face into the desk. He twisted his arm up behind his back and Ulrich cried out.

"Go ahead and scream," Ben said. "Get security up here. Get the cops. First thing I'll tell them, the first thing my lawyer will talk about in the press conference he calls, is the Caspers. And Ecologia."

He felt Ulrich freeze up at just the mention of the words. Whatever the Caspers and Ecologia were, Larison hadn't been bullshitting him.

Ben pulled Ulrich from the desk and shoved him into his chair. Ulrich wiped blood from his face and stared at his hand as though he couldn't believe what he was seeing. "What do you want?" he said.

"I want to know how you recognized me."

"I mean, why are you here?"

Ben realized Ulrich was too smart, and too tough, to answer questions based on assumptions. He tried to imagine the situation from Ulrich's perspective. Ulrich thinks the FBI is calling on him. Either he's confused by that or, more likely, scared. Then a guy shows up who Ulrich recognizes is definitely *not* FBI because Ulrich already knows him as something else. Something else that freaks Ulrich out enough for him to try to call security without saying another word. He hadn't gotten confused when he saw Ben. He'd gotten scared shitless. Why?

Because he recognized you as JSOC. Because he assumed you were here to kill him. And then he realized you weren't—because he's still alive, because someone who was here to kill him wouldn't have announced himself to a guard and let himself be recorded by all the security cameras in the lobby and at the front desk. Now he doesn't know what's going on. He's trying to find out.

"I've been tasked by the U.S. government with recovering some stolen property," Ben said. "And I have."

Ulrich's eyes widened. "You recovered—"

He caught himself before he could say more. But he'd already said enough.

"Yes," Ben said. "Larison's dead. I recovered the tapes. Now I want to know who I return them to."

Ulrich didn't say anything, but Ben could see the eagerness, and the calculation, in his eyes.

"You want them?" Ben asked.

"Why would you think I do?"

Ben was impressed by the man's discipline. But he'd already slipped, and Ben wasn't going to allow him to recover.

"My mistake," Ben said. He turned and started to walk to the door. "I'll give them to the Justice Department."

"Wait."

Ben turned and looked at him.

"I'm not saying I'm interested. But . . . what are you asking for?"

Ben waited a moment to let him sweat. "You can start by telling me how you recognized me."

Ulrich licked blood from his lips. "I've seen your picture."

"How?"

"Your file."

"Bullshit. There's no photo associated with my file."

Ulrich licked his lips again. "All right, look. I can see there was a mix-up here—"

"Just tell me the truth. Or I'll know I can't trust you with the tapes."

"Okay, okay. The CIA's been trying to get those tapes back. They—"

"The CIA might have a photo of me. Or maybe they could get one. But that doesn't tell me what you matched it to."

Ulrich didn't answer. Ben didn't give him time to think of another lie. He turned and walked toward the door.

"Lanier! Paula Lanier. She took the picture. While you were sleeping, on the way to Costa Rica."

Ben stopped and turned. He tried to make sense of it, but couldn't. "What?"

"She works for me, all right? Or she did, when I represented the vice president's office. Now I'm more of an asset for her because of my connections. Or, she's my asset. Sometimes it gets hard to tell."

"I don't understand."

"I knew the FBI was going to be involved in this thing, okay? I knew as soon as it broke, and I needed someone I could trust. So I pulled some strings and had Lanier assigned. She's been reporting developments to me. Including the involvement of a mysterious operative who wouldn't even acknowledge his affiliations."

"Who sent those contractors to Costa Rica? Who sent the two Ground Branch guys?"

"That was a CIA op."

"But you knew about it."

"In case you haven't noticed, I make it a habit to know about everything."

Ben thought. Someone had followed him from the airport that afternoon. The only person outside of Hort who knew he'd been selected as the courier was Paula. He could have kicked himself for his stupidity, for letting his guard down. She'd played him. And he'd fallen for it.

"What about the two guys who followed me from National today?"

"Ground Branch again."

"Who the hell's running the CIA? You?"

"It's not a question of who's running it. People have common interests. We work together."

"And your common interest on the tapes is the Caspers."

"That's everybody's common interest. Every American's, anyway."

"What are they?"

"Why are you asking me? You work for Horton, right? He knows as much as I do. Christ, he was responsible for their orderly disposition."

Ben was surprised but didn't show it. "I'll ask him when I'm ready to ask him. I'm asking you now."

Ulrich looked at him. "What do you think is on those tapes?"

Ben shrugged. "Waterboarding. Torture."

Ulrich laughed. "Waterboarding and torture aren't even news anymore. Over half the country supports torture, didn't you know? And over sixty percent of Evangelicals."

"Video would be different."

"Well, that's probably true. Seeing what American soldiers and spies had to resort to in the war on terror would have been painful. It would have damaged our self-image as a country, weakened our will to do what needs to be done. But the Caspers were the real problem. Asking the country to accept what we had to do about them . . . that would have been too much. People wouldn't be able to understand. And they shouldn't be forced to."

"What are you talking about?"

"You'll give me the tapes?"

"For the truth."

Ulrich nodded. "You know about the ghost detainees, don't you?"

Ben thought about what he'd heard. "Rumors. Detainees the CIA was holding without acknowledging their capture or detention. Shuttling them through Abu Ghraib and Bagram and Guantánamo and the rest so the Red Cross couldn't verify their existence, or keeping them at the black sites. That's what the Caspers were?"

Ulrich wiped blood from his mouth, then regarded his hand. "If you want to keep secret prisoners, you have to build secret prisons. After 9/11, we tasked the CIA with doing exactly that. And then we populated what they built."

"With the Caspers."

"Among others. Now, the way you hear about it in the media today, you'd think all the people we picked up in the war on terror were innocent. Because once the

Supreme Court decided terror detainees had the right to petition for habeas corpus, we had to start letting a lot of them go."

Ben thought of the Manila city jail. "Well, if you couldn't prove they'd done anything—"

"Just because we couldn't prove it in a court of law didn't mean it wasn't so. And look, okay, maybe some of them were innocent. Unfortunate, but unavoidable. But now they have a grudge. Meaning, even if they weren't dangerous before, they are now. You want to be the one who lets one of these guys go and then have him slaughter more Americans? You're JSOC, not the ACLU, I thought you'd get this. It's why I'm telling you."

Ben didn't answer. Not so much earlier, he would have gotten it. But now, hearing it out loud, he wasn't sure.

"So you captured these ghosts. What's the problem?"

"The problem is, the way they were interrogated might have offended the sensibilities of the armchair quarterbacks who've already forgotten 9/11."

"You waterboarded them?"

Ulrich tugged on his beard. "At first."

Ben had been waterboarded during his SERE—survival, evasion, resistance, escape—training. He'd consented to it, the people who'd done it had been his own instructors, he'd been provided with a safe word and a tennis ball he could just drop at any time to stop the whole thing, and it had only been once—and still it was one of the most unpleasant things that had ever been done to him, instantly stripping away his will and replacing it with paralyzing, childlike terror. He'd held out for fourteen seconds, which made him practically the class champion. And the Caspers had gotten the real thing, and who knows how many times.

"What do you mean, 'at first'?"

"Let's just say that, by the end, they *wished* they were just being waterboarded."

Ben looked at him, trying to imagine what you would have to do to a man to make him long to be waterboarded, instead. He couldn't come up with anything. He said, "And the CIA videotaped it."

"You got it. There's no genius like a CIA genius. Fundamentally, they created a whole line of government snuff films."

Ben imagined a bunch of guys watching God knows what through a viewfinder, recording it, watching it again later on a screen in a dark room. Rewinding it. Pausing. He thought of what Hort had said, about how torture is always about something else. He felt sick.

"And you're worried that if the public ever sees the videos, they're not just going to go after the people who filmed and starred in them, they're going to go after the producers, too."

Ulrich looked at him. "If I were you, I'd be a little more concerned about Muslim audiences on this than I would be with domestic ones."

"Yeah, I get that. But you're not me."

Ulrich didn't answer.

Something was tickling at Ben's mind. There were a lot of things you knew when you were in the unit, or at least that you'd hear about. But the Caspers . . . not a word. How had they covered it up so completely?

"What did you do with them?" he said. "The Caspers. When you were done with them. Done filming."

Ulrich didn't answer.

Ben said, "Tell me you didn't."

"Look, these were genuinely dangerous men—"

"Oh, man—"

"—who couldn't just be released. But they couldn't be tried, either, or they would have gone public with tales of torture. And besides, they'd go free in the end anyway because people would say their confessions had been coerced."

"What did you do with them?"

"They were disposed of."

"You mean, the CIA just executed them? Prisoners?"

"Not the CIA. JSOC. Your commander. Horton."

Ben blinked despite himself. "What? Why?"

"JSOC was being run out of the Office of the Vice President. The Caspers were just one of the operations your people were involved in. They were ghosts anyway—no records of their capture, movement, detention, or imprisonment. It was as though they hadn't existed. We just had to make de jure what was de facto. And now it is. They don't exist. They never did."

"Except for the tapes."

"Yes. That's why we wanted those tapes back. You ought to get a medal for recovering them."

For some reason, the thought of this guy proposing a medal, and for this, made Ben want to hit him again.

"What was Ecologia, then?"

"A company that devised an innovative way to dispose of cadavers. The Ecologia machine freeze-dries Aunt Betty in liquid nitrogen, vibrates her into dust, vacuums off the water, removes any dental or surgical metals with a magnet, and leaves you with nothing but compost. They recommend you plant a tree using Aunt Betty as the fertilizer. A memory tree, I think they call it."

"That's how you got rid of the Caspers. You killed them and then freeze-dried them."

"Actually, as I understand it, the Caspers were run through the machines alive. Drugged first. They didn't feel anything. They weren't afraid. They didn't know what was coming."

Ben shook his head. He'd been involved in some dark things, some things that crossed the line, he knew. But this . . . it was extreme.

"Are you starting to get it now?" Ulrich said. "Imagine videos worse than Abu Ghraib, worse than what's described even in the nonredacted version of the CIA inspector general's report. Videos that would have implicated our brave men and women in activities the liberal media would call murder. If those tapes had gotten out, it would have been a national security calamity."

Ben thought for a minute. He said, "Who signed off on acquiring the Ecologia units? That must have been a big purchase, right? Liquid nitrogen, high-powered vibration, and magnets . . . and there would have been training, too, right? It's not like you bought a toaster oven with an instruction booklet. This was big. Whose fingerprints are on the authorization paperwork?"

Ulrich didn't answer.

"Yeah, I thought so."

"If your point is that I'm motivated because I've got my own skin in the game—"

"That was my point. Yeah."

"—you should know that my own exposure or lack of exposure is hardly the point. The national security risk exists either way."

"Can you really tell the difference between one and the other?"

"Just give me the tapes. I'll make sure they're properly disposed of. And you might have noticed, I'm pretty well connected in Washington."

"You're kidding, right? You're a lobbyist. That's, what, one level higher on the food chain than a telemarketer?"

"I'm talking about influence. And if you don't think I have it, you're not paying attention. I'd say you deserve a promotion for what you've done. The posting of your choice. Maybe an assignment to the National Security Council, how would that be? The national security adviser is a personal friend. You'd have his ear, you could see how policy is really made. From the inside."

Ben looked at Ulrich's ego wall. His urge to hit the guy

had evaporated, leaving behind a sediment of dull nausea and a nameless feeling of being somehow . . . tainted.

"I've seen it," he said. He turned and walked toward the door.

"Wait," Ulrich said. "What about the tapes?"

Ben didn't answer. He opened the door and kept on walking.

Ulrich hurried to his side. "Then tell me what you want," he said, his voice low. "Money? The government was prepared to pay a hundred million to have those tapes back. You can have that, too."

Ben hit the down button in the elevator bank. His head hurt. He wanted to be alone.

"Just tell me what you want," Ulrich said.

A chime sounded. The elevator doors opened. Ben stepped inside.

"I'll let you know," he said.

"Wait, you can't just walk away. We're talking about the property of the U.S. government. You can't—"

The doors closed. Ben hit the button for the third floor. He'd take the stairs from there.

He considered that phrase, *property of the U.S. government*. He wondered if Ulrich intended, or even recognized, its sudden ambiguity.

39 MORE INSIDE

Ben walked through downtown D.C., feeling exhausted, adrift. This thing had seemed so straightforward at first. Why didn't it now? Nothing had really changed. There were tapes. If the tapes got out, it would be a terrorist recruitment bonanza. He'd been tasked with locating the tapes, and he'd carried out his orders. He hadn't managed a neat, final conclusion, there was no real victory to declare, but under the circumstances he'd achieved the best possible outcome, or anyway the least bad one. The information he'd uncovered had enabled Uncle Sam to avoid a checkmate in favor of a stalemate. And for purposes of keeping those tapes under wraps, a stalemate was just as good as a win.

So why did he feel so . . . empty? And unclean?

What had Larison said? *How can there be a conspiracy when everyone is complicit?*

He called Hort. One ring, then, "Where have you been?"

"Sorry. I couldn't check in earlier."

"Damn, son, don't make me hear from Larison before I hear from you. I'm old enough for that kind of shit to give me a heart attack."

"You heard from Larison?"

"I left him a note with the diamonds. I needed to tell him what you gave him wasn't the genuine article."

Ben was so surprised he shook his head as though to clear it. "What?"

"Yes, I know that's a surprise. I'll brief you on the rest when you're ready."

"They were fake? Do you know what he would have done if he'd realized?"

"I told you, I'll brief you—"

"I'm ready right now."

"Where are you?"

"Downtown D.C."

"I'm at the Pentagon. Platform, Farragut West Station? That's four stops for me, I'll be there in thirty minutes."

"I'll be waiting."

He clicked off. For some reason, beyond the obvious fact that Hort had put him in danger without warning him of it, it bugged him that Larison hadn't gotten what he was supposed to. Maybe it was a brothers-in-arms thing. Maybe it was because what Hort had done felt exactly like the kind of manipulation Larison had warned him about. He wasn't sure. All he knew was, he didn't like it.

Hort showed up on time. "Are you hungry?" he said, walking over to the wickets, where Ben was standing. "I don't know about you, but I could use a good steak."

They headed west on K Street, then north on Nineteenth, against traffic both ways. It was a small thing, but Hort had trained Ben never to give the opposition something for free, and Ben wasn't surprised he lived what he taught. After about five minutes, they arrived at a place called the Palm. White-linen-covered tables and booths, polished wood floors, cartoons of the celebrities who'd eaten there plastered on the walls. Seated maybe a hundred people and looked pretty full. The manager greeted Hort as "Colonel Horton." Told him not to worry that he didn't have a reservation. Ben wondered what it was all about. Hort didn't ordinarily debrief him at places like this one. Whatever. The aroma of well-seasoned steak was suddenly incredibly inviting.

They ordered a pair of sixteen-ounce New York strips. Hort chose a bottle of wine, too, a California Cabernet from a place called Schlein Vineyard.

"I don't get it," Ben said quietly after the waiter had departed. He had to suppress his irritation. "How could you give Larison fakes? Isn't he going to find out and just release the tapes?"

"I can't guarantee that he won't. But I couldn't guarantee it the other way, either. Overall, I think we're safer if he gets his payout as an annuity instead of as a lump sum. A modified version of your proposal."

"Safer for whom? You know what he would have done if he'd figured it out while we were still together?"

"You would have handled that."

"Come on, Hort, what was it, three days ago you were telling me I wasn't at his level?"

"Yet."

"Yet. I caught up to him in three days?"

"You were supposed to be just the courier. If you'd known, it would have affected your demeanor. Larison would have spotted that. So you would have been in more danger knowing than you were in ignorance. It was a calculated risk. And from the results, I'd say it was the right one."

Ben shook his head, wanting to say more, not knowing what. It was true, it had turned out well. And it wasn't the first time he'd been sent into the shit without knowing everything he would have wanted to, or felt he was entitled to. But still, that feeling of being . . . manipulated. It was settling in more deeply.

"I guess," he said, after a moment. "But I'll tell you, having seen the guy in action twice now, I wouldn't want to piss him off unnecessarily."

"You forget. I know him."

Ben thought of that phrase Hort had used on the flight from Manila: *I know people.* At the time, he'd thought he understood. Now he realized Hort hadn't been talking about contacts, or at least not only. He was talking about people's natures. He wondered, uncomfortably, what Hort thought he knew about him. Ben could be manipulative when he needed to be—he had been with Marcy Wheeler, in fact—but it had never been second nature to him. The thought that Hort's whole approach to everyone he knew involved assessment, and maneuver, and exploitation, and the realization that Hort probably wasn't atypical in that regard, at least among a certain class of player . . . it was making him feel naïve, and concerned, and disgusted, all at the same time.

The waiter brought the wine. Hort tasted it and nodded. The waiter filled their glasses and moved off.

Hort raised his glass. "Good work."

They touched glasses and drank. Ben barely tasted the wine. What he really wanted was a hot shower. And about thirty hours of sleep. And to not think anymore.

Ben set down his glass. "I was followed from the airport."

Hort nodded. "I wondered. There was something on the news about a shooting in Arlington. You think I had something to do with that?"

Ben shook his head. "No."

"Good. Although I wouldn't blame you."

It was awkward feeling so suspicious of Hort. He supposed he needed to get used to it. "I need to ask you some questions," he said.

"I want you to. It's why I brought you here. So we could talk."

"Larison told me about the Caspers. About Ecologia."

Hort took a sip of wine. "I thought he might."

"Why didn't you tell me?"

"You needed to find out in your own way."

More manipulation, then. He was seeing a side of Hort he'd never adequately appreciated. Or that he'd been willfully blind to. "How . . . you were involved in that?"

"Yes."

Ben waited. Hort said, "In the last administration, JSOC was reporting directly to the Office of the Vice President. There was a special class of detainees the CIA had rendered out of various Asian and European countries. Highly secret. Unacknowledged. People we picked up in targeted operations, not the wholesale bullshit we used to populate Guantánamo. The vice president wanted a specialist to interrogate them. One man, to keep things compartmentalized, to have a single source who could assemble the pieces and see through the lies. I went to Larison."

"Larison tortured them."

"That's . . . what it turned into."

"That's what you meant before. When you told me not to give in to that temptation."

"That's right. And I hope you were listening."

"Did you get anything from them?"

There was a pause. Hort said, "Nothing we couldn't have gotten using the *Army Field Manual*. If we'd wanted to. But like I told you, the vice president and his crew were after more than just the results."

"And when they were done, they couldn't let them go."

"That's right. Once the original mistake was made, we were faced with a variety of unpleasant choices. The least unpleasant was the Ecologia program."

"When was this?"

"September 2006. The same time the president acknowledged the existence of the black sites and the fourteen high-value detainees being moved from the sites to Guantánamo. And there was a bonus: the administration needed some actual bad guys in Guantánamo, which the black site detainees provided."

"A distraction?"

"Misdirection. All the president was doing was announcing what was already widely known. The black sites became the story, and while public attention was focused there, Larison was quietly eliminating the Caspers, the black sites' premier occupants."

"You used Larison for it."

"To maintain the compartmentalization. Plus, I thought he was hardened at that point. Another mistake. In fact, he was suffering. But too tough to admit it."

"But . . . that means he would be on the tapes."

"I doubt he cares at this point. Or if he did, he could just have deleted or obscured his face."

Ben was as fascinated as he was appalled. What Hort was telling him had really happened. It didn't get more inside than this.

"How did it work?"

"The program?"

"Yes."

Hort shrugged. "The CIA was holding the Caspers in various secret prisons—Thailand, Romania, Lithuania, a prison within a prison at Bagram. They were identified only by a number. Larison would show up with the prisoner's number and an authorization code. And the guards would turn the prisoner over."

"Like an ATM."

"Same concept. But without records of deposits and withdrawals."

They were quiet for a moment. Something occurred to Ben. He said, "Giving Larison fakes . . . was that authorized? On the call you had me listen in on, the national security adviser was on board with giving him the real thing."

Hort smiled. "No. It wasn't authorized."

"Then who has the real diamonds?"

Hort's smile broadened. "I do."

Ben shook his head. "What are you . . . what's going on here?"

"I'll tell you what's going on. The country is facing a perfect storm of vulnerability. The previous administration turned programs like rendition and torture that had always rightly been run at a retail level into a wholesale operation, an operation that couldn't be concealed. There's a public backlash now and the new administration is having trouble containing it. Meanwhile, intel demonstrates what common sense already told us: U.S. torture has been the greatest jihadist recruitment bonanza ever invented. We need new capabilities to address the problems we've created. Unfortunately, we've lost some of the old ones. For a while, there was an off-the-books operation run by someone named Jim Hilger that had been doing the country a lot of good, but that's been wiped out."

He took a sip of wine. "I and a few others are trying to rebuild. The military is going to have an increasingly influential role in the new order of things. Two active war theaters with no end in sight, the war on terror, military commissions for terror suspects, that's all bipartisan now. The last administration wanted to use the military in domestic law enforcement, and I expect we'll see more of that, too. I want you to be part of it all."

Ben thought. The management-style questions, letting him listen in on the conference call with the national security adviser . . . this is what it was all about. He didn't know what the hell to think.

"And Larison?"

"I want Larison to be part of it, too. A highly capable man and officially dead on top of it. There's a lot he could do. And a lot you could learn from him."

Ben thought about what Larison had told him, and wondered if maybe Hort didn't know the man the way he thought he did.

"You see the pattern?" Hort said. "We take the gloves off, it works, so we do more of it. What should be a retail program goes wholesale. You get force drift, mistakes, revelations, commissions, dismantling. Now we're unprotected, our methods have made things worse, and when we're attacked again, the public will scream for protection and won't care how. And we'll repeat the whole sorry cycle again."

Ben shook his head. "I don't get what you're trying to do."

Hort nodded. "This is all new to you," he said. "I get that. I want to explain a few things about how America really works. I think then you'll understand where I'm coming from."

"Okay."

"Number one, the country is run by corporate interests. I never understand when people get all worked up about socialism. There's no socialism here. There's corporatism."

"I don't follow you."

"Okay, pop quiz. Why do we give nearly three billion dollars a year to Israel?"

"So she can defend herself."

"Wrong. It's just a way of funneling a subsidy to U.S. arms manufacturers, which is where Israel, by quiet understanding, turns around and spends the money. But no one would support it if we called it 'Raytheon aid.' 'Foreign aid' just sounds so much more aboveboard."

Ben didn't answer. Hort said, "Okay, next. Health care reform. Why?"

"So more people will have insurance."

"Wrong. By requiring more people to purchase insurance, the government creates new customers for the insurance companies and big pharma."

Ben nodded, unsure. He still didn't understand where Hort was trying to lead him.

"And the AIG bailout was a way of funneling money to Goldman Sachs, which was owed thirteen billion by AIG and would have gone under without it. Hell, the government does this for its own, too. Without bulk mail subsidies, there would be no junk mail, and the post office would have nothing to deliver. And how do you think Halliburton and all the rest have made out from Iraq and Afghanistan? Think that's just a coincidence? None of this is even new, by the way. The Marshall Plan wasn't about helping Europe. It was about creating new customers for American corporations."

He took a sip of wine. "People don't realize it, but we have corporate interests so large they have foreign policy concerns. These corporations will pay for intel. And they'll pay for action. Hilger, for all the good he was doing, was beholden to several of them. With a hundred million in start-up capital, we'll be independent."

Ben shook his head, thinking this couldn't be true. "But . . . I mean, we're not supposed to be independent, isn't that right?"

"Theoretically, yes. We're supposed to be beholden. The question is, who are we beholden to?"

"Well . . . Congress, I guess. I mean, I know they're a pain in the ass, but . . ."

"Congress? You know what the turnover rate in congressional elections is? In the neighborhood of two percent. Even the North Korean Politburo has a higher turnover rate than that. So who are we beholden to? Not the people. In a democracy, voters choose their leaders. In America, leaders choose their voters. There's no competition anymore."

"Come on, Hort, Republicans and Democrats . . . they hate each other, right? There's competition."

Hort laughed. "That's not competition. It's supposed to look that way, so people think their interests are being looked after, they have a choice, they can make a difference, they're in charge. But they don't."

"That doesn't make sense."

"I'm afraid it does. You see, there's more money to be made in cooperation than there is in competition. It's the same dynamic that leads to cartels. You can argue that the cartels should be competing. But they don't see it that way. Their profit motive enables them to rise above the urge to compete. In the service of the greater good, naturally. People who think there's actual friction, and real competition, between Democrats and Republicans, or between the press and politicians, or between the corporations and their supposed overseers, they're like primitives looking at shadows on the wall and believing the shadows are the substance."

Ben thought of Ulrich. Were he and Hort on the same team? Is that what all this talk about cooperation meant?

"I went to see Ulrich," he said. "Just now. Larison said I should."

Hort smiled, obviously pleased. "I know you did," he said. "And how was the late Mr. Ulrich?"

Ben looked at him, thinking he must have misheard. "What?"

40 THREE NUMBERS

Ulrich cleaned himself up in the restroom. Now that the shock of the encounter was wearing off, pain was beginning to manifest itself. His jaw hurt, his nose hurt, and two of his teeth were loose. He felt nauseated and shaky.

What was killing him was the way he was being whipsawed. Hope, despair, then back again . . . you could reach the point where you just wanted it to be over, never mind how.

If what Treven had told him was true, there was still a chance. Talk to Horton, make a deal of some sort. Yes, there would be concessions—painful ones, certainly. But no one wanted those tapes out. In the end, that's what would matter. He'd call Clements, brief him, coordinate. They'd come up with something.

He walked back to his office. Clements was waiting inside, standing in front of his desk, examining the shattered remnants of the phone. Ulrich jumped when he saw him. "Christ," he said. "What are you doing here? I was just going to call you."

Clements looked at him. "The door was open."

Ulrich walked in. The door closed behind him. He turned and saw two burly men in dark suits that looked like they didn't get worn very often. He noticed someone had closed the drapes.

"Is this supposed to scare me?" he said.

"Just some private security. We've been using Black-water for a lot of projects lately."

"What do you want?"

"I want the audiotapes you made."

"You can't have them."

"I need you to open your wall safe."

"Even if I were inclined to open it for you, and I'm not, and even if the tapes were in it, and they're not, it wouldn't help you. I told you, I made copies. They're with a friend. Who will release them if anything happens to me."

"The problem is, I don't believe you. Look at you, you look down your nose at everyone, Ulrich, there's no one you trust that much. And you had them handy the other day when you were on the phone, right here. Remember? You reminded me recently it was a secure line. I'm calling your bluff."

Ulrich didn't answer. The burly guys started to move in. Ulrich opened his mouth to scream for help and Clements nailed him with an uppercut to the solar plexus. Ulrich went down, wheezing.

"It wouldn't have mattered if you'd screamed," Clements said. "We've checked all the nearby offices. Everyone's gone home. We checked the soundproofing, too. It's very impressive."

The Blackwater guys dragged him over to his desk. Clements watched, flexing his fingers open and closed. "I can't tell you how long I've wanted to do that," he said. "That, and more."

They pinned him stomach-up against the desk, his feet dangling just above the floor, each Blackwater guy securing an arm and shoulder. Clements opened a case on the floor and took out a battery-operated power drill. "I want that combination," he said. "One way or the other."

Panting, Ulrich said, "You're bluffing."

To that, Clements only smiled.

"You won't get away with this," Ulrich said. "The cameras in the lobby—"

"We've taken care of the cameras. When we're done here, I'm going to call some of my favorite *Washington Post* op-ed columnists and leak a few choice details about what you've been up to, and what terrorist group might have done this to you. Nothing that could be proven, of course, but you know how those columnists like to traffic in rumors. Makes them feel like they're savvy, isn't that what you said? And it's not as though you'll still be around to set the record straight."

He fired up the drill and came closer. "The good news, Ulrich, is that you're going to be seen as a martyr. We'll use your death to sow public fear and get more of what we want. See what I've learned from you? I hope you're proud."

Ulrich tried to kick, but the Blackwater guys braced his legs with their knees. He started to tell Clements to wait, just wait for a second, they could figure this out, discuss it, but one of the Blackwater guys covered his mouth with a callused palm. Ulrich struggled desperately, but the Blackwater guys were too strong, and too experienced. He tried to say something, anything, to reason with Clements, to beg him, to get him to just wait, wait, they didn't need to do this, he could explain, please, *just listen to me*! But he could only grunt into the meaty hand crushing his swollen lips and loose teeth.

Clements came closer. The sound of the drill was horrifically loud. Nothing was working. He felt a wave of horrible panic. He struggled harder. He began to scream. Clements reached him with the drill. The Blackwater guys pushed down harder. He watched through bulging eyes over the top of the hand smothering his mouth as Clements placed the drill against his left knee. And then the pain was so shocking, so total, that his thoughts were obliterated. The pain consumed him.

It went on for a long time—both knees and his left elbow. Breaks and questioning in between. Ulrich sobbed and begged. But he held on to the number. The one thing he knew was that once he gave it, they would kill him.

By the time Clements moved to do his right elbow, the desk and the floor around it were covered in piss and sweat and blood. The Blackwater guys were barely restraining him now, just keeping him from sliding off the desk. He'd lost his glasses, and the room and the faces were a blur. At some point he'd lost control of his bowels and the room stank from it, stank from shit and the smell of his own singed flesh. He couldn't even scream anymore. Something in his throat had cracked.

"After this," Clements said, "we do your face."

"Please," Ulrich croaked. "Please."

"We can't let those tapes come out," Clements said. "Think of the way they'd undermine people's confidence in government. Imagine what that would do to national security. Be reasonable now. Do what's best."

The drill came closer. A sound came from Ulrich's mouth, a sound he'd never heard before, a moan, a whine, the involuntary tenor of absolute despair. Clements paused and watched him.

Crying, Ulrich rasped three numbers, three numbers that a moment earlier had seemed so important to him. But they weren't important anymore. Nothing was important. Not the tapes, not the Caspers, not anything.

All he wanted was for it to be over.

41 THE OLIGARCHY

Hort hadn't responded. But he was still smiling, a smile Ben found increasingly chilling.

"What do you mean, 'the late Mr. Ulrich'? And how did you know I was there?"

Hort took a sip of wine. "I mean 'the late Mr. Ulrich' because Mr. Ulrich is dead now. I understand he was alive when you left him. Though I'm not sure the building's security tapes will reflect that."

Ben felt the blood draining from his face. "Did you set me up, Hort?"

Hort regarded him calmly. "How? By making you go to his office? Having him argue with you in the corridor, with blood all over his face?"

Ben thought of what Larison had told him. He imagined Hort, or whoever, whispering to a reporter, *He'd been under a lot of stress . . . family problems, an arrest in Manila . . . a grudge against the former vice presidential chief of staff . . .*

"How do you know this? What happened to him?"

"It turns out he had some damaging information about some people who used to report to him. Those people went and got the information back. They didn't ask nicely."

"You?"

"CIA."

"They tortured him."

"I think Ulrich would have called it 'enhanced interrogation techniques.'"

"What about everything you said, about how torture is always about something else?"

"I didn't do it, and I wouldn't have done it. Regardless, I never said torture could never work. Hell, it worked for the French in Algeria."

"But they lost the war."

"True. But if losing a war isn't your concern, and if you know for certain the subject has the precise information you're after, and if you can immediately test the quality of what you get from the subject without wasting your time on wild goose chases because torture produces a hundred times more chaff than wheat, and if the subject dies afterward so he doesn't spend the rest of his life on a personal jihad against the nation of the people who did it to him, and if no one ever knows about it so the practice doesn't recruit thousands more terrorists, sure, it can work. Now, the conditions I just described are almost entirely theoretical and have nothing to do with the program Ulrich and company designed, authorized, and implemented. Unfortunately for Ulrich, he seems to have been the rare exception to the rule that torture isn't worth the cost. At least, that's what the CIA thinks."

"And now someone's going to try to set me up for what happened to him."

Hort didn't answer. Ben thought, *You want to see a jihad? When I'm done with you, Larison's going to feel like your best fucking friend.*

"The CIA has the security tapes from Ulrich's building," Hort said. "Clements generously offered to hand them over to me. Professional courtesy and all that. But I imagine he made copies. By now I'm sure you've noticed, that's the way it works."

Ben felt sick. "Then I'm compromised. Permanently."

"No more so than most of the people in this town. It can be managed."

"Managed how?"

"I've bailed you out before, son. I think you can rely on me to do it again."

"In exchange for what?"

"I told you. I want you to work with me."

"I already work with you."

"I'm talking about a different capacity."

Ben didn't answer. If he understood what Hort was saying, he couldn't believe it. Didn't want to believe it.

The waiter brought their steaks and moved off. Hort picked up his knife and fork, cut off a juicy chunk, put it in his mouth, chewed, and swallowed.

"Damn," he said. "That's good."

"What capacity?"

"I think you need a little context first."

"I'm listening."

Hort took another bite of steak and washed it down with some wine. "The most important thing is this. America is ruled by an oligarchy. If you want to understand America, you have to understand the oligarchy. And if you don't understand the oligarchy, you can't understand America."

"I don't know what you mean."

"I mean a small group of people having de facto control over a country."

Ben thought of what Larison had said. "You're talking about a conspiracy?"

"Not at all. Conspiracies are hidden. The oligarchy is right out in the open. It's just a collection of people in business, politics, the military, and the media who recognize their interests are better served by cooperation than they would be by competition. There aren't any secret handshakes. Most of the people who are part of the oligarchy don't even recognize its existence. If they recognize it at all, they think of it as just a benevolent, informal establishment. They tell themselves it selflessly serves the country's interests rather than selfishly serving its own."

Ben was equal parts intrigued and horrified. "How does it work?"

Hort chuckled. "Arthur Andersen was examining Enron. The credit agencies were examining the subprimes. That alone ought to tell you everything you need to know about the way the oligarchy works."

"But it doesn't have—I don't know—rules?"

"There are a few unwritten ones. Number one, above a certain pay grade, a politician can never be prosecuted or imprisoned."

"What about Nixon?"

"Nixon would never have been prosecuted. He was told that if he resigned, he would be pardoned. And that if he didn't, he would be assassinated."

Ben shook his head. It seemed too outlandish to be true. "What about Clinton? He was impeached."

"Sex is the exception. Because it doesn't offer a patriotism defense."

"What about the Caspers? Ecologia? People wouldn't go to prison for that?"

"Some would have. After all, we know from Abu Ghraib that it's all about the pictures. No pictures, no proof. No proof, no scandal. No scandal, no convictions. But even with video proof of the Caspers and what was done to them, the real architects would never have suffered. The oligarchy wouldn't be able to whitewash it the way they did Abu Ghraib, but they'd just scapegoat a slightly higher-level target. The midlevel bureaucrats, the Ulrichs of the world, would be the sacrificial lambs. You see, when the oligarchy looks in the mirror and says, 'The State is me,' it's not inaccurate. It's not hubris. They're just describing reality. They've made it so."

"Hort . . . I don't understand. You just accept this?"

"I'm a realist, son."

"You don't want to fight it?"

"Maybe I would have if I'd been born fifty or seventy years earlier. But the establishment is bigger now, more entrenched. The Roosevelt and Truman expansions were ratified by Eisenhower. Kennedy's and Johnson's abuses were ratified by Nixon. Bush Jr.'s extraconstitutional moves have all been ratified by Obama. It's a ratchet effect. There hasn't been a federal law in the last sixty years that's done other than increase the government's power and influence, and the power and influence of the corporations that manage the government by extension. The leviathan only grows."

"You're saying it can't be beaten?"

Hort laughed. "You can't beat the oligarchy. You can't beat it because the oligarchy has already won. The establishment is like a virus that's taken over the organs of the host. Now it acts as a kind of life support system, and if you remove it, the patient it battens on will die. Remember the scene in that movie *Alien*? Where the creature attaches itself to John Hurt's face, runs a tentacle down his throat, and puts him in a coma, but if they cut it off, it'll kill him? That's the oligarchy. The establishment is a creature whose first priority is ensuring that if you try to remove it, you'll wind up killing the host."

"So there's nothing that can be done."

"No, there is, and that's where you come in. The only possible solution is to manage this fucked-up system from the inside. That's why I wanted the diamonds. And the tapes, if Larison comes around. They give us leverage. Then, if someone within the oligarchy is abusing his position so much that it's creating a problem for national security, we can quietly remove him, one way or the other."

"You mean Ulrich."

"For example."

"Sounds like the mafia. With me as an enforcer."

"You can call it that. I prefer to think of it as good management. Would you rather have to clean up another mess like the Caspers, a mess caused by a bunch of fools? I don't know about you, but I'm tired of being the cleanup crew. I'm tired of the board of directors being composed of dimwits and ideologues. The Constitution, the Declaration of Independence, the *Federalist Papers* . . . that's all just window dressing now, the artifacts of an ancient mythology, the vestments of a dead religion. We need something different now, something suited for the modern world. We need realists, men like us. We are the change we've been waiting for."

He took another mouthful of steak and chewed, nodding appreciatively.

"I don't buy it," Ben said. "You could blow it up if you wanted to."

Hort swallowed. "Suppose I could. Then what? You want a revolution? Chaos? Russia in 1917, China in 1949? Who knows what we'd wind up with in the aftermath. At least now we have order."

"Maybe order's overrated."

"Tell that to the folks in Somalia. You of all people ought to know about that. And besides, our oligarchy has a few things to recommend it. It's open, for one. Look at me. Descended from slaves, and here I am, a member in good standing. Anyone can join. You just have to believe in it. You just have to pay your dues and follow the rules. That's what we mean these days by 'equality of opportunity' and a 'meritocratic society.' "

"You're part of it?"

"Of course I am. I'm not fighting it, am I? I've accepted its inevitability. Now I'm just trying to make it run properly."

"Then . . . you're one of the good complicit people, is that what you're saying?"

Hort took another mouthful of steak. Chewed. Swallowed.

"There's always been an establishment, son. In every culture, every country. There's always going to be someone on the inside, pulling the real levers of power and influence and profit. You want it to be moral men, like you and me? Or do you want it to be the Ulrichs of the world? Because it's going to be someone. That's the only choice."

Ben thought of Larison again, what he'd said about how you have to suborn yourself. He wondered if there was ever a person who'd compromised himself without at some point offering up Hort's own words to the appalled reflection in the mirror.

"Hort . . . I don't know. You're telling me the Constitution doesn't matter? That seems . . . that's a lot."

"It's not that it doesn't matter. It's fiction, but necessary fiction. Part of what keeps America strong is the society's belief that we're a constitutional republic. That no one is above the law."

"That we don't torture."

Hort nodded. "Now you're getting it."

"You're saying people can't know the truth."

"And don't want to know it. Do you know anything about *honne* and *tatemae*?"

"No."

"Couple of Japanese concepts an exceptional man taught me a long time ago. *Honne* is the real truth. *Tatemae* is the façade of truth."

"You think our job is to maintain the façade of truth?"

"I do. And that's not a bad thing. Just like every society has an establishment, every society also needs *tatemae*. Think about Gitmo. What was that all about?"

Ben shrugged. "We needed a place to put the bad guys."

Hort shook his head. "No, that's a *honne* answer. The real purpose of Gitmo was to make the public feel safe.

Whether it was actually making anyone safe was a secondary consideration at best. Hell, the truth is, we didn't even know who we were putting in there, we just wanted a big number so we could announce to the public that we'd captured eight hundred of the 'worst of the worst.' Who wouldn't sleep better at night knowing so many of our enemies had been taken out of the game? But we knew most of them were innocent. But it didn't matter. We needed the number."

"But the Caspers weren't innocent. You said so."

"That's right, and if the public ever gets wind of what happened to the Caspers, the whole sorry story will come out, including the part about how most of the detainees were innocent. The public needs talismans, son, things like airport security, silly things like taking your shoes and belt off and leaving your six-ounce tube of toothpaste at home. On a *honne* level, those kind of 'security' measures are laughable. On a *tatemae* level, they convince people it's safe to fly, and the economy keeps humming along, safe and profitable for the politicians and the corporations they work for."

"I just . . . Hort, I can't believe what you're saying."

"Ask yourself this. If you're part of the oligarchy, what's more important: that Americans be safe, or that they feel safe?"

Ben didn't answer.

"Or what matters more: convicting a guilty man, or having society believe the guilty have been convicted? One guilty man going free is irrelevant, as long as society believes the guilty have been punished. But if society loses that confidence, you get anarchy. And the oligarchy doesn't like anarchy."

They were quiet for a few minutes. Hort ate. Ben didn't.

Hort gestured to Ben's steak and swallowed some of his own. "Try it, it's good."

Ben shook his head. "I'm not hungry."

Hort watched him. "I'm sorry to hear that. Well, when you feel up to it, there's something I want you to do."

"What?"

"I told you, we're rebuilding. There's you, there's Larison, I hope, and there are a few others. And there are two in particular I want you to track down."

"Who?"

"A former marine sniper, goes by the name Dox, is one."

"Who's the other?"

Hort took a sip of wine. "The same man who taught me about *honne* and *tatemae*. A half-Japanese former soldier gone freelance, named Rain. John Rain."

"The bartender in Jacó mentioned a guy named Rain. Said he knew him in Vietnam. Called him 'death personified.' "

Hort nodded, and for a moment his thoughts seemed far away. "I'd say that's an apt description."

"You want me to track this guy down. And Dox."

"They're the ones who took down Hilger's operation."

"This is retaliation?"

"Hell, no. It was unfortunate, but it wasn't personal. Hilger got in Rain's and Dox's business, which even for a man as effective as Hilger turned out not to be a very smart thing to do. No, I want them on our side. I want to make them an offer. But I have to find them first. Sounds like maybe you already have one lead, this bartender in Jacó."

So this was what all the praise had been about. All the grooming. To entice him. To make him want to be complicit.

"Hort . . . part of me, I'm honored. But I can't work for this thing you call the oligarchy."

Hort took a swallow of wine. "You've been working for it. You just didn't know it."

"I . . . whatever you want to call it. I don't want to be part of it."

"You want to stay ignorant."

"That's not what I mean."

"Because you're not ignorant anymore. You come a certain distance, you can't just turn around. It doesn't work like that."

Ben thought of Larison, asking him, *You really want that knowledge?*

He thought of what it would be like to kill this man, who'd been a mentor, a father figure.

He decided he could live with it.

"You threatening me, Hort?"

"I don't have to threaten you. You can work with me or get owned by the CIA. That's pretty much the deal right now."

Ben swallowed, his nausea worse. So this was what it meant to be an insider.

"You're not worried I'm going to expose this?"

Hort laughed. "You still don't get it, do you? There's nothing to expose. It's all right there to see, for anyone who cares to look. But nobody does. And there's nothing they could do, anyway."

42 FROG IN A POT

Ben left the restaurant ahead of Hort. He had a killer head-ache and he felt like the only thing keeping him from puk-ing was that he hadn't touched his food.

The last thing Hort had said to him before he left was, *Think it over.* He'd said it with complete confidence, the supreme unconcern of a man who'd had this conversa-tion many times before, and always with the same inevi-table result.

He stopped at a CVS pharmacy to pick up some fresh skivvies and a toothbrush, then spent the night in a downtown hotel. He was exhausted, but couldn't sleep. He stared at the ceiling and reran events, trying to make sense of them.

He wished Larison had just released the tapes. He hated that he'd prevented it. But then Al Jazeera would be broadcasting terrorist recruitment propaganda right now. And by commission or omission, Ben would have been part of what caused it.

You see, when the oligarchy looks in the mirror and says, "The State is me," it's not inaccurate. It's not hubris. They're just describing reality. They've made it so.

It was like a terrorist hostage situation. To take out the terrorists, you'd have to sacrifice the hostages. You want to go after the oligarchs and the self-interested, you have to take out the nation, too.

He rubbed his eyes, wishing he could sleep. When this thing had started, he'd so wanted to be on the inside. And then Hort had opened the door and showed him what the inside was really like.

You come a certain distance, you can't just turn around. It doesn't work like that.

Maybe I was stupid along the way to get in that position, to get in so deep I couldn't find my way back, only out.

There had to be a way out of this. There had to be.

He slept fitfully for five hours and was up at just after dawn. He showered, dressed, and headed out to get something to eat. His appetite had returned in the night and he was starving.

The air was already muggy and oppressive. Summer insects buzzed unseen in the trees. He fueled up at a diner and walked to the Lincoln Memorial. He observed Lincoln's stoical features, then zigzagged from the Korean to the Vietnam to the World War II memorials. He thought of his parents, of that long-ago Washington weekend. He wondered what they would make of their son now.

He walked along the Mall, past oblivious joggers and robotic early commuters, past pigeons and a lost-looking dog, past the sallow-eyed homeless who watched this scene, surrounded by monuments and marble, every morning and every night. He stared at the hollow dome of the Capitol.

Paula had told him she lived in Fairfax. Maybe she drove to work, but he doubted it. Traffic on 66 had to be a bitch. Why bother, when it was a straight shot on the Orange Line from Fairfax to Federal Triangle Station and from there just a short walk to the Bureau?

He set up in a coffee shop at the intersection of Twelfth Street and Pennsylvania Avenue. Unless she was in the habit of varying her routes and times, and he'd seen zero evidence of that, he didn't expect he'd miss her.

He didn't. He'd been waiting less than an hour when he saw her coming up Twelfth Street. He watched as she turned right onto Pennsylvania Avenue, eight lanes of traffic leading to and from the Capitol, then fell in behind her, squinting into the sun, cars and buses chugging past.

"Paula."

She jumped and turned around. "What are you doing here?"

She looked scared. He'd expected her to be surprised, but not scared.

"What's wrong?"

She looked around, then back at him. "Did you kill him?"

"Who?"

"You know who. Ulrich."

"No. Although I gather certain people might want to make it look that way."

"How are they going to do that?"

"I saw him right before he died."

She didn't answer.

"I know you worked for him, Paula. You sent him my picture. You kept him apprised. That was me they were going to take out in Costa Rica, right? No wonder you were so shaken up. Two guys who are supposed to take me out clean, and I dropped both of them right in front of you. Right on you, actually."

She looked away. "I didn't know. Didn't know that was going to happen."

"They tried again yesterday, did you know that? Followed me from the airport."

She pursed her lips. "Those two in Arlington?"

"So you knew about them."

"It was on the news."

He looked at her. "Why? I just want to know why."

"I don't know anymore," she said, shaking her head slowly.

"Well, try. Try to explain."

She sighed. "There are people who know what's going on, and people who don't. People who can get things done, and people who can't."

"That's it? That's why?"

"Look, I joined the FBI right after 9/11 because I wanted to make a difference. It took me about a year to figure out I couldn't. That no one can make a difference. The system's too big. The only thing you can make is a stand. And making a stand without making a difference is quixotic at best. More likely, it's suicide, like some Buddhist monk setting himself on fire to protest something that's never going to change anyway. So I went from idealist . . . to realist."

"How's that working out for you?"

"At least I see what's going on. Look at you, stumbling around in the dark, not even knowing why."

"This is what you meant by 'No one sees me coming.' And when you told me you know how to work a cover . . . your whole life is a cover. And all that bullshit about how you'd rather just be yourself . . . you think having natural hair is all it takes? Do you even know who you are?"

She frowned. "I know who I am."

"Bugged you when I asked, though, didn't it?"

"Oh, are you going to analyze me now?"

He looked at her. "Why'd you sleep with me?"

She shrugged. "You're a good-looking guy. Is that so hard to understand?"

"That was it? You had an itch to scratch?"

"What, you think I fell in love with you? Please."

"I think you felt something, yeah. If you hadn't, you wouldn't have been so fastidious about my kissing you or seeing where you live. You let me into your body but not into your apartment? What's that?"

"It's what I had to do."

"To get me to trust you. Drop my guard."

"Something like that."

"Something like that. So you found out I was the courier, and told Ulrich, and they set another team on me."

"I told you, I didn't know what they were going to do."

"And I'm the one who's stumbling around in the dark?"

She didn't answer.

"Look me in the eye, Paula. Prove to me you're not human, because I don't believe it. Tell me you didn't feel anything."

"What if I did? We call that 'two birds with one stone.' You have a problem mixing a little pleasure with your business?"

"So you fucked me for business. What does that make you?"

"But I told you, I enjoyed it, too."

"Good that you enjoy your work."

Again she said nothing.

"There's no other way for you, is there? You can't do something only for yourself. Even when you try, it's really for the people who are pulling your strings."

"You can think what you want."

"Exactly. That's the difference between you and me."

"You'll come around. Everybody does."

"You're confusing me with you," he said, shaking his head. "Look it up. It's called projection."

He walked away, past the traffic, the blank-eyed buildings, the commuter zombies.

He imagined a frog in a pot, the water getting gradually warmer, the frog never noticing any of it. He imagined people telling themselves they would never be part of something corrupt, then telling themselves they would only be part of it to make it better, then telling themselves, hey, the thing wasn't corrupt in the first place, it was just the way of the world, they'd been naïve before and now they were savvy.

He thought of Paula. He didn't hate her. He almost felt sorry for her. He wondered if she'd realized what was happening to her, or if she only saw it in retrospect, after it was too late to do anything about it. Or maybe Ulrich had something on her, the way the Agency now did on him, the way all of them did on one another. It didn't matter. At some point, she'd made a choice. Now she was part of it.

He wondered if he was different.

Maybe he had a way to find out.

43 THE POLITE THING

The next morning, Ben waited in another rental car outside Marcy Wheeler's house in Kissimmee. He was nervous in a way that was weirdly different from the familiar precombat jitters.

He didn't need to be here. He knew she wasn't really expecting to hear from him, or, if she was, that she didn't expect the truth. But he'd said he would tell her if he could. And he sensed that somehow, if he avoided that, rationalized it away, arrogated to himself the power to shape and distort and withhold, it would make him like what he now recognized in Paula. And in Hort. Maybe he was making too much of it, but even that consideration felt like the worm of a rationalization. He thought he'd have to be vigilant about things like that, disciplined. Alert to threats to his integrity the way he was to threats to his person.

At just past eight o'clock, Wheeler's front door opened, as it had a few days before. She kissed her son and watched him while he waited for the bus, then went back in the house, again with that wistful, sad look he'd noticed last time. He got out, walked over, and knocked on her door.

When she answered, she took a step back. "Agent Froomkin," she said. "I . . . I didn't think you'd come back."

Ben felt a weird tightness in his chest. He could tell her

anything, he realized. She'd have no choice but to believe it. Why make it hard on her? Why burden her, when she already had so much on her hands and on her mind? A little piece of fiction, a white lie, would free her from her doubts. Wouldn't anything else just be cruel? And selfish, too, to unload on her just to prove something to himself.

"It's not Froomkin," he said. "And I'm not FBI."

Her jaw tightened. "What are you?"

He shook his head. "I can't tell you that."

A little fear crept into her eyes. "What can you tell me?"

"What you wanted to know. If you still want to know it."

She looked at him for a long time. He thought maybe she was going to tell him no, don't tell me, it's too much. Free him from the responsibility. Free him from the choice.

"I want to know," she said.

He cleared his throat. "Your husband was having an affair."

She didn't blink. She didn't flinch. She looked at him, and he could tell without knowing how that she hated him.

"Who was she?" she said, her tone so flat it could have been produced by a synthesizer.

He hesitated.

Just fucking say it. "It wasn't a she."

Her pupils dilated. He could feel her sudden revulsion for him. He felt it for himself.

She said, "God."

He didn't respond.

A long moment passed. She said, "Well, I asked you to tell me, didn't I?"

She shook her head as though in wonder at her own stupidity.

"Still. I really can't believe you did. I can't believe it. I guess the polite thing would be to thank you."

Tell her the rest. Tell her he's not dead. Tell her.

But wasn't she indicating now that she didn't want to know? Didn't that change—

"Goodbye, Agent whatever your name is and whoever you are."

She closed the door in his face.

He stood there for a long moment, telling himself to ring the bell, get it out, finish what he'd come here for.

He didn't. Instead, he walked back to the car, feeling slightly ill. He wondered whether he'd proven something. If so, he wished he knew what it was.

He drove back to the airport in Orlando.

He had some tough decisions to make. Decide wrong one way, and he could take the fall for Ulrich. Decide wrong the other way, and he could spend the rest of his life anesthetizing himself like Paula. Or looking for some crazy Hail Mary way out, like Larison.

It seemed like the safest alternative was to do what Hort had asked. Track down the men he wanted. It would buy him time. After all, Hort couldn't monitor everything that happened in the field. He might learn something, the way he had from Larison. Speaking of whom, he could track him down, too. He'd done it before. He could do it again. There was no telling who else Hort had screwed along the way. Put together a few disgruntled former soldiers, and Hort could wind up on the wrong end of a fragging. With Clements and the CIA and the rest of the damn oligarchs or whatever they called themselves alongside him.

He hoped he was making the right decision. Hort said he knew people. Would he have seen this coming? Would he have known this was the way Ben would perceive the situation, the way he would persuade himself he still had free will even as he was doing Hort's bidding?

He didn't know. He'd have to be careful.

You come a certain distance, you can't just turn around. Yeah, he could see that now. He couldn't just walk away. He was too deep inside. But that didn't mean he couldn't find a way out.

But should he? There was a lot of damage you could do from the inside, if that's what you wanted.

He smiled grimly. Yeah, if damage was the objective, inside could be awfully goddamned good.

AUTHOR'S NOTE

Location photos of some of the places in this book can be found on my website at
    http://www.barryeisler.com/photo.php.
  During the year in which I wrote this book, various people privy to its plot were concerned the CIA interrogation tapes would surface and overtake the story. I told them not to worry: those tapes would never see the light of day. They haven't. And they never will.

ACKNOWLEDGMENTS

I couldn't have written *Inside Out* without the books and other sources I mention after these acknowledgments, and I couldn't have written it without the generous help of my agent, editor, friends, and family, either. My thanks to:

My agent, Dan Conaway of Writers House, and editor Mark Tavani of Ballantine Books, for getting what I was trying to do with this story from the beginning, enriching it considerably with their input, and for reading and rereading the sex scene beyond what editorial requirements could ordinarily explain.

A whole bunch of superb bloggers and other journalists, for the reporting and commentary out of which this story grew. To name just a few: Juan Cole, Informed Comment; Digby, Hullabaloo; Amy Goodman, Democracy Now!; Glenn Greenwald, Unclaimed Territory; Hilzoy, Obsidian Wings (Hilzoy, come back!); Scott Horton, No Comment; Josh Marshall, Talking Points Memo; Andrew Sullivan, The Daily Dish; Marcy Wheeler, Firedoglake. Some others I admire have characters named after them in this book and in my other books, too—see if you can spot them. And you can find even more on the blogroll of Heart of the Matter at www.barryeisler.com/blog.html. If you like your journalism independent rather than corporate-owned and corporate-addled, I recommend reading these people every day.

The Washington Post's Barton Gellman, author of the superb *Angler: The Cheney Vice Presidency,* for coining the term "information laundering" that appears in the prologue.

John Alkire, Tom Bourke, Jason Evans, Scott Gentry, and Ken Rosenberg, for their expertise on international banking, and for steering me toward uncut diamonds as an appropriate means of anonymous exchange.

Ron Winston, for sharing his peerless expertise on diamonds and the diamond industry.

Tom Hayse, for everything I needed to know about satellite phone security.

Peyton Quinn, for familiarizing Ben with the notion of the pre-violence "interview" that appears in chapter one—and more of which can be found at www.rmcat.com.

Jane Litte of dearauthor.com and Sarah Wendell of smartbitchestrashybooks.com—smart, insightful, hilarious critics—for terrific feedback on the sex scene. If there's something you don't like about the scene in question, I hope it goes without saying that Jane and Sarah are entirely to blame.

The extraordinarily eclectic group of "foodies with a violence problem" who hang out at Marc "Animal" MacYoung's and Dianna Gordon's nononsenseselfdefense.com, for good humor, good fellowship, and a ton of insights, particularly regarding the real costs of violence.

Alan Eisler, Judith Eisler, Tom Hayes, novelist J. A. Konrath, Naomi Andrews and Dan Levin, Owen Rennert, Ted Schlein, and Hank Shiffman, for helpful comments on the manuscript and many valuable suggestions and insights along the way.

Most of all, my wife Laura, for never being too busy to help me figure out a story point or to indulge my political rants. Thanks, babe, for everything.

SOURCES

When this book was in manuscript form, it contained over eighty footnotes. I was tempted to keep them in the text, but in the end I judged them too distracting from the story. As a compromise, I moved the references here. You can also find them on my website.

First *New York Times* report of torture tapes destruction.
http://www.nytimes.com/2007/12/06/washington/06cnd-intel.html?bl
&ex=1197090000&en=3a8e1ed53c7d157e&ei=5087%0A

Second *New York Times* report—not two tapes, but ninety-two.
http://www.nytimes.com/2009/03/03/washington/03web-intel.html

Torture tape time line.
http://tpmmuckraker.talkingpointsmemo.com/archives/004872.php
http://tpmmuckraker.talkingpointsmemo.com/archives/004887.php
http://www.slate.com/id/2179607/sidebar/2179658/

CIA urges suppression of documents related to the torture tapes.
http://www.washingtonpost.com/wp-dyn/content/article/2009/06/08/
AR2009060804117.html?hpid=topnews

Mainstream media's euphemistic contortions regarding U.S. torture.
http://www.salon.com/opinion/greenwald/2009/05/08/torture/

Senate Armed Services Committee inquiry into the treatment of detainees in U.S. custody.
"The abuse of detainees in U.S. custody cannot simply be attributed to the actions of 'a few bad apples' acting on their own. The fact is that senior officials in the United States government solicited information on how to use aggressive techniques, redefined the law to create the appearance of their legality, and authorized their use against detainees.

Those efforts damaged our ability to collect accurate intelligence that could save lives, strengthened the hand of our enemies, and compromised our moral authority."
http://levin.senate.gov/newsroom/supporting/2008/Detainees.121108
.pdf

What the Gang of Eight knew about the torture program.
http://www.salon.com/opinion/greenwald/2007/12/09/democrats/

ACLU Freedom of Information Act requests for information on treatment of terrorist suspects.
http://www.commondreams.org/cgi-bin/print.cgi?file=/news2007/
1212–04.htm

How the CIA dodged court orders covering terror prisoners.
http://www.law.com/jsp/article.jsp?id=1200594608313

The CIA destroyed records documenting torture.
http://www.motherjones.com/politics/2009/09/case-missing-torture
-documents

Dick Cheney admits to waterboarding.
http://www.mcclatchydc.com/staff/jonathan_landay/story/14893.html

Records of what was on the interrogation videos.
http://www.aclu.org/safefree/torture/39094prs20090320.html

Information laundering—how the government uses the media to turn talking points into news stories.
http://www.salon.com/opinion/greenwald/2007/09/11/petraeus_inter
view/

And another example of how the government and mainstream media cooperatively propagandize.
http://www.nytimes.com/2008/04/20/us/20generals.html?_r=3&page
wanted=1&hp

Manila city jail.
http://www.hurights.or.jp/asia-pacific/039/05.htm
http://kuwentos.wordpress.com/2004/10/06/manila-city-jail/

Pinwale, the NSA's illegal domestic surveillance program.
http://www.nytimes.com/2009/06/17/us/17nsa.html

Why bounty hunting isn't a great way to catch terrorists.
http://www.newstatesman.com/200610090029

The CIA's terrorist interrogation "mosaic."
http://www.thewashingtonnote.com/archives/2009/03/some_truths_abo/

CIA use of Boeing for rendition flights to black sites.
http://www.newyorker.com/archive/2006/10/30/061030ta_talk_mayer

Secretary of State Rice's version of "If the president does it, it means it's not illegal."
http://blog.foreignpolicy.com/posts/2009/04/30/condi_rice_defends_torture_as_legal_and_right

The torture memos.
http://lawprofessors.typepad.com/conlaw/2009/04/the-torture-memos.html

The CIA as fall guy for Iraq.
http://www.thenation.com/blogs/capitalgames/120112

Force drift.
http://www.newyorker.com/archive/2006/02/27/060227fa_fact?currentPage=all

How to turn permission to torture into a limitation on torture (and blame field personnel for exceeding it).
http://www.salon.com/opinion/greenwald/2009/07/22/colbert/index.html
http://www.nytimes/2007/10/04/washington/04interrogate.html?pagewanted=1

U.S. policy on sleep deprivation, hypothermia, stress positions, beatings.
http://www.nybooks.com/articles/22614

The U.S. torture program led to no useful intelligence.
http://www.nytimes.com/2009/04/23/opinion/23soufan.html

How the Bush administration used torture to try to establish a Saddam Hussein/al Qaeda link.
http://www.mcclatchydc.com/227/story/66622.html

Scapegoating of enlisted personnel for torture at Abu Ghraib.
http://www.law.whittier.edu/pdfs/cstudents/wlr-v27n3-smith-abstract.pdf

Jonathan Turley's article on Abu Ghraib scapegoating and the abdication of command responsibility.
http://www.usatoday.com/news/opinion/editorials/2005-06-06-turley
-edit_x.htm

Dan Choi, Arab linguist, driven from the military for being gay.
http://www.huffingtonpost.com/aaron-belkin/obama-to-fire-his-first
-g_b_199070.html

We can make a terrorist talk, but we can't get him to talk in English.
http://www.huffingtonpost.com/2009/05/15/dan-choi-daily
-show_n_203830.html

Assassination ring operating out of the Office of the Vice President.
http://www.minnpost.com/ericblackblog/2009/03/11/7310/investiga
tive_reporter_seymour_hersh_describes_executive_assassination_ring

The vice president's plan to override the Fourth Amendment and use active-duty military to arrest U.S. citizens on American soil.
http://www.secgov.info/2009/07/classification-and-constitution.html
http://www.nytimes.com/2009/07/25/us/25detain.html

CIA briefs Congress on a CIA assassination program.
http://www.huffingtonpost.com/2009/07/08/panetta-acknowledged
-cia_n_228321.html

CIA lies to Congress.
http://www.motherjones.com/kevin-drum/2009/07/lying-congress

Doctors assist in torture.
http://harpers.org/archive/2009/04/hbc-90004704

Outsourcing assassination to Blackwater.
http://www.nytimes.com/2009/08/20/us/20intel.html?_r=1&hp

Contractors rape with impunity.
http://www.cato.org/pub_display.php?pub_id=9342

How to destroy a citizen through trial by media.
http://www.salon.com/opinion/greenwald/2008/08/04/anthrax/

Over half of America supports torture.
http://www.huffingtonpost.com/2009/06/03/poll-slight-majority-of
-a_n_210700.html

Over sixty percent of Evangelicals support torture.
http://www.cnn.com/2009/US/04/30/religion.torture/

CIA black sites.
http://www.newyorker.com/reporting/2007/08/13/070813fa_fact_
mayer
http://www.washingtonpost.com/wp-dyn/content/article/2007/02/27/
AR2007022702214.html

CIA secret prison system.
http://www.nytimes.com/2009/08/13/world/13foggo.html?_
r=2&hp=&pagewanted=all

**CIA shuttled ghost detainees through Abu Ghraib, Bagram, Guantá-
namo, and other prisons so the Red Cross couldn't verify their existence.**
http://www.washingtonpost.com/wp-dyn/articles/A25239–
2005Mar10.html

Ghost detainees at black sites.
http://www.npr.org/templates/story/story.php?storyId=10819080

How the CIA built the black site prisons.
http://www.nytimes.com/2009/08/13/world/13foggo.html

**The Supreme Court rules terror suspects have the right to petition for
habeas corpus.**
http://www.salon.com/opinion/greenwald/2008/06/12/boumediene/

Government releases terror suspects it can't charge.
http://www.salon.com/opinion/greenwald/2009/07/31/detention/
index.html

Waterboarding someone 183 times in a month.
http://emptywheel.firedoglake.com/2009/04/18/khalid-sheikh
-mohammed-was-waterboarded-183-times-in-one-month/

JSOC run from the Office of the Vice President.
http://www.minnpost.com/ericblackblog/2009/04/01/7800/seymour

_hersh_cheney_left_allies_behind_in_national_security_posts_and_
may_still_influence_events

CIA inspector general's report on torture.
http://washingtonindependent.com/56175/the-2004-cia-inspector
-generals-report-on-torture

Schlein Vineyard wines.
http://www.schleinvineyard.com/

We didn't know who we were imprisoning at Guantánamo.
http://pubrecord.org/nation/4936/wilkerson-ive-conclusion-cheney/

Covering up that we didn't know who we had imprisoned at Guantánamo.
http://pubrecord.org/nation/4936/wilkerson-ive-conclusion-cheney/

We knew most Guantánamo prisoners were innocent.
http://www.thewashingtonnote.com/archives/2009/03/some_truths_
abo/
http://www.foxnews.com/politics/2009/03/19/ex-bush-official
Guantanamo-bay-innocent/

U.S. torture—a jihadist recruitment bonanza.
http://harpers.org/archive/2008/12/hbc-90004036

Torture radicalizes prisoners.
http://www.mcclatchydc.com/homepage/story/68872.html

Senator Durbin: Congress is corporate-owned.
http://www.huffingtonpost.com/2009/04/29/dick-durbin-banks
-frankly_n_193010.html

**Health care reform creates new customers for the insurance companies
and big pharma.**
http://www.latimes.com/news/nationworld/washingtondc/la-na
-healthcare-insurers24-2009aug24,0,4551786.story

The AIG bailout was a way of funneling money to Goldman Sachs.
http://www.rollingstone.com/politics/story/26793903/the_big_take
over/print

Halliburton profits from Iraq and Afghanistan.
http://www.halliburtonwatch.org/

Marshall Plan as corporate welfare.
Thomas J. McCormick. "Drift or Mastery? A Corporatist Synthesis for American Diplomatic History." *Reviews in American History* 10, no. 4 (December 1982).

Congress's turnover lower than North Korean Politburo's.
http://www.mediastudy.com/articles/av11-9-06.html

The mainstream media as "Church of the Savvy."
http://uscmediareligion.org/?theScoop&scID=185

Why France lost in Algeria even though torture "worked."
http://www.salon.com/opinion/kamiya/2009/04/23/torture/

The oligarchy includes journalists.
http://www.newsweek.com/id/191393/

Arthur Andersen was examining Enron.
http://www.huffingtonpost.com/terrence-mcnally/qa-with-michael-lewis-par_b_248357.html

The credit agencies were examining the subprimes.
http://www.washingtonpost.com/wp-dyn/content/article/2009/04/24/AR2009042402902_pf.html

Above a certain pay grade, a politician can never be prosecuted or imprisoned.
http://www.thenation.com/doc/20090914/hayes

Bipartisanship isn't all you might hope.
http://www.thenation.com/doc/20090914/hayes

The leviathan only grows.
http://www.salon.com/opinion/greenwald/radio/2009/07/02/savage/index1.html

BIBLIOGRAPHY

In addition to the sources listed in the preceding section, this story draws on a number of excellent books, all of which I would recommend to anyone interested in exploring the political reality behind my fiction.

THE U.S. TORTURE PROGRAM

Administration of Torture: A Documentary Record from Washington to Abu Ghraib and Beyond by Jameel Jaffer and Amrit Singh.

Chain of Command: The Road from 9/11 to Abu Ghraib by Seymour Hersh.

The Dark Side: The Inside Story of How the War on Terror Turned into a War on American Ideals by Jane Mayer.

Getting Away with Torture: Secret Government, War Crimes, and the Rule of Law by Christopher H. Pyle.

Ghost Plane: The True Story of the CIA Rendition and Torture Program by Stephen Grey.

How to Break a Terrorist: The U.S. Interrogators Who Used Brains, Not Brutality, to Take Down the Deadliest Man in Iraq by Matthew Alexander.

The Lucifer Effect: Understanding How Good People Turn Evil by Philip Zimbardo.

A Question of Torture: CIA Interrogation, from the Cold War to the War on Terror by Alfred W. McCoy.

Torture and Democracy by Darius Rejali.

The Torture Memos: Rationalizing the Unthinkable by David Cole.

The Torture Papers: The Road to Abu Ghraib by Karen J. Greenberg.

Torture Team: Rumsfeld's Memo and the Betrayal of American Values by Philippe Sands.

Torture and Truth: America, Abu Ghraib, and the War on Terror by Mark Danner.

Truth, Torture, and the American Way: The History and Consequences of U.S. Involvement in Torture by Jennifer K. Harbury.

Your Government Failed You: Breaking the Cycle of National Security Disasters by Richard A. Clarke.

GUANTÁNAMO

Guantánamo and the Abuse of Presidential Power by Joseph Margulies.
The Guantánamo Files: The Stories of the 774 Detainees in America's Illegal Prison by Andy Worthington.
The Guantánamo Lawyers: Inside a Prison Outside the Law by Mark P. Denbeaux and Jonathan Hafetz.
Guantánamo: What the World Should Know by Michael Ratner and Ellen Ray.

CIVIL LIBERTIES

Angler: The Cheney Vice Presidency by Barton Gellman.
Bush's Law: The Remaking of American Justice by Eric Lichtblau.
Justice at War: The Men and Ideas That Shaped America's War on Terror by David Cole.
Nation of Secrets: The Threat to Democracy and the American Way of Life by Ted Gup.
The Shadow Factory: The Ultra-Secret NSA from 9/11 to the Eavesdropping of America by James Bramford.
Standing Up to the Madness: Ordinary Heroes in Extraordinary Times by Amy Goodman and David Goodman.
Takeover: The Return of the Imperial Presidency by Charlie Savage.
The Terror Presidency: Law and Judgment Inside the Bush Administration by Jack Goldsmith.
The True Believer: Thoughts on the Nature of Mass Movements by Eric Hoffer.

GOVERNMENT/MEDIA COMPLICITY

Amusing Ourselves to Death: Public Discourse in the Age of Show Business by Neil Postman.
Great American Hypocrites: Toppling the Big Myths of Republican Politics by Glenn Greenwald.
The Great Derangement: A Terrifying True Story of War, Politics, and Religion by Matt Taibbi.
Hostile Takeover: How Big Money and Corruption Conquered Our Government—And How We Take It Back by David Sirota.
Manufacturing Consent: The Political Economy of the Mass Media by Noam Chomsky and Edward S. Herman.
A Tragic Legacy: How a Good vs. Evil Mentality Destroyed the Bush Presidency by Glenn Greenwald.

FILMS ON RELATED SUBJECTS

No End in Sight by Charles Ferguson. http://www.noendinsightmovie
.com/

Secrecy by Peter Galison and Robb Moss. http://www.secrecyfilm.com

Standard Operating Procedure by Errol Morris. http://www.sonyclas-
sics.com/standardoperatingprocedure/

Taxi to the Dark Side by Alex Gibney. http://www.taxitothedarkside
.com/taxi/

Torturing Democracy. http://www.torturingdemocracy.org/